The Cartel

By

A.K. Alexander

Cover Design: Damonza www.AwesomeBookCovers.com
Interior Design: Linda Boulanger
www.TreasureLineBooks.weebly.com

Published by D'Vine Press
Also available in eBook publication
PRINTED IN THE UNITED STATES OF AMERICA

To Dad. I love you and thank you for always believing in me. This one is for you because I know it's your favorite. Here's to being a New York Times best seller, even if it's only in our imaginations.

Helen your daughter speaks so highly of you, I can't wait to meet you

Michele Scott (AKA Alexander

BOOK I

1969-1976

Calí, Colombia

CHAPTER ONE

EMILIO ESPINOZA TRACED THE SCARS ACROSS THE undersides of his wrists, now white with time, but still visible. Not like the ones that remained on his heart.

Moving to the ornate wooden armoire, he picked up a framed photograph of his brother Antonio and his lovely young wife Lydia. He stared at his brother's face, his eyes becoming slits of hatred. He closed them, and threw the picture across the room, smashing the frame against the wall, his hands balling into fists as his vision clouded with tears. Glass shattered into small splinters across the adobe-tiled floor. Pulling the photograph from between the shards of glass, filled with rage and despair, Emilio ripped it into pieces.

Antonio was the reason the scars upon his heart never faded. What a fool his brother was! Antonio had no idea of his brother's true feelings toward him and Emilio planned to keep it that way—for now. But when he struck, Antonio would know. He would feel nothing but pain. The kind Emilio felt every day of his life.

Emilio's plans were long term. They had to be. He knew the desired effect might not come to fruition for years, perhaps even a decade. But he had plans and they had been brewing for nearly five years, since he was merely a boy of fifteen. He had been patient for this long. He would be patient for as long as it took.

He remembered that day five years ago so very clearly.

****

EMILIO CAME HOME EARLY FROM SCHOOL, DITCHING BECAUSE *he hadn't studied for a test. He did not want Antonio to find out that he'd left school early, so he crept quietly up the outside back steps to the guesthouse, which was several yards away from the main quarters, a place where he knew he could hide out until the appropriate time.*

He smelled the candles first. He smiled, knowing he was about to get a show from his Don Juan of a brother and some beautiful young thing. Antonio was known to bring women to the guesthouse and light a few rose scented candles, put on some soft music, and then, having set the mood, complete his conquest.

Emilio crawled along the balcony of the small villa, carefully rising up to peek into the window. The music playing—soft, low, romantic—

the woman's back toward him. Antonio held her close, stroking her long black hair, whispering something in her ear.

That hair, the lithe body. A shiver of delight slithered through Emilio as he watched in awe.

Antonio placed his hands on the woman's shoulders and easily slipped off her dress, letting it fall to the ground. Emilio closed his eyes, ashamed to be watching. But curiosity and raging hormones opened them. The woman stood completely naked. Antonio swept her up and carried her to the bed and laid her down on the red sateen comforter.

Emilio felt the first painful tug on his heart when he saw her face as Antonio put his hands on either side of it and kissed her. Emilio blinked his eyes, shook his head and looked again. Antonio pulled back, reached over to the nightstand by the bed and poured her a glass of wine. It was then, as Emilio watched her drink the velvet liquid, that he saw, understood and learned of betrayal of the worst kind. There, drinking wine, falling under his brother's seductive spell, laid Marianna. His Marianna. The girl of fourteen who was destined to be his wife, his lover. Emilio loved this girl and she'd sworn her devotion to him. They had been nothing but lies.

His body, which had shivered with delight watching the show, now, shook with rage. The sweat trickling from his brow ran down his face and into his mouth tasting salty and bitter. He made himself turn back to the window and watch.

After he watched the two people he'd loved more than life do the worst imaginable to him, he ran into the cacao fields and vomited, ached and cried. His clothing wet from sweat created from his anger and the intense humidity sweeping across the overgrown fields. Finally, he stopped, and falling to his knees he threw back his head. "Marianna!" He bellowed her name over and over again in such agony that it silenced the birds across the valley set in between two mountain ranges.

How could she have done this? His Marianna? How could Antonio have done this? Emilio had loved Marianna since they were seven years old. Even as a child, he'd known that God had placed her here on this earth for him, only him. Seeing them together, watching as they grew into young adults together, Antonio knew this, and still, he had stolen her from him, betraying them both.

Brokenhearted and filled with vengeance, Emilio waited for her to leave the villa. He stalked her path until she reached the edge of the fields where he grabbed her from behind, covered her mouth with a hand stronger than even he realized. Knocking her to the ground, he wrapped his hands around her tiny neck and strangled her to death as she struggled, watching him with knowing and terrified eyes. Then, snatching her up, he carried her to the river where he weighted her body with large rocks and tossed her into the rushing waters. She had never been found.

Emilio had sobbed, distraught, filled with remorse, anger, and fear. His brother, unaware that Marianna lay at the bottom of the river, consoled him. They'd find the lost girl, Antonio said, urging Emilio to move on with his life. No. Emilio wanted no life at all. He was beyond caring for anything life could offer him. A few days after killing his love, filled with irrevocable guilt, desperation, and hatred, he slit his wrists.

Antonio found him lying in a pool of blood by the river, and frantically sent for the doctor, begging him to save his brother. Emilio lost a great deal of blood, but with time and care, was healed. When he was well enough and out of danger, Antonio screamed at him, "You are a fool! There is not a woman in this world whose life is worthy of taking your own."

****

NOW, MANY YEARS LATER, HE UNDERSTOOD WHY HE HAD watched the entire seduction take place. He now knew why he had not bolted away at the first glance of her beautiful face, and why he bore the pain of seeing her in his brother's embrace. He had to completely fill his heart with his hatred of Antonio, fill it with the rage of betrayal. He'd succeeded, and he'd learned to hide that hatred. Emilio was as smart and conniving as his older brother. After all, it was his older brother who had taught him how to be evil.

As he looked out the large, paned window that faced the main house, Emilio vowed to seek revenge. He lived in that same dreaded guesthouse, the place where he'd watched his reality being pulled out from under him. But he didn't mind. Living there meant he could never forget. And living there meant he had a good view of Antonio and Lydia's bedroom, where he watched Lydia every morning as she took her coffee out onto the balcony. She dressed in sheer negligees, unaware of his watching eyes. She was gorgeous, truly magnificent. And she was part of Emilio's plan.

CHAPTER TWO
Costa Careyes, Mexico

THE MOUNTAINTOP FORTRESS, SURROUNDED BY LUSH GREEN jungle, palm trees, and armed guards, had been constructed to take in the Pacific Ocean views on the northern stretch of Costa Careyes, Mexico. The best way to reach the villa was by a ponga, which took over an hour from Manzanillo and over two hours from Puerto Vallarta, the two closest major cities to the area. It was the kind of place that caused outsiders passing by on pongas to look up at with awe and wonder at those who resided inside. It was only a vacation home.

The morning passed quietly and was uncharacteristically brisk as Javier Rodriguez sat out back on the veranda overlooking the steel gray sea below him, where waves crashed hard against the ragged edges of rocks etched into the mountain side by time. Looking a little to the north, he spotted fishermen heading out off the white sand beach in search of the evening's meal. The calming scent of orange blossoms and the richness of the jungle's soil, combined with the ocean breezes, would normally have eased Javier's troubled mind. Despite the lack of humidity this part of the world was known for, beads of perspiration trickled down Javier's back. He was drinking his second cup of coffee when Antonio, his longtime friend from Colombia, joined him in the idyllic setting. Antonio's dark eyes were alert, his black hair slicked back, and he was dressed immaculately in a white silk shirt and khakis. He sat down at the wicker-backed chair next to Javier, a slight smile easing across his genteel face.

"Ah, good morning, Antonio. I take it you slept well?" Javier set his mug down on the breakfast table.

"Of course. I always sleep well when I visit your home. The sounds of the ocean lull a man to sleep. Everything is comfortable here, and your servants are always so charming and friendly." Antonio raised his eyebrows, his smile widening. He rubbed his fingers together and then, with slightly longer nails than most men, began easing them back and forth underneath one another.

"I apologize that I could not greet you last night when you arrived. Cynthia and I were busy with my father."

"No need to apologize. I settled in quite nicely. How is your father?"

"He isn't well. Cynthia has been spending a great deal of time caring for him. He doesn't have long. If you'd like to see him while you're here, he's in the west wing of the house. I can take you there later."

"If he's up to it. It troubles me to hear that his health is failing. He was very good to me after my parents passed. I wouldn't want to disturb him."

"No. He would be happy to see you, Antonio. He loves you like a son. You remind him of when your father and he ran things. His memories are the only thing that I believe keep him alive."

Antonio sighed and nodded. "Those days are past. The old generation is nearly gone. When your father dies it will be only you and me to rule over our growing empire. And I'm here to tell you, in order to see it grow as we hope, we must rule with ferocity and wield an iron fist!" Antonio slammed his own fist against the glass table. He laughed, raising his head up and staring into his friend's eyes.

"You're a vicious man, Antonio," Javier replied teasingly, although he meant every word. Antonio was a ruthless man, had been since childhood when they'd grown up together in Colombia. After secondary school, Javier had gone to the university in Mexico City and then made the decision to move to Guadalajara and pursue politics. He and Antonio had remained friends through those years and recently had begun collaborating in business together, and they conducted much of their business at Javier's vacation home on the coast in Costa Careyes. Javier's fear of his compadre matched his love and respect for him.

"Yes and no. I prefer, my friend, to think of myself as a realist. My father is dead and yours is dying. You're the ruler here in Jalisco, and I believe it is very clear to all that I am the patrón. With good planning, you could go on to become the president of Mexico. The PRI is going through a crisis. Diaz Ordaz cannot even control the people," Antonio said, referring to the current president. "Together, my friend, we'll go far. But we need to be very clear on that. For our survival, it is vital for us to always work together and never against each other. Don't you agree?" Antonio lit a cigar between his manicured fingers and exhaled puffs of the acrid smoke into the morning air.

"Absolutely." There was no choice but to agree with his old friend. Even though Javier was the governor of the state of Jalisco, and the idea of becoming president interested him, it was Antonio Espinoza who ruled much of South America. Of course, he was not considered an official ruler, but in effect, he was clearly *seen* as the ruler, especially to those that it mattered to.

Antonio was the head of one of the wealthiest and largest coffee plantation families in Colombia. He'd taken over the empire at a young age, following the deaths of his mother and father in a boating accident. Antonio had expanded that empire by also dabbling in illegal businesses, in which Javier took an active role.

"Our families have known each other for a long time." Antonio leaned back in the chair, stretching out his legs.

"Of course, since our great-grandfathers."

Antonio arched his neck back, gazing up at the volatile skies. "That's why we have always remained like brothers and our business together is so successful. And now we have opportunities like never before." He smiled again. "I see something ahead of us that will make us far more wealthy and powerful than either of us ever imagined. You see, my friend," Antonio started, leaning in closer to Javier, lowering his voice, "there is a new wave approaching. The Italian mafia has ruled in the United States and Europe now for a long time. What they do not know is that there is competition on the horizon. And that is you and me."

Javier shook his head. "Come on, Cabrón. Do you really think the Italian mafia will allow us into their world?"

Antonio shrugged. "It doesn't matter if they welcome us with open arms. I don't think they'll be pleased to have any kind of competition. We don't need them."

"Aren't you afraid of death? They are ruthless men. The world knows this."

"I fear nothing, my dear friend. If I did, I would've been dead long ago. Besides, what we deal in does not hold interest for the Italians. And by the time they do discover us and what we have to offer, they'll want to do business with us because they'll have to if they want to get involved. For now though, I have no intention on dealing with the Italians. I want to get ahead of the game. However, we must move quietly lest we provoke their interest and they learn of the amount of money there is to be made. Go about this the right way, and they'll leave us alone. For now."

Javier wasn't so sure. He'd heard a great many stories about the Mafioso, and regardless of what Antonio said, he knew that they did have an interest in the drug trade. But he would continue to do as he always did and follow Antonio's lead, hoping it would all turn out as fruitful as his friend guaranteed him.

****

ANTONIO POURED HIMSELF A SNIFTER OF BOURBON.
He paced the floor of the guesthouse, and looked again at the clock. She was late.

He tossed back his drink, heat rising to his face, and he thought twice before pouring another. Dulling his senses was not what he wanted to do. No. Feeling every sensation, every nerve come alive as he touched her beautiful skin was his desire. *Feeling* was what he loved about being with Marta.

In an attempt to deny his need for her, Antonio stretched out on the downy sheets—white, satin. Cynthia hadn't missed a thing when putting a luxurious vacation home together for Javier. Even the guesthouse had the best that money could buy.

A faint tap on the door catapulted Antonio out of bed. He stopped himself. He had to regain his composure, to never let her know exactly how much she meant to him. He straightened his black silk pajamas, casually turned the knob, and pulled the door open.

There she stood. So lovely. The jasmine scented perfume that he'd given her on a previous visit enveloped his senses. It was indeed heavenly, a seductive intoxication. He shuddered inside as his hungry eyes absorbed the vision before him. She was indeed beautiful, clad in a flowing, light pink dress that only emphasized her essential purity. He could barely control himself, wanting to take the dinner tray from her and toss it aside and devour her instead. "Come in," he said, not liking the unmistakable anxiety in his voice. What kind of spell did this woman have over him?

She stepped over the threshold, moving to the coffee table where she set down his dinner and a bottle of wine. Antonio stood behind her and touched his lips ever so softly to the nape of her neck. It was useless continuing to try and control his passion. It was useless for her as well. She turned, her dark eyes hungry for him, she embraced him. Their bodies merged as he took her face in his hands and pressed his lips to hers.

"I've missed you, Antonio," she whispered, her voice like dew on morning leaves, soft, gentle, sweet.

"I've missed you, too."

"When can we be together? How much longer do we have to wait? And *why* do I have to wait? I do not understand this, Antonio. I know I am only a servant, but we're in love. You've said so a hundred times, and you've promised me that we would be together."

"It is far more difficult than you can understand," Antonio replied, not ready to delve into the politics of their relationship. He had one desire here.

"I'm not a stupid woman, Antonio. I may be young and therefore not wise in the ways of the world, as you've enjoyed reminding me." She smiled coyly. "But I am far from ignorant, and I am very confused at the length of time it has taken for us to be together. I need you." She pouted, her full lips making her completely irresistible.

He held her by her shoulders. "Soon, my sweet. All that I have will soon be yours." He sealed this lie with a long, deep kiss, and all her doubts seemed to disappear as she smiled, her face relaxing, and trust for him filling her eyes. His heart beat hard against his chest, not only filled with passion, but with guilt and panic, as well. How could he continue this?

Marta accepted both his lies and his desire and let her dress fall to the floor, exposing her delicate figure. Antonio took her up into his arms and positioned her on the bed. Their touching became feverish, quickly establishing a bond of intimacy.

Like a panther that had captured his prey, Antonio's passion was so intense that Marta could do nothing except surrender to his overwhelming sensuality. Starting with her mouth, he reacquainted himself with every inch of her. His tongue trailed past her neck, finding her breasts waiting. Quickly reacting to his touch, her nipples grew hard and she arched her back, aching for more. As his mouth devoured her breasts, Antonio's hand worked its way with slow expertise between Marta's thighs. She moaned when his fingers found her moist skin, and she dug her nails into his shoulders as he worked his hand against her. Then, when her arousal became overwhelming, Antonio heard the change in her breathing that signaled she needed more. He could tell by her trembling how much she needed the weight of his body pressed against hers, the feeling of him moving inside her, and the immeasurable pleasure he would bring to her. His firm masculinity replaced his fingers as he went on to sate both their erotic appetites. Later, when their desires were fully quenched, they clung together in the tangled sheets.

"I love you, Antonio Espinoza. I promise to always love you."

Antonio didn't have the heart to reply, knowing that any promises he had already made were futile.

CHAPTER THREE

MARTA DANCED AROUND HER SMALL QUARTERS HUMMING a tune she'd heard on Señora Rodriguez's phonograph earlier that day. Normally, giving up her free evening to work was an annoyance she didn't like to give into, but tonight was different. Two months had passed since Marta had last seen Antonio. She flitted around now, excited at the prospect of seeing him again. *Tonight*. Yes, tonight their lives would be changed forever.

The late afternoon sun sent rays of light through her window, making the hut feel less dim. Pictures of the Virgin Mary and Jesus hung on the walls. She turned away from Christ on the cross hanging over her bed and her stomach sank. The guilt stung her, knowing that she was living a life of sin by continuing a sexual relationship with Antonio outside of marriage vows. But she knew in her heart that their love was far deeper than simply lying together. They loved each other deeply. And how could God frown on that? He would forgive her. *Especially now*. She crossed herself.

She looked around the room she'd shared with her roommate Josefina for the last two years, since she was fifteen. It was worn with time, but they had done their best to fix it up, putting down bright colored rugs and drapes they'd sewn for the windows. The servant quarters sat below one of the cliffs on the north side of the estate. The village was not large and the Rodriguez vacation villa stood out on top of the hill overlooking the coastline. There were some smaller huts close to the beach and a restaurant that serviced the area where many of the workers from the estate would get together in the evenings for camaraderie. There was only one way in and one way out of the area, and it was by boat.

The villagers would take pongas in to Costa Careyes for supplies on a daily basis. The trip down the coast lasted about forty-five minutes. If Señor Rodriguez or his wife wanted to return to their main home in the city, they were taken by luxury yacht. They stayed in their vacation home usually about half of the month, but lately Señora had been staying the entire month to help take care of her dying father-in-law, who preferred the vacation home.

Marta cared deeply for Señora Rodriguez because the woman was compassionate and because she took an interest in both her and Josefina as human beings rather than simply servants.

Marta would miss La Señora when she left, but the knowledge of coming to visit her on Antonio's arm filled her, knowing that they would talk like old friends—knowing that no longer would she be on the level of a servant and that there would no longer be a need to hide their friendship from Señor Rodriguez. And like Señora Rodriguez, Marta knew she would be able to wear the finest jewels, along with the best clothes. She would have the best, like her *friend*, Señora Rodriguez, and she would soon be able to call her Cynthia.

Marta went over to her dresser and mirror, to pick up the silver brush Antonio had brought to her on his last visit. He was always so gracious and giving. The soft bristles moving through her long hair, reminded her of Antonio's graceful fingers running through it. Oh how she loved that, and she loved the fact that within a few hours she would be telling her lover the exciting news. She knew his eyes would shine brightly with pride and pleasure. Hopefully the baby would look like him, a son—a boy would mean everything to him. A son to solidify their love.

Oh! And how shocked her parents would be when they learned that their daughter, the one who had fled their home in shame and fear, was married to a great man like Antonio Espinoza. Certainly they'd want to be a part of her life then. But they did not have the right anymore. She had a new family, one she was creating, and one she would love with a fierceness and the protection her parents had denied her. She would soon prove to them and the rest of the world that she was destined to be far more than a lowly servant.

The middle child of three, Marta had always felt like the odd one. The other two were boys, which automatically made them worth more in the eyes of her family and her culture. Her parents never paid much attention to her, unless they were taking the time to tell her how stupid and useless she was.

She recalled with vividness the day she'd left home—her *quinciañera*, her fifteenth birthday. It was tradition and although her parents didn't have much use for her, they did like parties. And she knew that, if anything, it would be a good excuse for them to visit with family and friends to drink large quantities of beer and wine. Marta had known that it wouldn't be a fancy party like those who had wealth and prestige. Yet she looked forward to it, like most girls in Mexico did. It symbolized the crossing over from a child into womanhood.

But when the time came and there was no party, no celebration of her most special birthday, Marta tearfully questioned her grandmother, who had no choice but to tell her the truth.

"Oh Mija, I knew one day you would need to be told, and now it happens that it is on the day that should be most special in your life." The older woman reached her gnarled hands out and stroked the ends of Marta's hair.

Marta shrank back, not liking the sadness in her grandmother's voice. She had been the one person to love her throughout her life, never bullying or belittling.

"I told your mother I thought it was wrong to ignore this day, no matter the circumstance of your conception."

"I don't understand."

"Sit down closer to me." Her grandmother patted the side of her creaking old bed. Marta did as she was told. Her grandmother sighed, the lines around her eyes deepening and her lips tightened. "Your Papa is not truly your father." Marta felt her mouth drop open, not totally understanding the words she was hearing. But soon the picture became clear. "Your mother suffered a great tragedy at the hands of an enemy of your papa's when he took her dignity away. You were born nine months later."

Her grandmother went on to explain, but to Marta it was a jumble of words. She understood dignity and enemies and the significance of nine months. Her grandmother went on to say something about her papa being a good Catholic and vowing to raise Marta as his own. It was so apparent now why the ambivalence and, at times, anger was harshly directed at her from her parents. She was evil in their eyes. Created from evil.

"I must go," she heard herself say to her grandmother. "Now that I know this, I cannot stay here. They will see that you have told me and they will treat me even more harshly."

The old woman nodded and handed her a small amount of money, likely all that she had. Kissing her grandmother on her weathered cheek, she thanked her for the gift of both the money and the truth and gathered her few belongings. She then left the only home she'd known.

She discovered through a friend that the Rodriguez family was hiring servants at that time, and so she made her way to the great rancho and hacienda where she pleaded for the job and was hired to work at the villa on the coast. She was taken out by ponga and had been on the small stretch of beach for two and a half years now.

Antonio entered her life a year ago when he came to the villa to meet with Señor Rodriguez on business. He took her aside one night and told her how beautiful she was. Smitten with him from that moment on, he soon consumed her every waking thought.

Now, as she donned her pressed uniform, the one reserved for parties, Marta heard the engines of Señor Rodriguez's yacht approaching. She knew that Antonio was on the boat. The thrill of the coming evening with Antonio caused her to fumble with the buttons on her blouse. Tonight in her lover's arms, she planned to tell him the wonderful news. News that she'd been keeping locked tightly inside for an entire month, except for telling her roommate and friend Josefina.

Josefina came out of the bathroom, pulling her hair back.

"Today is the day, Josefina. I will see Antonio tonight and tell him about the baby. Soon I will leave this place and we will be married." She twirled around.

"You are a hopeless romantic," Josefina said.

"Hopeless or not, I am carrying Antonio Espinoza's child," she replied.

A pounding at the door interrupted the two friends. Marta ran to it, hoping it would be Antonio. Maybe he had been thinking of her and needed to see her before the party. Could it be that he knew of her circumstances? That his intuition told him of her need and the child growing inside her?

To Marta's dismay it was only their boss, Lupe. "Come. The guests are arriving and Señor Rodriguez wants us out front," she ordered, hands planted on her hips, not a smile to be found on her aged face.

Tonight's fiesta was a special one. Señor Rodriguez was hosting a celebration in honor of his wife, having recently found out that she too, was with child.

Marta bounced out of the room and kissed Lupe on the cheek, which the old woman wiped away at once. "What has gotten into you?" she asked.

"Let me say that this is the happiest day of my life."

"You are an odd girl. This wouldn't have anything to do with Señor Espinoza, would it?" Lupe's face darkened.

Marta wondered momentarily why the scowl, but dismissed it and giggled when Josefina interrupted, "Why, of course not. Where would you get an idea like that?"

The two younger women grabbed hands and breezed past Lupe, heading to the courtyard garden.

The garden was filled with flowers the color of passion fruit as servants busied themselves placing platters of food on the large, elegantly decorated tables. A waterfall in the center of the adobe tiles sprayed out crystalline drops of cascading water.

As the guests arrived, Marta served hors d'oeuvres. At one point in the early evening, while searching for Antonio, she caught a glimpse of one of the most beautiful women she'd ever seen.

The woman evidenced a grace that no other woman possessed at the party. She wore a flowing chiffon dress that matched her light green eyes. The dress covered what Marta knew a dress would soon be covering on her—an expanding midriff. She couldn't help smiling at the sight of this woman with child. Even in the woman's late pregnant state, she was dazzling. Her honey streaked hair glistened in the last rays of the afternoon sun. She looked like the women

Marta had seen in the fashion magazines Señora Rodriguez looked at from the United States and Spain.

Turning to pick up a tray of drinks, she spotted Antonio. Her heart surged. Maybe she should approach him right there and tell him she was carrying his child, but it would be wiser to wait until they were alone. The least she could do was serve him a drink.

Walking toward him with a tray full of drinks, including his favorite drink of tequila and orange juice, she witnessed a small child run up to him. He stooped down, and the little girl threw her arms around his neck. Behind the girl stood the woman she'd been admiring, her hands resting on her widening waistline. The woman leaned over and patted the child on the shoulder while whispering something in her ear. The girl kissed the woman on the cheek, and then went off chasing after a group of children. The scene mesmerized Marta, but something inside her began to ache right in the center of her chest. After the little girl ran off, Antonio pulled the woman in close to him and kissed her, long and hard, exactly in the way that he had kissed Marta on so many nights.

Marta dropped the tray of drinks. They crashed onto the tile floor. She felt the gaze of partygoers upon her. A silence fell as she bent down, struggling to clean up the glass. *Please don't look at me. No, please do not see me. God, save me from this moment.*

As if he'd read her mind, Antonio's eyes locked onto Marta's. She tried to divert her attention back to the mess. Biting back the tears was pure torture. As soon as her mind fully processed what she'd seen, the lump in her throat swelled, constricting her every breath.

Lupe jolted her with a cruel reminder of her actual station in life. "Clean up this mess, you ignorant girl."

Unable to control her emotions any longer, Marta fled the party, her vision distorted by confusion and tears. When she reached her room, the tears rushed forth. *My God, he is married. Married. He has a child, maybe more than one.* How? Why? Their love was a lie. It had never been real for him. Nausea overtook her, reminding her of the child growing within *her* womb. *A bastard child.* She would never tell Antonio of the baby. Her child deserved far better than a father who spouted deceit as naturally as if he were the devil himself.

Lying on her bed and staring at the painting of *The Last Supper*, Marta knew this was the harsh truth. It was not a bad dream. It was an unfortunate reality, and all of it constructed by a man she'd planned to dedicate her life to. How could he have looked at her the way he had? How could he have held her in his arms? Made love to her? Told her that they would be together soon? Lies. Nothing but lies.

The pleasant thoughts that had danced in her head only hours before dissolved when she looked into his eyes at the fiesta. The truth painfully revealed there. He could no longer hide behind his lies.

She'd forget him. She had to. Antonio Espinoza would mean nothing. Forget his face, eyes, words, touch, all of it. A life grew inside her and she realized she had to find a new way to live for herself, and *her* child. One in which this man would not exist for either of them. Regardless of everything else, she would love the child for what she knew it to be—a blessing from God. Decisions had to be made. Where to go? Where would she begin this new life? How would she get there? How would she provide for herself and her baby? Clearly, she could not stay here.

Suddenly, as if the good Lord himself planted it in her mind, she knew. She would go to where dreams came true. She would go to America.

CHAPTER FOUR

WHEN JOSEFINA CAME IN AFTER THE PARTY AROUND midnight Marta was packing. "What are you doing?" her friend asked.

"What does it look like?" Marta replied.

"I hope not what I think it looks like. Have you gone crazy? You're not planning on leaving."

"I haven't gone crazy, but I am leaving," Marta said. She placed a small crucifix around her neck.

"Think this through, Marta. Why must you go?"

Marta walked over to Josefina and wrapped her arms around her. "I'm sorry, but I cannot stay here now, not after tonight. Señor Rodriguez must be outraged with me. I ruined his celebration."

Josefina pulled away from their embrace but held onto Marta's arms. "You've ruined nothing. The fiesta went fine. Besides, if this is anyone's fault, it's Señor Espinoza's. He lied to you about everything, and now you carry his child. I was so afraid of this. Men like that don't marry girls like us. I'm sorry, Marta, but I knew this to be too good to be true. I wish it wasn't this way. But you can't let that man ruin your life. If anyone should leave here feeling disgraced and never to return, it should be him."

"That may be. But we both know that will never happen. Antonio will come and go as he pleases. Señor Rodriguez will not stop receiving him because he fathered my child and then broke my heart." Marta choked back her desperate need to sob all over again.

"Why can't you simply avoid him when he comes here? Señor Rodriguez is a fair man. He will make certain that your path never crosses with Antonio's," Josefina implored as she sat down on the edge of Marta's bed.

"Even so, I will know he's here, and he'll surely find out about the baby. I do not want my child to have any involvement with that man."

"Please don't go. You're the only true friend I have here. You're my family."

"I'm so sorry," Marta whispered. She went back to putting the few things she had left into a small duffel bag.

"Where do you plan to go? How do you plan to get to wherever it is that you're going?"

"I'm going to America, and I have no idea how I'm getting there." She let out a quiet chuckle, realizing how foolish that sounded, but it didn't change the fact that she was going.

"It's obvious that your mind is made up. I suppose I'll have to help you," Josefina said, picking up one of her friend's sweaters and folding it for her.

"What do you mean?"

"Exactly what I said. Now, make sure you pack only what you need, because the trip you're about to make will be long and grueling. I suggest you get a couple of hours of sleep, because it may be all you are able to get for awhile."

"What are you talking about?"

"A plan. Don't worry. I know how to get you where you need to go."

Marta shook her head. Surely her friend had lost her mind, but she trusted Josefina. After packing, she rested for a bit, her mind racing with thoughts of what lay before her, then with memories of Antonio—memories that now seemed so distant and unreal. She finally fell into a fitful sleep. But no sooner had she done so than Josefina was shaking her awake.

"Come on. We've got to go," she whispered. "Hide your money in two separate places. It can be dangerous out there. Are you certain that you really want to go?"

"I haven't changed my mind."

"Hurry up then. We don't have a lot of time."

Marta quickly got up and dressed. She wore an old black skirt and blouse. Pulling her long, thick hair up into a bun at the nape of her neck, she secured half of the four hundred dollars she'd saved into the hair and net. She was thankful for her long thick hair. If anyone tried to rob her, they wouldn't think to look there. She placed the other half of the money into a jewelry bag, which had been her grandmother's, and tucked it inside her duffel. If she were robbed, that *was* where the thieves would look, and assume that was all she had.

Josefina grabbed her by the hand. They slipped out of the servants' area to the back gate of the estate leading to the shore. A guard with a rifle greeted them. He looked at Josefina who called out, "For the people." The guard nodded his head knowingly, and scanned Marta up and down. A look of suspicion crossed his face.

"She's okay. Señor Rodriguez said that she could work with me tonight. He said that extra help is needed." The guard didn't budge. He stared hard at the two women. "If you think I'm lying, go ask him yourself. I'm sure he'd be thrilled with you for waking him at this hour, especially after he's spent his evening hosting a fiesta."

Muttering to himself, the guard opened the gate, letting them pass through. Marta held tightly onto Josefina's hand as they descended the rock stairway in between overgrown bushes. When they reached the sand, Marta tried to ask Josefina about the incident with the guard.

"Don't worry about that. It's nothing. And remember, anything you might see or do tonight is secret. Don't ask any questions, not one. You may not want to know the answers. Now let's hurry. We haven't got a lot of time."

This was not normal behavior for her friend. The warning to protect secrets that she didn't even know about was frightening.

They walked along the dark beach for a couple of miles, guided by moonlight. Marta, unsure and intimidated, hesitated at one point, almost telling Josefina that this was a ridiculous idea and they should turn back. However, Antonio's face flashed through her mind, followed by an image of his pregnant *wife*. Her resolve hardened and she even picked up her pace.

They passed through the village and heard the songs and laughter of drunken stragglers in the palapa restaurant. Lights from the palapa reflected off the ocean's rolling waves, their shadows following the women as they walked against the shore. The rest of the village was dark now, except for the outlines of huts spread throughout from the shore on up into the jungle's mountainside about a quarter of the way up.

They came around a point at the south end of the beach where Josefina led them back up on a path and into the jungle. The path eventually gave way to a dirt road where they saw the headlights of a truck. It was headed in their direction. Marta's stomach twisted.

Josefina squeezed her hand and smiled at her. "It's fine. When the truck reaches us, climb in, and don't say a single word to anyone."

Once in the dark bed of the truck, Marta made out a group of men and women huddled together. She looked at her friend, who put a finger to her lips. The loaded truck took off up the winding road, its passengers jostled around by its rough surface. The truck started climbing shrouding them in humidity, its denseness filled with a pungent and dank sweetness.

They stopped nearly an hour later, deep in the heart of the jungle. Alarming, unfamiliar sounds echoed throughout the lush thick foliage—screeches from some undeterminable animal, a monkey maybe, and alarming bird calls. Marta shivered. Was this really the right thing? And what in the world were they doing in the jungles of Costa Careyes?

"Act like you belong, and do as I do," Josefina whispered in her ear.

The driver motioned them out of the truck and led the group down an embankment, crossing a stream. Through the trees lights reflected on the water. Marta tried to get a better look at what lay ahead of them. It looked like a factory of some sort.

Baffled, Marta eventually set aside her fear as curiosity took over. What was this place? And why in the world had Josefina brought her here? They walked into the small concrete building and once Marta's eyes adjusted to the lights inside, she carefully looked around her. There was an assembly line of about thirty people putting a liquid substance into vials, and then stuffing the vials into chili peppers. At another row of tables there were about a dozen more people placing the peppers into wooden crates. She looked at Josefina, who shook her head and handed her a crate.

"Start working."

"But, I..."

Josefina held up her hand. "Trust me."

After a couple of hours of working at the task, Marta began to tire. No one said anything. They worked tirelessly. Josefina had to be crazy. How in the world was stuffing these peppers going to get her to America? And, what were they stuffing the peppers with?

As she was about to ask Josefina what was going on and insist on some answers, Josefina tapped her on the shoulder. "It's time to go."

Marta followed her outside with some of the others. They balanced crates on top of their heads or carried them in their arms. Marta held hers in front of her, staggering under the weight of the heavy crate. All she wanted to do was lie down, to not take another step. The day, the emotions, the grueling trip into the jungle was catching up with her.

They reached the road where five trucks were parked. The workers set their crates in the back of the trucks. Josefina took Marta's out of her arms and put it in the back of one of the trucks, then took Marta by the hand and walked up to the passenger side and opened the door.

"Fernando, this is my friend Marta. She has a problem and needs to get to the States. Can you help us?"

The driver leaned forward over the wheel. He had a craggy face and a long black beard, but his eyes looked friendly. "Sure, I'll see that your friend gets to where she needs to go."

Josefina smiled and turned to Marta. "Fernando is a good man. He will take care of you. They take this stuff into the United States all the time. He'll make sure that you get there safely. Don't worry, I wouldn't lead you astray."

Marta hugged her friend for the last time and climbed up into the truck with her small bag of belongings. Moments later the convoy pulled away. Marta, unsure of what she'd experienced, closed her eyes, attempting to sort out everything she'd been through in the past twelve hours. It was strange how things could change in such a short amount of time. How could one go from the happiest moment in life, to the most miserable? Those twelve hours felt more like twelve years.

Fernando spoke, startling her. She opened her eyes. "You might as well settle in, we've got a long trip ahead of us." He smiled at her. He was missing several teeth, and the ones he wasn't missing looked pretty rotten.

She tried to muster a return smile. What in God's name had she gotten herself into?

****

LATE THAT SAME NIGHT, ANTONIO LAY AWAKE STARING AT the blades of the ceiling fan raking the air above his bed. Thankfully, its swishing sound had lulled his wife to sleep. But *nothing* would put *him* to sleep tonight.

Marta's eyes captured his thoughts, and he knew he would never forget the way they'd looked when she'd discovered the truth. God, how he wanted to go to her, comfort her, tell her that he did truly love her, unlike any love he'd ever felt. He knew as he stared into those pain-filled eyes, that the moment would be seared upon his heart and mind forever. What he'd done to her was irreparable. As much as he yearned to go to her, he knew he couldn't. He had already hurt one woman he held dear that evening. He certainly wanted to spare Lydia the proof of his infidelities. They would devastate her. He truly loved her as well, but with a different kind of love. The passion wasn't what it had once been. Marta filled that void.

Would his weakness for beautiful women be his downfall? Marta hadn't been his only affair, but she was the only one, other than his wife, that he'd fallen in love with. He'd had it all for a while, the best of both worlds. There'd been no real need before to tell Marta that he was married. She never asked. He thought that she should have figured it out, a man of his stature and eminence, but he knew damn good and well, deep in his heart, that his Marta did not have any idea that he had a wife. She was naïve and he'd reveled in the fact that she trusted him so deeply. It was that type of innocence that attracted him to her in the first place.

Why had Lydia nagged him so badly to come to the party? She'd left him no choice. He'd tried and tried to convince her that it wasn't in the best interest for her and the baby. But it was to no avail. When Lydia wanted something bad enough, the damn woman knew how to grind on him until she got her way.

Lydia had begged, nagged, pleaded, wanting to see Cynthia and hating being left alone, complaining of his brooding brother Emilio. Lydia had to have been the one to put Cynthia up to the phone call that she'd placed to Antonio, insisting he bring her friend with him so the two could spend time together before they both were occupied with new babies.

Antonio hoped to see Marta before she discovered the truth on her own. He wanted to break it to her gently. He had searched for her during the party, knowing that he had to tell her the truth and convince her that they could still be together when he visited Javier's. But he did not find her in time and by the look in her eyes he knew that any thought of further intimacy between them could not occur. She hated him now. He was certain of that.

If only he could have explained. Lydia hadn't let him out of her sight the entire time they'd been at Javier's. He wondered if her woman's intuition had warned her. Sadly enough, Marta discovered this painful revelation in the worst way. Maybe that was the best way. It would be over, and Antonio could concentrate more on the future of his and Javier's ever-growing empire. Marta took up a lot of space in his mind even when they weren't together.

Lydia rolled over, letting out a groan, her discomfort obvious. He stroked her forehead and silky hair. Lydia loved him, but something drew him to Marta. The girl who was barely a woman had captured his heart. She possessed a power over him that frustrated him beyond words, because he didn't want to desire her. He should not desire her. But he did. Even at that very moment, he craved her.

Logic told him that it was as well that things were over between them, but the spiritual side of him knew that he would never be the same again. Marta had touched him in a way that no other woman had, and he would miss her deeply.

CHAPTER FIVE

THE TRIP FROM COSTA CAREYES TO TIJUANA WERE THE longest days of Marta's life. Even longer than when she'd left her home, brokenhearted after finding out the truth about her parents. She was cursed, she was certain of that now. The trip had been hot, dirty and miserable. Marta was sick a good share of the journey. Fernando had been the Godsend that Josefina indicated he would be, trying his best to keep her nourished and hydrated, but the infant growing inside her sucked everything from her. Constant pangs gnawed at her stomach. Even when she did eat, she wanted to vomit. There were a few times when she did exactly that, and Fernando had to stop and help her clean herself. The men in the convoy grumbled at her, complaining that she was holding them up.

Fernando growled at them to leave her alone. "She's my sister, and she's with child. Back off, all of you!"

They left her alone after that and she looked at him in consternation, surprised that he knew of her condition.

"I have six sisters, and at this point I've lost count of how many nieces and nephews I have. But I figured with all that puking you're doing, you must be carrying a baby," he replied.

Marta nodded, knowing that her face was turning red. She wondered briefly what he thought about her not having a husband, but she felt too sick to really care anymore.

When they arrived in Tijuana, Marta was horrified to see such filth. The stench in the air was one of rot—coppery and foul. It looked nothing like Costa Careyes. Certainly there were poor people there, too, but nothing compared to the poverty she witnessed here. Even the poor where she came from lived reasonably well. They survived on fish, living in small villages where people understood the meaning of family and neighbor. Crime remained low in these villages because it was dealt with in swift, harsh fashion.

Tijuana was far removed from that type of rural poor. As they drove through the main street, Marta noticed how many people, including children, sat on the street corners and begged—encased in dirt. They obviously had no shame. Her feelings went back and forth from sympathy to indignity that anyone would allow their child to beg. It was an indecent thing to do. How could such conditions exist? She had lived a luxurious lifestyle in comparison.

Fernando pulled away from the convoy and over to the side of the road. He glanced at Marta, but didn't look directly at her. "This is as far as I can take you." His eyes were filled with empathy.

She must've misunderstood him. "But we aren't in America yet," she said.

"You're right, but I can take you no further. You must understand we take a big risk crossing the border with what we're carrying. You're an illegal. I can go to jail just transporting you. If I get caught with you, they're certainly going to pull us over and discover what we're transporting. I become a risk to everyone then."

"But I can hide," Marta pleaded, patting down her disheveled hair.

"If I could, I'd take you all the way, but the others insisted that I let you out here."

"But you promised me, and Josefina."

"I know, and I'll make good on my promise," he replied.

"How? Certainly not by letting me out here." Marta grew angry with this man she'd grown to trust in such a short amount of time. He was simply more proof that men were not to be trusted. She was so foolish.

"There is a friend of mine named Tito Velasquez. He takes people across the border for a few hundred dollars. I'll take you up the road he lives on. Then you'll have to walk the rest of the way, because the truck won't make it to the top."

Marta fumed. How could Josefina have entrusted her to this man? Why was Fernando letting her down? To hell with Antonio. This was all his fault. Marta cursed him under her breath, while she nodded her head, defeated again. She had no other choice but to go. She'd come this far, and she was certainly not going to remain in this hellhole a minute longer than necessary.

When Fernando stopped and let her out, he apologized again and described the house that she would be looking for just over the hill. He handed her fifty dollars. "Take this."

"I don't need your money."

"Please. Take it. You may need it. Don't be foolish."

She grabbed the money from him. He told her to tell Tito Velasquez that Fernando had sent her, and then he would cut her a deal on how much she would have to pay to cross over to the States. Marta reluctantly thanked Fernando and slammed the door to his truck.

She climbed the hill ahead of her, and by the time she reached the top and found the shack of a house she was looking for, she was exhausted and longed to be back home. *Home. Home?* She had no home. She swallowed the lump in her throat and summoned up all her courage, lifting her shoulders back and holding her head high.

Shacks dotted the hillside; many of them made of cardboard and scrap material. After coming from one of the finest haciendas in all of Mexico, this was overwhelming. She bit her lower lip and sucked back the emotion choking her.

The house she was looking for turned out to be one of the better ones. It was small, but made of wood and had wrought iron around the windows. There were a handful of children playing in front of the house, ranging from toddlers to teenagers. A man stepped out of the doorway. The first thing Marta noticed was his facial hair and bald head. He reminded her a pirate she'd seen in a book that Señora Rodriguez had read to her and Josefina. There was a large scar across his chest, which she could see through his open shirt. His eyes were dark and close together. He squinted them, watching her as she approached the house.

"Hello. My name is Marta. Fernando sent me here." The man nodded. "He said that you could get me to America." He nodded again. "I am at the right house, aren't I?"

"Yes. I'm Tito Velasquez. Please come in. We can discuss business. You look tired."

"I am. It was a long ride here and not a very comfortable one," Marta replied.

"You came from the Governor's?"

"How did you know?"

"I know Fernando works for him. I have helped others who have come along with him, wanting to cross the border. To be honest with you, I don't have any idea why you would want to leave the beauty you came from for the world you're headed for." He waved his thick arms in exaggerated fashion as if she were a fool.

"Oh, I don't plan to stay here. As I said, I want to go to America," she replied. She thought that he understood this.

"I know. That's what I meant. Come, my wife can make you something to eat. I'm sure you're hungry, and then you can get some rest."

Marta nodded. A few moments later seated at a small wooden table, a plate of beans, rice and tortillas was placed in front of her. The food nourished her and took away the nausea she'd experienced all morning.

She learned from Tito that it would cost her three hundred dollars for him to get her across the border. Usually it took five hundred, but because she was Fernando's friend, he had agreed to cut her a deal. The three hundred would include getting her across safely, because as he explained to her, many times bandits got hold of people and robbed them, and even worse, sometimes raped the women. The thought produced goose bumps on her slender arms.

"Once you get across, you will meet up with my partner, who will take you to Los Angeles. Jobs are plentiful there." He winked at her. "We'll be leaving soon. Right after the sun sets. We will walk most of the night, and it will be long and hard. I set a certain pace, and expect you to keep up with it. It's necessary to move quickly in order to avoid immigration and bandits." Marta's heart raced at the thought of what dangers may lie ahead. "Of course, you can change your mind if you'd like, and stay here in this beautiful city we call Tijuana," he mused, a smirk on his face.

"No. I look forward to going," she replied. She searched his eyes for confirmation.

"Then don't look so scared. I make this trip often. Like Fernando said, you are in good hands."

Weren't those the same exact words that Josefina had used when she'd handed her off to Fernando? But what did she have to lose? She'd come this far; she would keep going. There really weren't any other options. Antonio had already stripped her of her dignity, friends, job, and home. She handed Tito the money and he got up from the table, muttering under his breath about stupid people and their silly dreams.

Tito's wife let Marta lie down on a cot, and told her it was necessary to get some sleep for the crossing. His wife was portly and aged. Her face, lined with crevices, made Marta want to reach out and touch it. She wondered if it felt like the sandpaper it resembled. However homely, the woman treated Marta in a gentle way, which she greatly appreciated after the hardships she'd encountered so far.

As soon as her head hit the cot, she was sound asleep. Around four o'clock, the sun beating in through the open window woke her, and Tito came in shortly afterwards to let her know that it was time to go.

Walking to the border took only an hour. On the way Marta saw more of the poverty locked inside Tijuana. She was ashamed that this was even a part of her country. Many of the people she saw didn't look Mexican. They possessed darker skin and more angular faces. They appeared to be the poorest of the lot, and Marta knew they were Indians. Tito spit on one as they walked past. The sight caused Marta's stomach to rumble and feel that all too familiar feeling of wanting to vomit.

When they reached their destination, they met up with a few other people who'd obviously had met with Tito beforehand. There was another woman, a little older than Marta. She smiled shyly at Marta when they exchanged glances. But Marta wasn't in the mood to make friends. She'd already been forced to trust enough strangers in the last week to last her a lifetime. No more.

There were also three other men in the group, as well as a girl of about thirteen traveling with one of them who had to be her father. Marta could see the sad desperation in the girl's eyes. She instinctively wanted to comfort this frightened child.

She found it odd to see at least a hundred or more men, women, and children lined up at the border fence, like a group of dogs wanting to jump over to the other side. The Tijuana River before them was nearly dried up, but it disgusted her all the same. It smelled putrid from feces and rot. A dead dog, its guts hanging out, added to the dreadful odor. Marta averted her eyes. There were several abandoned old cars up and down the river bottom for as far as she could see, and trash was strewn everywhere.

Tito faced them, "This is not where we cross. We go further along the fence away from all of these ignorants. There is a much less chance that we get caught going in a little further before crossing over. And many times the fencing is down the further we walk, so we won't even need to cut through."

At first Marta wasn't too sure about Tito's idea of waiting to cross the fence. Surely they could run fast enough and then they'd be there—America. It was only a stone's throw away. Why was he so cautious? So many others were taking their chances.

As the group continued to walk along the fence line, she looked back for an instant, and could see some of the people who hadn't been quick enough after getting through the holes cut into the fence, and she now understood why Tito took such great care. Because her entire life savings was on her, and because she'd already spent so much money and time getting to the promised land, she grew grateful for this man's caution. She could see those unfortunates who had been rounded up like herds of cattle by Immigration officers. She heard angry shouts and screams coming from them.

As her group pushed forward, others who also decided to travel further inland before crossing made their attempts, and before long it was Tito and his handful of travelers trekking through the dust and chaparral alone.

After some time, they stopped and Tito let everyone have a drink of water. He then pointed to the mountain they would be climbing. "Follow me at all times," he said sharply. "Once we are over the mountain, we are out of any danger of being caught by Immigration. They have yet to find these trails, I've made. But there are other dangers out here, and you need to all be close to me and be aware."

The last thing Marta wanted was to climb that intimidating mountain. And she certainly didn't like the sound of whatever dangers might lie ahead. But there was no looking back now.

Climbing the rough terrain was hard on Marta's pregnant body. Barren bushes snagged her skirt and produced small cuts on her legs. Her muscles, stiff from the hike, began to spasm, causing her to groan in pain.

Finally, around ten o' clock at the top of the mountain, Tito let them have another rest and some dinner that his wife had packed for them.

"Hi, my name is Elisa. What's yours?" the other woman asked.

Marta answered hesitantly. She wasn't eager to meet anyone new, and she felt so miserable from the climb that she glared back at Elisa. "Marta," she replied, biting her lower lip at the sound of her irritation.

"Are you excited?" Marta looked at her dumbfounded. "I mean, about the United States."

"Yes."

"Do you have a job there?"

"No."

"This is my third time crossing. I already live there. My two boys are citizens, because they were born in the States, but my family lives in Mexico, so I try to go down once a year to visit with them." The woman buzzed on.

She spoke so rapidly that Marta had to concentrate to understand her. Her Spanish sounded much different than the Spanish that Marta spoke, and she couldn't help but view Elisa as being a member of a lower class. Marta smiled at the thought that she'd lived in a beautiful mansion. She figured it wouldn't hurt to be congenial for a few minutes with the woman. The fact that she'd crossed the border before aroused Marta's curiosity. "You've made your way across other times?"

"Yes, I always I have Tito take me, because he's for real, you know. Some of these men take your money and drive you to the border. They're thieves. Take everything you've ever worked for. You think they're going to cross with you, and you get ready to go, then turn around to find your leader gone. Gone with your money and everything else you owned. It's crazy. I tell you, I've seen it before. And he is wise not to cross back there in Tijuana. It's too risky. And so hard after you always get caught and they send you back, you try again..." She waved a hand in Marta's face. "This is a longer way, but worth it. You're lucky you found Tito on your first time across, 'cause otherwise you don't know what could happen. It happened to my cousin, when Immigration caught her. Scared her so bad, said she'd never do it again. Not me, though. I'm lucky I know Tito. He gets me safely across every time."

"You're not scared?"

"No. The first time I was. The second, a little, but not anymore."

"Where do you live?" Marta asked intrigued by how worldly this woman was, even if she was only a peasant.

"I live in Los Angeles. There are lots of factories up there, you know. My boys and me live there. I sew clothes. It's a hard job, but better than most. At least I don't have to work in the meat factories. I make much more money there than I could anywhere in Mexico. Why are you coming to the States?"

Marta briefly explained to her that she lost a job cleaning house for a rich man, and heard there were lots of jobs in America.

"This is true. Lots of rich *gringos* need you to clean house. They pay pretty good too, I hear. I couldn't get one of those jobs, though. I'm not so pretty, you know. But you, no problem. In fact, I know some friends who could help you out."

Marta grew more interested, while she wrapped her trash up, and stuck it neatly into her pack.

"You got some money, don't you?" Elisa asked her.

"A little, why?" Marta wondered, touching her bun, making sure the money she'd secured several times during her trip was still there.

"To get a place to live in Los Angeles, you need money. There is a place next to mine you can rent for two hundred dollars a month."

Marta thought that sounded like a lot of money, but after all, it was the United States, and she was sure she'd be making a lot, too. *The place must be pretty nice.* Marta nodded yes, and was then jolted out of her senses when Tito hollered at the two women to quiet down for a moment—his voice taut.

They obeyed him, sensing something must be wrong. They could see by the moonlight that he and the other two men were cocking their revolvers. The young girl clung tightly to her father's side. Marta's insides rattled at the prospect of what could be out there.

Tito suddenly yelled, "*Bandidos*! Get down!"

Marta felt Elisa push her down and bit her lip; she tasted blood as she fell to the ground. She heard men yelling and cursing, and gunshots echoing around her. Elisa pulled Marta closer to her and then grabbed her by her hand, urging her to come with her. While the men were busy fighting, they didn't notice the two women slipping away. Marta and Elisa could see that bandidos outnumbered the men in their group. Marta wondered where the young girl was. She even turned to go back for her, but Elisa stopped, holding on to her fiercely. So she couldn't do more than hope that the girl had managed to get away.

Marta's heart beat rapidly, her blood racing with terror. She and Elisa ran as fast as they could, holding onto each other. They found a small cave and hid in it.

A few moments later, they heard distant laughter coming from the ambush site. Silently weeping in each other's arms, they heard a shrill scream. With a jolt of fear, Marta realized the bandits had the young girl. It seemed an eternity before the screaming turned into mere echoes of a whine. Marta desperately wanted to save the poor girl. She prayed to the Virgin Mary as the sounds of torture filled her ears.

She'd never heard sounds like those before. They were inhuman, made even more so by the cruel laughter of the men.

Marta cringed at the thought of what they were doing to her. She and Elisa continued to hold each other tightly, squeezing harder each time they heard the keening of the girl, who now sounded like a whipped dog. The men cried out names like *bitch* and *whore* at her. Marta prayed they would leave, so they could rescue her.

Suddenly, however, they heard a gunshot, followed by wave after wave of vicious laughter. They had killed the poor girl. Marta cried for her, praying that her soul was now in Heaven, and the acts that she'd been forced to endure forgotten along with the memories of the world's cruelty.

****

MARTA AND ELISA DIDN'T MOVE THE ENTIRE NIGHT, waiting instead until dawn before they decided to leave the safety of the cave. Marta wept throughout the night, fearing for her life and that of her baby's. And she grieved the girl who'd suffered such a violent death. Elisa comforted Marta, stroking her hair and telling her that things were going to be all right. The men's laughter died down after a time, and Marta assumed they must've gone away.

When the sun came up, the women decided they had to move on.

"Come on, Marta. We're not going to get anywhere by staying here. I've crossed often enough. I think I know where to go."

"I'm so afraid. What if those men come back?" Marta asked, feeling uncomfortable in her skirt, which was now soaked in her own urine.

"I know you're afraid, but if we stay here, we'll die. We must be careful, that's all. I don't think those men are anywhere near. They got what they came for," Elisa replied scornfully. She took Marta by the hand and led her out of the cave.

Marta held on to the end of Elisa's skirt as they hiked up the hill. The stout, buxom woman didn't seem to mind. With her long hair twisted up into a braid, she reminded Marta of her grandmother. Following in her footsteps, a wave of gratitude came over her.

Halfway up the hill, they witnessed the effects from the night before. Tito lay half hidden in a bush, his shirt torn from the thicket he'd fallen into. There was a gunshot wound in the center of his abdomen and a trickle of blood dried on the side of his mouth.

"Don't look, Marta."

"He looks so awful."

"He's with Our Lord now. Turn away. I'm going to see if he has any food left in his pack."

"Elisa, no."

"If we don't get it, then surely the coyotes will. I don't know how long we'll be traveling, and we're going to need some food and water."

For a minute, Marta wanted to continue her protest. But then she thought about her unborn child, and realized that what Elisa said was the truth. She turned away. As she did she could see another one of the men they'd been traveling with. She went over to the corpse, even though she feared the sight of the man. However, she was smart enough to realize that it was her life that mattered now. She approached the man while Elisa scoured Tito's pack.

"What are you doing?" Elisa hollered.

"It's another one of the men. Maybe he has some food."

When she moved closer to the body, his chest heaved, gasping to fill his lungs with air. He was still alive. She rushed over to him. He looked up at her with glossy eyes. She knelt down. *Dios Mío. My, God, My God.* A gaping hole in the man's pants exposed his bullet wound, blood oozing from it puddled onto the dirt beside him. The pain in his eyes sent an ache through her body as she placed her hand on his forehead and stroked back his hair, doing what she could to provide him with some comfort.

The wretched stench of death permeated the air—the blood around her—and its odor was metallic and sour. It burned her nostrils, causing her eyes to water. She pulled her hand away and jumped back from his body when he flinched. Then, nothing.

She wiped the tears from her face and looked away only to be brought back to her knees by the sight of the body of the girl a few feet away. Marta brought her hand to her mouth covering both her need to wretch and scream. Then she covered her eyes and let out a wail. Elisa came to her side. Marta forced herself to look again at the girl, her nude body barely recognizable, covered in bruises and dried blood.

"Turn away," Elisa commanded, in a voice taut with dread.

"What should we do now?" Marta asked, as they backed away from the carnage and looked northward.

"We keep moving."

CHAPTER SIX

SIX MONTHS HAD PASSED SINCE JAVIER HAD HOSTED THE
party for his wife Cynthia. His father had passed away three months
earlier and they were now back in their home in Guadalajara,
mountains surrounding them on either side. Their home in the city
was not the palatial vacation villa they owned on the coast. Like
Guadalajara itself, their home was reminiscent of the entire city
itself—colonial and historical. Javier and Cynthia's home had been
built over a hundred years earlier for a general in the Mexican army
who had spared no expense. When Javier and Cynthia had moved in
as he took the office of governor, Cynthia had had the place
refurbished, maintaining its history. Much of the artwork placed in
alcoves consisted of antiques from the colonial time period.

There were twelve bedrooms in the house and one of them had
now been decorated as a nursery and another a playroom. The
Rodriguez's baby would have every comfort imaginable.

Javier sipped sangria from his glass as he sunbathed near the pool located in the Saltillo tiled courtyard. While soaking in the incredible heat, he could not stop thinking about the large amount of money he and Antonio were making by shipping heroin and marijuana up north. The distributors loved the stuff, and they couldn't supply it fast enough to keep up with the demand. The Vietnam War was in full force, and American kids were smoking a lot of the weed, and almost as many were shooting the brown poison into their veins. Javier and Antonio were living in grand style because of it. It amazed him that so many people wanted to change their state of mind, their emotions, whatever it was that made their life unbearable that they wanted to escape it through drugs. He shook his head and figured it was not about him. If people were honestly so stupid to buy the drugs that he and Antonio supplied, then so be it. Money was money and the money was fantastic.

"*Señor* Rodriguez," Lupe screamed. "*Señor*—come quick. The baby. Señora is having the baby."

What? No, that couldn't be. It was too soon. He bolted from his lounge chair, spilling his glass of *sangria* all over his white shirt and shorts. He raced to Cynthia's room, where several of the maidservants were gathered and pushed his way through. There his wife lay on the bed, covered in a pool of sweat and screaming out in pain.

"The doctor! Where in the hell is the doctor?" Javier barked.

"He's on his way, *Señor*. We called him. It happened so suddenly."

"Javier," Cynthia cried out.

He rushed to her side, and held her clammy hand—her face drained of color. "I'm so hot. The baby is coming too early." She turned to him, tears pooling in her beautiful green eyes. Javier could see that his wife was caught in her own pain- filled world. Something wasn't right.

He sat with her, stroking her hair back off her forehead and telling her how much he loved her as they waited for the doctor. Soon after her water broke, the doctor rushed in, immediately commanding everyone to leave the room, adding to Javier's deep fear. After an initial examination, the doctor sent for Javier. Taking him aside, he told him, "I'm afraid she has a very high fever. I believe it is caused by a condition known as toxemia. It's very dangerous for her and the baby."

"What is that? I don't know what that is. How dangerous?" he asked unable to keep the panic out of his voice.

The doctor didn't look at him. "I'll do everything I can." He pushed his bifocals up his long nose.

"Let's take her to the hospital," Javier demanded. "Right now. We must go now."

"It's too late, Governor. An hour ago, yes, maybe so, but the baby will be born soon. We can only pray."

"Pray? What do you mean, that's all we can do? There must be something, *anything* you can do. You have to help her."

"I will do what I can," the doctor replied, shaking his head and walked back to Cynthia's side.

Javier felt the walls closing in on him. Slumped against the door like a beaten dog, he prayed, tears running down his face. He could not believe his lovely wife could die. He had to be with her and comfort her. He pulled himself up and went to Cynthia, taking her by the hand again, praying his own life force would seep into her body through the warmth of his hands.

She weakly squeezed his hand and murmured, "I know something is wrong, Javier. I can feel it. I see it in your eyes."

Javier shook his head. "No, love, you're fine. Everything is going to be all right. I'm a nervous father-to-be, that's all."

"Please, Javier, please have them save the baby. Let the baby know how much I loved and wanted..."

"You are talking nonsense now. You need to rest, love," he said.

"Bring me the priest," she whispered.

Javier sighed and sobbed quietly. His life passed before him. He could not lose his wife and child. He kissed her cheek, knowing it was useless to protest. He closed her door behind him, and had one of the maids call for Father Felipe. The priest came within the hour. By that time Cynthia's fever had risen and the sheets were soaked with her perspiration.

The priest went to her and read the last rites at her bedside. As he made the sign of the cross, Cynthia went into convulsions. Javier yelled out. He was powerless and grief-stricken as he watched her die. He held her hands tight as the priest finished giving the sacraments. And as if she'd been granted permission to die, she did so with grace. Her hands went limp, her breathing shallow until she took a last breath and her eyes fluttered closed.

The doctor placed a hand on Javier's shoulder. I am so sorry, Governor. You must go now, though. Please go and wait outside. "I have to deliver your baby. We do not have much time."

Javier wiped the tears away and nodded. He didn't want to leave Cynthia there. It didn't feel right but he knew there was no other choice. Cynthia had specifically asked that her baby be saved. He left the doctor alone with her.

Standing outside Cynthia's room, Javier fell to pieces. She was gone. Grief and shock traveled icy cold through his body. His mind numb, his heart pained as if it were being held in a vise. How could this have happened? Tears blurring his vision, he punched a wall and yelled out.

His misery was shattered with the sound of a baby's cry coming from the other room. He pushed open the door, and witnessed the doctor holding up a tiny, red infant. He gazed at the scene for a moment. Cynthia covered with the bloodstained sheet, not moving. He pulled the sheet off her peaceful face and kissed her tenderly. "I love you always," he whispered. He then turned around to see his new baby daughter wrapped in woolen blankets.

The doctor said, "She's tiny, only five pounds, but that's because she's a bit premature. I don't see anything wrong with her, however. She's breathing well and has good color. Give her to one of your maids and she should do fine. But if you'd prefer, I can take her to the hospital, where we can monitor her."

Cynthia's nursemaid, Consuela, began to walk forward to take the baby, but Javier intercepted her, gently lifting her out of the doctor's arms. He cradled his newborn daughter. "No," he said firmly, holding his hand up to Consuela. "I will take care of my daughter."

****

AT THE MOMENT JAVIER LAID CLAIM TO HIS BABY DAUGHTER, hundreds of miles away, Marta Peña lay in a twin bed covered with a patchwork quilt she'd made over the months. She kissed the top of her small son's head. He'd been born the night before.

"He looks so perfect," Elisa said.

"Mhhm. He is perfect," Marta replied.

The dark-haired baby slept comfortably next to the warmth of his mother. His birth had been easier than she'd expected. Elisa had helped deliver him, along with a midwife. The labor had only lasted four hours in the bedroom of their apartment.

"I'll bet you never thought you'd make it." Elisa interrupted her thoughts. "Especially when we were stuck out in the middle of nowhere, with no idea how to get here."

Marta let out a sigh of sheer exhaustion, mixed with the bliss she felt over the birth of her son. "I owe it all to you. If not for you, I would've never been able to settle here in the United States."

Marta remained grateful to God and to Elisa for getting her across the border, and that the rest of the trip had gone along without incident. Once in Los Angeles, Elisa convinced Marta to rent the room below hers, in the duplex where she and her boys lived. There were four families living in the small area, but it was clean, and they all treated each other well enough. Marta had taken on several jobs cleaning houses and made a decent living for a while, but now that the baby was here, she was afraid she'd lose those jobs.

"No one will want me back to clean now that I have a baby, and I can't afford child care."

"Don't worry about it, Marta. I have some good news for you. I am marrying Jefé, and he says that I don't need to work outside the house any longer. I will take care of the baby." Elisa looked so excited that she blushed like a schoolgirl. "He has a good job, and said I could stay home with the boys from now on. I'm sure he wouldn't mind if I take care of the baby, too."

"Why didn't you tell me?"

"He only asked me last night, and then you decided to surprise us not long after with the little one here." She bent over and kissed the baby.

"I can't ask you to take care of him."

"And why not? We are like sisters, you and I. God has brought us together for a reason. We've already conquered much together. I would be honored to take care of our little baby. By the way, what are you going to name him?"

"I don't know."

"What was his father's name?"

Marta paused for a moment. "Antonio." The name sounded foreign to her. Although she and Elisa had a bond, she never spoke of Antonio and it seemed as if Elisa knew not to ask, until now.

"That is a powerful name. So your son here must have one equal to it. Let me see. How about Jesús? Or Mañuel?"

"No," Marta answered, thinking hard for a moment for a befitting name. Finally she said, "I think I'll name him Alejandro after my grandmother's father. She always told me he was a strong and brave man."

Elisa nodded in approval. "I like that. Very strong." She made a fist and held it up high.

Marta smiled. "Good then, I will name him Alejandro. Alejandro Peña."

CHAPTER SEVEN

ANTONIO WATCHED HIS FIVE-YEAR-OLD DAUGHTER ROSA
picking flowers in the garden, while he held his nine-month-old
daughter, Felicia. The cherubic baby slept soundly in her father's
arms. Lydia had gone into town for the day. Since it was Sunday, the
nanny was in town with her family.

Antonio enjoyed this time alone with his young daughters. He
loved both of them dearly. He did, however, want a son and although
his passion for his wife was tempered with the loss of Marta, he
would soon suggest to Lydia that it was time to try for a son. He
desired to have someone carry on the Espinoza name. Even though
there was always the possibility that his only brother Emilio would
marry and have a son one day, he wasn't going to bet on it.

Antonio glanced down at his watch. His brother was supposed to
have met him fifteen minutes ago. Apparently, Emilio had important
news for him. What that news might be didn't particularly interest
Antonio, as what was important to Emilio was usually fairly trivial to
Antonio. More than likely his younger brother had run out of money.

"Antonio." He heard Emilio's voice ring out from behind him. He turned around to see his brother descending the stairs at the back of the house. It was no wonder he hadn't married. The man was so good looking, why should he settle for one beautiful wife when he could have many women? Plus, he was still quite young. Emilio walked toward them. He wore nothing but white, his usual attire. He told Antonio that women loved the innocence of white. Antonio laughed out loud, remembering his brother carrying on endlessly about women and what they loved.

Emilio strode up to his brother. Antonio put his finger to his lips and glanced down at the stirring baby.

"Hi," Emilio whispered, running his palms through the natural waves in his hair.

Antonio nodded. Rosa followed closely behind her uncle while she tugged on her father's pant leg. "Come pick flowers with me? Please, Papa, please."

"In a moment, mija. Your uncle and I need to speak first. Why don't you see if you can find your mama the prettiest one?"

"Okay, Papa," the reluctant child sighed.

Antonio patted Felicia while keeping a close eye on Rosa, and then asked Emilio what was so important.

"I received word earlier today that Simon Levine wants to meet with you and Javier."

"Who did you hear this from?"

"A fellow working for him down in Cuba. Levine says the Italians in New York are getting nervous with us running drugs down here. He claims he can keep everyone happy."

"Fucking Spics," Antonio said, spitting. He knew that no matter how badly he wanted to control the industry, the big guys would always be the Italians. The Italians had laid out a lot of money to begin their partnership with the Latino Mafia, and they obviously didn't like the fact they were losing some of their profit to Antonio's group. He'd miscalculated their interest in drugs coming from his country. Simon Levine was a man who had his hand in all things that could make him money. He'd been involved with La Cosa Nostra to an extent, but he was also his own man. He did business with the Italians but kept them at arm's length. Was he planning to do this with Antonio and Javier? Likely he wanted a piece of the pie, too. Levine couldn't be ignored. He had too much power, wealth and was well connected.

"What are you going to do?"

"Meet with him," Antonio growled, causing the baby to wake up. He bounced her against his shoulder for a moment and she quieted down.

"What about Javier?"

"What about Javier? He'll meet with him, too."

"Haven't you heard?" Emilio cocked his head, looking at his brother intently.

"Heard what?"

"Cynthia. She died in childbirth a few days ago. I thought you certainly would have known."

"Oh, my God. No. The baby? What about the baby?"

"I guess she's fine. Javier hasn't let anyone besides the wet nurse touch her. He says he's to take care of her, and no one else."

"Ay, he's gone crazy. How did you find this out before I did?"

"I have a connection who knows somebody who works for him," Emilio replied.

"I see. Go to the house; tell the maid to have my bags packed and the helicopter ready."

"You're going there?"

"Of course I am. Javier is like family. It's time we help him. Besides, his wife needs to be buried, and we have to get back to business. The longer we wait, the longer Levine waits, and I don't feel good about that."

*****

WIIEN ANTONIO ARRIVED AT JAVIER'S HACIENDA, THE SUN had set. He was escorted into a wing of the house he'd never seen before. Walking down the long hallway, he realized it had been designed for the children meant to occupy it. Along the corridors were painted murals of carousel horses and teddy bears. It was filled with pastel colors.

He wasn't quite sure what he would say to Javier and he hesitated a moment before following Lupe, who led him to the last door on the left.

He tapped on the door and walked in. Sitting there in a rocking chair was his friend, with a tiny infant wrapped in a pink blanket. Javier slouched slightly over the child. To Antonio, he appeared smaller, older, weaker. He slowly looked up at Antonio. The grieving father's eyes were lined with deep, dark circles, and the whites of his eyes were bloodshot. Dried tears on his face reflected a quiet vulnerability.

Antonio walked over and placed his hands on Javier's shoulders. Javier shuddered beneath them. "My friend, I'm so sorry about your loss. I know that you must be in very deep pain." Javier nodded. "Please let me and my family help you. Come stay with us for a time. Lydia and the nanny...." Antonio didn't have a chance to finish his sentence, when Javier held up his hand.

"Isabella is my daughter. No one will take care of her except me." He looked at Antonio defiantly.

It was apparent Javier had made up his mind. Antonio respected that. Once Javier recovered a bit from the loss of Cynthia, he would come around.

"When is the funeral?"

"Day after tomorrow."

"Is there anything I can do?"

"No."

"I know this is a terrible time, but you need to be aware that Simon Levine is coming to see us."

Javier sighed, obviously not wanting to discuss business. "When?"

"Some time next week. Would it be easier for you if he came to Colombia?"

"I'd prefer here. The baby will not be ready to go anywhere by that time."

"I understand." Antonio leaned over and kissed the baby on her forehead. "She is beautiful, my friend. Like her mother." He placed a hand over Javier's for a moment. "All you have to do is ask. Anything. Anything you need for you, your daughter..." He nodded and removed his hand from his friend's.

As Antonio reached the door, Javier called out to him, "Thank you, brother." Tears filled his eyes.

****

AFTER A BITE OF SUPPER, ANTONIO RETURNED TO HIS ROOM and reflected on Javier's loss and of his own long-lost Marta, which kept him tossing and turning through most of the night. He had no idea where Marta had run off to, and didn't feel that it was appropriate to ask Javier.

He got up to pour himself a drink when he heard a young woman's voice outside his door. "*Señor Espinoza?*" His heart skipped a beat. He wondered for a moment if it were Marta. He parted the door slowly, and there stood Josefina.

He'd seen her several times in the past with Marta. The two were obviously close. She wasn't pretty like Marta, but rather plain, and Antonio had no interest in her whatsoever.

"What can I do for you?"

"I came here to tell you something, *Patrón*," she said, her close-set eyes staring down at her rather large feet.

"Yes?" Antonio asked, amused that such a silly looking girl might have the courage to approach him.

"I'm not sure how to tell you this, but I don't feel right keeping it from you."

"What is it? I am tired."

"Marta has given birth to your son."

Antonio stared at the young woman for several seconds. She did not look at him. "What?" He finally said, his voice raised as a nervous and angry energy turned his blood cold. "Is this some joke? I will have you fired for this. You imbecile!"

Josefina shoved a fistful of letters into his palm, then abruptly disappeared, leaving Antonio startled and confused.

Antonio sat down at the desk and read the half-dozen letters Marta had sent to Josefina. They expressed her deep love for Antonio, and the powerful effect his betrayal had had upon her. The letters clearly described the details of Marta's experience crossing the border, and how she blamed Antonio for all her hardships. It was obvious that she never wanted to see Antonio again.

He was impressed with her perseverance. He never would have imagined that Marta had the nerve to go alone to the United States.

And when she mentioned how much she missed Mexico, his stomach sank, knowing he was responsible for her leaving. If only he had been honest with her from the start, she never would have had to go through so much pain.

He'd had no idea what a strong and determined young woman she was, and he felt a renewed yearning for her, a desire to go to her and comfort her for all that she'd endured.

His eyes raced across the words of Marta's last letter in which she described her pregnancy and her newborn son. Josefina told him the truth. He sat stunned. He had a son? He had a *son*. The reality came over him, lifting away lies and tucked away emotions. Anguished, he cried out, frightened at the sound of the pain in his voice. He couldn't believe he had a son. The son he'd always longed for finally existed. Bittersweet tears stung his eyes as he dropped his head into his palms and sobbed.

CHAPTER EIGHT

THE DIESEL FUMES FROM THE CHARTERED PLANE GAVE
Antonio an intense headache. As a remedy, he drank a few measures
of Scotch before takeoff. Once under way, he felt the calming effect of
the alcohol, and he let his mind focus on the problems he'd been
trying to avoid. However, no matter how hard he tried, he could not
get over the fact that somewhere in this world, he had a son—a son
he longed for but could not rationalize claiming as his.

The last few weeks with Javier had been horrendous. Cynthia's
death had taken a severe toll on him, and the fact that he'd insisted
on staying up throughout night after night with the baby made
matters worse. There were now dark shadows under his eyes; eyes,
which, at one time, were vibrant and alive, now contained an
unbearable sadness in them, aging Javier beyond his years. Yet,
Antonio couldn't help but admire him. The devotion he had shown
his daughter was nothing short of miraculous. Antonio realized that
the infant filled the void Javier felt so deeply. Antonio could
understand this because he himself felt such a void. He wondered
what his son looked like, how he was faring. He'd obtained the

address where he and Marta were living through the labels on the envelopes. Many times in the two weeks since he'd discovered that he had a son, he longed to fly to Los Angeles and visit them, if only to hold his son. But he knew that the love he still felt for Marta, compounded by the birth of their son, could lead him so far astray that he might never return to his family. He could not bring himself to carry out such a cruel injustice. His wife was a good woman, and he loved her and their daughters.

So, he buried himself in his work. Javier's interest in their business and his own politics waned in such a short amount of time that Antonio had witnessed their operations slipping. At the behest of Javier, he'd taken over the production of heroin in their jungle factory, managing all phases of that portion of the business.

Heroin was such a strange drug. Why in the name of Jesus would people want to stick themselves with a needle, and inject foreign venom into their bodies? *Crazy.* Nonetheless, the Mexican Mud produced quite a substantial amount of cash, and profits were growing larger by the day. If the *pinche gringos* wanted to get high off the brown poison, it was surely none of his business, as long as the cash kept rolling in.

The struggle for power between the Mexican and Italian families was growing fiercer, and now Simon Levine had summoned Antonio and Javier, insisting that he was no longer willing to wait. Antonio was able to postpone the meeting for a few weeks, in the hopes that Javier would rid himself of his grief. The last thing Antonio needed was a bereaved widower on his hands.

Antonio arrived in the Bahamas and slid into the back of a limousine, which delivered him to the entrance of a lavish hotel, where Levine's driver informed him that Señor Rodriguez had already arrived. Antonio shuddered when the man also mentioned sarcastically what a cute baby Señor Rodriguez had brought with him. Antonio could see the man's white teeth glow against his coal-black skin as he flashed a mocking smile.

The massive hotel spanned a good portion of the picturesque beach overlooking a pale turquoise sea. Once inside, guests were dazzled by dozens of slot machines, flashing and glittering. Hundreds of American tourists, zinc oxide spread over their noses, poured money into the machines, passion fruit drinks in their hands. The Bahamas had become all the rage since Castro had taken Cuba away from the Mafioso, but Antonio was a bit shocked. He hadn't realized the extent of its success. There was evidence all around that Nassau was fast becoming a haven for the wealthy and the high-stakes gamblers alike.

A courteous gentleman from the front desk escorted Antonio to the Presidential Suite. "Is everything to your satisfaction, sir?"

"Yes." A mirrored ceiling reflected an enormous round bed covered in black velvet. There was a built-in hot tub in the center of the room.

"Is there anything I can get for you, Mr. Espinoza?" the man asked.

"No, I think that will be all," Antonio replied, tipping him.

"Thank you, sir. Mr. Levine will see you and Mr. Rodriguez in the private dining room at seven. Is that time suitable to you?"

Antonio nodded, hoping that Javier had hired a nanny by this time. Calling the desk, he was put through to Javier's room.

Javier's tired voice answered the phone. "Hello?"

"What do you think you're doing, bringing Isabella down here while we're about to deal with Simon Levine? Where in hell did you leave your senses?"

"Leave my daughter out of this. She goes with me no matter what, no matter where. I brought a nurse along to be with her when I can't. She is my daughter, my responsibility. I expect you to understand that. And if you and the hardball playing Jew don't like it, then you can both go fuck yourselves."

Antonio was taken aback by the vehemence of Javier's outburst. Never in his life had he been spoken to like that—and certainly not by Javier. For a moment, Antonio wanted to shake some sense into his head. Instead of retorting, he calmed down and replied, "Fine. Be in the dining room at seven—alone." Antonio hung up the phone with a newfound respect for his partner and friend.

ᛇᛇᛇᛇ

SIMON LEVINE WAS A SMALL MAN, BUT HIS MERE PRESENCE commanded respect. Although his gnarled features and razor-thin body gave him the appearance of fragility, his gravelly voice boomed when he spoke, causing all within his range to stop what they were doing and pay attention. Antonio couldn't guess his age, perhaps sixty, maybe even seventy. His salt-and-pepper gray hair receded behind his ears, with only a marginal tuft left at the very center. His narrow eyes didn't reveal much—a skill that Antonio figured Levine had learned from years of experience in this dangerous business. He offered his hand to Antonio, who found to his surprise that the man's seeming weakness was only a facade. The stoop shouldered man had a strong grip.

"Please sit down, gentlemen." Levine motioned to the table inside the elaborate dining room, aglow with candlelight. "I'm pleased you could both make it here. I hope your flights were pleasant and that everything is to your liking." He poured each of them a glass of expensive French wine. "This is my finest," he said, taking a sip and sending the waiter away with a flip of the hand.

Antonio glanced over at Javier, who hadn't cracked a smile and obviously wasn't in the mood for congeniality. Antonio nudged him with his knee underneath the table, and Javier brought himself to the proceedings with reluctance. He smiled on cue and drank his wine. The formalities dispensed with, Antonio viewed this as an appropriate time to approach the subject of their presence there.

"Mr. Levine, you did not ask us here to drink your wine and to lounge in the luxury of your hotel."

"Call me Simon, as I will surely call you Antonio. You are right. I have not called you here for these things. However, I do enjoy seeing to your comfort, and I want you to feel free to ask for whatever you like while you are here in the Bahamas. Do so at my expense, please." He smiled at Antonio and Javier, flashing the brilliance of a gold cap on one tooth. "Allow me to explain to you why I have invited you here. I think I can do as much for you gentlemen as you can for me. You've been running illegal immigrants through here for years now, as many other families from Mexico have. But I like the way you do it. You're honest. You give your people, no matter how simple, what they pay for—a one-way trip to Miami. Many of the other families aren't nearly as fastidious. They steal their clients' money, leaving me with a heap of uneducated foreigners I don't want hanging around my doorstep. You understand?"

Antonio and Javier both nodded.

"Therefore, I'd like to make you a few propositions that should increase your business tenfold. The first is, we make a deal. I allow *only* your organization to transport your people up here. In return, I see to it they get to the States. Together we shut down all the other organizations. *Voilá*, you and yours monopolize the trade, my friends."

"And what do you want out of this?" Antonio asked.

"Smart man," Levine replied, shaking a finger at him. "I want a mere five percent off the top, nothing more, nothing less."

"And how do we know you don't set this up with all the others?"

"As I said, I like the way you gentlemen do business. I'm not in the game to fuck anybody over. If I can find a couple of honest partners who feel the same way, then why do I need anyone else?"

"How do we get rid of the others?"

"Force. If they don't back out peacefully, we use a little force. Nothing commands more respect than a well-placed threat. Wouldn't you agree?"

"I like it, Antonio. I think we should see how it goes. Besides, we can still run them through Mexico into San Diego," Javier said.

"Javier is right,' Simon said. "I don't need any part of that. I'm only talking about the Colombians, Brazilians, those people wanting to go to Miami."

Antonio nodded his head in agreement. The words of the deal sounded good, but he still wasn't sure he trusted Levine. The man had been in bed with the Italians and he wondered if they weren't indirectly behind this idea. And he didn't like the idea of sharing money with anyone. But if it would help flush out some of the competing organizations back home, it would be well worth it.

"You mentioned something about more business?" Antonio asked, intrigued by Levine's offer.

"Yes, but first we feast. A man cannot think on an empty stomach. Eat, my new *compadres*. Isn't that the word you use?" Levine snapped his fingers.

Three waiters appeared, setting down trays of food. Antonio's mouth watered as he realized he hadn't eaten anything all day. Letting down some of his defenses, he decided old Levine might not be so bad to do business with, after all.

He and Javier filled themselves on the dishes before them, downing medallions of beef in a Bordeaux sauce, sautéed vegetables, garlic potatoes, and cheesecake dripping with raspberry glaze. By the time the meal was finished, Antonio patted his stomach and loosened his belt.

He noticed Javier's demeanor had changed drastically, seeming to relax for the first time in weeks. Antonio smiled at the sight of the familiar twinkle in Javier's eyes.

After the feast and the table were cleared, the men shared cognac, while three gorgeous native women, clad in nothing but chiffon skirts, danced for them. After a few dances, Levine ordered the women away and got down to business.

"I want to help you organize. I know you dabble in marijuana and heroin, but I think I can see to it that your dabbling turns into a lot more. Enough to profit all of us greatly all the way around."

Antonio leaned in, curious as to what offer Levine would present. He motioned for him to continue.

"You are esteemed men in your countries—respected, good businessmen. Politicians." He eyed Javier. "Would you be interested in setting up plans with me to run the drugs in a much larger volume through the Bahamas, and then into the States? Then you could put the money back into my investments here, such as the casinos and hotels, and we launder the money clean."

"It sounds like an expensive venture to me. I don't know if we have that kind of cash ready to invest," Javier commented.

"Not a problem," Levine replied, holding up his hands. "I'll loan you the initial investment, with a small interest applied on the payback, of course."

"How does this benefit you?" Antonio asked, wondering again if Levine could be trusted. "Other than the interest on a loan that I'm not certain we would need anyway."

"Your investment in my casinos for one thing, and I want a thirty percent cut as well."

"Thirty? You can't be serious?" Antonio said. "Why in God's name do you think you should take a thirty percent cut of our business? We're the ones taking all the risk. You want us to move the drugs and all you do is take our investments, accepting it into your casinos? That sounds like bullshit deal for us, if you ask me."

"I didn't mean to offend you, Tony. Please, let's all relax, and see if we can't make a deal which suits us both," Levine remarked in a cool, even tone. He wiped a trace of sweat from his upper lip. "I certainly don't want to screw you."

"I take my business very personally." Antonio crossed his arms and leaned back.

"In this business, that can either be a great asset or a serious detriment. It all depends on how you want to play the game. I'm counting on your playing of the game so both of us can participate and come out as winners."

"There's no way in hell I'm going to offer you thirty percent of my business. I'd be willing to go ten."

"Ah, come on, let's be fair here. I may not be taking the same amount of risk as you, but I am putting my business and myself on the line. I'm willing to offer you a substantial amount of cash to set up a big operation, plus give you an exclusive to use my paradise here for you to process your business ventures through. Ten is too low for me."

"Twelve."

"Nah, still too low." He shook his head, a sly smile on his face.

Antonio sighed and a silence fell across the table. He eyed Levine. "I'll go as high as fifteen and that's it. You're still getting cash off the top of the immigrants we run through. As far as I can see, I'm offering you one hell of a deal."

"You drive a hard bargain, my friend, but I'm anxious to do business with you." Levine stretched out his hand and, with a handshake, closed the deal. He leaned back in his seat. "I think some good ground rules have been laid here this evening. Now I would take great pleasure if you would both partake in having another cognac and sharing some fine Havana cigars with me, given to me by none other than Batista himself. This was before Castro got his grubby hands on that unfortunate country. I tell you, the fucking wops are still having a hard time getting over that one. They want Castro so bad, they can taste it."

Levine handed out the fine cigars, and as they sat puffing on them, Antonio hoped the deals he was making with the Jew would not be the cause of his own downfall. He was sure that somewhere in those percentages that the Cosa Nostra would be getting a take. First things first. If they could get rid of the competing Mexican families, life would be easier. He'd later deal with Levine and any of the mafia he needed to.

Once back in his suite, Antonio was able to relax. Levine had put him on edge. No matter how Levine referred to the Italians, Antonio knew the old man had an affinity for them. He admired them. If there was one group of people Antonio didn't want to work for or with, it was them. They were sneaky, not to be trusted. The only honor they recognized was within their families. They were too well known for causing wars, and Antonio had no desire to be a part of that.

The meeting had done one thing for him, and that was to take his mind off Marta and his son, Alejandro. What a good and powerful name, he mused in his near drunken state. The cognac the men shared together after dinner eased through his body, warming him.

As he went over the evening's events, there was a knock at the door. When he opened it, there stood one of the island princesses who'd danced for them earlier. Her sensuous beauty sent the blood rushing through his veins.

"Señor Espinoza, I'm so glad we could spend some time together," she said in a soft voice tinged with an exotic accent.

"Please call me Antonio. I'm pleased you could join me. Would you like a drink?"

"No thank you, Señor."

He poured her a brandy anyway. The implication was subtle, but the message was clear: he was in control, and if he wanted her to have a drink, then she would have one. As they savored their brandies, Antonio walked across the room and turned on the stereo. Frank Sinatra was humming in his smooth voice.

When Antonio turned around, the green-eyed beauty was loosening her pale yellow chiffon skirt. "No, no." He approached her, setting his glass down on the coffee table. He took her by the hand and led her into the bedroom, where he began his seduction. He pulled her close, kissing her lightly on the neck; her scent brought back old memories. His mind wandered as the smell of jasmine filled his nostrils, traveling directly to his brain. Marta had smelled so similar. His mind tried to deceive him, telling him this was Marta he was making love to, but his heart knew the truth.

Even though the island princess succumbed to each request, his heart still ached for the one woman who would always hold his heart, the woman who had given life to his only son. Had it been possible, he would have gone to her. But that could not be. His loyalty to his wife and daughters was fierce. He also knew from Marta's letters that she had no wish to ever see him again.

CHAPTER NINE

MARTA FINISHED CLEANING THE WINDOWS INSIDE THE
Beverly Hills mansion, making them look as though you could walk
through them. Her work was hard, with a long daily bus trip, but she
felt fortunate to have a job. Elisa was home taking care of Alejandro.
She wished she could be home with her baby but she knew that she
had to earn a living and make a good life for her son.

"Marta, how are you?" Mr. Johnson, the owner of the home, asked,
startling her. She hadn't heard him come up behind her.

"Fine, sir," she replied.

"I see your night school is paying off."

"Yes, I like it very much."

"Uh huh. Say, is my wife around?"

"No, sir. She's shopping."

"Of course, I might have known. As you can see, I'm on my way to
the golf course," he replied, motioning to his golf bag sitting in the
entryway. "Do you like golf?"

"I don't know," Marta answered, feeling a little nervous talking to the man of the house. After all, he never spoke to her when his wife was around.

Mr. Johnson walked closer to her. Smelling his cologne, she wondered if he'd bathed in it—strong and too sweet for a man's cologne. Mr. Johnson was a pleasant looking man with salt and pepper hair, and very tall. His square jaw and high cheekbones reminded her a little of Antonio.

He brushed against her shoulder. "You are a very pretty young woman, Marta. I've noticed you often, cleaning around the house."

"Thank you, sir, but I really must get back to the cleaning."

He waved his hand through the air. "All work and no play..." He arched his eyebrows. "Visit with me. Certainly, you can spare a few minutes. Remember, I am the guy who pays your bills."

"That would be nice, but please, sir, I need to get back to work. My bus leaves in only two hours and I still have so much left to do."

"Now, Marta, you wouldn't want to upset me, would you?" Mr. Johnson pressed his large hand down hard on her shoulder.

"You're hurting me," she whispered through trembling lips.

"I don't want to do anything to hurt you. In fact, you'll like what I want to do with you."

"Please. No. Your wife is coming home soon." Marta could see his demeanor changing. He looked larger than he had before and her instincts told her to run. Her mind flashed back to the night she and Elisa crossed the border, and the screams of the young girl being raped and tortured to death.

"Come on, Marta, she won't be home anytime soon." He yanked her around and held her tight, kissing her on the lips. She pursed her lips together and struggled to free herself. She smelled alcohol on his breath. Her stomach coiled tightly as she pressed her hands into fists against his chest.

"Don't fight it. You'll love it." He threw her against the wall and she yelped in pain. He came toward her again. But as he manhandled her breasts, she kicked him square in the groin, causing William Johnson to double over in pain, leaving him gasping for breath. Marta could hear him yelling obscenities at her as she ran out the door, her vision blurred by her tears.

*****

JAVIER STROKED ISABELLA'S THICK BLACK CURLS ON TOP OF her head. The baby's hair felt like the fine tendrils of a silken web. He beamed when he held her, looking into the green eyes that were so like her mother's. Javier made the sign of the crucifix across his chest as he prayed for Cynthia's soul to rest in peace.

That day, as on every Sunday since her mother's death, Javier took Isabella to Cynthia's grave, where he would place fresh flowers, lingering for a while with his daughter. Antonio had often told Javier to let the memory of Cynthia go, arguing that Javier wouldn't be able to move forward with other women if he kept living in the past. Javier ignored Antonio's nonsensical advice. He wanted his daughter to grow up knowing her mother, even if it was in a different sense than all of them had expected.

The baby was almost six months old now, and Sunday was their day of rest. "Come on, Isabella, it is time to go visit Mama."

The child's bright eyes focused on her father from her crib. She'd been busy studying her hands and fingers, beginning to realize that they were a part of her. As soon as she heard her father's deep voice, her attention was diverted, and she smiled widely up at him.

"Her love for you is so obvious," Lupe said as she walked into the room. She went over to one of the white wicker drawers and pulled out a pale pink sweater, along with white tights and a beautiful pink flowered dress, intricately detailed with lace sewn along the bottom. Lupe handed the clothes to Javier.

"That's all right," he told her. "You can bathe and change her this morning. I think I'll go out to the garden and pick some fresh flowers for Cynthia."

"Very well." Lupe's surprise was clearly audible.

"I think it is time I start to ask you for more help. I'm officially making you Isabella's nanny as of today. I am too tired to keep this up by myself. Will you help me?"

Lupe beamed at the prospect and nodded her head. "Of course, Governor. I would love to take care of the baby."

"I will still tend to her a good deal of the time. We'll go over specific duties tomorrow morning. Have her ready in half an hour."

"Of course."

He headed to the garden thinking about what he'd heard recently about the Torres family. Rumor had it that the family from Mexico City was not happy about the deal he and Antonio had made with

Levine. Rumor also had it that they were going to strike back unless they were included. Antonio told him not to worry about it, but that was impossible.

He would feel safer now that Lupe would be with the baby at all times. He was afraid Manuel Torres might make him a target. Manuel was noted for being a vengeful man. Wars didn't frighten him. In fact, he thrived on them. However, if Manuel didn't have the backing of some of the other families, then he wouldn't get very far. His power was limited. But Javier knew that if he could convince at least one other family of his plight, he and Antonio could be in trouble. He therefore wanted to keep Isabella as far away from danger as possible.

As he finished picking a rainbow of roses from the garden for Cynthia's grave, Lupe brought Isabella out to him. He gently lifted her out of the nanny's arms, handing the roses to Lupe. Isabella cooed at the sight of her daddy. "Ah, *mi princessa preciosa*. Papa will always keep you safe from harm's way. This I promise."

CHAPTER TEN

"YOU SEEM SO DISTANT LATELY, ANTONIO. WHAT'S WRONG?"
Lydia asked.

Antonio looked up from his desk where he was going through the numbers from his coffee fields, oil reserves, and some of his illegal businesses. It appeared their venture with Simon Levine was paying off. He glanced up at his wife. She was scantily clad in a white lace nightgown. "Why haven't you gotten dressed?" Antonio asked, lighting a cigar. He looked up at the clock. "It's already eleven o'clock."

"I know what time it is. You've been down here in this study all morning. I'm tired of waking up alone, and going to bed alone. I need you."

"I'm busy," Antonio replied curtly. He didn't have time now for her nonsense. He'd been occupied with his new business deals, and thoughts of his son had become something of an obsession.

"Yes, I know. But even when you come to bed, you don't touch me any longer. At least, not like you used to."

"For God sakes, you've just had a baby," he replied.

"No, I did *not* just have a baby, Antonio. Felicia is nearly a year old now. Believe me, I am completely healed."

Antonio knew she was right. But ever since Felicia's birth and his discovery that Marta had borne his son, Antonio didn't view his wife in the same light. She was the mother of his children, but the loving feelings he once had for her weren't quite the same as before. His heart was elsewhere. "I'm sorry, I figured you weren't interested." He didn't know what else to say to her. "You seem so tired from caring for the baby."

"Not interested? My God, Antonio, are you blind? And as for being tired, that's what nannies and maids are for. Every night, I come to bed wearing almost nothing at all. Instead of wrapping your arms around me when you lay down, you fall asleep at once, on your side of the bed. Am I that horrifying to you now? Is your mistress so beautiful that she has ruined you for me?"

"There is no other woman."

"I am not ignorant, Antonio. Of course, there are other women. Just remember who is the one who has given birth to two beautiful daughters for you." She sighed. "But that is the problem, isn't it? I have not given you a son. How can I give you a son if you no longer make love to me?"

He stood up from behind his antique desk and walked around it, grabbing her by the arm. The rage he saw in her eyes surprised him. He knew he had to put out her fire before things grew any worse. Flinging her upon the gold-colored chaise opposite his desk he tore at her negligee. "Antonio," she breathed. He kissed her neck sliding his fingers down her body and in between her legs where he caressed her. His lips traveled to her breasts. She called out his name again. He closed his eyes willing himself to become aroused along with her.

Lydia wrapped her hands around his soft penis and she gasped. "Antonio?"

He pulled away from her and stared angrily. "I can't."

"Why? Why can't you? It's me! It's me?"

"No. No." He reached out to her, trying to grab her by the shoulder. "Please. I'm sorry." She walked out of the room. "Lydia," he called out. "Come back. Please."

He heard the door slam to their bedroom at the other end of the house. He placed his head in his hands. He had to go to her, find a way to make love to her. She was his wife and maybe if they had a son, this would all change. He could forget about Marta, forget about the boy he wanted to know and raise.

Picking up the phone, he dialed the number of the best jeweler in town and asked him to send over his finest piece, something that would impress his wife. Tonight he would make all of it up to Lydia—his affairs, his love for another woman, and the son whose blood was his own.

*****

LYDIA DIDN'T LIKE BEING IGNORED. IT ANGERED HER MORE than anything else. She'd always been the princess, and now here was her husband, the man she doted on and had been completely faithful to, ignoring her and unable to make love to her. It was clear that his heart belonged to another. Lydia was not Antonio's special princess any longer, and she knew it.

She walked through the flower garden, stopping to smell a yellow rose, which had come into full bloom. She looked back toward the house and could see the silhouette of her husband at his desk—always working. When they'd first met, she'd only been sixteen. He was ten years older than she was, and very powerful. The attraction between them had been like an irresistible magnet pulling them together. Out of respect for her and her respect for the Church, they waited until their wedding night to consummate their relationship. But when they did, the passion was incredible. There weren't any words to describe the feelings that had encompassed her. Now, however, those feelings lay dormant within her, but for Antonio they seemed to be dead. It was obvious in the way he didn't look at her, didn't talk to her, did not hold her. She longed and burned for someone to make her feel like a woman again—someone with warm, gentle loving hands.

She stood up from smelling the rose bush and was startled by hands that abruptly encircled her waist. She turned around in fright to face the culprit. It was Antonio's brother Emilio. "You shouldn't have done that! You scared me."

"I'm sorry. I didn't mean to. What are you doing out here, looking so sad, like a lost soul?"

"Smelling the flowers and thinking."

"Ah, *thinking*, something you women seem to have such a knack for."

"What does that mean?" Lydia giggled, playfully pushing her brother-in-law so that he nearly lost his balance.

"It means women think *too much*. And it must be true, because it brought a smile to your face."

"You're incorrigible."

"And you're beautiful."

"Emilio . . ." she protested, feeling her face blush from the compliment.

"That's another problem with you women."

"Oh, and what's that?"

"You have no idea how to take flattery."

"That so?"

"Mhhmm. Look at you. I tell you that you're beautiful and you act like a schoolgirl."

"But coming from you..."

"I'm a grown man now. Besides, it's not like you're my grandmother. I know you're not even five years older than I am. So for you to keep treating me as if I were a little boy is ludicrous."

"But you *are* a little boy. Grown man! Twenty-one is not a grown man for you. You are a silly little boy as far as I am concerned, and that won't ever change." She laughed and tossed a yellow rose at him, then turned to run from him. He chased her throughout the garden, until he caught up with her and forced her to the ground. While he tickled her, both burst into laughter, until she faced him and their eyes met. Lydia struggled underneath him. Butterflies swarmed in her stomach and electricity ran down her spine. Her heart pounded through her silk blouse. She was certain Emilio could hear it.

"Emilio." It was Antonio, yelling for his brother from the house. A smile spread across Emilio's face as he released Lydia. They stood up immediately and brushed themselves off.

"That was fun," he whispered to her.

She turned around and stormed off in the direction of the house, angry with herself for being so weak and easily manipulated. But all the same, her pulse beat rapidly. She quickened her pace as she heard Emilio's laughter.

*****

"WHAT ARE YOU DOING DOWN HERE IN THE GARDEN?" Antonio asked his brother when he caught up to him.

"Actually, I was visiting your wife."

"Ah, and where is she?"

"She said she had to go back up to the house for something. I don't know, maybe to check on the baby."

"I see. I have some things to discuss with you." Antonio put his arm around Emilio's shoulders and together they strolled out of the garden and into the fields where cocoa leaves grew abundantly. Emilio was a couple of inches taller than his brother, and lankier, both handsome men. Emilio had always been considered "the pretty one." As a child he was often mistakenly referred to as a girl. His deeply hooded eyes were a caramel color, framed by long thick eyelashes. He had a slender nose and high cheekbones. His thick hair, which he wore somewhat long, he would slick back into a sleek ponytail many nights before venturing out on the town. He *was* beautiful to look at. This bothered him when he was a child, for he ached to appear more masculine. But as a young man, he discovered that his looks were an attribute.

"What did you want to discuss?" Emilio asked.

Antonio hesitated before beginning. "You know the situation with Javier has been rather tenuous of late. He is distant, withdrawn. He only cares about one thing."

"His daughter."

"Yes."

"That's understandable, considering the circumstances."

"But I am worried about him. I am also worried about the Torres clan. I just spoke with Javier and they know of our meeting with Levine. Needless to say, Manuel Torres is not pleased. My instincts tell me he is a man who thinks with his *cojones* and who will seek our blood if he isn't cut in on the deal."

"Manuel Torres is unlike you. I agree that he's led around by his balls."

"You understand."

"If you recall, I've had dealings with Torres before," Emilio remarked, referring to Magdalena Torres, Manuel's daughter. Emilio had deemed her irresistible one night. When he didn't bother to see her again, she retaliated with the force of her father. Emilio was badly beaten by the Torres thugs. When he sought help from Antonio, Antonio told him that he wasn't going to begin a war with the Torres family because his baby brother couldn't control where he put his dick. More than likely, he deserved the beating.

"True," Antonio chuckled.

Emilio straightened his back and with smug confidence asked, "What is it you're asking me to do?"

"Keep an eye on Javier. Torres will go for the weak link, and right now I believe it to be Javier. I also want you to find out everything you can concerning Torres what he thinks, which families he may be trying to convince to ride with him, and so forth. The last thing I want is bloodshed." He pointed a stern finger at Emilio and looked him squarely in the eyes. Eyes that looked at so many as mere prey. Antonio was finally giving his younger brother the chance to prove himself by becoming a predator. Little did Antonio ever guess that he was still Emilio's biggest quarry.

CHAPTER ELEVEN

JAVIER ROCKED ISABELLA TO SLEEP, WHICH HAD BECOME his nightly routine. The day had taken its toll, like all the days since Cynthia's death. The precious child stirred as her father stood up and placed her in her crib. A cross above her head, pictures of the Madonna, along with one of Cynthia, made Javier feel that a force other than his own strength continually protected Isabella.

He stretched his arms after he placed the baby down and turned her light out, leaving the door cracked open. Lupe slept in the room next to Isabella and woke whenever the child cried out in the night.

He headed straight for his room, undressed, and went to bed. Exhaustion had gotten the best of him. As soon as his head hit the pillow, he was sound asleep. Slightly after three in the morning, a scream from down the hall near Isabella's room echoed throughout the house. Javier jumped out of bed, nearly stumbling over his own feet. He ran down the hall, blinded by the darkness. The screaming was coming from Isabella's room. He stormed through the door to find Lupe standing in front of the baby's crib in hysterics. She looked up at Javier, wide-eyed and obviously shaken.

"*Dios mío*, what has happened, woman?" Javier shouted at her.

"The baby, the baby! Some men came and took her away. They held a gun to my head."

"What? What are you saying?" He couldn't believe what she was telling him. It was too outrageous. No one could've gotten inside his fortress. "I don't understand."

"They left this." She handed him a letter.

Javier's hands began to shake as he read it: *We don't like having our throats slashed by traitors like you and Antonio Espinoza. We suggest you come to your senses. You and your Jew must bring us in on your deal, if you want to see your precious daughter alive again.*

Javier crumpled up the letter and chucked it across the room. A rage like none he'd ever felt before enveloped him. "Manuel Torres is a dead man."

*****

ONCE ANTONIO RECEIVED WORD OF ISABELLA'S KIDNAPPING, he and Emilio flew to Guadalajara, where they met with Javier, who, within twenty-four hours, was becoming completely unhinged, pacing back and forth like an animal filled with fury and pain.

"We will find her," Antonio told him.

"I will kill that son of a bitch."

"Let me do it," Emilio interrupted.

Antonio shot him a disapproving glare.

"He will return your daughter, and he will have to pay some kind of penance for this. If he doesn't, we have other ways of handling him." He nodded his head in Emilio's direction.

His younger brother smiled and cracked his knuckles, knowing full well what was to be done with Manuel Torres.

Antonio realized he was taking a big step by allowing the possible murder of Torres and a couple of his henchmen to take place. But Torres had started this fight by kidnapping innocent Isabella. Nothing enraged Antonio as much, nor was anything more outrageous or disgusting to him than enemies who would involve children in the wars between them. Rules of respect dictated that this was out of line. Kill a boss, kill a partner, but don't touch the wives or children. Manuel Torres had broken that law. For this, he would pay. Isabella was Antonio's goddaughter, the daughter of his best friend. Her safe and immediate return was the only acceptable solution. If this did not happen and a war between the families resulted from Torres's bad judgment, then so be it.

CHAPTER TWELVE

"**YOU DID WHAT**?" **MANUEL TORRES'S VOICE ROSE AN OCTAVE** when he learned about the kidnapping.

"I thought you wanted us to threaten him." His youngest son Pedro tried to reason with the old man.

"A threat, yes, but kidnapping Javier Rodriguez's baby? How fucking stupid can you be? What do you think this will mean for us?"

"That we'll get what we want," Pedro shot back, searching his father's eyes for any sign of forgiveness. At the time, Pedro and his pal José thought that taking the baby was a great idea. Granted, all the tequila they drank helped convince them of the soundness of the plan. And carrying it out hadn't been easy, either. And now this was the thanks he got. His father was never proud of him, never satisfied with anything he did to win his respect. That's why Pedro had the most menial of jobs, doing all the family's dirty work. All his brothers had positions of authority. All he ever got were promises that were never fulfilled.

"Are you listening to me?" Manuel shouted at him.

Pedro hung his head in despair.

"How do you suppose I'm going to fix this one? For God's sake, this is the man's *child*. I'd rather you'd killed the son of a bitch himself than take his baby. He and Espinoza will be out for blood now. We may have some pull with the smaller families, but after this…" He flung his arms in the air. "You're a fucking imbecile!"

"I'm sorry, Papa," Pedro responded, trying to choke back tears mixed with bitter rage.

"You'd better be, you stupid asshole. Now get Sergio in here. I need to get in touch with Antonio to see if we can fix this disaster."

Pedro left his father's office, swearing silently to himself. He hated him so much that he hoped Antonio *would* do away with him. His father was nothing more than a small-time crook. Everyone knew that Manuel was playing with fire, trying to become involved in Javier and Antonio's game.

The other families lied when they said they would support Manuel. When push came to shove, they'd back down as soon as they saw the whites of Antonio Espinoza's eyes. But Pedro had to hand it to his father. The man was either completely out of his mind or else he had huge *cojones*.

He sent Sergio, his father's righthand man, into the office, and went to check on the baby. He'd given her to one of the nursemaids who took care of his sister's kids. One thing about the Torres family, they never believed in having homes for themselves. Parents, grandparents, children, spouses—everyone lived under one big roof. His father seemed to like it that way. Pedro didn't know what his mother thought. She was a quiet woman who lived the sacrificial life of the good wife. Pedro always felt sorry for her and longed to comfort her. But not only was she quiet, she was cold as well. She never responded to his affections. Pedro decided that maybe it was time to get out of this place.

"Let me see the baby," he ordered the nanny.

She handed the bright child to him. He stroked her hair and gently pinched her nose. She smiled and giggled. "You are so cute. How would you like to go with Uncle Pedro on a little trip?" The nanny looked at him quizzically. "I'm going to take her for a walk. I'll be back in awhile. Pack me up a bottle."

The nanny did as she was told and prepared the baby to leave the house. Soon, he and Isabella were in his car, heading for his new life. "If they don't want me," he said aloud, "then I'll find a family who'll be proud of what I can do for them." He glanced over at Isabella sleeping in the basket next to him, and smiled. "And you, precious one, are my ticket."

*****

MARTA SPOONED RICE INTO ALEJANDRO'S MOUTH.
The baby kicked his round feet, smiling at his mother, who was obviously the light of his life, as he was hers.

Most nights, once the baby was asleep and she'd finished cleaning their small home, she'd find herself lying in bed, exhausted from the day's work, but still unable to sleep. Her mind inevitably drifted to thoughts of Antonio, of their lovemaking, things he'd said, and his betrayal that last day. Eventually, tears would fall, and physical exhaustion would win out. But even after she would finally drift off, dreams about him would invade her sleep. She hated and loved him at the same time, hated and loved those dreams as well.

On those nights when she couldn't sleep, she would write down pages of poetry about Antonio. At times, she thought about sending these poems to him. But then the vision of him kissing his pregnant wife and their daughter kept her from making that mistake.

Tonight, she felt especially lonely once she put the baby in his crib. Elisa and her husband had taken her boys and gone to visit cousins up north in the Redwoods. She was the only one who understood Marta and was always there to comfort her. Marta heard Alejandro stir in the crib next to her bed. She peered in on him. Angry tears blinded her as she thought of Alejandro never knowing his father.

She balled up the poems she'd written over the months and tossed them into the fireplace. She struck a match, but couldn't bring herself to set it under her poems. She took them from the fireplace, unfolded them, and tried to smooth them out.

Then she made a decision. If she must suffer in this hell, he, too, should pay a price. She neatly gathered the poems together, placed them in an envelope, and addressed it to Antonio. This was not the time to send them, she was aware of that. But soon she would mail them. Soon he would know about his son and about the suffering he had caused them—all in the name of his own selfish pleasure.

CHAPTER THIRTEEN

JAVIER WAS GOING MAD. HE COULND'T BELIEVE THAT
Manuel Torres would do such a thing. He paced restlessly when the telephone finally rang and he grabbed it at once.

"Javier Rodriguez?"

"Yes?"

"This is Pedro Torres." Javier fumbled with the phone. "I am Manuel Torres's son."

"Yes, I know. Where is my daughter?"

"With me. Don't worry. She's safe. I'm bringing her to you right now."

"What?"

"Yes. What my father did was very cruel. He should never have taken the baby away from you. So I took the baby, and I'm bringing her back to you."

"Where are you?"

"I can't talk any longer. I will see you soon." With that, Pedro hung up.

Javier was baffled by this call. Why would Pedro care so much about his baby? And why would he want to betray his own father? It had to be a trick.

*****

ONE OF THE GUARDS ENTERED JAVIER'S QUARTERS AND TOLD him that Pedro Torres had arrived, and that he had the baby with him. Javier immediately rushed downstairs, where Pedro sat playing with Isabella on the floor of the lavish living room. Large bay windows in the room gleamed with reflections of large palm trees surrounding the courtyard.

Javier ran to the child and picked her up, cradling her in his arms. He kissed her and cuddled her tightly.

Pedro stood up. He was a handsome young man, with classic Latin features. He was thin, with shoulder-length raven hair. Javier didn't know whether to kiss him or kill him. First, he called immediately for Lupe to take Isabella away, and not to let her out of her sight.

"*Sí Señor*," Lupe replied tearfully as she took the baby from him.

Once Isabella was out of the room, Javier stared at the young man, who extended his hand to him. "I am Pedro Torres."

Javier hesitated before shaking it. "Yes, I know. Why have you done this?"

"I told you on the phone. I thought taking the baby was wrong. I wanted to make things right."

"And your father?"

"My father, as I'm sure you know by now, has no respect for other people. He is a man who thinks only about himself."

"I hear bitterness in your voice..."

"I have never loved my father. He has never loved me."

"Is this the real reason you brought my daughter back?"

"I would be lying if I said no, but it's only part of the reason. Taking the baby was wrong. She belongs here. And neither family wants a war."

"Then your father should've thought long and hard before he did something this stupid."

"I agree."

"What do you want out of this, Pedro?"

"A job."

"But you have a family. Go back to work for them."

"I have no family now."

Javier paced back and forth in the room, contemplating his next move with the finesse of a chess player. "All right, I will tell you this. I believe someone should pay for this crime against me and my daughter."

"Yes," Pedro replied.

"What do you think I should do?"

"I think you should kill the man responsible." Pedro tried to keep his hands from shaking.

"You do? And, you want a job? And you say you could be loyal to another family besides your own? I will give you a chance to prove it. You kill Manuel Torres. If you do this for me, in such a way that the blame will lie on someone else, then you will be welcome in my family."

Pedro nodded and left Javier's house, on his way back home to murder his own father.

CHAPTER FOURTEEN

PEDRO ENTERED THE HOUSE SILENTLY ONCE EVERYONE was asleep. He knew that his family would have figured out by this time what he had done, and that if anyone had seen him at Javier's home, he would be dead. But he also knew his way around the crevices and shadows of the old hacienda, and therefore was none too concerned about being caught. He'd worked himself up into actually wanting to kill his own father: the bastard deserved to be sent straight to hell.

He approached the old man's suite, his hands trembling.

Once inside the bedroom, Pedro could see his father sleeping alone in his large bed, covered with the best silk sheets money could buy. Pedro let out a sigh, relieved to see that his father did not have a guest for the evening.

His father's heart medicine was on the nightstand, next to the bed. Pedro took the small receptacle of pills and emptied half of them out. Once that was done, he replaced them with amphetamine capsules that looked like the medicine for his father's heart.

Pedro knew that henceforth, each morning after his father had taken his heart medication, he had only a fifty-fifty chance of surviving into the next week. And no one would be any the wiser. They'd assume that the son of a bitch had had a heart attack. It was beautiful and it was foolproof.

Pedro stealthily exited his father's room and left the hacienda as quietly as he'd entered it. Sweat trickled from his forehead while he walked away from the compound. It was over. His life here, with a family that had never taken the time to know him, with a father who despised his very presence, was over. Relief engulfed him. Pain, sadness, happiness, and anger swirled together in a vicious brew as he headed toward a new life and a new family.

Book II – 1976-1983

Los Angeles, CA

CHAPTER FIFTEEN

MARTA WORKED DILIGENTLY AT HER SEWING MACHINE IN A small warehouse, surrounded by more than a hundred workers bent over their tables. Dust particles and lint choked the air, making her sinuses run constantly. She stopped for a moment and wiped away the sweat dripping from her forehead. The summer heat hung heavy throughout the warehouse, her clothes sticking to her, and the smell of people working fast and furious in the poor conditions grew sourer by the hour. But the job paid the bills.

The highlight of the day was arriving home to see Alejandro. He made life worth living. His cheery attitude and bright smile could wipe away the hardships of the worst days. It had been a long five years since the day she and Elisa had crossed the border. Unfortunately, not much had changed.

Marta and Alex were still living in the same small house where he was born on Washington Street, in a constant struggle to achieve a meager existence. America hadn't been the land of opportunity she once thought, but she knew that because her son was born an American citizen, he would have chances in life that he never would have had living in Mexico. Every once in a while, Marta's memories of Antonio would weave in and out of her mind, taking her back to a time when she felt full of life, her heart young and naïve. She could not help but still wonder on occasion how Antonio was doing, never forgetting the love they once shared. But her pleasant memories soon turned dark as she recalled the bitter discovery of who Antonio really was—a liar and cheat. There was no way around that. Denying it would be lying to herself. Facing realities was what helped to keep her working and motivated in a country she had not fallen in love with as she'd hoped. She missed her home, her culture, her life in Costa Careyes. She was grateful though that she had a job and a child who adored her, as well as her friendship with Elisa.

When she arrived home by bus, she checked the mail. Like clockwork every month, there was a check for five hundred dollars. The name on the check was from a company in Colombia called "*Por el gente,*" which meant, *For the People.* She knew that Antonio must be the one sending the checks. Marta was certain that he had somehow found out about Alex, because the money began arriving shortly after her son's first birthday.

Her initial instinct was to tear them up, but after thinking it over, Marta realized that she could use the money for Alex, to buy the things that he deserved. She saved the money each month, only taking out what she needed for her child. She put away the rest for him, hoping that someday, she would be able to send him to college. However, there was a part of her that didn't feel right about taking the money. Yes, the man was Alex's father, but Marta could not help feeling that by taking that money she was almost as much of a liar as Antonio was. She knew there would come a day when Antonio would want to see his son, and the money would then become an issue.

She and Elisa worked busily in the cove of a kitchen making tamales. Marta sighed.

Elisa stopped stuffing the masa with pork and looked at her. "What is it?"

"What do you mean?" she asked.

"Why such a heavy sigh. Why are you troubled?"

"I was thinking again about Alex's father, and I wish I didn't feel guilty about using Antonio's money."

"Guilty. Ha. I think you're stupid. You should take all that money and move into a nice place. Get out of this dump. He owes you so much more than five hundred dollars a month. That money though could get you into a small house, Marta. You should do it."

"And where am I supposed to tell Alex the money came from?"

"Tell him the truth. He deserves to know, Marta. He needs to know he has a father." Elisa scooped out seasoned meat into the masa, and handed it to Marta who rolled it and tied a husk around it.

Marta shook her head. "I can't do that. I've told him since he was very little that his father was a hero, who died trying to save people in a building that crumbled during an earthquake."

"That's very creative of you, Marta." Elisa smiled. "I didn't know you had that in you." She winked.

"Please. Leave me alone about this."

"Leave you alone about this? Then stop talking about him and thinking about him. Consider the money a gift. Treat is like it is. I've only heard this story a million times. Either use his money or quit complaining."

Marta sighed and gave her friend a dirty look. They didn't speak for a few minutes as they went through the repetitive motions of making the tamales, which they would take down to Olivera Street and sell .

"You still love him, don't you? You wouldn't think about him, talk about him and have these guilt feelings if you didn't."

"Stupid, I know," Marta whispered. Elisa walked around the counter and embraced her. Marta wiped away her tears, and let out a little laugh. "If something should ever happen to me, I would like you to hold the money for Alex in a savings account and give it to him when he is old enough and wise enough to handle it."

"Why would you say something like that?" Elisa pulled away from her. "Nothing is ever going to *happen* to you."

"I have to think about these things, even so. I have to make certain that Alejandro is provided for. I'm his mother and I, I mean we are all he has. No matter what I still may feel for his father, he has no right

to my son and if something ever happens to me, I do not want
Antonio near him."

"Ridiculous. You're talking crazy words."

Marta stopped set her tamale down and took her purse from the
kitchen counter, pulling out an envelope, handing it over to Elisa.
"This is the paperwork and information you would need. Promise
me that you'll do this if needed."

Elisa stood her jaw dropped. "I don't understand."

"Take it." Marta shoved the envelope at her.

"Of course I would do anything for you. You know that. We're not
only friends, you and I. We are sisters."

"Thank you." Marta kissed her cheek and then looked at her
watch. "It's time for me to get ready to meet Alex."

"My goodness. I didn't realize it was so late." Elisa wiped her
hands on her apron. "Hector!" Elisa yelled to the little boy tossing a
ball around in the street. He came running in, panting.

"What, Mama?"

"Do you want to go with *Tía* Marta to meet Alex?"

"Yes!" the six-year old responded, grinning from ear to ear. His
love for Alex was obvious as his face lit up with the prospect of
seeing him soon so they could play.

Both children were unhappy that Alex was going to a new school,
but Marta, wanting the best for her son, had arranged for him to be
bused to one of the better public schools in the city. She knew that by
doing so, it would give him more opportunities for a better
education, and she'd studied what made successful people in

America. Education was a key factor. It was why she took as many night classes as she could, when she could, and why she'd become an avid reader of history, politics, culture and anything else she felt would better her for her son and for herself.

"Go change your shirt first, and wash your hands and face. You look like a filthy pig," Elisa ordered.

Obeying his mother, Hector quickly did as he was told. With her hands on her hip, Elisa turned back to Marta. "I really think you should put Alex back in school with Hector. He is sad and anxious lately. You must see it. You know that they tease him there. He isn't white and he never will be. In their eyes, he's nothing but a poor wetback."

"I don't think it's all that bad. I think he simply misses Hector during the day. It'll take him a little time, but once he gets used to it, he'll be fine."

"You never get used to people making fun of you. You don't, Marta. This is a harsh world and I know you want to give Alex the best opportunities possible, but putting him in a white school won't help him. It's going to hurt him."

Marta leaned her head to the side feeling the crack in her neck, her face burning slightly. Her friend always spoke her mind. They definitely didn't always agree. "They'll stop. He's getting a good education. What more can he ask for?"

"To be happy," Elisa replied. "He deserves to be happy and you know that." She took off her apron. "I have to get my shoes."

Marta couldn't respond as Elisa walked back into her bedroom to put on her shoes. She knew that Alex hadn't been happy since he started going to the new school about a month earlier. But she was only thinking about him. The schools in their area were poorly structured, with teachers who couldn't manage the overcrowding problem. Marta knew that he was still having a hard time adjusting. She hoped that before long, he would fit in with the other children.

"Come on, let's walk to the bus stop," Marta called out to Hector, who was still in the bathroom, scrubbing up.

"I'm coming. Don't leave without me." Hector came bouncing out, a huge grin on his face. He grabbed Marta's hand and they set out on the mile-long walk to the bus stop.

She said a silent prayer that her child would come home with a smile on his face today.

CHAPTER SIXTEEN

ALEX WATCHED THE TRAFFIC OUTSIDE AS HE SAT ALONE
on the bus. The girls across the aisle were whispering about him.
Every once in a while, he could hear one of them say *beaner* or
wetback, and the words sliced right through him knowing they were
bad words about him. He swallowed hard and bit the side of his
mouth. He wanted to cry. His mother always taught him to be proud,
so he certainly wasn't about to let these *gringos* see that he was
upset.

A large boy, a couple of years older than Alex, came and sat down
next to him. Alex didn't bother to look up at him, because he knew
what they were going to do. The boys in the seat in front of him
turned around.

"My dad says that greasers are good for nothing but weeding his
lawn. He can't believe they let you into our school," the freckled-
faced kid remarked.

"Yeah, you're a wetback, right? Look at you, all dark and
everything. You look like a monkey," another bucktoothed boy
taunted him, while the girls across the aisle laughed.

Alex wanted to get up and get off at the next stop. He ached for his mother to appear and rescue him. She would make everything all right.

"Beaner! Beaner! Beaner!"

"I bet your mama is fat and ugly, and makes you beans every day. That's why you're a stinking beaner!"

"Stinking beaner, stinking beaner—with a big ugly mama! Big, ugly, stupid, beaner mama! Beaner boy has beaner mama," they jeered.

That was enough to push Alex over the edge. No one made fun of his mother. He shoved the huge kid as hard as he could, sending him off the green vinyl seat where he landed on the floor of the moving bus.

"You little son of a bitch!" the kid yelled getting to his feet and punching Alex in the face. Alex's head snapped back, smacking hard against the window. A surge of pain shot through his skull and he tasted blood on his lips.

The entire busload of kids whooped and hollered. The bus driver, hearing the commotion, pulled off to the side of the road, and walked back to see what was going on. The woman with three chins stormed over to Alex's seat. Everyone on the bus grew silent.

She looked at Alex, then at the other kid, and bellowed, "Who started this?"

All the kids pointed to Alex, who fought back his tears—a humiliation worse than the physical pain from the bump on his head.

The woman reached down and took Alex by the hand, walking him up to the front of the bus. She bent down, inches away from Alex's face. She took a tissue from the box on the dashboard and wiped his bloodied nose. In a lowered voice she said, "Listen, kid, I know you didn't start the fighting. It's not your fault, but take it from someone who knows, it won't stop. Kids are mean. They tease and hurt and well, it might be best if you talked to your mother about driving you or doing something else other than riding the bus. I'm sorry. Why don't you sit up here the rest of the way?" She pointed to the front seat directly behind hers.

Alex nodded his head. His mom couldn't drive him. Although she'd been going to school at night to become a citizen, she'd never learned to drive, and even if she could, they didn't have enough money to buy a car.

When he reached his stop, he saw Hector and his mama waiting for him as usual. His mother lingered behind as Hector ran to the door of the bus.

"What happened?" Hector asked, his eyes widening at the sight of his beaten friend. Alex burst into tears and could hardly steady his breathing. He finally gained control of himself and told his friend the whole story. Hector jutted out his lower lip. "I'll have my daddy beat them up. He will, too. He will beat them up and their dads too."

When Marta approached Alex and saw that something was wrong, she cried out, "Oh no!" She pulled him into her arms. "Horrible, horrible children! You don't have to go back to that school. Never again, *mijo*!"

With his mother's comforting arms wrapped around him, he sighed and leaned into her. After a few moments the event on the bus was on the way to becoming a distant memory. Alex let go of his mother and took Hector's hand as they walked home together.

CHAPTER SEVENTEEN

THE SUN FLOATED ON THE MOUNTAINTOPS TO THE WEST
like a misplaced beach ball as Emilio watched his beautiful sister-in-law gaze at the fiery sky. He decided to make this the night that he would take her into his bed. His flirtation had gone on long enough. Unfortunately, she was a proud and faithful woman, and although there were a couple of times over the years when he thought she would succumb, she had not and he hadn't pushed it. The timing had never seemed right, and instead of pursuing her wholeheartedly, Emilio occupied his nights aplenty with little girl whores that succumbed to everything he asked of them, and were easily tossed aside when he was finished.

He liked them young. Fourteen was a nice age, it reminded him of his first love, his Marianna. But those memories were growing dangerous with each young girl. The night before he'd almost gone over the edge after finding a girl who looked so much like Marianna he found himself watching her for nearly an hour. He'd studied her as she stood next to a fruit crate talking to the boys and men who walked by. She obviously hoped to lead one to her bedroom in order to more than likely provide dinner for her family—a family who'd surely been the ones to send her out into the violent streets of Calí. What an insane and cruel world. Emilio found himself wanting to reach out and save the girl.

He'd approached her. "Hello."

She smiled. Very sweet. He took her hand.

"No," she said. "You can come to my room."

Emilio didn't let go of her hand or listen to her protests, which although quiet, were also firm. Probably a rule her parents had taught her, due to the dangers of the violence this part of the world witnessed on a daily basis. When she saw the luxury hotel he was taking her to, she stopped the protesting. He made her wait outside until he'd secured the room. It was a risk by bringing her there, but he wanted her to see the finer things in life. Maybe she would realize there was so much more to the world than the piece of filth her family had chosen to make her into.

Once inside the suite with its decadent furniture, fine silks and breathtaking view of the mountains the girl couldn't stop giggling. This delighted Emilio who ordered wine for them. "What's your name?" Emilio asked.

"Violetta."

"Beautiful."

She blushed.

"Tonight, your name is Marianna."

She nodded. He took the glass from her and set it on the nightstand table and he took her hand and led her to the bed, where he undressed her and made her lay on the sheets while he looked at her for several minutes. The longer he looked, the more she reminded him of his dead Marianna and the day he'd killed her—the day his brother stuck the knife into his heart and back. Memories flooding him, Emilio brutally took the girl and with every thrust she cried and begged him to stop, until he wrapped his hands around her neck and she stopped saying anything. As he watched her face, he was shaken from his fury and he uncurled his hands from her. She gasped for air, her hands going to her neck. Emilio gave her five hundred dollars and told her if she ever spoke of what had happened he would kill her and her family. He knew his threat and giving her more money than she'd probably ever seen in her lifetime would keep her quiet and keep her family from asking her too many questions. She nodded and ran out of the room.

Thinking about it, Emilio knew he'd gone too far with the girl and now he had to focus on the woman who'd become his ultimate challenge. The one who would help him gain all the power he desired and bring down Antonio.

Lydia had grown even more gorgeous during the past few years. He knew how his brother ignored her, too busy for his attractive wife. He was certain that tonight she was ready to take the sinful plunge. He also knew that she'd finally realized that she could never have the same Antonio whom she'd once known. Her disillusionment was complete.

"Beautiful."

"Hmmm," she turned around, startled. "Oh, the sunset? Yes, it is."

"No, I mean you."

"Emilio."

"I'm serious, Lydia. You're the most beautiful woman I've ever known."

"Please, Emilio, I'm your brother's wife. Your silly flirtation has to stop."

"But why? I'm only telling you that you're beautiful. Why should Antonio care? It's only the truth, no?" He moved closer to her and caressed her golden face. She shook her head, backing away from him.

"Don't do that," she whispered. She glanced out the window.

"Why not? You can't tell me you don't want to be touched. I see my brother with you. His mind is always on business. He flies here, there. He doesn't take the time to be with you. I understand how you must be hurting. He has obviously forgotten what a treasure you are. Although I find that impossible. I could never forget."

Lydia avoided his eyes, her own filling with tears.

"I don't mean to hurt you, but you must know that he has other women. Why else wouldn't he come to you every night? My brother is a fool."

Lydia leaned her body against the oak wood bar, her breasts pressed together between her arms that she had tightly wrapped around herself. Emilio poured her a drink.

The girls were with their grandmother for the evening, all the servants had long since retired to their quarters or gone home to be with their families. His timing was perfect. Antonio was out of town again, meeting with some distributors in the States.

He walked back around to the other side of the bar standing closer to Lydia again. "You need a man. I see it in your eyes. I see the way you look at me. Your eyes burn through me every time I walk into the room." Lydia shook her head. "Don't deny it. I feel it when I'm around you."

She took a sip from her drink, her scarlet lips leaving an imprint on the glass. "Emilio, you must stop this now. Not only am I your brother's wife, but I am much older than you are."

"What, five years? Quit denying your feelings with lame excuses. You want me as badly as I want you. No one will know. No one ever has to know."

Emilio reached behind Lydia's head and pulled the white ribbon out of her hair. The long, honeyed strands fell past her shoulders, framing her sculptured face. She began to back up again, but he grabbed her by her small waist and pulled her close to him. Kissing her hard on her mouth, Emilio could feel her resisting, trying to pull free. This aroused him further.

To have his brother's wife—*ah! That would be ultimate achievement.* The struggle for power between them would dramatically decrease, and the painful memory from his youth would become irrelevant. He would be able to stand up to the man whom all Latin America referred to fearfully as *El Patrón*, knowing that he, Emilio, had slept with that man's wife, his powerful brother's wife.

Emilio whispered in her ear, "A woman as special as you are deserves a man who can give her all of his attention. You are so lovely, so very lovely. Let me make love to you. Let me show you how lovely you are." Those words were exactly what she needed to push her over the edge. His roving hands began to explore her body, caressing her arms, her back, her waist, and then moving lower. He moved the tips of his fingers to her inner thighs, teasing her with a light touch. Lydia shivered and he knew she was his. He touched his lips to her neck, feathering her with kisses and letting his tongue sweep across her skin, as he untied the halter knot in her aqua summer dress. The dress fell to the ground.

He moved his hands up again and pulled her tightly into his chest, enjoying the feel of her breasts against him. Then Emilio moved his lips to hers, kissing her hard, making that ache she felt for him almost intolerable. She moaned when he pulled away, her eyes still closed, and Emilio gently lowered her to the rug next to the bar.

His touch grew more passionate now, slightly rougher, his hands squeezing hard, letting her know how strong his desire was. When his hand finally moved between her legs, her found her moist and ready. Lydia moved her hips up to meet his hand, silently begging him not to stop. She wanted more. She wanted everything. He began to work his hand against her, and Emilio smiled as he heard her gasp. So, as the sun disappeared beneath the horizon, Emilio made love to the woman he had coveted for so long. His tongue roved all the crevices of her sensuous body, making her squirm with ecstatic pleasure. He took a great deal of pleasure in observing her resist the orgasm her body wanted so badly, but that her mind and heart told her she mustn't allow herself. But the way he was grinding into her, the way he felt inside her, was too much and Lydia could not stop herself from surrendering to the pleasure. She was hot and breathless now, digging her hands into his back and so obviously desperate to reach that peak of ecstasy. When she finally lost the struggle and gave herself up to an incredible climax, Emilio was delighted to hear her groan with a mixture of satisfaction and grief.

Before she could catch her breath, Lydia stood up and dressed, tears clinging to her eyelashes. But Emilio knew that she'd loved every second of it.

"There's no need for tears. It's our secret."

She glared at him and stormed off to her room. He knew she'd be back for more, and he'd be waiting to give it to her.

CHAPTER EIGHTEEN

ANTONIO RAN HIS HAND OVER THE ENVELOPE ON THE SEAT next to him, the one with Marta's and Alejandro's address written across the front. He swung the car down the street into the Pico Union area, shocked that they lived in such a slum. Surely Marta would've used the money he'd sent her all these years to rent a decent home, but it didn't appear so. His stomach ached. He had been so nervous about seeing his son for the first time, he couldn't even think about eating.

He and Javier were in town to meet with Levine. Antonio knew that they were going to discuss the prospect of smuggling more heroin into the States, but Levine had actually made a subtle suggestion that they begin working with the Italians. Not an idea that was making him happy.

He slowed down to read the numbers on the tiny houses. This was the kind of shabby neighborhood in which many of his dealers lived. It disgusted him to see that his only son resided in such a place. Their lives could be so different if he could only convince Marta to return to Mexico, and allow him to provide a nice home for she and his son.

Thoughts of dragging Marta and their son back to Colombia ran through his mind. This street was so run down; the undeniable stench from the sewer was sickening. There were bums scattered about the sidewalks as Antonio slowed down for a bunch of kids playing broom hockey in the middle of the street. That was when he spotted him.

Oh my God, it's him. It's my boy. He knew him instantly. There was no mistaking those dark eyes and that tough exterior. He was the best looking kid out there, of course. Antonio smiled to himself as his heart swelled with joy, overwhelmed by the urge to rush out of the car and hug him. But as he reached for the door handle, he saw Marta walking toward the boy. He sat staring, watching. She still amazed him—her beauty, her grace, and strength. She was not as young nor innocent looking. The hardships of her life had taken their toll, but there was an undeniable confidence in her now, evident in her posture.

He contemplated his next move as he saw how wholeheartedly his son ran into her arms. The two hugged each other tightly and Marta gave him a big kiss on the cheek. The scene brought tears to Antonio's eyes, because he realized that he had no right to intrude on them. There was a bond between these two, which he wouldn't dare break.

Antonio wondered what Marta had told their son about him. *What if he thinks I'm dead? Or worse yet, what if she told him that I deserted them?* With his aching head resting in his open palms, Antonio felt his guilty heart shatter.

*****

LYDIA DIDN'T LIKE BEING DECEPTIVE, BUT SHE *HATED* BEING deceived. She had known for some time that something was wrong with her marriage. Now that she herself had been unfaithful, her guilt urged her to search frantically through Antonio's personal things, where she knew she would discover evidence of her husband's infidelity and thus be able to justify what she'd done. She ransacked his desk, all the drawers in his room, and went through his closet, but came up empty-handed. As a last resort, she decided to look through the books in his library.

Lydia remembered seeing Antonio in the library with a pile of letters on his desk the day she confronted him about not wanting to make love to her anymore. He'd shoved those letters into a desk drawer and locked it when she walked into the room, claiming that they were only bills. But her woman's intuition told her that those letters were much more important than that.

After flipping through several volumes, Lydia came across a book of poems. And that was where she found them, concealed in the middle of the book. There were at least twenty hand written poems stuffed inside the book, in addition to a long letter. Apparently, some young servant girl named Marta had become pregnant with Antonio's child—*a son*. Lydia couldn't help feeling sorry for this innocent, unworldly girl, and she suddenly hated her husband for leaving her all alone to raise his child.

Lydia felt connected somehow to this Marta, perhaps because they had both been deceived by Antonio's charms. Stupid. It was no wonder that Antonio wanted no part of her or their daughters. Bitter tears streamed down Lydia's face as she placed the letters back in the book, and replaced it on the shelf. After carefully straightening up Antonio's quarters so that he wouldn't suspect she had gone through his things, Lydia returned to her room, where she could be alone with her thoughts. She needed to plan a fitting revenge, one that would cause Antonio to feel the same pain that was now planted in her heart and soul forever.

CHAPTER NINETEEN

ANTONIO SAT WITH JAVIER AT THE LOUNGE INSIDE THE
Beverly Hills Hotel and reached for the fourth gin and tonic the
waiter had brought to the table. Unable to find the courage to
approach Marta and their son, he could only try to get as drunk as
possible in order to avoid dealing with the painful situation.

"You might want to slow down on that stuff," Javier suggested.
"Levine will be here at any moment."

"Fuck him," Antonio replied sourly. Levine was becoming greedier
in his old age, and Antonio was about ready to cut him off, literally.
"You know what, Javier? I want you to handle it. I'm tired and I need
some rest tonight." Antonio watched a shocked expression spread
over Javier's face. "Knock yourself out. Play the head honcho for the
night. But don't give that pendejo everything he wants. You should
know how to deal with him by now. You've watched me long enough.
Don't make any fucking decisions before consulting me first. Tell me
what he's asking for, and we'll go from there."

"You sure?" Javier asked.

"Of course. You are my partner and my friend. I trust you to do right."

"Do me a favor then, will you?"

"What do you need?"

"Call the nanny, and check to make sure Isabella is all right. Let her know that I will be calling later on tonight." Javier picked up his glass of wine and toasted Antonio.

Antonio dragged himself up to his room. Business was getting him down. It seemed that everybody always wanted something from him. But he knew that the real reason he felt so exhausted was because of what he'd witnessed that afternoon. He admired the fact that Javier had the courage to raise Isabella on his own.

After Cynthia died, Javier balanced his time between his young daughter and their business, along with his political career. But Isabella always came first. She was a sweet, intelligent, beautiful child, and Javier had done an excellent job raising her. Antonio always urged him to find a woman and settle down, but Javier was bound and determined to keep things the way they were.

Feeling lonely, Antonio decided to call his wife. The phone rang many times before Lydia finally picked it up.

"Hello," she answered wearily.

"Hello, how are you?"

"Antonio?" she asked, suddenly sounding wide awake, a slight quiver in her voice.

"Of course it's me. Who the in hell did you think it was?"

"You woke me up."

"I'm sorry. I called to say that I miss you. Even though I don't tell you very often, I do love you." There was silence on the other end, and then he heard her murmur, "I love you, too," in a voice that sounded like she was near tears.

"Are you all right?"

"I'm fine. See you soon."

Antonio replaced the receiver and wondered why his wife sounded so strange.

CHAPTER TWENTY

JAVIER ENJOYED BEING THE MAN IN CHARGE FOR A CHANGE.

"Good to see you again, Javier." Levine sat down. "Where is Antonio?"

"I'm afraid he's not feeling well."

"I am very sorry to hear that."

Javier detected a hint of relief in Levine's face, as the older gentleman smiled and leaned back in his chair. He knew that Levine didn't care much for Antonio's tough demeanor.

"He would like me to fill him in on the details of this meeting. I should let you know beforehand that no decisions will be made without my consulting him."

"Of course." He folded his hands together and tucked them under his chin, his gaze never leaving the rim of his wine glass as he spoke. "You people are passing a lot of dope through my port lately, not to mention people."

"That's the idea," Javier replied, wondering where Levine was headed.

"Of course it is, but the locals are causing a ruckus, and the police are taking some interest in our activities."

"That's why you get such a large percentage. It's up to you to make sure we get protection."

"Sure, I understand this. We've been doing business for, what, five years now?"

Javier nodded. "Something like that. Why?"

"Well, it would seem to me that with the demand increasing and all this heat on *my* back, a bigger cut for me would be in order."

"Simon, I don't know. You know Antonio. He isn't going to like this. He doesn't like sharing much of anything. He's going to tell you that you get more than your share as it is." Javier didn't know what else to tell the man. He knew Antonio wouldn't give an inch when it came to their deal. He was constantly telling Javier that he'd like to do away with Levine as their middleman.

"Fuck Antonio," Levine said under his breath.

"Excuse me?"

"I do a lot for you people. I don't need *you*. There are a lot of people like you out there, dying to do business with me. As a matter of fact, a man named Pablo Aguilar called me last week to ask about the possibilities of our working together. I told him that I was a loyal man, and I intended keeping my business the way it is. But I feel sure he'd give me the share I want without any problem."

Javier wished Antonio were present. He didn't particularly care for confrontations. In a way, however, it was as well that Antonio wasn't there, because in his current state of mind, he might have strangled Levine right then and there.

"Look, I like you, Javier. I think that together we could work something out. We don't need Antonio. He's another goddamned big shot trying to run the world. Together, we can shut him down." Levine took a long drink from his glass of wine.

Javier stared at him, unable to find the right words to say. A young large-breasted blonde girl winked at Levine as she cruised through the nearly deserted lounge.

Levine scooted closer to Javier. "That's my date for the night, and it looks as if she's eager to get going. My apologies that I can't stay for dinner, but duty calls. Think about what I said and get back to me. I'm telling you, we don't need Antonio. You can make a lot more money with only one partner. A lot more money."

Javier sat frozen as he watched Levine and the girl stroll away. How ignorant was Levine? Or was this some type of setup? He knew that he wouldn't turn his back on Antonio. They had been friends for far too long for Javier to betray him. As soon as he recovered from his unpleasant meeting with Levine, Javier went straight to Antonio's room.

After Javier stood pounding on the door for several moments, Antonio finally pulled it open. He stood in the doorway in a silk robe, rubbing his eyes. "What do you want? I told you I was going to bed."

"You're not going to believe this," Javier replied. Maybe he should have waited until morning for Antonio's sobriety to return.

"It better be good."

"Believe me, you need to hear this."

Antonio walked over to the bar and poured himself a glass of water.

"Levine wants more money."

"You're kidding me, right?" Antonio chuckled. "You're getting funny in your old age." Javier didn't crack a smile. "Jesus Christ, you're not joking."

Javier could see Antonio's eyes bulge, as if he had suddenly been jolted into his old sober self. "That's not the best part."

"There's more?"

"Oh, yes."

Antonio motioned with his hand to continue. Javier told him about the entire meeting: the threat to go with Aguilar, and, finally, the attempt to cut Antonio out and make a deal alone with Javier.

"Who the fuck does he think he is? That goddamned piece of scum. I'll kill him! I'll kill the son of a bitch! Trying to undermine me, trying to make my own partner, my friend—deceive me! That piece of shit!" Antonio's face burned with rage, his fingers tightening around his glass. "No one, I mean *no one* fucks with me. Correct me if I'm wrong, but didn't I tell him that when we first started doing business together?"

Javier agreed with Antonio, afraid to get in the way of his wrath. "What are you going to do?"

He shook his head and after a moment of silence, he looked at Javier. "Don't worry about it. I'll take care of Simon Levine."

CHAPTER TWENTY-ONE

PEDRO TORRES WAS HOME WITH BELLA DURING JAVIER'S trip to Los Angeles. She was sick when her daddy left, and Pedro himself didn't feel too well either, so he offered to stay and help the nanny care for her.

Actually, he liked being home with Bella. She was such an intelligent and curious child. There was a clear bond between the two. After all, she was the reason he now had a *real* family. As he had hoped, once he'd disposed of his father, Javier had accepted him with open arms. He'd treated Pedro like a son and had come to trust him. It hadn't been as easy to win over Antonio's trust, however. But through time and perseverance, even Antonio had come around. Pedro knew that someday he would run their empire. After all, both Javier and Antonio only had daughters. And as the business partners aged, Pedro figured that he would only have Emilio to contend with. Emilio was such a hothead that he was bound to screw up sooner or later. Pedro, whose instincts were usually on the mark, felt that Antonio loved his baby brother, but for some reason he didn't completely trust him. That would be Emilio's downfall and Pedro's winning ticket.

"Pedro," a soft voice called out to him. It was coming from the garden below the balcony, outside his room.

He knew that Bella must be up and feeling better. Her long, dark hair was pulled back with a yellow bow. She wore a t-shirt with a pair of denim overalls as she stood below, looking up at Pedro on the balcony, squinting her bright green eyes against the sun.

"Buenos días, Bella. How are you this morning?"

As if she didn't have time for this small talk, she replied, "Come quick! I think the mare is about to have her baby."

Pedro set his coffee down and hurried down the stairs. He met Bella in the garden, where he grabbed her hand and they jogged down to the barn. The two of them shared a love for the horses. There were stables and training facilities both at the main house in Guadalajara and at the coastal home in Costa Careyes. Pedro gave Bella riding lessons as often as possible, knowing that one day she would make an excellent equestrienne.

As they approached the stables, they could hear the mare pawing at the ground. They peered quietly into her stall. The horse sensed them, glancing up at her audience, her dark brown eyes full of anxiety. She let out a groan as she lay down on the fresh straw, which crinkled under her weight.

Bella and Pedro watched in fascination and awe as nature took its course. Within twenty minutes, a shiny new colt was born, and his mother licked his chestnut coat dry. Within forty more minutes, the new colt was standing on his wobbly legs, nursing from his mother's teats.

Bella looked at Pedro. "When I grow up I'm going to have a whole bunch of horses."

"You mean your daddy doesn't have enough here for you?"

"No, I'm going to raise them and have a hundred million."

"My, but you are ambitious. I certainly hope your husband will like horses."

"He will, silly."

"Oh, really."

"*You* like horses."

"Yes."

"*You'll* be my husband."

"Isabella, I'll be an old man by the time you marry."

"No you won't. You'll never be old."

"We *all* grow old, Bella."

"I don't care. I want you to marry me," she declared.

"You'll grow up, Bella, and meet the handsome young man you'll marry."

"No, I want to marry *you*," her demands grew louder.

"Okay, Bella. You win. I'll marry you," he said laughingly, appeasing the little girl.

However, as Pedro watched the child feed the mare a sugar cube from her pocket, something twisted in him at that moment, almost like a vision. For a second he had to wonder if Bella's wishes weren't a bizarre prophecy that he was truly *destined* to fulfill.

CHAPTER TWENTY-TWO

THE MORNING SUN SOOTHED ANTONIO'S BACK.
It had been a while since he'd simply sat outside and relaxed.
Business was so hectic he'd almost forgotten what life was all about.
He needed to spend more time enjoying it.

Antonio loved his city of Calí. It was the home of his ancestors,
and he vowed he would always remain here. The estate was well
hidden, in the vast blue mountains above the Cauca Valley. The view
from the mountaintop a radiant one. On a clear day such as this one,
Antonio could easily see the Pacific Ocean to the west. Sitting in his
favorite lounge chair, he didn't hear Emilio come up behind him.

"Antonio."

"Hey, little brother, how are you?" Antonio asked, surprised to see
him. "It's been a while."

"That's no fault of mine," Emilio replied as he sat down in the
chair across from Antonio.

"I know, things have been crazy lately."

"A little *too* crazy from the sound of it. You look tired."

"It comes with the trade."

"I think maybe I can help you," Emilio replied.

Antonio had never known Emilio to be so direct. There was something oddly different about him. "What do you mean?"

"I'd like to be your righthand man," he announced confidently.

Antonio laughed, "You what?" Where was this coming from? In a way, it was impressive, or at the very least endearing. He leaned back in his chair, waiting for Emilio to make his pitch.

"I am telling you that you need me. You're working all the time and you have no time for your family. I can alleviate some of the work load for you."

"What about Javier?"

"What about him? He's your business partner. He makes sure the product gets to the States and the distributors get it. That's it. Finito. It's a done deal."

"Well, little brother, what does a righthand man do?"

"I'm glad you asked. I would be the one to make sure everyone's happy—you, Javier, the distributors, Levine. Everyone."

"Screw that bastard Levine. I don't give a shit if *he's* happy or not."

"But you *do* have to make him happy. And so we might as well make the best of the situation."

"That's the last thing I want to do. That *pendejo* Simon does nothing but steal my money. He's a no-good bastard."

"I apologize. Forget I even mentioned him. Let me finish what I came to say. I want to be the man you can count on. You may love your partner like a brother, and, yes, he does a good job for you, but when it comes down to it, he isn't your own blood. I believe that he would likely screw you the first chance he got, if a better deal came along." Emilio leaned in closer to Antonio, his white silk shirt sticking to him.

"I very much doubt that he would."

"You know as well as I do that business is not his number-one priority. It's still his daughter."

"As it should be."

"Dammit, Antonio, all I want to do is help you, and you can't even let me do that. What in hell did I ever do to you?" Emilio paced back and forth, his hands flailing wildly as he spoke.

"Calm down and shut up. You're not talking to some ignorant idiot. I am your brother and you will show me some respect."

"Respect, respect. All my life it's been about respecting you, Antonio. What about me? All I get from you is a bunch of bullshit about 'watching over the fort while I'm gone,' or 'do this, do that.' But you never give me anything really important to do."

"Listen to me. I have done the best I could by you. I've sent you to the finest schools, given you a grand place to live, let you have your freedom, and loved you. What more could you ask for?"

"Respect."

"How can I respect you when you've done nothing to prove your worth? Not once have you ever thanked me. You played around when I sent you to school, and you're still playing around today."

"Give me a chance to prove myself. Please, I won't let you down."

Antonio sat quietly for a very long time. He thought over the things Emilio had said, and slowly began to consider that Emilio might be sincere. Maybe it *was* time to give him a chance. "Okay, you want a chance, you say. One chance?"

"That's all I'm asking for."

"Good, then. There's something I want you to do for me, and if you can do it without messing up, then we'll see what happens. But if you mess up, I'll see to it you'll never be more than a deckhand on my yacht."

"I won't let you down, brother. What do you want me to do?"

"Kill Levine." Antonio smiled.

"What?"

"You heard me. I want that old pig dead. I don't need him any longer. In fact, if you do this for me, I might just move *you* over to the Bahamas and put *you* in charge of Levine's operation."

"Jesus Christ, Antonio. Won't we be starting a war with the Italians?"

"No one cares about the Jew anymore. In fact, I'm surprised the wops haven't done away with him yet. Besides, no one will be able to figure out who did it. And by the time they figure out that he's dead, we'll already have set up shop." Antonio looked deep into his brother's eyes, wondering if he was up to such a challenge.

"I'll do it."

"If you breathe a word of this to anyone, then I'll have you by the balls. Understood?" Emilio nodded. "Good. For your sake, I hope that you do."

CHAPTER TWENTY-THREE

LITTLE ROSA STOOD AT THE DOOR OF HER MOTHER'S SUITE, watching her sob. Her daddy had left again for America that morning, and she was certain her mommy must be missing him. Even though she was only six years old, Rosa felt the urge to comfort her.

She padded over to the side of the Victorian bed with its yards of antique lace hanging from the canopy. It was a room like no other, and Rosa loved it. Unlike her little sister, Felicia, who enjoyed bouncing on the bed and getting into their mother's dresser drawers, Rosa would come into the suite whenever she could escape the clutches of her nanny, but was content to simply sit in the room, dreaming of stories about princes and their fair maidens. Her mother's room allowed for such dreams. Sooner or later though, Chata would always find her, and then Rosa would be reprimanded.

One day, Lydia found out that the child enjoyed coming into her room to think and dream about other worlds. She'd found Rosa sitting in the middle of the peach-colored antique rug that was placed over the hardwood floors. She heard her singing and talking about a princess who was searching for her prince. Lydia held her breath as she quietly stood watching her child at play.

Rosa had no idea that her mother was looking at her, until Chata stormed in. "There you are! I've been looking everywhere for you. You are a naughty little girl," she scolded her, shaking a gnarled finger at her, as her sparse eyebrows furrowed. She picked the child up with one swoop of her arms. But Chata's face, which had fumed with anger only moments before, drastically changed when she laid eyes on Rosa's mother.

Lydia instantly grabbed Rosa out of Chata's arms. "She is welcome here whenever she pleases. To sing, play and dream." She winked at Rosa.

"I thought that, well…" Chata tried to explain, her weathered face wrinkling as she tried to hide her shame.

"You thought wrong. She is allowed in here without your supervision, or even your permission, for that matter. Don't you have something else you could be doing?"

"*Sí, Señora*," the old woman replied.

Lydia waved her hand, dismissing the woman from her presence, and then set Rosa back down on the floor. She bent down, placing herself at eye level with her eldest daughter. Tears streamed down Rosa's flushed cheeks. "Shh, *mija*," she murmured as she pulled Rosa to her chest, hugging her tightly. "As I said, you can come to my room day or night to play and dream."

"You're really not mad at me?"

"Of course not."

"And Chata can't yell at me?"

"No, because if that old *bruja* yells at you again, I'll kick her in the behind so hard, she'll fly straight to the moon on that broom of hers." They both laughed, and Lydia straightened Rosa's hair. "No more crying, okay?"

"Thank you, Mama."

"Anything for you." With that, Lydia left the room and let Rosa continue playing.

The memory of that day made her mother's bedroom a sanctuary for Rosa—not to mention that her little sister wasn't allowed the same privileges as she was.

But now her mother was in tears, and Rosa wished to console her. She climbed up on the high bed. Her mommy didn't even glance up. She wrapped her small arms around her.

"Oh hello, *mija*," sobbed her mother.

"Mama, why are you crying?"

"Don't worry about me."

"But Mama . . ."

"I am missing your daddy, that's all."

"I know, Mama. I miss him, too. But remember, he always comes back."

Lydia glanced up at Rosa, who took her mother's face in her tiny hands and said tenderly, "Please don't cry."

Her mother smiled. "All right, no more tears."

"Promise?"

"Promise."

"Good mama," Rosa replied, placing her hands on her hips. "No more crying. You promised."

Her mother smiled. "Yes, I did. Now run along."

*****

LYDIA WATCHED AS HER CHILD CLIMBED DOWN OFF HER BED and scampered away. *Ah, my golden one, my baby. But she is not a boy, not the son Antonio desperately longed for. Neither Rosa nor Felicia will be loved as much as Antonio would love the son he has with another woman—the son I am certain he has gone to see.*

*****

IT WAS ALL FALLING INTO PLACE FOR EMILIO.

With some ingenuity and determination, the whole lot would be his. But now was a time for patience.

Killing Levine would be simple, even enjoyable. What his older brother didn't know was that Emilio had killed men before—often for as small a favor as a good screw or some fine tequila.

Emilio had scoped out Levine's rather massive home, as well as all the guards around it, and knew how to accomplish the murder. He'd studied Levine's habits for a week through a set of binoculars.

On one occasion, he had even disguised himself as one of Levine's gardeners. Nobody had been any the wiser. Levine's guards were a bunch of goons, and he knew that he would be able to get around them easily enough.

It was a Sunday night, and all the servants were out of the house. Levine always went to bed around nine. Once asleep, his two bodyguards would invariably venture into the game room to shoot pool.

Access to the house was fairly easy. Emilio scaled the eight-foot concrete wall, leading down to a mountain path overlooking the Caribbean. As he reached the other side of the wall, he paused, making sure he hadn't been spotted. Dressed in black from head to toe, he went around to the side of the house, where he found a bathroom window partially opened. He quietly opened it all the way and wriggled his way through.

He snuck up the stairs, his ears tuned to the movement of the bodyguards below. He paused when he heard one of them say, "Did you hear something?"

"Nah, man. It's probably the old man getting up to take a piss. Come on, it's your turn."

"Yeah, okay."

Thank God. The last thing he needed was to take out a couple of big Jamaicans. He wanted it to be a clean job, free of any mess.

The master bedroom was located in the far end of the house. Its wide doors were locked. He worked the lock with experienced hands, and silently let himself in. There was Levine, sleeping soundly in the large bed.

Emilio walked over to the side of the bed standing inches from his face. He grabbed a pillow and stuffed it over Levine's face. The old man coughed, choking as he squirmed like a wild animal caught in a trap. The resistance excited Emilio, and he pressed the pillow harder into Levine's face. After a few minutes, Levine gave up and his body collapsed. Emilio smiled with satisfaction at a job well done. He pulled the pillow off Levine's face, exposing his rolled-back eyes. He then took the man's pulse to make sure he was dead. Yes, he was dead.

Fifteen minutes later Emilio was back at his hotel, drinking a whiskey next to a large-busted redhead.

"So what do you do for a living?" she asked him.

"I kill people."

"Oh, really?" Her southern drawl revealed that she was a tourist.

"Really."

"Sounds interesting," she remarked with a laugh that indicated she didn't believe him.

"It is. It really is," he replied. He broke out in a laugh that joined hers.

CHAPTER TWENTY-FOUR

LYDIA THOUGHT ABOUT EMILIO CONSTANTLY:
his smile, his touch—the passion they shared. At times, it seemed
like a distant dream. A month had passed since they'd been together,
and as much as she hated to admit it, she couldn't wait until she
could be with him again. While she was filled with shame about their
indiscretion, the excitement and fear of being caught made her want
him all the more.

He had been gone for a week in the Bahamas, and a part of her
wanted to fly there and see him, but she had no idea what she would
tell Antonio. She knew it would take all her resourcefulness to
prevent her husband from finding out anything. Not that he'd notice
or even care. He was always so busy with his life, and now that Lydia
knew the truth about his other family, it alleviated some of her
feelings of guilt.

Lost in her daydreams as she lay by the pool, Lydia didn't hear
him approach. She opened her eyes when she felt the sun being
blocked.

"Hey, gorgeous," Emilio greeted her.

She tried to conceal her happiness, but found it difficult. "You're in my sun," she remarked testily.

"Am I?"

"Yes."

"I am so sorry, *Señora*," he answered. He straddled her lounge chair. Lydia sat back, pulling the towel up around her. Emilio sat down.

"Emilio, what are you doing?"

"This."

Emilio reached out his hand and lightly stroked Lydia's cheek. She turned away from him in order to avoid his eyes. He then pointedly turned her toward him again, placing both his hands on her face and kissing her softly on the lips. She momentarily resisted, but as the kiss became more heated, she quickened to his desires, which had now become her own.

Abruptly she pushed him away. "Not here."

"Why not?" Emilio asked.

"There are servants everywhere."

"That's what makes it so much fun."

"And risky. My God, Emilio, what we're doing is so wrong."

"Do you really care?" His finger traced the outline of her breasts inside her bikini. "I want you. Now."

"No."

"Come on." He grabbed her hand. She knew it was a losing battle, and her only choice was to follow him. He led her into the poolside cabana.

"I don't think we should," she continued her weak protests.

"Shh, relax." Emilio placed her down on one of the sofas, where she closed her eyes and gave in to her desires.

Emilio wasted no time. He quickly unfastened the tiny cloth scraps that covered her breasts, and began to caress them. He ran his tongue over her nipples making Lydia squirm in ecstasy. She tried as hard as she could to keep her breathing quiet. His tongue traveled down across her flat stomach, which showed no signs of the children she had borne.

Once again, Lydia attempted to resist him by sitting up. But he pushed her back down and lightly placed his tongue upon her soft mound of flesh. With expertise, Emilio brought her to an orgasm. She tried with all her might not to let out a sound, but as much as she resisted, she couldn't stop the soft moans that escaped her lips.

Now it was Emilio's turn. He stood and unzipped his suit pants, and even before completely removing them, he was inside her. With heated passion, his rough side took over. Emilio pulled out and turned Lydia onto her stomach where he entered her from behind. As he made love to her hard and fast, Lydia climaxed again. Emilio felt satisfied enough to achieve his own release.

As soon as he was finished, he stood up and zipped up his trousers. Lydia was still on the couch, stunned and exhilarated.

"You and I were meant for each other. Mark my words," Emilio said. "I will see you at dinner. Antonio is expecting me now. Thank you, my love." He bent down and left her with one last kiss.

*****

JAVIER WATCHED HIS DAUGHTER RIDING HER HORSE, SALSA.
He hated the thought of her getting hurt, but the image of Bella on that horse was amazing. Pedro led both horse and rider around with a lead line.

The young man had surprisingly turned out to be an asset to their organization. Pedro had a great future with their business, and Javier was prepared to put him in control of all of the marijuana distribution within the Los Angeles area, as long as Antonio concurred. It was important for Antonio and Javier to appear to be a legitimate business. Even though the cops, immigration, and anyone else who needed to be, were paid off, and no one gave them any real trouble, it was still important, since Javier was seriously considering running for the Presidency. It was something he wanted to discuss with Antonio, who he expected momentarily.

He'd been concerned about his friend lately. Something seemed to be distracting him. Minutes later, he arrived. "Ah, Antonio. I didn't hear you."

"Comes with practice," Antonio replied.

"I'm pleased you are here. I am worried about you. You seem troubled lately, my friend. Your age has begun to show."

"Thank you," he said with a smirk.

"You know I am only concerned."

"I know."

"Talk to me. We are like brothers. If you can't talk to me, then at least talk to God."

"God cannot save me from the torture I am going through."

"What on earth do you mean?"

Antonio looked away.

Javier reached across the table and poured him a glass of cola he'd had brought out prior to their meeting. He patted Antonio on the hand.

"Marta," Antonio finally said.

"Marta?" Javier asked.

"Yes, Marta."

At first, Javier was very confused. Who was Marta? Then, as if a bucket of cold water had slapped him in the face, he realized who he was speaking of. "You mean that pretty servant girl who used to work here, the one who left suddenly without giving any reason?"

"Yes."

"What about her, Antonio?" Curiosity overcame some of his concern.

"We were lovers."

"I knew as much." Javier picked up his cola and took a sip.

"It was more serious than that. I made promises to her."

"What kind of promises?"

"Promises I couldn't keep."

"I see," he replied.

"There is more." Antonio took his cigarettes out of his shirt pocket and lit one. Javier stared at him in silence. "She left here because of me."

"Why?"

"The lies. I never told her I was married. I told her that she and I would be married, and I would take her away from her servant life."

"You knew you could never do that."

"Yes, but part of me *wanted* to believe that I could do these things for her. God knows, *part* of me wanted to." He paused for a second and looked at Isabella on her horse. "She's growing up."

"Yes."

"She's as beautiful as her mother."

"Thank you."

"Javier," Antonio continued, "I fell in love with Marta. She was like a forbidden treasure. She filled a void in me that no other woman, including Lydia, ever has."

"What happened?"

"You know that I could never leave my family."

"Why didn't you keep her as a mistress?"

"I would have, but because I failed to tell her the truth from the beginning, she left here when she saw me with Lydia at the party you gave for Cynthia, shortly after she became pregnant with Bella."

Memories flooded Javier's mind. As soon as Antonio mentioned it, Javier remembered the fiesta as if it were yesterday. He remembered how happy he'd felt, how his wife had looked. He even remembered the teal dress she'd worn, loose around the midriff where she was beginning to show. That dress had matched the color of her eyes—eyes their daughter now possessed.

"I'm sorry, I know how much it still pains you to talk about it."

"It's all right." The lump in his throat made it difficult for him to say anything more.

"She was pregnant, my friend. Can you believe it? Pregnant with my child."

"How could you let her go?"

"I had no idea she was pregnant. I would've seen to it that she'd been taken care of if I had known."

"How did you find out?"

"It doesn't matter. I didn't find out until after the baby was born. By then, I felt wrong about going to see them. My loyalties were to the family I already had. Believe me, I wanted to go to her, to take care of her and my only son." Javier raised his eyebrows. "Yes, that's right. My son. She bore me a son. I found out their address, and I've been sending them money every month. A few weeks ago, when both of us were in Los Angeles, I finally worked up the courage to go and see where they lived."

"Did you see them?"

"Yes."

"What was their reaction?"

"They didn't see me."

"I don't understand."

Antonio explained to Javier what had occurred when he went to see Marta and his son.

"So you never spoke with them?"

"No."

"Now I understand why you have been so distracted. This, along with the Levine fiasco, must be very difficult to deal with. How have you remained sane?"

"I don't know, but I am going back to Los Angeles today, and I have decided to confront Marta."

"What about Lydia?"

"I don't know. I don't know anything anymore. Marta may throw me out. I wouldn't be surprised if she hates me, but I have to see her again. She has to know how sorry I am. If there is any way I can make it up to her, I will."

"I wish you luck, my friend, I really wish you luck."

At that moment, Bella came running up to them. "*Tío* Antonio," she squealed with delight.

"Hello, sweetheart."

She climbed into his lap and gave him a big hug. A bittersweet mixture flowed through him. He thought of Rosa, who was close to Bella's age, and of his son, who was also around the same age. He questioned himself as to whether or not he was betraying his wife and daughters by desiring to know his son better.

But perhaps the real betrayal was to the woman he had lied to, and the son who had never known his father. He prayed that the answers would come to him soon.

*****

ANTONIO SLEPT THROUGH THE ENTIRE FLIGHT FROM
Guadalajara to Los Angeles, his subconscious plagued by dreams of
Marta and his son, and of Lydia and their two daughters.

A limousine picked him up, taking him to the Century City Plaza,
where he checked into a tower suite. After tipping the bellman who
had brought up his bags and checked to see that all was in order, he
closed the door and rang for room service. "A gin and tonic, please.
Yes, room 1274."

When in the United States, Antonio was always very conscious of
his accent, and he made sure to restrain himself from speaking any
Spanish. Javier had once chided him about being embarrassed about
his own nationality and culture.

"Embarrassed? Ha. Never. I know how much hatred the *gringos*
have for us. And to get ahead in their country, you must play their
filthy *gringo* games. If that means acting like a filthy *gringo*, then that
is what I must do."

A knock on his door signaled the arrival of his drink. Again, he
saw disrespect in the eyes of the boy who held both the drink and
the bill. His pride made him leave a large tip.

"Marta, Marta, Marta," he whispered as he stood on the balcony,
staring twelve stories below at the swimming pool. "What have I
done? The agony I've put you through." He walked back into the
room, leaving the sliding glass door open for the cool, spring breeze
to flow. He sat on the bed and stared at the phone. He took the piece

of paper with the number on it and fingered it, trying to decide whether he should call her or go there.

He had no idea what her reaction would be either way, so he picked up the phone and dialed Marta's number with trembling fingers. It rang three times, until a child's voice answered.

"Hello?"

Antonio froze. For the first time he was hearing the voice of his son. He closed his eyes and pictured the child he had seen a few weeks earlier.

"Hello?" he said again.

Antonio could not speak or move, and his son hung up the phone. His mind was made up for him at that moment. He had to see his boy. Tears formed in his eyes, tears that had accumulated from all the years he'd never known his son.

*****

MARTA WAS TIRED FROM HER DAY'S WORK, WHICH SEEMED more brutal than usual. The foreman yelled all day long for the sewers to work faster.

No matter how much Elisa harped about her using that money Antonio sent each month, Marta was determined to save this money for Alejandro. Her dream of sending him off to college one day could only come true with that money. If Antonio did only one thing for his son, it would be to provide Alejandro with an education.

Alex was a good student, and since Marta had switched him back to the neighborhood school where most of the students were Hispanic, he improved day by day—learning his arithmetic and how to read. Each day, she thanked the Lord for blessing her with such a beautiful, intelligent son.

As she made *menudo* for their supper, she glanced out the kitchen window to see Alex and Hector playing stickball. *I wish I could give him more. I wish he had a father. Maybe I should never have run from Mexico. My child has a right to a father, like any other boy.*

Marta's mind traveled back to the day she had seen Antonio's pregnant wife. Alex not only has a father out there, but sisters or a brother and sister. Marta's insecurities about keeping Alex away from his father weighed heavily on her mind. She felt selfish for preventing the boy from knowing him. Then she stiffened and thought about how selfish Antonio had been. She reassured herself that he had no right to her child, none at all. However, she knew that was wrong as well. As much as she tried to hate Antonio, she couldn't.

The aroma of the *menudo* filled their small home. As Marta began making the tortillas, there was a tap on the front door.

"It's open, Alejandro." There was no response. "*Ay, niño.* Mama is too busy for your games today." There was another knock on the door. This time it was louder and more decisive. "Okay, okay, silly boy, I'm game." Marta opened the front door, expecting to catch Alejandro hiding behind the oak tree in the front yard. Instead, it was Antonio. She jumped back, feeling her jaw drop open as she let out a startled yelp. It was as if it were only yesterday. He looked the same: that regal stance, that chiseled face and those serene eyes, looking right into her. There he stood—Antonio Espinoza. She had dreamed about this day for years, but now that the day had come, she was at a loss for words. Her shaking hands covered her open mouth.

"Hello," Antonio said, finally breaking the silence.

"Hello," she uttered through her palms.

"May I come in and speak with you?"

"I don't know." She dropped her arms and shook her head.

"Please, Marta. Please, let me talk with you." His heart raced, studying her. He couldn't force her to let him in, but standing there with her, seeing her—she hadn't changed. She was more beautiful than he'd remembered.

"You can't stay long. We're getting ready to eat." She didn't know what else to say, how to respond or act.

"*We*, meaning your husband and son?"

"No. Only Alejandro and me. I've never married."

"Alejandro. A beautiful name."

"He is a beautiful child."

"I know."

"Well, this is my home. It is nothing like you're used to."

"It is lovely, Marta."

She took him through their small home. The old hardwood floors creaked beneath their shoes. They were clean but badly in need of repair. Their furniture was sparse and old, and the blue-and-white curtains had doubtless been handmade. But the home was immaculate, and held a charm that only Marta could've given it.

She led Antonio into the family room, which appeared to also serve as a bedroom for Marta. The couch, shabby and lumpy, was a sofa bed from where he sat down on the sofa, he could see the hallway leading to a bathroom and his son's bedroom.

Marta saw him looking at Alex's room.

"Would you like to see it?"

"Yes, very much."

"Go ahead."

He peered into his son's bedroom. It was the one room that was bright and cheerful. There were posters of Mickey Mouse and Donald Duck on the walls. A small rocking chair sat in the corner next to the closet. There was a large wooden box filled to the brim with toys, and his stuffed animals lounged on the red comforter that covered his twin-size bed. There were several children's books on top of a white wicker dresser.

The toys that filled it and the colors of the room made up for its small size. He thought of Rosa and Felicia's rooms at home, which were three times larger. His daughters had toys galore, but he saw that his son was far from neglected, and this pleased him.

"He likes Mickey Mouse," Marta remarked.

"I see. Has he been to Disneyland?"

"No. I've been wanting to take him, but with work and everything... I'm saving our money as well."

"I understand."

"Would you like some coffee?"

"Yes, please."

Marta went back into the kitchen, while Antonio lingered in Alejandro's doorway. When he turned around to see Marta walking into the main living area and setting down two cups of coffee, the light came through the window and caught the ends of her long, dark hair, making them glisten.

He walked over and sat down in the chair across from her. She smiled, and he knew that she felt as uncertain about this meeting as he was. Yet in an odd way it felt comfortable being together again. The love they'd felt for each other hadn't dissipated over time. It couldn't have.

"Does my son know about me?"

"Not much."

"I see. You've been saving the money I sent you?"

"For his education."

"That's good. Do you need more?"

"No, thank you. We do fine."

"I've missed you," he blurted. "I would have helped you with the baby. Why didn't you come to me?" If only she had come to him.

She paused before answering. "Is that what you would have wanted, Antonio? Come to you and your wife to tell you both the news that I was going to have your baby? And what would you have done?"

"Helped you."

"Helped me *how*? By seeing that I got out of the country and out of your life. Helped me. I didn't want your help. I did what needed to be done without you."

"You know I never would have caused you so much pain intentionally."

"But you *did*. And you *did* do it intentionally, regardless of what you say now. You knew I loved you. You made promises to me—promises that you knew you could never keep. You lied to me. And your kind of help is not what my son and I need. The only reason I even accept your money each month is to fulfill a dream I have of seeing Alejandro graduate from college one day."

"My love for you was never a lie." She was being foolish. How could she doubt his love? "Your pride stands in your way."

"You expect me to believe you about loving me? I may have been naive then, but I am not ignorant now. And as for my pride, all I can say is, if you call honesty pride, then you are the one who is ignorant and shameful."

"I am not lying to you. I did love you. I still do," he whispered. "I've always loved you. You have to understand who I am, and what I represent. I could not hurt my children in such a way."

"But you did hurt your child. Your son. Do you think it has been easy for Alejandro to grow up without a father? Do you think this has been easy for me? I am both his mother and his father."

"The truth is, I felt scared and trapped. I loved you, yes; but I also loved my wife. I wanted to come to you, be with you. But by the time

I came to my senses, you had already left, and I had no idea you were pregnant. If I had known, I would have searched for you."

"But you did find me, and you found out about the baby."

"Yes, but by that time I realized that you hated me."

"I did."

The tears in Marta's eyes betrayed her. She had never hated him. Hatred was not part of who she was. "Did you really?" He leaned in close to her and touched her hand.

"You bastard." She looked down at the floor and back up again. Tears flooded her eyes. He kissed her gently on the cheek.

"You bastard," she repeated, balling her fists up.

"I am so sorry I ever hurt you. I would give my life if I could take away the pain I have caused. I would do anything for you. I have suffered, and thought about you, and longed for you every day since you left. You are the only one who has ever seen my soul. I know now what a mistake I made, letting you go out of my life. I am not happy, Marta."

"I am sorry. But you made your choice long ago."

"There is still time."

"There is no time."

"Listen. Please. Hear me out." She protested. He placed a finger over her lips. "Life passes quickly each day, too quickly. You are the one who made happiness a reality for me. I want you back in my life. I want you and Alejandro to come back to Colombia with me. I want you to be my wife."

"You are not thinking."

"No, it's true. I didn't plan this, but as soon as I saw you again, I knew."

"You have a wife. Go back to her. Leave us alone."

"She knows I am not happy. She is not a spiteful woman. She will go easily, once I pay her a lot of money."

"Money and a great deal of pain. Spiteful or not, I could never hurt someone else to benefit myself. You see, Antonio, I am not like you."

"Please think about it."

"There is nothing to think about."

"Give us another chance."

"Why? So you can tuck me away in some apartment and make me your prostitute whenever you feel the urge?"

"You were never that. I have already told you how much I loved you, and love you still."

Marta grew silent and stared at him. He felt as if she were looking straight through him. She sighed. "I have waited to hear those words for so many years—too many, maybe. Now that I hear them, they don't mean what I once thought they would. I may live here with Alejandro in this small house in this rundown neighborhood, which really isn't so bad because we all know and take care of each other here. We help one another when it is necessary. I may not possess much, and I work long, hard hours for what I do have. But to be honest with you, I like my life here. I have only myself to depend upon. And my child is happy. We have clothes to wear, and food to eat, and, yes, Alejandro is quite intelligent and getting a good education. As much feeling as I may still have in my heart for you, I

169|P a g e

can't go back with you. I will not take another woman's husband. It would be wrong and deceitful. It would ruin any love we ever had or might rekindle together."

He smiled at her, although he felt like crying—his heart breaking. She was still the good-hearted and loving woman she'd always been: never putting herself first, but always caring about what might happen to others. She was the one pure person he'd ever known. "I understand." He wished he didn't.

"Thank you."

"Answer me one thing, truthfully."

"Yes?"

"*Do* you still love me?"

She folded her hands in her lap and crossed her legs. "Antonio Espinoza, you would have to be a fool not to know the answer to that. But if you must hear me say it, then, of course, I still love you. I always have and I always will. You do not see another man in my house, do you? Nor will you, ever. I gave you my heart as a girl, and that love was true and will be forever. No man could ever take your place."

Antonio nodded. A mixture of relief, bliss, and sadness engulfed him as her words penetrated his heart. She stood up and walked into the kitchen to stir the *menudo*. Selfishly, he liked the fact that there had been no other men in her life. But he also pitied her because, like her, he knew what it was to have your heart stolen, so that you could never truly love another.

"Would you like to have dinner with us?" Marta asked him from the kitchen.

He wanted to, to see and talk with his son, look into the child's eyes and maybe in some way the boy would recognize him and simply by seeing him would on some level know that he was his father. "I can't. I have to go." As hard as it was to leave her, and not have the pleasure of meeting child, he knew the pain of having to leave Alejandro after meeting him would far outweigh the pain of going now. Antonio wasn't sure that he would be able to leave after having dinner with them.

She nodded and opened the door.

He kissed her on the cheek and walked away, tears blurring his vision.

CHAPTER TWENTY-FIVE

EMILIO SIPPED A DRINK AND SILENTLY COUNTED HIS blessings: Levine was dead. Antonio was preoccupied, as usual. Javier was the big fat pushover he'd always been. And as for him, he was regularly getting laid by his brother's beautiful wife.

"Beautiful but tragic, tragic but beautiful," he muttered. One day his brother's entire empire would be his. But he realized that patience was a virtue. Meanwhile, he would take all that he could for as long as possible.

He wasn't ready to make any major moves yet. But he *did* need another player on his side, so he decided to meet with Pedro. If the two of them could get together, it wouldn't take long before Emilio was running the show. He knew that Javier thought of Pedro like a son; but he also knew that Pedro was a sneaky weasel, a man who'd murdered his own father—a fact that endeared him to Emilio.

"*Señor?*"

"*Sí.*" His thoughts were interrupted by one of his handful of regular whores.

"*Señor* Torres is here to see you."

"Show him in, please."

Emilio was seated on the balcony outside his large apartment, overlooking the town of Calí leading back into the sparsely populated jungles of Colombia. As usual, Pedro appeared in a charcoal designer suit and tie, attire he had adopted in imitation of his mentor, Javier.

"Hello! Hello! So good of you to come, my friend." Emilio held out his hand, which Pedro grabbed and shook forcefully. "Good morning." He smiled. "You may go," he said to the fair-haired Spanish girl who had shown Pedro out to the terrace. He took a cigar from a small case on the glass table next to him. "Would you like one?"

"No, thank you," Pedro replied.

"A drink, maybe?"

"No, nothing, thanks. I'm curious about why I'm here. You said it was an urgent matter. And more so, I'm curious about why you instructed me not to inform Javier of this visit. I had to jostle my way around his questions, and I've reserved a flight back home early in the morning."

"You see, my friend, I have a proposition for you."

"What kind of proposition?"

"Business."

"We both work for Antonio and Javier. I'm certain that if there were something we needed to meet about, *they* would have called the meeting themselves. So let me set you straight before you say something that may turn out to have repercussions. I respect my job and I value your family. I honor all the good both Javier and Antonio have done for me. But I know you, Emilio. You are a greedy man who will sacrifice anything or anyone to achieve your goals. But I am loyal, and I will not harm those who have treated me well."

"My, my, my, but you are suspicious. I only invited you here so that we could get to know one another better. It is my understanding that we will be working more closely together in future. And I agree with you completely. Loyalty is vital. I understand you value *loyalty* in the same manner you value your family." Emilio watched Pedro flinch.

"Javier *is* my family."

"Hmmm, I see. I'm not trying to harm anyone. I thought it might be a good idea if we became better friends. You *do* realize that someday all of this will be *our* empire," Emilio remarked, gesturing to the streets of Calí. "Right now, our organization is nothing compared to that of, say, the Italians. But in time we too, will be able to compete with each and every organization, until *we* are the ones on top. We will own South America. There is no doubt in my mind that the Colombian crops have the potential to make us more money than we ever dreamed of, and they will make us the kings of the world."

Pedro pulled his chair closer to Emilio and got right in his face. "You are as transparent as a guilty woman who has betrayed her man. I will not have any part of this scheme you've hatched against your brother and Javier. I have no desire to take down the two people who have put me in my present position. If you were as smart as you think you are, then you would hang onto the coattails of your superiors. That is the only way you will ever be in charge of this organization. If you'll please excuse me, I have a real meeting in an hour. I would like to go back to my hotel for a few moments. Thank you for your hospitality." Pedro got up from his chair and casually strolled through Emilio's apartment and out the door.

Emilio slammed his fist against the glass table and took a large swallow of his drink. "Pedro Torres had better watch his back, because the prodigal son will be sorry someday his *new* loyalty is so goddamned pure!"

CHAPTER TWENTY-SIX

MIGUEL CARLOS DIAZ DIDN'T NECESSARILY ENJOY BIRTHDAYS as much as other six-year-olds did. Everyone always wanted to kiss him on the cheek and pinch him. His mother would fuss over him, slicking his hair back with some kind of yucky stuff. Worst of all, she made him wear a coat and tie.

Today would be different than those other miserable birthdays, because Isabella Rodriguez would be coming. Weeks before, his mother had told him that Isabella's family would never allow her to attend his party. "They are different from us, Miguel; better, very rich. She'll never be allowed to come to the village for your party." Miguel knew that couldn't be true, however, because Isabella was his best friend.

They didn't go to school together, of course. Bella attended private Catholic school, while Miguel always made the trek down the road to the small house next to the church, which had been converted into a school. It was on Sundays that Miguel normally saw Bella at church and in the Sunday school. Next week, they would both be in Catechism class and then he would see her every day.

Miguel liked Bella because she was as weird as he was. She told him that no one at her school played with her. Instead, they teased her because she didn't have a mother, or because she was so small. Their bond formed one Sunday morning during a lesson on the resurrection of Christ, when a precocious Bella kept asking questions, and the liturgy teacher became angry with her for asking them. The teacher finally told Bella to go sit in the corner. Miguel had never known a kid to be so brave, and from that day on, he decided to be her friend.

They soon discovered they had common interests in jacks, marbles, and much to Miguel's surprise, collecting bugs. They tried to meet at least once a week, whenever they could get out of the house without being noticed, which was much harder for Bella because she had to get past the nursemaid and the guards. She was a smart girl and had told Miguel that she watched the guards and learned when they took breaks to smoke cigarettes or have lunch and getting past her nursemaid was not so difficult as all Bella had to do was create a giant mess in her room or somewhere else in the house to distract the woman. Once she made it through that maze, she would meet Miguel and they would travel to a swampy pond not too far from Bella's hacienda, and collect crawdads and all sorts of peculiar pond life.

Bella would talk about her father and Pedro, about the horses she rode, and the animals that lived at her house. Miguel in turn would talk about God. Of course, his mother instilled a belief in God and Jesus every day. Bella was the only one he might consider higher than God, but he knew that was wrong, and that God would think that a sin, so he told himself that God was the most important being of all.

Miguel's mother suddenly dashed into his room, wearing a silk type of black dress. Her lips were painted red like a movie star, which Miguel saw once in awhile in one of the magazines Bella would sometimes sneak out of the house and show him. Miguel and his mother didn't have much extra money but his mother saved a little from her job as a maid in the best hotel in Guadalajara, where she told him that movie stars sometimes came. After buying the groceries and paying the bills, she then would spend what they did have on her dresses, hair, and makeup. His mother Carlotta was a very beautiful woman, and Miguel thought she could be a movie star herself. She was that pretty. But he had never remembered seeing her so fancy before, not even for church on Easter Sunday.

"Oh, Miguel, how does Mama look? Can you believe that *Señor* Rodriguez is coming to our home and bringing his lovely daughter to your party? We are so lucky. He is such a handsome man. I saw him look at me in church one morning. Maybe he'll like me. Maybe we'll even go out for dinner some night . . ." Carlotta Diaz glanced down at her son, who was glaring at her, transfixed by how oddly she was behaving. "Don't mind me. I'm being silly." With a flip of her manicured hand she pushed her long, dark hair back behind her shoulders; hair made all the more beautiful because she'd taken the time to curl it today instead of pulling it tight into a bun. "This is your day, *mijo*, your day. Now come here and let me fix your tie."

He reluctantly shuffled over to her. He hated this part. After fixing his tie, she wet her fingers and smoothed a strand of hair that was sticking up on top of his head. She then wiped his face clean until she was finally satisfied with his appearance. "My sweet boy, you look so handsome."

Miguel walked out of the room and into the one room, the living room, where his three aunts, two uncles, grandfather and grandmother were gathered, as well as a few dozen kids of all ages who dashed in and out of their tiny home. It was clear that his mother was determined to make a big splash because Bella was going to be attending his birthday party. Their house was small but his mother kept it clean. They shared a bedroom because there was only one room other than this main one. They each had their own twin bed, and there was a tiny bathroom and a kitchen that wasn't much larger than the bathroom.

As all his relatives gushed over him, Miguel's mother rushed back into her kitchen to boil the lobsters his Uncle Eduardo had caught for her. The terrifying noise of the crustaceans' hideous screams sent Miguel tearing out of the house.

It was only a few minutes before he saw the dark sedan easing down the road. A wave of excitement stirred in his stomach. He didn't know if he should laugh or throw up. Before he could figure out which, the car came to a slow stop in front of him.

The driver got out of the front and came around to the rear of the car to open the door. Out stepped Isabella in a pretty, yellow dress trimmed in lace. Her hair was pulled back into a ponytail with ringlet curls dangling from a large white bow. She wore white patent-leather shoes, and in her hands was a neatly wrapped gift. Her regal father then stepped out of the car. He held a large present in his arms.

"Happy Birthday, Miguel," Isabella said in her soft, sweet voice, handing him a smaller gift.

"Thank you," he replied, his hands trembled a bit as he accepted it.

Bella's father knelt down and shook Miguel's hand. "This is for you, amigo."

"*Gracias, Señor Rodriguez.*"

"Ah, *Señor* Rodriguez..." Miguel heard his mother's excited voice outside the house, one that Miguel knew Javier Rodriguez would consider a shack. "We're so pleased that you could come today. I am Carlotta Diaz, Miguel's mother." Carlotta stepped in front of the children and held out her hand to shake his.

Señor Rodriguez smiled and kissed her hand. Miguel had never heard his mother sound so nervous or speak in such an elegant way.

"And your husband, is he here today?" Señor Rodriguez asked.

Carlotta turned her face downward and shook her head. "I am sorry; my husband is with our Lord now for five years. When Miguel was barely a year old he died."

"I'm so sorry."

She took Javier by the hand. "Thank you. Come with me, bring the present. I have *cerveza* and *ceviche* all ready. Before long, the lobsters will be ready as well."

Javier smiled and replied, "Sounds delicious."

"I do hope you like it. My wonderful son is always telling me what a good cook I am."

"I'm certain you are."

Miguel could hear his mother's laughter all the way into the house. He was so embarrassed by his mother. However, Bella soon made him forget about her obnoxious behavior.

"Want to go down to the pond?" she asked.

"Uh-huh, but what if we get in trouble?"

"We won't. Come on." Bella took Miguel by the hand and led the way.

By the time they reached the pond, Bella's dress had a tear in it and Miguel had lost his tie. That didn't matter to either one. What did matter was who could find the largest crawdad and catch him.

"There's one right there," Miguel yelled.

"I'm going to get him," Isabella hollered back. As they ran around the pond, mud spattered their good clothes. Bella's tights and patent leather shoes would never be white again.

Getting carried away, Bella followed the crawdad right into the water. But there was a steep drop at the edge of the pond, which soon pulled her under. She clambered to swim, crying out for help. Miguel started to cry, not knowing what to do. He had only succeeded in swimming with the aid of his uncles before now. He did the one thing that he'd been taught so well: he prayed.

He watched, horrified, as Bella slipped under the water. She cried out for him. Without further thought, he went in after her. God would get them out. Miguel struggled toward her. As he got close enough to reach out his arm, she went under, and for a second he thought he'd lost her. But he reached down and grabbed the top of her hair, pulling her back up. Holding her with one arm, he paddled back to the side of the pond and laid her down on the grass, struggling for air. Isabella's eyes were closed and she wasn't moving. He screamed out at the sky, "No, God! Please don't take Bella away like you took my papa. Let her be okay. Please, God, please!" He looked down at Bella, who spurted out a stream of water as her eyes fluttered. In his relief and joy, he hugged her. "Bella, Bella, are you all right?"

Her eyes opened, "I'm fine, silly. Boy, you should've seen the pretty angel I saw. She told me she was my mother."

Hearing Bella utter such strange words, it came to Miguel that Bella had almost died and gone to heaven. At that moment, he vowed to God he would never betray Him and would always serve Him. *Always*. He also vowed to watch over Bella and keep her safe for the rest of their lives.

CHAPTER TWENTY-SEVEN

ALL THE SIGNS WERE THERE: NAUSEA, DIZZINESS, TENDER breasts, and the fact that her period was ten days late. Lydia didn't have to see a doctor to be certain she was pregnant.

Her emotions were mixed. One moment, she felt elated at the prospect of having another baby. But she also knew full well that there was no possibility that the child could be Antonio's. But what could be a more perfect revenge than to conceive a child with his brother? The fact that she was in love with Emilio only made her long to bear his child.

She sat at her vanity, carefully applying her makeup, contemplating which outfit she would wear. She would meet Emilio for lunch, planning to tell him about the baby then. Lydia sprayed herself with the White Shoulders perfume Emilio had given her last Christmas. She finally decided on a pair of black crepe pants and a white silk shirt with a plunging neckline. She knew it wouldn't be long before her midriff expanded, and wearing anything revealing would then be out of the question. At least she knew that Emilio would not be the type to seek out other women when she was pregnant. He loved her too much for that, she was sure of it.

As she drove to his apartment, Lydia pondered Antonio's reaction to this situation. He would be angry, naturally, but would he be hurt? That was what she really wanted him to feel, the same pain of rejection and betrayal he had caused her.

She hoped Emilio would be as happy as she was, and want her to move in with him immediately. Her only problem was Rosa and Felicia. Rosa was her favorite. How would this affect her? Antonio would *have* to let Rosa go with her mother.

Felicia seemed to like Chata better than she did her own mother, perhaps with good reason. Lydia never paid the same attention to Felicia as she did to her oldest daughter. But for the past year, Lydia had been so wrapped up in her own life that she allowed that *bruja* of a nanny to take charge of both children. She was sure Rosa, too, was feeling neglected and she was sorry for that, but she would make it up to her. No, she would not give up her parental rights to Rosa even when this new child was born—a son, possibly. Oh, she would relish in that. The one thing she couldn't give Antonio, she would give instead to his own brother.

When she opened Emilio's door, classical music from the stereo resounded in her ears. "Emilio," she sang out, but there was no reply. She walked through the living room and back toward the bedroom suite. As she reached his bedroom door, she could hear the shower and smiled. He would certainly be surprised to see her. She slipped out of her clothes. Opening the bathroom door, she felt the steam hitting her dewy skin, making her tingle all over.

She moved the curtain away and stepped in behind him. He was facing the showerhead, washing his face. She wrapped her arms around his waist and whispered in his ear, "Guess who?" She moved her hands down his body and began to stroke him.

Emilio turned around to face her. He pulled her close and kissed her as their clinging, wet bodies awakened to the heat of their passion. Within the past few months, Lydia had learned very well what pleased Emilio. Her long red nails traced the outline of his body until she was on her knees. As she took him in her mouth, an erotic moan escaped his lips. The water from the shower sprayed them while Lydia brought Emilio complete satisfaction.

Once out of the shower, he tossed her on the bed and took her aggressively. Her mind flashed on the baby growing inside her. She murmured, "Emilio, please don't be so rough."

"You know you like it this way," he replied, as he took her from behind and slapped her buttocks hard.

"Yes, but..."

"*But nothing!* Be quiet and enjoy."

She tried to relax and revel in their lovemaking as she had done in the past, but this time was very different. A child was growing in her womb, which would provide her the insurance to get out of her failed marriage.

However, no matter how much Emilio tried to please her, nothing could bring her to ecstasy today. Her mind was on her baby: their baby. As she lay in the bed next to Emilio, thoughts of how she would tell him this news plagued her.

The silence between them was broken when Emilio asked, "What's wrong, love? Is my technique failing you?" he joked.

"Oh, God, no," she replied as she rolled over onto her stomach and up onto her elbows.

"Aren't you feeling well?" Emilio asked, turning to face her.

"Something like that."

"What does that mean?"

Lydia knew that this was the right time to tell him. There was no easy way to say it, and it came out before she had given it a second thought. "I'm pregnant."

"What?"

"We're having a baby."

"A baby?"

"Yes. Are you angry?"

"Angry? No. I'm amazed. You're certain this is my child?"

"Emilio!"

"I'm sorry. I'm in shock. I wasn't expecting this. I thought we'd been so careful."

"We were, silly, but sometimes these things happen." He reached over and stroked her across the cheek. "You're not angry, then?"

"Not at all. This is wonderful news."

"You're happy?"

"Of course I am. I'm going to be a papa."

"We do have a problem, though."

"Antonio?"

"Yes."

"Don't you worry about him. I'll handle him."

"What if he tries to take my girls away from me? Especially Rosa?"

"Do not worry about Antonio, *querida*. Leave everything to me."

And in Lydia's blind naiveté and her hope for a blissful fairy tale life, she decided to do just that.

*****

ONCE LYDIA LEFT, EMILIO KNEW HE DIDN'T HAVE MUCH TIME to figure out what he was going to do. Thankfully, he was blessed with a devious mind. The moment Lydia told him she was pregnant, his brain had shifted into overdrive.

He had to devise a plan to get rid of her. It was the wrong time in Emilio's scheme of things for Lydia to become pregnant. Love or not, as of late he'd realized this thing with Lydia had been far more about power and sex than genuine romance. And he'd been rapidly tiring of her and her neediness. He would get rid of her, and fast, before Antonio found out. An open break from his brother at this time could destroy everything for him. If her pregnancy could only have occurred later, perhaps, once Emilio had fashioned Antonio's downfall, such an event might have been an asset. Possibly, Emilio would've even arranged a divorce for her and married her himself, as the final coup.

He pulled on his trousers and a T-shirt, and walked over to the bar to pour himself a drink. This was a very delicate situation, which had to be handled just so. Picking up the phone, Emilio regretted what he was about to do, because, once done, he would no longer have the immense satisfaction of screwing his brother's wife.

"Rico?"

"Emilio?"

"Sí."

"I'm certain this isn't a social call."

"Very astute. I have a job for you, and it's a delicate situation."

"Who do you want me to kill?"

"I don't think that'll be necessary this time."

"A job without blood and gore? What kind of fun will that be?

"Come to La Casa and I'll leave instructions with Jorge," Emilio responded. La Casa was a tiny bar near the docks. Emilio had only met Rico a couple of times, but he knew he was both trustworthy and greedy.

"I don't know if I like the sound of this, Emilio. You know my game—hit and run."

"I'll pay you twice your usual rate."

"This must be really important."

"More than you'll ever know. You can pick everything up in a few hours. I want this taken care of within the week."

"My curiosity is piqued."

"Above all else, I need you to use the utmost discretion."

"Nothing but."

"Thank you."

Emilio devised his plan, writing out instructions for Rico. He left his apartment and headed down Avenue de Las Banderas, crossing the street at the intersection and heading west toward La Casa. Emilio hated loose ends and Lydia could become one if she wasn't taken care of properly. However, his conscience would not permit her to be murdered.

After leaving the instructions with Jorge and downing a shot of tequila, Emilio walked across the street, jogging along the shore. He knew that Lydia could be handled. Now he had to come up with the second part of his plan—taking care of Antonio.

His brother would have questions after he'd disposed of Lydia. If he didn't have the right answers, utter chaos could erupt. Control was crucial. Once Lydia was shut away from the civilized world, he would be able to concentrate on Antonio.

CHAPTER TWENTY-EIGHT

THE VISIT WITH MARTA AND SEEING HIS SON LEFT ANTONIO
full of emotion. He longed to spend more time with her and really
have a chance to meet the boy. He ached at the thought of how
abandoned Marta had felt. He always considered himself a man of
honor, but now visions of himself in a different light haunted him—
visions he did not care to see.

On his way back home, he thought about ending things with Lydia,
but he couldn't hurt her. Lydia had always been good to him: kind,
sweet, and loving. But their passion for one another had long since
disappeared. If he could discover a way to rekindle it, then he might
try.

For the first time in his life, he felt all of his fifty years. He had
worked hard to build his empire but now he wondered if the power
and the money were worth the price he had paid. As he was
chauffeured toward his home, he made the decision to do the right
thing. He decided to become responsible, respectful to his wife and
family. No matter how badly his heart ached and yearned for things
to be different, he realized what needed to be done.

He asked his driver to take him to his favorite jeweler in town, where he purchased a beautiful emerald necklace for Lydia. He then picked up a dozen red roses and a bottle of her favorite wine. If Marta did not want him in her life, then he could shut her out of his. He would become as honorable as she had always been.

As they pulled into his driveway, Antonio saw several cars there, including two police vehicles. His heart sank, because he knew there must be serious trouble. The entire police department and the local justice system were on his payroll, so he knew that whatever they were there for had to be serious. His first thought was that something had happened to one of his children. Stepping out of the back of his car, Emilio came toward him.

"What is going on here?" Antonio barked.

Emilio put his arm around his brother. "It's Lydia."

"What are you talking about?"

"There is no easy way to say this," Emilio sobbed.

"What's happened?"

"She was in a car accident last night. The police are investigating, but it looks as if her brakes went out, or possibly she took a corner too fast and lost control. I am so sorry, but her car went over the side of the cliffs."

"Is she . . ." Antonio couldn't even finish the sentence.

Emilio nodded. "They haven't found her body yet. They think it drifted out to sea."

"Oh, my God!" Antonio cried. His shoulders sank as he stood staring at the ground. His mind went numb. The faces of his precious girls flashed through his mind. "Do the girls know?"

"No."

"Where are they?"

"Playing with Chata."

"How do I tell them? How am I supposed to tell them that their mother is gone?" Antonio cried aloud. A group of men whom Antonio recognized as part of the police department turned around to look his way with sympathy.

The police chief approached him. "*Patrón*, we are so sorry for your loss." He reached his large hand out to Antonio. The jowls of his face seemed more noticeable with the look of concern in his eyes. He was an enormous, balding man with a mustache that curled at the sides. He was famous for always possessing Cuban cigars, claiming that Castro sent them to him personally in large quantities and that he saved them for special occasions. Everyone knew this to be pure fabrication, but he was friendly and a good storyteller, and therefore well liked, not to mention being an easy payoff.

"Thank you," Antonio whispered.

The other men came over one by one to give their condolences, each extremely respectful of the man they had come to call *Patrón*, including the local priest, who was indebted to Antonio for all he had given to the church. The priest tried to ask Antonio about memorial service arrangements, but Antonio waved him away, beseeching Emilio, "Will you please take care of this for me?"

"Of course I will. You can count on me."

"Thank you. I need to be alone, if you'll excuse me."

"*Sí, Patrón*. We understand," replied Father Morales.

Antonio walked through his front door in a complete daze. He took the necklace out of his briefcase and clutched it in his hands. "I have been a horrible man," he said aloud, "and this is my punishment—to tell my daughters that their mother is dead."

He sat down on the velvet sofa that faced the bay windows, which looked out on a small, bubbling fountain that tended to attract all sorts of birds, Lydia's favorite place to sit. There were many nights he'd found her there, staring out into the distance, or during the day, reading to her children.

As he lifted one of the pillows from the sofa, smelling it to see if her perfume lingered on them, he discovered a faint whiff of vanilla and rose. Tears began to flow more freely now that the shock was lessening. He slumped down into the sofa, crying in silence. No one dared bother him, except one.

He heard a tiny voice ask, "Papa, why are you crying?" Antonio turned around to see his seven-year-old daughter, Rosa. "What's wrong Papa? Where's Mama?"

His heart felt as if it would collapse upon hearing Rosa's words. God was punishing him. Not only did he have a son without a father, but now he also had two daughters without a mother. He knew that today was the worst of his life. He sat his oldest daughter on his knee and told her about her mother's death.

*****

BELLA WAS PUNISHED FOR DAYS AFTER THE POND INCIDENT.
Neither she nor Miguel ever told their parents the whole truth about
what had taken place. They had made a pact to keep it a secret. With
that pact, their friendship was sealed forever.

The worst part of her punishment was that she wasn't allowed to
play with Miguel for an entire week, and had to be supervised by
Pedro, her father, or her nanny at all times. She wasn't allowed to
visit the horses, and dessert was out of the question.

As for Miguel, he was sent to his room without being able to open
his presents, or to have any food until he went to church and
repented for bringing such disgrace upon his mother and their
family.

A few days later, while Bella thumbed through her favorite picture
book about horses, her father came into her room.

"Hello, Bella."

Bella wondered why he was dressed in a tuxedo, his hair slicked
back. She tried to act uninterested, but she couldn't remember ever
seeing her daddy so dressed up. He looked like a prince out of one of
her stories.

"Hi, Daddy," she muttered while she kept flipping through her
book.

"I'm going out for dinner this evening. Pedro and Maria will be
here to look after you."

"Oh." She was dying to know where he was going but she bit her lip, because she had to pretend she was still angry with him for punishing her so harshly.

"Would you like to know who I'm taking to dinner?"

"Uh-uh."

"Are you sure? I think it might make you happy."

"Well, fine," she replied, knowing that the only people her papa ever took to dinner were Pedro, sometimes Antonio when he was visiting, and her.

"Miguel's mother, Señora Diaz."

Bella stared blankly at her father. "Oh," was all she could muster.

"I thought you'd be happy about this. I know you and Miguel are such good friends."

"Have a good time, Papa," she responded, returning to her book once more.

Bella was so furious that once her father left, she threw all the stuffed animals off her bed, and then took every single toy out of her chest, tossing them onto the ground and nearly breaking off one of her doll's heads. When she was finished, she sat down in the middle of her mess and cried.

It was Pedro who found her. When he walked into her room, he stumbled over one of the toys strewn about. "What happened here?"

"A monster did it."

"What a bad monster. Why did this monster do this?"

"She was mad."

"And why was she so angry?"

"Because her papa went to dinner with a really big lady monster."

"Oh." Pedro tried to stifle a laugh. "Well, I see now. That is horrible."

"Yes, it is," Bella replied, placing her hands on her hips.

"Now, why do you think this lady monster is so bad, and what is your monster so afraid of?"

"See, she has a real nice little boy, and she's so mean to him. And my monster says if she likes her papa and marries him, then she'll also be mean to her."

"I understand. Why don't you tell your monster not to worry so much. It takes a long time before papas ever decide to marry someone. Besides, they are only having dinner. Speaking of which, yours is ready. Tell your monster she needs to clean up her mess, so that you can come eat. I'll tell you what, if you help her, I'll let you have dessert tonight."

"What kind of dessert?"

"Your favorite."

"Chocolate cake?"

"Of course."

"Fine. I'll be down in one minute." Bella watched Pedro leave her room. The chocolate cake interested her, but it didn't ease her mind about the matter of her father and Señora Diaz having dinner together.

She was not a stupid child. Although papas could take a long time before they married someone, Señora Diaz liked her father a lot, and Bella knew that her father sorely missed her mother.

"Don't you worry, Mama, I won't let her in your house," she said aloud, "I promise."

CHAPTER TWENTY-NINE

THE PAIN IN LYDIA'S ABDOMEN WAS IMMENSE.

She could feel that her panties were damp and the metallic stench from her blood burned her nostrils. Opening her eyes, she found herself shrouded in darkness, sounds of moans and cries surrounded her. In her state of mind, she was unable to determine whether these sounds were even human or not. She curled up into a fetal position, paralyzed with fear. Instinct told her that the life she'd been carrying inside her no longer existed. But she couldn't understand why. The last thing she remembered doing was driving her car from her doctor's office.

Dr. Martín had congratulated her on the impending birth of her child. She'd smiled gleefully to herself as she left his office, jubilant at the prospect of being with Emilio forever. On her drive home, she'd had car trouble and pulled off to the side of the road. Two men stopped to help her. The next thing she remembered, one of them was putting a gun in her side. She pleaded for their mercy as they forced her into their car.

One of the men was very tall, with narrow eyes and a high-pitched voice. His hair was scraggly and hung in his face. She didn't get as good a glimpse at the other one, because once she was inside the back seat of their white Mercedes, they blindfolded her. But she did remember that the other one exuded a distinct odor of garlic and tequila.

The men laughed at their victim as she fought tooth and nail to escape, even though she knew there was no way out. She must have kicked one of them in the testicles when she was struggling to free her hands, because she heard him cry out in pain before he slapped her. After that, she felt a slight sting in her arm, and instantly everything became hazy. The only things she was able to remember were the sounds of what she thought were wounded animals.

The smell was antiseptic. She distinctly remembered a sharp, horrendous pain in her pelvic region. Trying to scream, she found she could make no sound. They were tearing her baby away from the safety of her womb.

Now she lay in a dark, dismal room, a mental fog blurring her senses. As she faded in and out of consciousness, she began to resign herself to the fact that this was not a nightmare, but a reality. Antonio must have done these horrible things to her. He must have found out about her affair with his brother and about their baby. She couldn't imagine him capable of such an atrocity. If he could do this to her, what would he do to Emilio?

Lydia couldn't help crying over her loss. The baby was gone, and she would probably never see Emilio again. She wanted out of this hellhole. Who was going to save her? She heard a door open, and a crack of light beamed through. Lydia couldn't make out who was inside her room and she started to perspire and shake. She closed her eyes, hoping that whoever it was might think she was asleep and go away.

"Hello, pretty lady. I am pleased that you could join us," the voice said.

In her distorted state, Lydia thought it sounded like a man, but there was a softness that made her believe that it might be a woman. All that she knew for certain was that whoever it was needed a shower badly. She felt the room shrink smaller than it already had been before the person walked in. He or she must have been quite large.

"Oh, my, you're so beautiful," the androgynous voice said as the person stroked Lydia's hair. "You're in pain. Yes, I know. This will make you feel much better."

Before Lydia could protest, she smelled alcohol and felt a prick in one of the veins of her right arm. Whatever it was that was flowing through her body felt chilling at first, before a strangely warm sensation flooded her entire body, beginning with the back of her legs and quickly numbing her pain and senses as if neither had ever existed. Even the emotional trauma she'd endured subsided. The room's atmosphere lightened and she was calm as if she floated in a warm pool, and her worries became distant. The strange presence left, shutting the door. The sound of echoing laughter resounded in

Lydia's ears, but the laughter didn't matter. Emilio didn't matter. Antonio didn't matter. Nothing did.

*****

THE LETTER CAME ON A SATURDAY AFTERNOON AND MARTA tore it open. It was from Antonio. She hadn't been able to shake him from her thoughts since he'd come to see her. It wasn't as if she had ever gotten him out of her mind, but at least she had been able to distance herself from him for all those years.

However, ever since his visit a week ago, she had thought about him constantly. Seeing him had stirred up emotions long since repressed. When he'd asked her to go back to Colombia with him so that they could be together, the temptation was nearly irresistible, but she knew in her heart that it would destroy her self-respect if she were to take another woman's husband. She could never do anything so deceitful.

Marta read the letter. It was horrendous news. Antonio wrote of Lydia's death, and how her body hadn't been recovered. He described his confusion, pain, and guilt. She was devastated to learn that Antonio's eldest daughter, Rosa, hadn't spoken since her mother's death, and that the little one wouldn't let her father out of her sight. It was clear that Antonio was suffering, and Marta wanted nothing more than to go to him. And he made it clear that he wanted her to come and be with him.

He'd enclosed a check for her airfare. Marta didn't know what to think. The one thing she knew was that Lydia's death changed the situation, even though what hadn't changed was the pain Antonio had once caused her. And, even though she ached for him, Marta didn't know if she could bring herself to go to him, unsure that she could trust him.

*****

JAVIER DIDN'T RECEIVE WORD OF LYDIA'S DEATH UNTIL he'd returned home from yet another dinner with Señora Diaz. Carlotta was quite a woman, a bit eccentric, but she made him laugh and she was so beautiful. She had a Sophia Loren look about her that Javier couldn't help but be attracted to. Sophia Loren was Javier's absolute favorite actress. He'd "fallen in love" with her when he and Cynthia had seen one of her movies on their honeymoon in Italy many years ago. They had seen her walking in a piazza in Venice where her movie *Black Orchid* was being hailed as wonderful and Javier insisted they go to her movie. He'd been enchanted by her and Cynthia had teased him about his crush on the movie star. And now, in Carlotta he saw so much of the Italian beauty that he found himself on occasions when they were out together, fantasizing that Carlotta was indeed the actress. He knew it was insane, but it did feel good to be out laughing with a woman again. He hoped Cynthia understood his need from her place in the Kingdom, but he had honored her memory through celibacy now for six years.

There was one who was not pleased at all about Javier courting Carlotta: Bella. He really couldn't understand why. He thought she would be happy about it. It allowed her to spend more time with her best friend Miguel, who Javier found to be a charming little boy. Bella had expressed quite forcefully more than once that Señora Diaz was not fit to be seen with her father. This made him laugh, hearing his daughter's opinion on who was fit, or not, to be seen with him.

However, at that moment, there was no time to think about Bella. Once Pedro informed him of Lydia's death, Javier immediately made plans to go to Antonio. The day of Cynthia's death flashed before his eyes. He told Pedro to pack bags for the three of them. He hoped that Bella's presence might be a good distraction for Antonio's daughters. They always played well together.

It was late when the three of them reached Antonio's home. Emilio let them in. He seemed to be almost jovial, probably due to the booze he was drinking. He smiled at them, picking Bella up and swinging her around.

Pedro immediately lifted the sleepy child out of Emilio's arms and muttered, "She's very tired."

"I see. Who's the papa here?" Emilio joked, slapping Javier on the back.

Javier winced and squinted his eyes at him. "Where is Antonio?"

Emilio pointed toward the living room. "I can take her and put her in the girls' room, since she's so tired."

"No, thank you," Pedro answered. "You can tell me the way."

203 | P a g e

"Go down that hall and turn left. It's the second room on the right."

"Thank you," Pedro murmured, holding Bella protectively.

"Thank you, Pedro," Javier said.

"No problem."

As Pedro carried Bella to bed, Emilio walked into the bar to pour himself another drink. Javier went into the living room, where he found Antonio seated on the sofa, his head down.

Javier sat down quietly next to him, taking hold of his hand in silence. No words were going to ease Antonio's pain.

After a few moments, Antonio said, "My baby won't speak. Rosa says nothing. She will speak to no one."

"In time, my friend. Give her time."

"I'm so worried about her. She loved her mother so much."

"She's in a great deal of pain. She will speak once again, once the pain eases. How are *you* holding up?"

"I'm doing what I can. It's my little girls I'm concerned about more than anyone. None of this seems real to me yet. It's like a bad dream. I can't believe she's actually gone."

"I understand."

"I know you do."

"I have come to be with you, Antonio, to help in any way that I can."

"Thank you."

"I brought Bella with me. Maybe she can get Rosa to talk."

"I hope so, Dear God, I hope so."

****

ROSA WAS AWAKE WHEN PEDRO PUT BELLA DOWN NEXT TO her. He smiled at Rosa, and she closed her eyes. Usually she would be happy to see Bella. They had played together so often. But she didn't feel like seeing, playing, or talking to anyone. She was angry at the world and at God. How could He take her beautiful mother away from her? She vowed never to speak again until God brought her mama back home. Rosa couldn't believe she was dead. She wished that she were dead, too.

Bella reached over and patted Rosa on the head. "Hi," she whispered.

Rosa looked at her.

"I'm sorry about your mama."

Tears welled up in Rosa's eyes.

"I'll tell you a secret about what happens to mommies when they go to Heaven. If you close your eyes for a long time and you think about her, she'll come and talk to you. She'll probably be dressed in white and look real pretty. At least, that's always what my mommy looks like." Bella smiled at Rosa. "Trust me. I promise that it's the truth."

For the first time since before her mother's death a few days earlier, Rosa smiled and closed her eyes. She tried and tried to see her mother, but it would not happen. She didn't come to her as Bella said she would. Rosa could not understand why.

CHAPTER THIRTY

LYDIA HAD FINALLY FIGURED OUT WHAT WAS HAPPENING
to her. She discovered that the obese creature who occasionally
visited her was actually a transvestite who injected all sorts of drugs
into Lydia's bloodstream.

Far worse than the abuse her body felt from the effect of the
drugs, was what happened as she lay on her back, stoned, semi-
conscious, when the smelly, hideous man repeatedly plunged himself
deep inside her numb body, until he finally ejaculated and climbed
off. His repulsive breath stank of beer and cigarettes, and he laughed
at her while he zipped up his trousers. Most monstrous of all was the
awareness that she couldn't feel much of anything, nor did she care.
The loss of her baby, combined with the continuous injections, left
her lethargic, drifting, and oblivious to her surroundings.

She struggled to sit up, but collapsed back onto the creaking bed,
her head whirling around. The stranger burst into more laughter at
her intoxicated stupor. She couldn't bring herself to care.

All Lydia wanted was more of that peace potion. The drug took
her pain and fears away, replacing them with calm and a sense of
ease. It was as if the drug knew exactly where the pain in her heart
and mind were. It seemed to hit those spots first, and then her entire
body fell into sync, like nothing she had ever experienced before.

Sometimes when she was administered a shot, Lydia would try to
decipher whether or not she was in heaven or hell, but even this

thought process drained her of too much energy. Instead, she would stare at a steel crucifix above the small cardboard dresser in the corner of the room. A red light from the bar across the street flashed against the cross every few seconds, keeping her both entranced and confused. She wanted to grab the symbol of saved souls and throw it across the room. The red light also irritated her, yet she couldn't take her eyes off it.

*****

MARTA LEFT ALEJANDRO IN THE CARE OF ELISA AND FLEW down to Colombia. She was concerned about returning back home to Alejandro quickly. However, Antonio assured her on the telephone that this would not be a problem.

This would be Marta's first visit to Antonio's home. Their meetings had always taken place at Javier Rodriguez's vacation estate in Costa Careyes when she was merely a girl. A certain amount of anxiety boiled in her stomach as the car pulled up to Antonio's home. She hoped she hadn't made a terrible mistake in accepting his invitation.

She knew that he was extremely wealthy, but when she saw how exquisite his home was, she was astounded. The lush gardens surrounding the massive home were like none she had ever seen. There were all types of beautiful, bright flowers, requiring the care of several gardeners.

A young woman who reminded Marta of herself only six years before led her around back, to the patio with a breathtaking view of the ocean far off in the distance. Although she had lived in Los Angeles, Marta's trips to the ocean had been few and far between. Each time she saw it, the appeal was always overwhelming. When she had lived at Javier's home, she was able to see it every single day, and now she realized again how fortunate she had been. The ocean off of Los Angeles was equally beautiful, but she seldom went near it, for the memories it evoked were too painful. The green mountains that were almost a teal blue stood to the east. Nothing about where she was at that moment seemed real, but as if a painter was at his canvas painting the scene before him. Marta brought her fingers to her lips, and then looked at her hands to make sure that she was real and not in the middle of some artist's strange rendering of her life.

She found Antonio sitting in a lounge chair, his head raised towards the sun, and his eyes protected by sunglasses. She hadn't noticed when he last visited, but with the reflection of the afternoon sun, she could see that he was beginning to lose some of his hair. She sat down in the chair across from him.

Antonio didn't turn to look, but after a few seconds, he said, "Thank you for coming."

"There was no other choice."

Antonio nodded his head. "Javier is here. He and his little girl."

"And Señora Rodriguez?"

"No," he replied, taking off his glasses to look at her. "Oh, yes. You couldn't have known."

"Known what?"

"Cynthia died during childbirth with Isabella."

"Oh, God," Marta cried out, horrified by such unexpected, terrible news. Marta had always been very fond of Señora Rodriguez. She had taught Marta to read, and had always let her borrow records and illustrated books. She had even given Marta a few of her discarded dresses, which were the nicest clothes Marta had ever owned. The news that such a lovely woman had died, compounded with the death of Antonio's wife, left her momentarily speechless.

As he turned to look at her, she placed a hand on Antonio's face. He tried to smile. "I am so sorry for what you must be going through," she told him.

He nodded. "It is an ending to a period in my life. Not the kind of ending I would've desired, but still, an ending. I have to move on. I have no other choice. This is part of the reason I've asked you here." He sat up, taking both her hands in his.

"Antonio..." she began.

"Please don't say anything until I've finished. This is fate, you realize. Granted, there is cruelty in it, but can't you see that this is the way things are meant to be? God has brought us back together, Marta. There is no doubt about it. He knows of my love for you and how powerful it is. We are destined to be a family. I want you to bring Alejandro here to live, and as soon as it is appropriate, you and I will be married."

Marta looked away, not knowing how to respond. Giving an answer would not be as simple as either one of them would've liked. "We have a home there," Marta replied.

"*This* would be your home. You could have all *this*."

She looked down and then into his eyes again, "To be honest, Antonio, I don't know if I want all this. It is beautiful and long dreamed of, but I can't forget . . ."

He interrupted, "The past."

"Yes," she whispered.

"I'll do whatever it takes to convince you that my love is a true and faithful one. Whatever you need or want from me is yours."

"I need time to think."

"Of course you do."

Neither spoke as they held hands. Marta knew what her answer would be, if Antonio would agree to abide by her conditions. That would be a true test of his love—if he could truly do what she was going to ask of him.

CHAPTER THIRTY-ONE

LYDIA'S MEMORIAL SERVICE WAS SMALL AND DISCREET, attended only by the immediate family. Rosa didn't shed a tear. In fact, she hadn't shed a single one since she'd been told her mother was dead. Rosa stared at her Uncle Emilio and remembered a day in the garden, not so long ago, when she saw him kiss her mother and had hated him for it. She noticed that he didn't cry now, either. Everyone else cried, but *not* Uncle Emilio.

Emilio glanced at her once, across the living room, back at the house and smiled. She turned around and headed outside into the garden, where she prayed that the memory of her mother would become clearer to her.

Watching the red and orange fish in the small pond, her uncle walked up behind her. He placed an arm on her shoulder. She shivered at his touch. However, she was bound and determined not to let him see that she was afraid of him.

"Your mother loved you very much, Rosa. She wouldn't be happy to see you so sad, not talking to anyone. Listen, I know what you think you saw here, not too long ago. You know, your mama and me?

But it was nothing but a simple kiss. You don't need to tell your papa about it, either now or later on. He's already so sad. If you told him something like that, he'd get mad at you because he wouldn't believe it. I know you'll be a good girl and not say anything, because if you do, not only will your papa be mad, but so will I. And I don't think you want to make your Uncle Emilio mad, because I can be very mean. We don't want that, now do we?"

Rosa kept staring at the fish. She hated her uncle so much that she wanted to hit him. The weird thing was that she could remember a time when she thought he was so wonderful. He ruined her image of him the day she saw him kissing her mama. Even though she was still only a child, Rosa's instincts told her not to trust this man, ever again. She even felt that, in some way, he was the cause of this terrible mess. Rosa couldn't even imagine her mama dead. She thought of the whole situation as *the badness*. She wished it would go away—all this *badness*.

Emilio patted her on her head and walked back to the house. Yes, she knew that somehow, in some way he was responsible for her mother being gone.

CHAPTER THIRTY-TWO

MARTA STARED AT ANTONIO'S COMPLEX FACE AS HE LAY IN A deep slumber, after hours of passionate lovemaking. She was amazed and pleased that a man who could be so full of intensity—almost to the point of rage—could also be so gentle and kind.

The past few hours together were much more than either had expected. They certainly surpassed all Marta's expectations. Years ago, she had come to him as a girl. Now she was a woman, and even though her experience remained limited to him from years before, the mere presence of womanhood added a tinge of sophistication, which lent itself to her new confidence as she explored her sexuality with Antonio as she never had before.

Marta leaned over and gently kissed his cheek. He murmured something as he wrapped his arms around her. An involuntary smile spread across her face.

The prelude to their lovemaking had been a promise sealed with a kiss. Antonio had agreed to her stipulations, in order that she and Alejandro join him in Colombia. By doing so, he had proven his love for Marta. Antonio had promised to become a legitimate businessman.

Marta had known of Antonio's illegal trade and brutal business tactics, along with the dirty money it produced, since the day she'd climbed aboard Fernando's truck on her way to cross the border. Fernando had told Marta that he was transporting heroin for Antonio and Javier. At first, her shock and dismay at the prospect of Antonio being nothing more than a dirty criminal seemed ludicrous. But as the hours passed, and Fernando's words sunk in, it all made sense to her. Of course Antonio delved into a life of illegal activity. He was nothing but a liar, a cheat, and a thief. Those were her feelings about him for nearly seven years.

Now, as Marta looked over at her lover, the thoughts of his cruel and evil ways began to dissolve in the aftermath of his promise and their lovemaking.

"If you want me and your son to come live here with you, then you must turn all of your business dealings into legitimate enterprises," she had told him.

"Marta, that would be very difficult," he'd replied.

"Perhaps so. You told me to name my price. That's it."

"Please try to understand, I'm a very important man. To do what you're asking of me won't be easy."

"Fine, then I'll leave tomorrow morning." She had stood up, nearly knocking over the chair she'd been sitting in.

"No, wait a minute. I didn't say I wouldn't do it. I only said it could be complicated."

"But not impossible, no?" Marta had placed her hands strategically on the table and leaned over, revealing just enough cleavage beneath the cream silk dress he had ordered for her earlier that day.

"No, not impossible."

"I'm waiting for an answer, Antonio."

He sighed, reaching out for her he grabbed her, pulling her into him. "Only for you. I will do this only for you."

"Thank you, my love. Thank you. This means everything to me." She'd thrown her arms around him and he'd picked her up off her feet and carried her into his bedroom.

And, now lying in Antonio's bed, loving him more than ever, Marta prayed that he would keep his promise to her and their son.

*****

ROSA WAS NAUSEOUS. MAMA WAS GONE ONLY A FEW WEEKS and Papa already had another woman in the house. He tried to keep her out of sight, and he told Rosa she was an old friend who'd come to pay her respects. But Rosa had witnessed the two of them exchanging private glances. She was smart enough to know they weren't simply old friends. She burned with rage at her father's disrespect and betrayal. She wanted to scream at him, and give him a piece of her mind. But she wouldn't. She still wasn't speaking to anyone—especially *not* her father.

Frustrated, annoyed, and hurt, Rosa decided to walk to her mother's gravesite outside the rose garden, on top of a rolling hill. Rosa had chosen the place herself. Her mother's body had never been retrieved, but to be able to go to a place where she felt her mother would have liked to be buried brought her a sense of comfort.

When her papa had asked her where she wanted her mother placed, she instantly led him by the hand to the grassy knoll where she and her mother had sat on so many occasions, telling stories to each other.

Now, after scrambling up to the mound, she sat down. A cool March rain had fallen the night before, causing the air to smell fresh and exhilarating. She sat on the lush grass that only the jungle humidity and rich Colombian soil could produce. Sunlight warmed her shoulders and back as she folded her arms, resting her head on them.

Her tears came so freely for her beautiful mother. How could this have happened? She would neither understand nor believe in a God who would take away the one special person in her life.

She didn't hear her uncle come up quietly behind her until he sat down next to her and placed a hand on her head. She looked up then scooted away from him.

"Now Rosa, you don't need to be afraid of me. Uncle Emilio would never hurt you. You know that."

She didn't know that. She couldn't muster the smallest amount of trust for this man who called himself her uncle. Remembering the scene in the garden between him and her mother made her shudder, wrapping her arms tightly around herself as she got up to walk away. He grabbed her small shoulders, turning her around. "Rosa, I know you're not deaf. Now, Uncle is speaking to you."

Trying to squirm out of his powerful grip, she gave in and looked directly into his deceitful eyes. Her parents had always teased her about the mean looks she could give when she didn't get her way. She stared him down.

"Such an intense child you are, little Rosa." Her uncle reached out and touched one of her long strands of hair. "And so beautiful, exactly like your mother."

A sickening feeling swelled in her stomach, as though it had been festering there for some time. She could taste her lunch again and actually wished she could vomit it all over him.

"Yes, so pretty," he whispered, stroking her cheek. She struggled against him once more knowing that what he was doing was wrong. He began to finger the buttons on her dress with one hand, while his other one grabbed her arms and held them behind her back. She tried to cry out, tried to struggle, but all of her protective senses seemed to have abandoned her. Shock took over, to the point that she became unable to defend herself. The only thing she could feel was fear—a fear so amazingly forceful, it completely succeeded in immobilizing her.

Her uncle's hand soon found the lace trim of her panties. As he put his fingers inside them, Rosa began to pray to the God who had abandoned her. *Please, Father, don't let him do this to me. Make him go away.* She closed her eyes and suddenly no longer felt that she was inside her own body. It was as if she had drifted away from her wicked uncle. She no longer felt his fingers or anything else about him. She could neither smell him nor hear his voice as she safely floated above the beautiful place where her mama and she had spent so much time together.

*****

"MARRIED?" ISABELLA PRACTICALLY CHOKED ON THE WORD. Her father had just told her that he was going to marry Miguel's mother. They were sitting down for dinner—Bella, Papa, and Pedro. Señora Diaz's absence had made the evening all the more pleasant, as she so often dined with them these days. Bella hadn't seen her father by himself much since he and *that* woman had begun courting, usually leaving early in the evenings, and almost always returning quite late. Bella hated her. She was always nice when her father was around, but as soon as he was out of the room she turned into a mean *bruja*. Bella was certain that her mother, about whom she'd heard such wonderful stories, wouldn't like this change in Javier's taste in women either.

"I'm so happy for you, Javier," Pedro interrupted, glancing furtively at Bella.

"Thank you. And what about you, Bella? You should be very happy. You'll be getting a new brother very soon."

"That lady is *not* my mother."

"Of course not, Bella, but she does like you, and I expect you to treat her with respect. Think of all the fun you and Miguel will have."

"Not with her around here. She doesn't let us do anything fun. And you are dumb to marry her."

"Isabella, I forbid you to speak to me in that tone of voice."

Bella stood up and shoved her plate aside, knocking over her glass of milk. "You can't do this to my mommy. That ugly, stupid lady will never be my mother, and I don't have to listen to her, no matter what you say!" Bella ran from the dinner table. "And you are dumb!"

Javier stood up and yelled, "Bella, you come back here!"

Pedro placed a hand on the older man's arm. "Let her go. She is upset and sad for the mother she's never known. Give her some time. I know her. She is a very sensitive little girl."

"Don't tell me about my own daughter." Javier glared at Pedro, who sank slightly in his chair.

"I would never do that. It's only that I know how much she's longed to have a mother. She tells me all the time she wishes she could have known her *own* mother. This is hard for her. You've been mother and father to her. I think she may feel like she's losing you as well. Please give her the time she needs right now."

"Perhaps you're right. I really thought she would be happy about this. You know how close she and Miguel are."

"Yes, but a brother is much different than a friend. Things may change when you marry Miguel's mother."

"I never thought about it that way. I don't know what to do. This is more complicated than I thought, but I really like this lady. She's funny. Yes, a bit different, but I've been so lonely, and she really is very..."

"Beautiful. It is impossible for one to overlook that, isn't it?"

Javier didn't answer Pedro at first, not liking the tone of his words and what that tone implied, but as the words ate at him for a moment he had to say something. "I am not so shallow as to marry a woman for her beauty."

"Many men have."

"You are overstepping your boundaries here, Pedro."

"Maybe this is none of my business, but before you do this, you may want to really consider which head you're thinking with."

"You're right, it *is* none of your business. I've suddenly lost my appetite. Good night."

"Good night."

Pedro watched Javier disappear around the hall corner. He pondered what might take place in this household in the near future. He knew Javier was lonely for a woman, and that Carlotta Diaz wasn't even close to Javier's class. But as he himself had done, she had been able to worm her way into the exclusive confines of a powerful, wealthy family. Pedro had to admire and respect her for that. He also had to ache for the sense of abandonment he knew his little Bella was feeling at the moment. He remembered that feeling all too well from his own upbringing.

CHAPTER THIRTY-THREE

MARTA PREPARED TO FLY HOME AND BRING ALEJANDRO BACK with her over the weekend. She knew that Elisa would be surprised and happy for her. But there would also be overtones of sadness. She dreaded the trip home and the impending conversation she would have with the dear woman who'd been her best friend for the past seven years.

As she was folding the last of her things into her suitcase, Antonio flung open the door in an excited rush. "You can't go until Monday."

"Why not?"

"Javier has moved up his wedding date. Carlotta is pregnant, and they're getting married this weekend. Go and buy yourself the most exquisite, expensive dress you can find. The plane will be ready to take us to Guadalajara this evening. Be ready to leave by five o'clock. I've already telephoned some of the finer boutiques and called around a car. They're waiting for you."

"Oh, but Antonio, I really wanted to get home. It's been two weeks, and I miss Alejandro so much. He was so excited when I talked to him last night. I told him I was coming home. I can't break his heart like that."

"He'll be fine. What's two more days? Besides, he told you himself how much fun he was having with Elisa and her boys. Please do this for me."

"I don't know. I really *do* miss him."

"It's important."

"I'll tell you what. I'll call home and talk to him first. If he becomes upset, I'll go home. If he says it's okay, then I'll stay."

"Who runs your house?"

"We've never been away from one another." She frowned.

"Oh, all right, if that is the way it must be, then call him."

Antonio hovered over her as she called home to talk to Alejandro about her plan to delay her return to Los Angeles. Antonio found it humorous, and knew he was going to love and appreciate this boy who already ran the roost.

He could tell by Marta's responses that Alejandro had granted his permission, as long as she brought him back some really good presents. When she hung up the phone, Antonio laughed. "I can't help but love that kid."

*****

BELLA AND MIGUEL DID IN FACT ENJOY THEIR RESPECTIVE parent's wedding. They played and danced, but each knew there was sadness in the other's heart. Miguel was actually elated to be gaining

Bella as a sister and to be moving into such a grand home, but he couldn't help experiencing her pain. He realized that she felt as if she was losing her father, and he thought she was, as well.

There was no doubt that his mother could be quite overbearing. She'd already made it clear to Miguel that he was to stay out of her way and out of his new father's way.

Before too long, Miguel knew that his mother would also make sure that Bella was alienated from her father's life. But for today, the two of them would dance and be happy.

*****

MARTA ENJOYED HERSELF. IT WAS AS IF HER DREAM HAD finally come true. Fond memories swirled in her mind of girlish daydreams that she'd long ago set aside for mundane realities. But now those dreams *had* become her reality.

The fruity sangria she sipped warmed her soul, but sent her to the bathroom for the third time in an hour. Passing by Javier's home office, she could hear Antonio's voice. Knowing it was silly and immature, but being a curious woman by nature, she casually leaned against the door to overhear.

"They did what? How many of them were there?" Antonio asked, anger rising in his voice.

"Five or six of them, and I've so far received the names of three of the men."

"How much was stolen?"

"A street value of hundred thousand dollars."

Marta heard a bang, like his fist being slammed against a desk.

"I want them dead, all of them. You find out who they are, have them located and killed. I will not have anyone stealing from this operation," Antonio said.

"I agree. I've already put out the order on the street in Tijuana, where I've heard they've run to. I don't know what to say. These are men who have been driving for us forever and to think they've betrayed us is unthinkable."

"But they have. And, who do they say is the leader of this mutiny?" Antonio asked. "Do we know?"

"Yes. They say his name is Fernando."

Marta gasped. They had to be speaking of the man who'd driven her into Tijuana years earlier from Costa Careyes. They were going to have him killed. She sunk against the wall. A lump caught in her throat as bile swirled in her stomach. How stupid could she be? Antonio was never going to change. Not for her, or their son. Not for anyone. For a man like Antonio Espinoza all that mattered was wealth and power, and if it meant lying to those he claimed to love, then that is what he did. Marta clenched her teeth and bit back bitter tears. He was a criminal and he would always be that—a killer and a drug dealer. Marta ran for the bathroom and wretched.

She walked out of the bathroom and glanced around, hoping to escape undetected. How could she have been so ignorant as to believe this man, who knew his way around lies as much as any card shark knows the tricks of his trade? Without any further thought, she went into the guest room they had settled in, found a wad of cash Antonio had placed inside one of the dresser drawers and took it. After making certain everyone was back out on the patio involved in the festivities, with tears stinging her eyes, Marta grabbed the overnight bag she'd brought with her, and headed for the front door.

*****

TERRIFYING SCREAMS SOARED FROM THE ROOM BELOW, awakening Lydia from her stupor. Although dreams and reality often fused together now, she could tell that these sounds were real.

Lydia had heard screams and laughter coming from other rooms before tonight. She knew that she was nothing more than a whore, living in a brothel where such sounds were commonplace. The thought of it almost amused her: Señora Espinoza. Whore. She once had the finest in everything: jewels, clothes, cars, houses. But she had been vengefully punished for her transgressions by a vicious and vindictive husband.

Panic subtly overcame her as she dragged her lethargic body to the door, cracking it open with the uncertainty of a just-punished child who has been banished to her room. Lydia had been told, on more than one occasion, never to leave her room until she was sent for, yet she retained enough sense to realize that real trouble lurked outside her door.

A scantily clad woman ran past Lydia's door yelling, "Fire! Fire!"

Lydia's clouded brain processed the scene before her. As quickly as she could make herself react, she wrapped a blanket around her body. Turning back from the door, she saw a cloud of white smoke swirling up beneath the floorboards. Like a demon in the shape of a snake, the smoke curled up from the floor, winding its way into vicious coils, preparing to strike whatever victim stood in its path.

Suddenly her mind began to clear and a will to fight and gain back all she had lost returned. For a second or two, the power of clarity entranced her, silencing the demons that had been so much in control of her mind and body during the past few months. As the coils of the snake attempted to wrap around her lithe body, constricting each and every organ inside her, she began to search for a way out, for someone to rescue her. Weakened she collapsed to the floor, gasping for air.

With her eyes shut, she prayed to her sweet Jesus for salvation. As if the sun had extended a ray of energy from its own light, she found herself crawling to the window, pulling herself up, and struggling to open it. It wouldn't budge. In one last effort, she reached up and took the metal crucifix from the wall, smashing it against the window. Blood dripped from the tiny cuts in her hands, but the pain they inflicted was of no consequence. Lydia stared down at the ground, two stories below, and knew she would rather die right now than suffer the ravages of that fiery demon.

Without further thought, she flung herself out of the small window.

BOOK III-1989-1993

Los Angeles, CA

CHAPTER THIRTY-FOUR

WALKING TO THE OUTDOOR MARKET TO BUY THE GROCERIES their mothers had sent them for, Hector and Alex roughhoused with each other along the way, shoving and pushing their way through crowds of people. Hector ran into an old man, who yelled at them, *"Pinche batos."*

The boys laughed, although Alex tried to stifle his mother's voice in his head cautioning him about respecting his elders. He knew she was right. She was right most of the time, but Hector was his best friend and it was plain hard to tell Hector that most of what he did wasn't right.

After they bought the necessary groceries, they went to the park. "Wanna smoke?" Hector asked as he rolled a joint.

Again, one of those things he knew his mother wouldn't approve of. "Nah. I better not."

"What you afraid of, your mama?" Hector chided. He lit the joint and took a long drag.

Alex took it from him and even though a sense of guilt hit him square in his gut, he smoked the pot with his friend. "Man, where does your bro get this stuff?" Alex asked, making ringlets of smoke out of the pungent herb. The drug was swimming on his brain now, and the guilt dissipated, but Alex had a keen sense that it would be back and maybe tomorrow he would go to the confessional.

"His boys, man. You know he said we could join if we want. They're bad, really bad, you know."

"Nah, we oughtta make our own gang. It'd be real cool. All the chicks would be begging for us." He knew that wouldn't be the case, but he wanted to be cool, even though he wasn't.

"Yeah, right. You and that ugly mug of yours." Hector laughed.

"Who you callin' ugly?"

"You."

"No way, man. You'll be callin' me *Patrón* one of these days."

"Yeah, right, cuz."

"I like that, *Patrón*. Sounds good, doesn't it?"

"*Patrón*, my ass." Hector pushed Alex to the ground and they both burst out laughing. "Maybe you don't have such a bad idea. We should create our own gang. We could get better stuff than *this* shit, and sell it out there on the streets."

"Right, man. I was kidding. No way am I gonna sell dope. I think you're crazy."

"There you go again, man. You so afraid of your mama that you can't even see straight. We start slinging dope and I bet you'll be able to buy your mama a real house."

"I'm not scared of my mama." Alex respected his mother and she'd had so many disappointments, not that she ever spoke of, but Alex could see it in her eyes and the way she looked so tired every night after working for hours on end and then insisting on making him dinner. She was dedicated to him. But, the idea of being able to move her out of the ghetto appealed to him. He'd do about anything to get her out of there and into a home and neighborhood where she deserved to live. He might even cave to Hector's ideas if it meant that his mother wouldn't have to work anymore. "Come on, we'd better get home before our mamas get mad at us for taking so long."

"Pussy," Hector said.

"Shut up before I break your face. Now come on." Not wanting his mother to discover his extracurricular activities, Alejandro decided to run up to his room and change his clothes before her keen sense of smell caught on. Mama continually hounded him about drugs, and not falling into the same traps as most of the other neighborhood kids managed to do.

"Alejandro, you are way too intelligent to be involved with drugs. I have plans for you."

"Like what, Mama?"

"College."

"Right. The only way I'm getting to college is if we win the Publishers Clearing House Sweepstakes."

"We'll see about that." She'd shake a finger at him. He knew that underneath her laughter, there was a purpose to her words. His mother was a mystery to Alex. It was as if she had some huge secret, which she kept even from him. But that couldn't be true. His mother was simple and pure. She wouldn't keep secrets from him. If appeasing her about college made her happy, then that's what he would do. The thought of selling drugs and making some real money came to mind again. If he did it for a little while, then he could probably make enough to go to college. He could make her dreams for him come true.

Over dinner, at the small table with pictures of Christ hanging on the surrounding walls, his mom gave him the same old lecture. "Alejandro," she said in that tone of voice that only mothers used. Alex looked down at his bowl of *menudo*. "As you know, I received your report card today in the mail. You can do much better than C's. You are a smart boy."

Alex couldn't look at her, because he knew she was right. He knew that he could do much better. He did well on the tests. It was the homework he never finished. Hector always distracted him in the afternoons and he let it go.

"You'll have to try much harder. I want you to start thinking about college and your future."

"Mama, even if I could get into college, we don't have the money to pay for it."

"Don't you worry about that," she replied. "The money will be there for college."

"How do you know? Do you have a night job I don't know about?" Alex teased her.

Marta didn't smile. "I am serious, Alejandro, you must start thinking about college. I also want you to get a job this summer. I'm going to be working double shifts at the factory, and I won't be here to babysit you. Not that I should have to at your age, but I don't want you stuck in this house, or out palling around all summer with your friends."

"You mean Hector?"

"Yes, I do mean Hector. As much as I love Elisa like a sister and both her boys like my own, neither one of them has proven to be worth his salt. She has done everything for those two, and they repay her by doing criminal things."

"Mama, don't be silly."

"Don't talk back to me. You will do as I say, and that means getting a job for the summer, and start thinking about college."

"Yes, Mama."

"Good boy."

After dinner, Alex climbed out his bedroom window and met Hector down the street.

"My mom says I gotta work through the summer."

"Yeah, well, did she say what you have to do?"

"No."

"I got a job for us then. I talked to my brother about *our* ideas."

"*Our* ideas?"

"You know, us selling pot. There's a lotta profit there."

"Yeah?" Alejandro asked, the word *profit* piquing his curiosity.

"He told me he knows of a guy who can set us up real nice, you know, and we can make a lot of dinero." Hector rubbed his hands together.

"You sure about this?"

"Hey, cuz, when did I ever lie to you?"

"You lied to me about Gabriella liking me," Alex replied.

"Yeah, but I was foolin' you. Hey, you know that Acapulco Gold stuff the gringos like so much?"

"Uh-huh."

"He says he can get us some of *that.*"

"Really?" If Hector was telling him the truth, then the possibility of him going to college and eventually getting his mother out of the ghetto could become a reality for them, and he wanted that for her. He'd bring up his grades and he'd live the dream she wanted. "It sounds better than working in a donut shop."

"No shit. You in?"

Alex slowly nodded his head. "But if my mom finds out anything about it, I'm dead meat."

"You're mama won't know nothin'."

"I hope not." The thought of his mother finding out worried Alejandro, but he attempted to fool himself into believing that once she saw all of the money he was going to have to buy her a beautiful home and money for him to attend college, she wouldn't be so angry. Alex and Hector shook hands on the deal.

CHAPTER THIRTY-FIVE

"*COCA, COCA, COCA.*"DO YOU KNOW HOW MUCH MONEY THE
wops are making off of it?" Emilio asked Javier, who'd been in
Colombia for meetings all week.

"There is a lot of money to be made."

"You're so right. But the problem is old habits die hard, and I don't
think my brother is going to be too keen on getting into it."

"Is that why you asked me here without Antonio's knowledge?"
Javier sat back in the chair and crossed his arms in front of him.
Antonio was his dearest friend and partner, but this ruffian of a
brother of his left a bad taste in Javier's mouth.

"Precisely."

"I don't think he'd like us meeting without him. I was under the
impression when you phoned that he would be here."

"Yes, I know, but he took the girls on a vacation. You know Rosa
has been so upset, so withdrawn since her mother died, even now—
this many years later." He shook his head. "The poor girl needs to be
in an institute. She is out of her mind. My brother has felt so guilty
about her despair. Life is unfair. I believe he keeps hoping she'll

regain her senses." He shrugged. "He's taken them on their annual trip to Europe. I thought you knew that. He said something about their going to visit Bella in Paris."

Javier looked away, his own guilt consuming him. He missed his daughter dearly. Every time he looked at Carlotta lately, he couldn't help despising her for putting a wall between Bella and him. Carlotta had convinced him late into her pregnancy with Stefan that it would benefit Bella and Miguel to attend boarding schools. After much deliberation and argument, Carlotta won out, and Bella was sent to France to a girls' school that evolved around an equestrian program.

"I won't have time for the other children when the baby arrives and you are traveling so much these days. It will be best for all of us, and then by the time they come home for holidays, the baby will be old enough to be taken care of by a nanny and we'll be able to bond again and all of us will have a lovely time together. All of the wealthiest families in the world send their children away for their education. It is the best for Isabella and Miguel. They can't get what they rightfully deserve in an education here in Mexico," Carlotta said. "And, we'll be able to dote on our new baby without making the other children jealous, which would be natural. You know how Isabella can be. To be honest, I'm not so sure she wouldn't harm the baby."

"That's ridiculous," Javier retorted. But he knew that she had a point. Bella was not happy that her stepmother was having a baby and had told Carlotta one night when she went into her room and offered to read her a bedtime story that she would hurt the baby when her father or Carlotta wasn't looking. When Javier asked Bella about it, she stared at him and said nothing. Javier at that point had acquiesced to Carlotta's suggestion, and he'd sent his beloved daughter and the boy he'd come to know as his son away to their respective schools in Europe.

By the next year, after the baby was born, Javier had begun pleading with Bella to come home, missing her terribly and knowing that he'd made a huge mistake. However, she made it perfectly clear to her father that she had no intention of coming home. She'd held her grudge for nine years now, only visiting during Christmas and spring breaks, and during the summertime. Javier doubted, after all this time, that they would ever share the closeness they once felt for each other.

As for Miguel, he'd been sent to a boys' Catholic school in Spain, preparing him for the seminary and priesthood. Javier knew that Miguel was pleased with this arrangement. He'd expected his mother to send him away. Javier realized that the only real despair Miguel had felt about it at all was leaving his stepsister when she was still so upset about everything. Fortunately, according to the letters he received from Miguel, the children spent at least one weekend a month together. His stepson usually went to France via the train to visit Bella. He was a good boy who took care of his sister. At least they had each other.

"Javier, you listening?"

"Yes, I'm sorry. I knew Antonio was going to Europe, but I hadn't realized so soon. I wish he had contacted me before he left. I would've sent along a gift for Bella."

Emilio squirmed in the leather chair across from Javier, while they continued to converse in Antonio's study, as if he had something to hide.

"It's not like him to not let me know when he is leaving."

"Yes well, he was very busy right before he left. I'm certain he planned to phone you. Regardless. Look, Javier, I'm not going to waste your time here. You know my brother is an old-fashioned sort. He likes being the *Patrón*, but times are changing, and our organization needs to change with them."

"We're making enough money selling *mota*, and with our other businesses. Leave it at that, Emilio." Javier didn't like where this conversation looked to be heading. Since Emilio had come on board, he'd seen the cocky bastard try to weasel into running everything. He should've brought Pedro along on this visit. Pedro seemed to be the one person who intimidated this little *pendejo*. Unfortunately, Pedro had come down with the flu, and at the last minute couldn't make the trip.

"You're wrong on this, Javier. We have the land and the manpower. Don't think like a dinosaur on this one. Cocaine is going to be the drug of the future. I'm telling you, I've tried this stuff. There is nothing comparable to it. The high you get from this white powder is excellent. When you're on it, the power you feel is immeasurable. I swear that it actually increases your intelligence."

Javier shook his head. "We don't use drugs in this organization, and I doubt there is any drug that can make you more intelligent."

"The money will pour into our laps." Emilio stood up and paced back and forth. "We have the means, right here in our own backyard, to produce the purest, highest grade available. I don't think you realize how much money people will spend for this stuff."

Javier looked away. This did not interest him in the least.

"Listen to me. You think selling *mota* for five hundred a key is big? It isn't anything compared to *six thousand* a key for the white gold."

"Did you say six grand?"

"Ah, did I find your number?" Emilio laughed.

"You've got my attention, anyway." A number like that would get anyone's attention.

"Good." Emilio walked over to the wet bar and poured two shot glasses of tequila.

"What would my role be in all this? What do you want from me?"

"First, to convince Antonio that this is the wave of the future, where the real *dinero* is. Once you've achieved that, you would head up the political end of it. Since you're a government official, it's important we make nice with the police and the Immigration."

"What kind of risk are we talking, as far as Stateside goes?"

"A little more than the *mota*. Shit, man, a drug bust is a drug bust, but it's not a problem if you've got the right connections. I've got some guys in the States ready to deal, and they'd make damn sure we don't have any problems."

"I'll think about it. But I think we should talk to your brother before we decide anything."

"Yes, I agree," Emilio replied. "That is your department. I think the way to handle him is not to even let him know this is my idea. You take all the credit for this, man. He still sees me as a snot-nosed kid. And, you after all are my brother's keeper."

"And you, Emilio are exactly what your brother and I think you are and that is a snot-nosed punk."

"Fuck you."

"I think I know your brother better than anyone—lies don't go over very well with him."

"Who's lying? It's worth a little fib to me if it's going to bring in that much more money. Think about it."

Javier nodded. "I'll consider it."

"You won't be sorry." Emilio handed Javier some tequila.

Javier shot back the tequila and wondered what Emilio was really after.

CHAPTER THIRTY-SIX

THE SEVENTEEN HAND GREY HANOVERIAN MARE CLEARED the four-foot-six-inch jump with graceful ease. Bella's petite stature only enhanced the giant's height and build. The two together were equestrian perfection. They turned the tight corner and cleared the next two jumps, making a difficult feat appear effortless.

Bella trotted Samson's Delilah to the center of the arena, where Jean Luc, her trainer, stood with his hands fixed upon his khaki breeches. "Wonderful, *cherie*."

He patted the horse on the neck. Bella swung her right leg over the saddle and slid down Delilah's side. "You, my dear, will be ready for next month's horse trials in Italy if you and Delilah keep this up. Tomorrow we go out on the course." Jean Luc playfully slapped Bella on the rump.

Bella took no offense at this. The entire school knew that Jean Luc maintained a preference for men. The girls at the school had a running bet going, to see if they could convince this gorgeous specimen to change his ways. But he never swayed. He chided and teased them about their incorrigible hormones, but Bella was different. She'd set her sights on becoming a world-class rider from the day she arrived at the school as a little girl, and had never wavered from that goal. Jean Luc had seen her potential from the start.

She never missed a lesson, rarely complaining of aches and pains like the other girls. If she fell, she always got right back on and rode the fences.

With any luck, Bella would make the Olympic team and head to Barcelona in a few years—riding for the French. She had done all her training in France so it was appropriate that she ride for the French. She would be France's "golden girl." Not only was she a talented equestrienne, but she was also intelligent as well as beautiful.

Even though Jean Luc desired men instead of women, he knew a beautiful woman when he saw one. He also saw the way other men looked at Bella when they would go shopping together or go for a *café au lait*. She was still only a child at nearly seventeen, with eyes as green as emeralds. Her long hair made everyone in the street stare. Bella never seemed to pay much attention. Her thoughts were a constant mixture of horses, fences, strides, dressage tests, cross country courses, saddles to clean, and breeches to wash. She never allowed anyone to mess with her tack, much less her prized possession—her Delilah.

Her father had bought the mare for her five years earlier as a birthday present. Delilah was four years old at the time, and was sold because her owners had gone bankrupt in a bad business deal. Javier was fortunate to grab her for Bella. The horse had come from wonderful bloodlines, and although her jumping lacked the experience that Jean Luc would have liked her to have for his star student due to the fact that Delilah was still a baby at the time, he had seen the horse's possible abilities and felt that with the proper training the horse and girl could go far together. And he could also see that a quick and certain bond had formed between the two "girls." It didn't take much to convince Bella's father to make the purchase.

Jean Luc walked beside Bella, who led the mare to the barn to be put up in the cross-ties. She stripped off the saddle, bridle, and protective boots from Delilah's legs. Since the breeze was quite cool, Bella decided against a bath and reached for a large sponge in her tack box, and sponged her horse down.

Jean Luc went into the small room off the barn and poured them each a cup of coffee. He set Bella's down, until she came in to wipe off her saddle and bridle she carried in.

After blanketing Delilah and giving her a handful of carrots, she led her horse to her stall. Bella then dragged the heels of her boots along the ground on her way back to the office, where she carried in her tack and sat down across from Jean Luc. He handed her the coffee, which she quickly drank. The warm liquid satisfied her aching joints. Although complaints weren't a part of her makeup, the aches she chose to ignore were still there.

After drinking half the coffee, she picked up a sponge and a container of leather cleaner from the cleaning box and began rubbing down the saddle.

"Quite some ride today," Jean Luc remarked.

"Thanks. She's an amazing animal, isn't she?"

"You can say that again. You know that I believe that your dreams of becoming an Olympic champion aren't so farfetched."

"You really think so, Jean Luc? Do you really believe I have a chance?"

He set his cup down on the desk next to him and crossed his arms over his chest. With his legs out in front of him, Jean Luc leaned back in the worn leather chair. "Now let me think about that question for a minute," he teased as he tried to assume a serious expression.

Bella threw the sponge at him and they both laughed. His crystalline blue eyes were full of amusement at her playful gesture. He pushed away a strand of his straw colored hair, which continually fell into his eyes, and threw the sponge back at her.

"Seriously now," he said. "I don't only think you've got a chance, I *know* you do. You and that mare of yours are destined to be winners. It's all up here, Bella." He tapped his finger to the side of his head. "And in here." He tapped his chest. "It is will and belief that will make you achieve your dreams. I believe you can do it, but it isn't up to me. It's up to you. What do you think?"

There was a slight pause before she answered. "I think you're right."

"Good. Then half the battle has been won. Now I'm late for an appointment," he murmured, glancing at his watch and thinking about Pierre, who would become impatient if he were kept waiting. "And I'm certain you have a great deal of homework to do."

"Some. I'm also meeting old friends from home for dinner—my godfather, actually, and his daughters."

"Great. Well, have a good time. I'll see you tomorrow, same time, same place."

"I'll be here."

As Bella finished her daily ritual, her mind tiptoed back home to her father. She tried not to think about home very much, but with Antonio and the girls visiting that evening, it was hard not to.

She missed him dearly, but she would never let on. He'd made his choice nine years ago, when he chose Carlotta over her. She had hated being sent away, even though now, when she reflected on it, she knew it had been the best thing for her. However, she would never give either her father or her conniving stepmother the satisfaction of knowing that this was how she truly felt.

She realized she would've never had the experiences or the opportunities she had in France if she'd remained at home in Mexico. The only thing she regretted was she sincerely missed Miguel and Pedro, both of whom she wrote to on a regular basis. Miguel's visits had slowed because his schooling was increasingly difficult as was hers, and any spare time she had she spent it with her horse.

Her dad had done everything he could to appease her, as when he bought her the horse. But the pain and jealousy of being replaced by her stepmother angered Isabella every time she thought about it.

Maybe one day she would find it in her heart to forgive her father for this betrayal, but she didn't see it happening anytime soon. She knew Antonio would lecture her about it once again tonight, but she was a strong-willed young woman. On this topic, her mind was made up.

CHAPTER THIRTY-SEVEN

MIGUEL CLOSED HIS BIBLE AND GLANCED OUT THE SMALL
window of his airplane seat. All he could see was dense fog. The
plane hit a pocket of turbulence, and Miguel fingered the cross
around his neck. Flying wasn't one of his favorite experiences.

He was glad to be going home, though. Finished with school, he
was now ready to go to work for the church and for God. The thought
thrilled him.

He would be going to work for St. Peter's and in time he knew that
he would be bringing God's message to the masses. His only regret
was that he would now be so far from his dear sister. He thought
about her often. Even though they still communicated through
letters, and occasionally by telephone, it never seemed enough.
Although there were no bloodlines between them, she was his sister
in every sense of the word. In Miguel's mind, after God and the
church, Bella was next in line.

He still remembered the stricken look on her face when his
mother and her father had told them they would be going away to

school. Bella had stared in disbelief and total shock at her father. Javier had broken Isabella's heart. Miguel had made many attempts to persuade her to forgive her father and make peace within her family. Although forgiveness was at the top of his code of ethics, he could not in any way judge his sister for her anger.

As his flight descended into Guadalajara, he prayed for a safe landing and for guidance in the work he was about to do there. He would have a few days at home with his family before traveling a few hundred miles south to St. Peter's Church, a small church and rectory. He realized how important his work would be, and how much he could affect the people.

CHAPTER THIRTY-EIGHT

HECTOR AND ALEJANDRO STRUTTED THROUGH THE DRUG- infested area off Pico and Hoover. The respect they were gaining with the younger boys in the 'hood was apparent. Talk of the money these two were making had become a hot topic for the young gang members. No longer little boys, they were big men on the block. They were supplying the blacks in Watts, the Asians in Little Korea, and anyone else interested in their product. The only people they didn't supply were their own.

When they began this venture, Alex made Hector promise they would never corrupt their own people. However, that was only part of their reasoning. Bigger, smarter thugs than themselves already owned the Pico, Hoover and surrounding areas. They realized that in their line of work, it wouldn't be too cool to cut in on anyone else's territory.

The stench of raw meat and urine hung in the air on Olympic Avenue. Alex couldn't wait until they had enough money to get out of the hellhole they'd called home for so many years. They'd only moved once during that time and he never understood why or questioned it.

It was right after his mother had returned from her only trip to Mexico to visit friends. She'd been so happy about going. But the day she came back, something of the sparkle in her eyes was gone and he never saw it return. They moved that day, to another small house only a few miles away.

Usually, his precocious, curious nature would have manifested itself into a lot of questions. But his instinct had told him not to push her—that something painful must have occurred for her to make such a radical change. She told him she was out of money, and that the rent on the other house was less. He didn't argue, but he also had the feeling that she was lying. His poor mother worked her fingers to the bone to keep them going, and Alejandro was determined to give her a better life.

"Hey, man, you know what I hear?" Hector said as they stopped to buy a pack of cigarettes.

"No, what did you hear?" Alex asked. His hair was slicked back and he was wearing a new pair of Levis he bought with the money they'd been earning. He'd been squirreling away most of the money underneath his mattress and told his mother he was working at a McDonald's in Brentwood, and she had believed him. He'd kept it from her all summer and now well into the school year. He'd been able to convince her that he worked after school, which in a sense he did. He was also now making top grades and working toward his plan of going on to college.

"I hear they got great parties down at USC. You know chicks with big tatas." Hector motioned with his hands cupped in front of his chest.

Alex pushed him. "Right, like a bunch of fraternity boys are going to let a couple of spics like us into their party. You're crazy."

"Nah, we'll dress up real sweet and all."

"Where we gonna get the threads?"

"We got some money now. Let's spend some of it."

"Uh-uh. Won't work." Alex shook his head, surprised by his friend's brazen attitude.

"I know one sure way we'd get in."

"What's that?"

Hector held up a small vial of cocaine.

"Put that away, you idiot." Alex slapped his hand down. "You want to get busted or what?"

"Oh, come on. There's no cops around here. Even if there was, they wouldn't bother us."

Alex knew he was right, but he didn't like him flashing the stuff in front of children and mothers. And he didn't want his mother to hear about it, either. "You really think that stuff'll get us into a frat party?"

"Are you kidding? The gringos love it. My bro turned us onto the good stuff, man. Those frat boys will welcome us with open arms into their fiestas. We'll get more *chicas* than we ever imagined."

Alex blushed at the thought of women. Hector always talked about women and having sex with them. It embarrassed Alex, because he'd never done anything other than kiss a girl. Oh, he talked the talk, but so far, he hadn't walked the walk. He knew how uncool it would be if anyone knew the truth. Women scared him half to death.

"Who knows, bro, this may be your big night," Hector said, slapping him on the back.

"Up yours."

"I'm jokin', man. So come on. You in?"

"Okay, but if we get our asses kicked I know who to blame."

"No problem."

*****

ALEX PUT ON A WHITE SILK SHIRT WITH HIS NEW JEANS.
His mother hadn't come home yet, so he was able to get out of the house without her wondering where the new clothes had come from. He wrote her a note, saying he'd gone to the library to study. That would please her.

He looked much older than his eighteen years with his hair slicked back and his golden skin. He looked at himself in the mirror and liked what he saw. Alex especially liked his eyes. "Amber," his mother called them, "like your father's." All Alex knew about him was that he was some great man, and that he died saving some people from a building during a big earthquake. He never understood why his mother didn't date or try to find someone else, but he always respected that. In a way, he was glad, because he always had her full attention.

"Hey, you ready, man? Come on."

Alex could see Hector through the reflection in the mirror standing behind him. He wanted to laugh but he knew it would hurt his friend's feelings. Hector wore a light blue silk shirt with wide lapels, and a navy polyester jacket and a pair of dark jeans. The gold chain around his neck made him look like a pimp from ten years earlier. "Hey, you look good."

"Yeah, I know, man. Chicks love this stuff. I'm looking hot. Gonna get me some good looking white girls tonight."

"Right," Alex replied, thinking his friend would get nothing more than his ass kicked looking like he was going to a Halloween party.

When they arrived at fraternity row, driving their low-rider Chevy, they decided it would be wise to park on a different street after seeing the Mercedes, BMW's, and other fancy cars.

The first house they came to had a bunch of people out front drinking beers and dancing. Everybody looked blonde and light skinned. A couple of the girls glanced their way and laughed. The fair-haired guys they were dancing with flipped them off. Uneasy about their reception, Alex convinced Hector to keep on walking down the row.

The houses on the street were large and magnificent. They all boasted perfectly manicured lawns with ivy growing up the sides of their brick walls, leading to the second story windows. Alex's mother had spoken of the homes she used to clean looking like these. Alex knew this was the type of home he would one day soon buy for his mom. She deserved this kind of luxury.

"Can you believe this? Look at these places, man," Hector whispered, not wanting to appear in the least impressed.

"I'll have a house bigger than all of these someday."

"Yeah, man," Hector replied grabbing himself. "You and me both."

About halfway down the row, they stopped in front of the crummiest looking house. The lawn was covered with beer cans scattered all around and the paint was chipping off its walls. It was the sore thumb of the block.

There was a group of guys out front with a couple of girls hanging around. The sweet aroma of marijuana wafted into the night air. One of the guys on the front porch appeared to be doing a ridiculous imitation of The Beastie Boys as the stereo in the background blasted out "Fight for Your Right." It looked like the party was just getting started.

"Man, this looks like our kind of fiesta," Hector said strutting up to where the group was sitting.

Alex walked coolly behind Hector, his head held high, hands shoved in his pockets like he owned the place, even though he wasn't too sure about this whole venture.

"Hey, man, name's Hector. What's yours?" Hector asked extending his hand out to a guy with a big nose and medium length blonde hair.

"*Me llamo Jay.*"

The group giggled.

"Cool. This here's my friend Alex."

Alex let out a clear, "Hi."

"Excuse me, but were you guys invited?" a redheaded girl asked.

"We're about to be," Hector replied.

"Really? And why is that, dude?" asked a guy with offensive acne and long brown hair.

"'Cause man, we got something you want," Hector said, pulling out the small vial of coke. Everyone's eyes grew large, as a cloud of silence swept through the crowd. The guy named Jay reached out to grab the vial. Hector slapped his hand away. "Uh-uh. I don't believe we've been officially invited yet."

"You got any more of that stuff?" Jay asked.

"Do we have any more of this stuff?" Hector asked, sarcastically rolling his eyes at Alex. Alex noticed he was trying hard to conceal his accent from these kids, but it wasn't working.

"We've got plenty of it," Alex interrupted. All the kids turned to gaze upon him.

"Well then, I guess you guys are official guests of the ΣĖ for the evening. Let our house be yours."

An hour later, there were at least a hundred eighteen-and-nineteen-year-old sweaty men and women crammed into the place. Rumor traveled quickly out on the row that a couple of Mexican dudes at the Sigma Epsilon house were selling some high-grade powder.

Alex sat in Jay's room drinking a Coke. Jay was boasting about being the president of the house. Hector was downstairs, making connections with kids buying drugs.

"So, Alex, isn't it?" Jay asked. He cracked open another beer and sat down on a red velour sofa. "Where you getting your stuff?"

The pizza faced kid leaned in and Alex gave him a dirty look.

"Back off, Stein," Jay said and the kid sat back in his chair.

"I really can't say."

"I see. You're dealing with some power?"

Alex lied, knowing it was Hector's brother who helped them get the drugs. "Yeah, the biggest."

"Huh. Well you know that this stuff is becoming pretty popular around campus."

"Apparently so," Alex replied, looking around at the posters of naked women on the wall and the red light that cast a glow throughout the room. The lava lamp sitting on the desk hummed like an aquarium.

"I'm a businessman like you, Alex, and I thought, you guys willing, we could do business together." Jay smoothed back his greasy hair.

"Specifically?" Alex asked. He kind of liked this new sensation of power. This white boy was actually showing him some respect.

"You guys sell to me, and I get it out to the kids here. You could make a killing."

"Sounds interesting."

"I bet it does. I can increase your beaner pockets by hundreds."

Alex looked at him, astonished at what Jay called him. After being in elementary school with white kids, he'd vowed to never let anyone call him names again. He felt the anger boil as he stood up to leave, not wanting to lose his cool. It was clear that Alex was outnumbered.

"Hey, man, where you going? What's up? I thought we were talking biz."

Alex grabbed Jay by his shirt collar—his cool gone. "Yeah, man, we were talking *biz*, until you called me something I don't let anyone call me."

Jay looked stunned, not knowing what to say. Then he let out a nervous laugh and said, "Oh you mean beaner? Jeez man, I thought you guys liked that. I figured you all call each other that."

Alex let go of his shirt and gave him a little shove. "We call ourselves whatever we like. You will address me as either Alexander or Mr. Peña. You got it?"

"Yeah, sure man, no problem. I didn't mean anything by it." Jay wiped the sweat off his forehead, and retreated to his chair.

"Good, I didn't think so." Alex relaxed and sat back down in the chair. "Now, how much product do you think you could buy?"

"A couple of kilos monthly," Jay replied, his voice still sounding shaky.

"Uh-huh, and you're sure about this?" Alex studied him.

"Yeah, man. Kids here love this stuff," Jay answered, holding up a small mirror with five lines of cocaine on it. "Want some?"

"No thanks." Alex never touched the stuff. Jay passed the mirror back and forth to his brothers in the room. Alex could see the euphoric effect developing immediately as their eyes glazed over. "When will you be ready to buy?"

"You provide the goods next week for me, and I'll come up with the cash."

"Where you going to get that kind of money?"

"Shit, man, my old man's in the jewelry business. He puts money in my account all the time. I got plenty. Don't you worry about it."

Alex couldn't believe that a twenty-year-old could get the kind of money it would take to buy that much cocaine, and from his own father, too. But he didn't question it. He decided to take a chance and call his bluff.

"All right, I know we're getting a decent supply in on Tuesday. I can deliver to you Wednesday, as long as you have the cash."

"No sweat, man. Can you meet me at the Jack In The Box on Vermont? I don't want you bringing it here. It might look a little suspicious, if you know what I mean."

Alex knew what he meant. He meant it would look funny for a couple of Mexicans to come into their white-bread fraternity in the middle of a Tuesday afternoon.

"No problem."

"Great." Jay reached over and shook Alex's hand. About that time, a raven-haired girl wearing tight jeans and a halter top walked in and hung all over Jay.

"If you guys will excuse me, we would like some privacy. Hey, stay around, Alex, and have some fun. There's a bunch of cute girls downstairs by now."

Alex nodded and walked out the door. He wanted to leave this place and return to his own neighborhood, where things were familiar. Even in this frat house's disheveled appearance and the kids with their hair longer than most on the fraternity row, Alex couldn't help but feel the gap between those who'd come from homes where parents passed out money seemingly without a care, and those who struggled on a daily basis to put food in the mouths of their children.

Coming down the stairs, he could see a group of girls standing around Hector. He couldn't believe it.

Hector, obviously wired, insisted, "Hey, come meet my new friends."

Alex nudged the girls aside and grabbed Hector by the shoulders.

"Easy, what you doing, man? Hang out, be cool, meet Treena over there," he said, pointing to a buxom blonde drinking a beer.

"What am I doing? What in hell are you doing?" Alex asked, amazed his friend had been coking up.

"I'm having a good time. You should too."

"You're high, man. I thought we agreed not to do this stuff. It's bad for business."

"You're too uptight. A little toot now and then won't hurt nothing."

"Come on, we're going home." Alex pulled on Hector's arm.

"You go. I'm having a good time."

"I'm not going anywhere without you. Now let's go."

"Fuck you, man, I'm about to get lucky with one of these little babes, and I'm not about to let you ruin it. And if you weren't such a stupid square-ass, you'd join the fun," Hector muttered, pushing Alex away.

Alex couldn't believe he was fighting with his best friend. Hector glared at him, his nostrils flaring like a wild horse.

"Hector, don't do this. I need to get home."

"Why? So your mama don't get mad at you? Man, you crack me up. You're one of the biggest dope dealers around here, and you're still worried about your mama. Fuck your mama, she'll get over it."

"You know what, Hector? You go do whatever you want. Get high, get laid, get stupid, I don't care." With that, he turned around and walked away, holding back his anger, his tears, and his frustration—due not only to a bull-headed friend but to a life that he really didn't want to lead but knew that he was destined for.

*****

WHEN ALEX ARRIVED HOME IT WAS A LITTLE PAST MIDNIGHT. Marta was waiting up for him. She stood in the doorway with her hands on her hips as he came through the door. "Where have you been? And don't you go telling me about the library, because I know you've been lying to me."

Alex stared at her in amazement.

"I know what you and Hector have been doing, Alejandro, and I can't believe my ears." Marta was torn between slapping him, hugging him, and crying. She'd been told earlier that day by a friend about Alex and Hector selling drugs, and they'd been doing it for several months now.

"What are you talking about, Mama?"

"You know exactly what I'm talking about," she answered him. She shook her finger at him. "I thought I raised you better than this, but I see you disappoint me. Selling drugs, for God's sakes. Alejandro, couldn't you have found something better?"

"Mama, I'm trying to make enough money to provide a better place for us."

"What. You think drugs are the answer? You break my heart. I can't believe you would do this."

Frustration and anger from years of working for a better life for her child who wanted to throw it away made Marta feel much older than her thirty-six years. She looked at her handsome son, thinking how much he looked like Antonio. Her disappointment was tremendous. Not only did he look like his father, but he also had the same kind of ethics as his father. She'd prayed her strong hold over him would have overcome any of the bad blood that ran through his veins. But staring at him now, she realized she'd obviously failed to save him from the fate of being Antonio Espinoza's son.

He'd lied to her about his job. When she'd found out the truth, she'd cried. Then anger set in upon discovering he wasn't home when she walked through the door after a hard day's work. Waiting up for him for a couple of hours gave her time to think about where she'd gone wrong. Maybe she should've ignored Antonio's deceit and moved to Colombia. Obviously, if her son was to be corrupt, he should've been able to do it in the lap of luxury his father wanted to provide them all those years ago.

The day she left Antonio behind for the second time in her life played through her memory. She'd made it out of the compound and had taken a cab to the airport, where she bought a ticket home with the money she'd taken from the dresser. Then she'd phoned Elisa and asked her to find a new place for her and Alejandro to live and to start packing for them.

"Why?" Elisa asked, her voice laden with fear.

"Please, do this. I wouldn't ask you for something so important if it weren't urgent. But it is. I'll explain everything later." Once together, she told Elisa everything, who called her a stupid fool for running from a life that could provide everything she had ever dreamed and longed for, all because of one small lie.

She'd looked her friend in the eyes while drinking a cup of coffee and said, "At least when I wake up in the morning I feel good about myself, knowing that I have nothing to do with cheating or lying, killing or stealing. Antonio Espinoza cannot wake up with that same satisfaction. And I may live the life of a poor fool, but I'll find every piece of gold I could ever dream of waiting for me in the Kingdom of God."

"Maybe so, but you're still a fool."

Marta wondered now if her friend had been right, all these years.

After she had returned to the States, she'd written Antonio a letter explaining why she and her and son couldn't live with a man who felt that lying to his wife and family was acceptable. She also made it clear, in no uncertain terms, that he wasn't to contact her or Alex. She considered him dead because of his blatant dishonesty. She knew it was harsh, but there could be no other way. And now she wondered, as she looked into her son's eyes, if she had to be as harsh with him as well.

"Sit down." She patted him on the knee as he sat down on the tattered, green sofa. "There's something I need to tell you, and I should have done so long ago. If I had, maybe you wouldn't be in this mess."

Alex gazed at her with a baffled look on his face, "What is it?"

"I don't know how to tell you this, so I'm just going to say it." Marta paused as anxiety caused her adrenaline to flow. "Your father wasn't a hero who died trying to save people in that earthquake."

"What?"

Marta could hear the amazement in his voice. His eyes grew round as he stared at her in disbelief. "In fact, he is not dead. He is still alive today."

A gravelly sound escaped from the back of Alejandro's throat. "What are you telling me?"

Marta told him bits and pieces of the ugly story. She left out the part about when she'd stayed with Antonio after Lydia had died, and how she'd planned to move Alejandro and herself to Colombia to live with him until she'd discovered that living a life with Antonio would be living a lie to her people. She also left out the part about when Antonio visited so many years ago.

"Please understand, Alejandro, I couldn't stay with your father. If I'd known he was married, I never would've been with him in the first place."

Alex held up his hand. "I don't want to hear any more. I can't believe this. You lied all this time, and he deserted me. You say he even knows where we lived and used to send us money. But he never came to see me. What kind of man is he? I don't understand this. You mean we don't have to be living here in this dump, but we do because you are too proud to live an *ugly life*, as you say—taking money from a guilty man who took you into his bed and left you to this horrible life where you work like a slave?"

The words sliced through Marta's heart like a jagged dagger. She bowed her head, choking back her tears. She reached over to hug Alex. "It wasn't like that at all. Your father and I loved each other very much. It's that sometimes people can't get past their differences."

"He certainly didn't love you enough, and I can see he didn't care about me."

"Please, don't say that. Please."

"I don't want to know anymore. I'm going out for awhile." He stormed out of the door without looking back.

Marta ran to the door, crying in desperation, "I'm sorry, Alex. Come back. Don't go, please don't go." It was too late. She collapsed in the old rocking chair next to the fireplace, the same one she'd used to rock Alex to sleep in for many years. Her heart ached as she longed for those days once again.

She'd never felt so alone before, not even when she'd left Mexico for the first time. She knew she'd made a mistake telling Alex the truth. But the biggest mistake, she now realized, had been keeping the truth from him all along. Her lies were as bad as Antonio's.

She longed to hold Alex and comfort the hurt she knew he was feeling, but she had no idea where he'd gone so she rocked herself rhythmically in the old rocking chair, until she finally drifted into a restless sleep.

CHAPTER THIRTY-NINE

JAVIER THOUGHT OVER EMILIO'S PROPOSITION. HE HAD MADE some good points. Maybe it *was* about time the business did expand. How could Antonio refute the case for making so much more money? After all, Antonio had always been greedy, but when Marta left him that second time, making it very clear that she and her son wanted nothing to do with him, Antonio had become hungrier for the almighty dollar. It was as if, in his mind, only buying all the goods in the world could make him happy.

Javier shook his head as he sat behind his desk going over his financial statements. It seemed that his second wife shared Antonio's philosophy, forever buying something, decorating this or that. She claimed to be bored at all times, and her complaining was beginning to drive him crazy. Her looks, once akin to Sophia Loren, had changed drastically, as she'd never lost thirty of the fifty pounds she'd gained during her pregnancy with their son, Stefan, who sadly enough had not brought their family together as she'd insisted he would. Instead his birth had driven quite a wedge between the two of them, which had begun the day she'd won the argument to send

Bella and Miguel away, and now she constantly nagged him to have another child.

"That is really what we need, Carlotta. The children we already have, you send away to expensive schools. And you say you want another one?"

"I know why you won't have any more children," she remarked as she paced back and forth, her hands on her richly clad hips. "It's because of Stefan. You're afraid I'll have another retard."

"You selfish woman," he yelled. "How *can* you speak of our son that way? He is not retarded. He's deaf. You certainly ought to know the difference, because there is a huge one. He is anything but stupid. He's extremely intelligent. I've spoken to his instructors at your expensive school for the deaf. They say that he is bright, and very popular with all the children and teachers."

"What is your complaint then?"

"My complaint is that you, Carlotta, are an uncaring mother."

"I certainly don't see any of our children complaining. Not even your own sweet Isabella who, from everything I've been told, is very happy she's in France."

"The only reason those children like it better where they are is because they don't have to live with you. Unfortunately, I do. I wish you'd find *me* some school to go to!"

"That shouldn't be too hard to arrange. I'll send you to the school for the mentally incompetent."

"That's it. Get out of here! You will not speak to me like that in my own home."

"Fine, Lord and Master." She'd stormed out of his office and hadn't spoken to him in days. This suited Javier fine. He had come to realize by now that the biggest mistake he'd ever made in his life was marrying her. Pedro had been right about Javier thinking with the wrong head when he'd put that damn ring on her finger. Lately, that particular head didn't seem to get much exercise, anyway. His reasons for marrying her turned out to be basically futile ones, except for the son their marriage produced.

He loved his son as much as he loved the estranged Bella, that is to say, with every fiber of his being. In a way, he was glad that Stefan was living in the United States, at a school in Texas where he was receiving the attention and special skills he would need in order to make it in such a difficult world.

As he was finishing going over his reports, Javier heard the front door open and the sound of Miguel's voice. "Hello, I'm home."

Of course, Carlotta had stormed out of the house to go shopping, so Javier went to greet both him and Pedro, who had always been fond of the boy.

"Miguelito. Ah, look at you." Javier smiled and held his arms out wide to embrace the young man he thought of as his own—and a man of God at that.

"Papa, I missed you," Miguel responded, wrapping his arms around Javier. "And I missed you, too," Miguel told Pedro.

"Come, sit down. You must be exhausted," Pedro remarked as he slapped Miguel on the back.

"I am," Miguel replied. He walked into the living room with them and sat down on the white leather sofa Carlotta recently purchased. "Where's Mama?"

"Out spending my money."

"Some things never change," he laughed. "I've missed this place so much."

"How long are you staying?" Pedro asked, sitting down in a chair across from him.

"Not long. They're expecting me in a few days at St. Peter's Church. Believe me, if I could, I'd stay longer. But the Lord doesn't like to be kept waiting," Miguel said with a chuckle. "I wish Bella were here."

"We all do," Javier replied.

"And Stefan, too."

"Yes, but Christmas will be here before we know it, and we'll all be together again," Javier said.

"But you're surely going to see Bella before then," Miguel replied.

"I hadn't planned on it, unless she's making a surprise visit I'm not supposed to know about."

"I thought you'd be going to see her next month, when she competes at the horse trials in Italy."

"What?" Javier's mouth flew open. Isabella had never said a single word to him about a major horse trial event. She'd always let him know about her big events in the past, and he always made a huge effort to attend each one of them. He knew of her Olympic dreams and he supported her completely. He couldn't understand why she hadn't made him aware this time. Yes it was true that they weren't as close as they once were, but she'd always kept him abreast of how she was progressing with her riding. He sighed heavily.

"You mean, you didn't know?"

"No, we didn't," said Pedro, answering for Javier, seeing the shock and disappointment in the old man's eyes.

"Oh, Papa, I'm so sorry. I assumed she'd written you about it when she wrote me. Once I received her letter, I called to let her know I would be coming back here, and going to work for the Church. She sounded a little upset. I was certain that she would want you to be there."

"I don't know. I guess I don't know my daughter as well as I once thought I did."

No one said anything. Javier looked out the large bay window to what now appeared to be an ominous sea. He knew Bella had drifted from his life, but he'd hoped he'd remained in her heart as she had in him. He'd rather die than consider that he'd lost his daughter forever.

CHAPTER FORTY

ROSA AND FELICIA WALKED BESIDE ANTONIO, EACH HOLDING
a hand on either side of him. There was a light drizzle along the
Seine, whose beauty had always entranced Rosa, inspiring her to
draw it many times. Shortly after her mother's death, Rosa had
retreated so severely that her one means of communication became
her drawings.

The first time Antonio heard her speak again was two years after
Lydia's death, when he took both girls to Paris. It was the first time
Rosa had seen the Seine.

"It's beautiful, Papa," she had whispered.

His eyes filled with tears hearing his daughter speak for the first
time in so long. He thought he had lost her forever, as he had lost
Marta. He took her in his arms. "You spoke! Merciful God, you
spoke!" They cried together while holding onto each other for a long
time. She still spoke only when absolutely necessary. Antonio knew
she'd never be quite the same. There would always be an underlying
sadness in the child's heart.

But now it was her art that made her happy. He had asked many times if she wanted to go away to school, where she could learn to develop her gift, her talent. But she'd always refused his offers. He knew that going away to learn her trade would benefit her, maybe get her to open up to others. And, although her talent was evident, the morbid and dark themes that seemed to be the focus of her art frightened him a bit and he wished she'd paint more lighter, brighter scenes. She did a lot of paintings with dead angels who looked remarkably like her mother, and other paintings with what Antonio could only classify as demons who looked to be battling child-like angels. Out of fear of putting her work to a halt, Antonio never made any suggestions about her art, and she continued to deny the need to go to art school. It was as if she were afraid to be around people, unlike her younger sister Felicia, who was the outgoing wild one. She had bright eyes and her mother's beauty. Possessing a mind full of questions, she was a perpetual chatterbox.

"Papa, Papa," Felicia said as she tugged at his coat. She always needed to be the center of attention.

"Yes?"

"I'm going to be a famous French model."

"Really? How interesting."

"You're not French," Rosa interrupted her tartly.

"So? When I was out shopping today, while you were wasting your time doodling, a man from the Marie Claire agency approached me. He told me that I was very beautiful, and that I should come to see him. He said he would take photographs of me to see if I am as beautiful on film."

"He was probably a con man," Rosa commented, as they walked across the street to the restaurant where they were to meet Bella.

"No, he wasn't. He gave me his card." Felicia pulled a card out of her coat pocket and dangled it teasingly in front of Rosa.

"Let me see that," their father ordered, taking the card from Felicia. Scanning the information on the card, he saw that it bore the name "Mark Le Blanc" on the front. At the top of the card were the words *Marie Claire.*

"See, told you so. Can I at least go talk to the man, Papa?"

"I'll think about it, but understand that I will go with you. You will not go alone."

"Oh, thank you, thank you. You wait, big sister, I'll be on the cover of every magazine in the world!"

"Good for you," Rosa muttered. She couldn't stand Felicia's childish antics, and prayed that she'd curb her obnoxious behavior in the restaurant. Even though Bella and Felicia were closer in age, her friend had always seemed to gravitate more toward Rosa. Bella was special to Rosa. She was the only one who never asked her why she had stopped speaking during all those years. Whenever Bella had come to visit, she would play with Rosa quietly in her room, as if she, too, were mute, a normal condition. Rosa had always appreciated her friend's consideration.

As they walked into the candlelit restaurant, mouth-watering aromas teased their taste buds. Antonio approached the *maitre de* to ask if Bella had arrived. Finding she hadn't, they made their way into the bar near the main room of the restaurant to wait for her.

Not long after taking their seats at a cocktail table, Bella arrived. Although disheveled from wind and drizzle, she still appeared as feminine and pretty as ever.

If anyone should be a model, Rosa thought, it should be Bella. However, Bella did not possess the height and trendy beauty her sister Felicia had. Bella was beautiful in both an exotic and classic way. Her green eyes and dark looks made her exotic, but the elegant bone structure of her face gave her a classic look, the kind even age couldn't diminish.

"Hello," she greeted them breathlessly. "It's so good to see all of you." She kissed each on the cheek as they stood to greet her. "I'm so sorry I've gotten you wet," she said to Antonio, holding out her raincoat. The *maitre de* walked over.

"May I?" he asked.

She handed her raincoat to the man who asked if they'd like to be seated in the dining room. Antonio nodded and they all followed him into the restaurant.

Antonio laughed. "No need to apologize." He held out a chair for her.

"Thank you," she replied. "Tell me, what is new with all of you?"

Immediately, Felicia answered, "I'm going to start modeling."

"Really?" Bella inquired, smiling knowingly at Rosa.

"Yes, haven't you heard? She's going to color her hair blonde and become the next Cheryl Tiegs," Rosa teased.

"Shut up. You're jealous. You wish you were me. All you do is waste your time drawing your stupid pictures."

"Girls," Antonio warned.

"How *is* your art coming along, Rosa?" Bella asked.

"It's wonderful. She draws and paints such beautiful pieces of work, it never ceases to amaze me," Antonio said.

"I'd really like to see some of them. You know, my horse trainer has a friend who is an art dealer. Maybe I could put you in contact with him."

"Oh, no, Bella you don't have to do that," Rosa protested. She shyly looked down at the *hors d'oeuvres* the waiter placed before them.

"Why not? I think it's a wonderful idea," Antonio said.

"Don't be silly, Papa, my art isn't nearly good enough yet to be seen by an art dealer."

"Now there you go again, doubting yourself. Your art is magnificent. If Bella can help, then let her."

"He's right, Rosa. I'm sure your art is very promising. I'd love to help in any way that I can."

"Well, all right, thank you, Bella," Rosa whispered.

She could not help but remember the words her demon uncle had spoken to her years ago, the words that echoed in her mind the whole time he'd committed his sins against her: *You will never be anything, Rosa. Only a mute child. And if you ever tell anyone about our private meetings, I will see to it that everything you've ever loved will be destroyed, everything.*

274 | P a g e

It was that same day Rosa saw him playing with her sister
Felicia's hair in the courtyard. He'd glared at Rosa, but she'd vowed
to protect her sister from harm, and thus far she had. Now Felicia
was grown, and Rosa felt certain Emilio had never harmed her. He'd
started leaving Rosa alone as well, once she turned fifteen. There had
been no explanation, and she certainly didn't ask. She had been
enormously grateful she no longer received his unwanted attention.

"Wonderful, I'll speak to Jean Luc about it tomorrow. He'll talk to
Pierre, and see if we can't set something up for you."

Rosa was elated about the idea of a real art dealer seeing some of
her work, but her self-doubt still plagued her, and Uncle Emilio's
words haunted her memory.

"Tell us, word has it that you'll be heading for the Olympics,"
Antonio said.

"I don't know about that," Bella replied. Her cheeks flushed.

"Come on, tell the truth."

"Well maybe in a couple of years to Barcelona. I hope." She held
up crossed fingers. "I have an important trial next month in Italy, and
Jean Luc says there's a good possibility I could actually make the
French team if Delilah and I have a good go."

"That's wonderful. Absolutely wonderful. I think we'll have to
make a special trip to come and see you and cheer you on. Your
father will be here, won't he?"

"I don't know," Bella paused, picking at her chateaubriand with
her fork.

"Of course he'll be here. I know how proud he is of you, Bella. He wouldn't miss this for the world."

"I really don't think he'll be here. I wrote him a letter telling him about it. When he didn't write or call me back, I figured he couldn't be here. I finally called him yesterday, and Carlotta said he wasn't in. I asked her if she knew whether or not they were coming. She said that they couldn't because they were going to visit Stefan in Texas. I think he has a soccer tournament going on with his school."

"I can't believe your father would choose to go to Stefan's tournament, instead of seeing you in a major horse trials, young lady. In fact, if I know your papa, he would bring Stefan along. Your brother would want to see you, too. It's too important for them to miss."

"I mentioned that to Carlotta, but she said the teachers at the school had told her that the soccer matches were really important to Stefan's self-esteem. How could I argue with that? He's such a sweet little boy, and he *is* my brother. I believe anything that would help him is all for good."

After they'd finished dinner, Antonio sat back in his chair and pulled a cigar from a long silver tube in his coat pocket. He mulled over Bella's story. Something didn't sound quite right. He doubted Javier would miss such an important event in Bella's life. He would make an appointment to visit him when they returned, and find out the truth. Antonio suspected that Carlotta was behind this slight. He hadn't liked the woman from the beginning, when she had been so unscrupulous about sending Miguel and Bella away. He hated the way Javier allowed her to control his life like that. Thinking about this made him recall Marta's attempt to control his own life, as the girls chatted on about horses, modeling, and art. Antonio tried to convince himself over the years that he was happy that Marta left after her attempting to make him change his ways. What a fool she was for leaving him. He would've given her everything she'd ever wanted. It angered Antonio that he hadn't even been allowed to raise his own son. However, it was clear to him that it had all worked out for the best. But how sad that his daughters suffered so much at that time, especially Rosa. Springing Marta and Alejandro on them might have caused them irreparable harm. Yet his heart still ached for them both. He wondered how they were and what they were lives were like now.

"Papa, are you listening?" Felicia needled him.

"Hmmm, what? I'm sorry. Guess I'm a little tired."

"Bella was saying that she'd get us a box at the trials if she could."

"That would be fantastic."

"I can't make any promises, but I'll talk to Jean Luc and see what he can do."

"Excellent. We will definitely be there to see you win, then to go on for the gold at the Olympics in Barcelona!"

Bella squirmed in her seat. "I think you're assuming a great deal, Godfather."

"Don't be silly. You will certainly win the gold, I can promise you that." He tapped his finger on the table to make his point.

The waiter came by and took their dessert orders.

"Oh, no, thank you. I'm watching my figure," Felicia gushed.

Rosa rolled her eyes at Bella, who couldn't help giggling. Felicia shot the two of them a sharp glance. Antonio watched, amused by his grown daughters acting like children.

"Nonsense," Antonio said. "We'll all have the *crepes Suzette*, please."

*****

"FOR SOMEONE WHO HAD NO DESIRE TO EAT DESSERT, YOU nearly licked the plate clean," Rosa remarked teasingly to her sister.

"I have a right. At least I don't look like a cow."

"Stop it," Antonio demanded.

Rosa was far from being a cow. Bella couldn't help noticing that she'd turned into a pretty young woman. She wasn't beautiful, exactly, but she was certainly no cow. Neither as tall as her sister nor as petite as she was, Rosa had been gifted with deep, dark eyes, framed by long, thick lashes. But it wasn't the dark hue that made her eyes stand out. Bella always thought there was a sadness in Rosa's eyes, as if some dark secret dwelled within them. Bella assumed that this tinge of sadness was caused by the death of her mother. But as time wore on, her instincts told her that her friend yearned for lost pieces of a life she never truly enjoyed. Bella recalled those years when she and Rosa would play together as being dismally quiet. Rosa had forgotten to be a child. Looking at her across the dinner table, Bella was certain that the sadness in her eyes ached for those lost years.

"I hate to eat and run..." Bella started up.

"Then don't," Antonio replied.

"I have to. We have a curfew at our school. I had to get special permission to come here as it is."

"All right, if you must. But we'll see you again before we leave."

"Definitely. I'll talk to Jean Luc first thing tomorrow about your art, Rosa, and also about getting all of you a box for the trials."

"Grand," Antonio said.

They all stood up to kiss her goodbye. Bella had a knack for spreading goodwill among people. She left them sitting in the restaurant, finishing their espressos, feeling as happy about seeing her as she had been about seeing them.

279 | P a g e

CHAPTER FORTY-ONE

THE WOMAN'S DREAMS HAUNTED HER AGAIN: GHOULISH, distorted images holding her down while she screams and pleads for her life, but no one helps her. She can't see who the people are. All she knows is, they are evil, and all she sees in the nightmares are her face horrified that anyone would torture her in this way. Through it all, the only thing she can do is watch it unfold, nothing escaping her lips but whispered, weak whimpers.

Finally, she is being shaken back into reality. As her eyes slowly open, she realizes once more that the nightmare is over. Before her stands the Mother Superior, the nun's kind, worried eyes staring down at her on her small cot.

"Wake up, child," the older woman said in a soft voice. "You're only dreaming. Remember? You're safe here."

The woman knew the words Mother spoke were true. The convent and church were her safe haven and the place where she earned her living as a cook. For her to leave now and return home would mean nothing less than total destruction.

Drowsily, the woman the nuns called Susanna sat up, trying to smile at the mother superior who'd treated her better than anyone she could remember.

"Oh, my girl, I wish you didn't have those awful dreams."

"I'm all right, Mother. Please don't worry," Susanna replied, her hands shaking. "Please, I am fine. I'll wash up and make my way to the kitchen."

The older woman frowned.

"One day we must talk about what it is that chases you like a demon and tries to possess you so."

Susanna nodded. Mother Superior turned and walked from the room. Susanna knew there would never come a day when she could speak of the demons haunting her. To speak of them would bring back the past and so much of it Susanna couldn't remember, and knew in her soul that she didn't want to remember. To recount and remember the past would mean certain death for Susanna. No, Susanna liked it here in the convent in this small village in central Mexico where she could live her days in peace with the past buried, and where no one ever asked her for her real name.

CHAPTER FORTY-TWO

ALEX DIDN'T RETURN HOME THAT ENTIRE NIGHT. MARTA worried herself sick. She knew her son was hurting, and all she wanted to do was to find him. In the morning, she'd traveled throughout her neighborhood, trying to hunt him down. She hoped he would get over his anger soon, forgive her for not having years ago told him about his father, and for not taking him home. All she wanted was to talk to him, to try to make him understand why she'd done what she had to do.

She stopped by the corner market to get a soda and ask the grocer if he'd seen Alex anywhere. When he told her he hadn't, her sense of desperation deepened.

He'll come home today. He's a good boy. He's hurting right now, that's all, she kept telling herself, trying to take comfort from these thoughts. She looked down at a picture of him she'd taken from her wallet from his twelfth birthday party, and he was smiling, holding up the football she'd bought for him. He was so happy then. *He's such a special boy. I have to get him away from selling drugs.*

She was jolted out of these thoughts by the shrill screeching of brakes. The next few moments were nothing but a blur. Loud popping noises of gunfire sprayed the street, as a reckless blue Chevy halted in front of the market place. Marta stood in disbelief witnessing the atrocity. She saw a young boy hit the ground, the bullets tearing through him. Running to help, she heard one last shot. A teenager lurched out of the way of the bullet. The victim it captured was Marta. Time slipped into slow motion. She felt no real pain as she reached for her chest, the warmth of seeping blood covering her hands. The people, the street noises, her life spiraled into a motionless blur, as she sensed her life draining from her. Her son's face, his sweet sounding voice—his essence surrounded her. She needed him to know that she loved him. She could not leave him. Not like this! He needed her. Damn God for this. Damn Him! And although she cursed God knowing that she would never again hold her son in her arms, an incandescent peace draped over her—a warmth so brilliant that her desire to allow it to take over her entire body soon outweighed her need to remain on Earth and be Alejandro's mother.

****

ALEX HAD HEARD THE SCREECHING TIRES, THE GUNSHOTS and had been watching from an empty warehouse window at his mother all morning searching for him, still sulking and angry with her. He'd almost come down twice, but his anger hadn't subsided enough to talk to her. With those first round of gunshots he dashed out of the building to protect her, but he was too late.

Now she lay dying in his arms. Tears streamed down his face. "No, Mama. No," he sobbed.

She reached up with the palm of her hand and stroked his face, "I'm sorry, so sorry. She gasped for air. "I love you, Mijo," she struggled to say. Her body shuttered and then without any fight left went limp against her son.

"No! Mama! No! No!" Alex screamed as the only secure world he had ever known left him. He cradled her body, rocking her back and forth as she'd done with him for so many years. His entire being frantically willed her body to return to life, but she didn't move. His loving mother was gone.

*****

THE DAY THAT MARTA WAS BURIED WAS A TYPICAL Southern California day—warm and hazy. The funeral was attended only by Elisa, her family and a few of Marta's friends. Hector stood next to Alex, who hadn't uttered more than two words since his mother's death.

He couldn't believe she was gone. She was the only person in his life who truly loved and accepted him. She was loving, kind, and always understanding. She did everything for him. Listening to the priest, he heard him talk about what a good lady and mother she'd been. Images danced in Alex's mind of his mom playing with him when he was a small boy, kissing him and holding him when he felt hurt or sick. She'd stood by him no matter what, even when he wanted to change schools because the white kids had teased him so bad. He was so afraid of letting her down, but she'd soothe him and tell him whatever he needed to hear to make him happy.

And then the last night that he saw her alive, when she told him about his father, he'd been so angry and unforgiving. "Mama, please know I am so sorry. I never meant to hurt you. Forgive me, please forgive me," Alex whispered, tears rolling down his face onto his black suit sleeves. He didn't bother to wipe them away.

In despair Alex cried out as her coffin was lowered into the grave. "No, Mama! No, don't go. No!" He stepped forward and put his hands on the coffin, shaking his head, his body trembling. Several people tried to ease his pain by talking to him, asking him to let her go that she was now in a better place. The pain remained hot and paralyzing. The priest laid a hand on Alex and allowed him grieve over his mother until he'd exhausted himself. Then more loving hands quietly lifted him and walked him away from his mother's grave.

He didn't know what he would do now or where he would go. There was only one thing he knew for certain. He would find the man who had turned his mother into a wage slave and get his revenge. His mother would still be alive if the man who called himself his father had lived up to his end of the bargain, and provided for them so they wouldn't have had to live in the dregs of hell, where insane, angry people shot and killed on the slightest whim.

Alex would see to it that his father took responsibility. That man would pay for what had happened to his mother. This man, who had so cruelly deserted her, would pay for what he'd done. Alex would find him and see to it.

CHAPTER FORTY-THREE

DRIVEN BY HIS WIFE'S NAGGING AND HIS OWN URGENT NEED to get away, Javier offered to escort Miguel to San Rios. He thought he would also fly down from San Rios to Colombia and speak to Antonio about the idea of getting involved in the cocaine business. And he wanted to see whether Antonio had visited Bella while he was in Paris. He knew they'd recently arrived home and was anxious to hear all about their trip, especially any news regarding his daughter.

The pain of hearing about Bella's horse trials from Miguel still disturbed Javier. He'd drunk himself into a stupor afterwards. But Miguel and Pedro convinced him that drinking over his problems with Bella would do nothing to change things.

Miguel took the bottle away from him. "Go to her, Papa. Make peace. She loves you. God doesn't want either of you to be in such misery."

"You're right," Javier replied, slurring his words and glancing at Pedro and Miguel through glazed eyes. "That's exactly what I'm going to do. But first," he sighed, "I'm going to take you," he pointed at Miguel, "to the convent in San Rios."

"You don't have to do that, Papa."

"Shhh, now. Of course I do." He held up his hand in protest, and then leaned back in the chair. He closed his eyes and murmured something about Carlotta having destroyed his relationship with his daughter. Miguel was certain he'd heard his stepfather say, "That fat, dumb bitch." The sad thing was that Miguel could understand Javier's feelings, and couldn't really blame him for them.

*****

JAVIER PEERED INTO MIGUEL'S ROOM, SEEING HIM HUG HIS mother goodbye. She was on her way to visit the newest spa in the Caribbean. She turned around, smiling her artificial smile at Javier. He smiled back at her with the knowledge that it had been arranged for Carlotta to suffer a massive heart attack while sitting inside a heated sauna that horrifyingly enough would become too hot for anybody to withstand.

"Are you ready?" Javier asked Miguel.

"In a minute, I have a few more things to pack."

"All right. Pedro and I will start putting our things in the car."

"Have a nice trip, dear," Carlotta said as she kissed her son on the cheek. "And don't let your father drink too much, worrying about his spoiled Isabella."

"All right, Mama." Miguel shook his head as she turned around to leave the room and shrugged his shoulders.

Javier no doubt didn't blame Miguel for his mother's shortcomings. The boy would certainly be saddened by the loss of his mother, but in the long run he would be far better off without her.

"Drive carefully," she told Javier as she passed by him.

"Of course," he replied. He walked over to the edge of Miguel's bed to zip up his duffle. "Have a wonderful trip yourself."

*****

SUSANNA SAT IN THE DARK. SHE'D FINISHED CLEANING UP after supper and the cool air had the tendency to relax her troubled spirit. The church and courtyard were beautiful. The church was built of stone, and the courtyard had a water fountain where birds drank their fill and perched on the sides to warm themselves during the day. Trellises lined this side of the church where ivy grew and honeysuckle flowers sprouted from large clay planters. The honeysuckle was orange and yellow and she loved watching the hummingbirds buzz into the long tube of the flower for its nectar. Comfort was where she was now. Secure comfort—and although her painful past weaved in and out of her memories regularly, she was able to let much of it go while listening to the water fountain and gazing out onto the desert-type mountains as the sun's last rays cast a silvery glow onto them.

She spotted headlights approaching along the winding road down the mountain. Yes, changes were coming—as much change as there could possibly be in this little convent nestled against the foothills of San Rios.

She knew that since Father Frances had passed away and Father Juan had replaced him, they had been looking for an intern to take Father Juan's place, as he was being requested by a larger church in Mexico City. She figured that the visitors pulling into the convent must be bringing the new intern. Rumor had it that he came from a wealthy family. She could make out three men taking bags out of the trunk. Father Juan and Mother Superior walked into the courtyard to greet them.

"No, thank you. We'll go into town and stay at the hotel," Susanna heard one of the men say. Something about his voice sounded familiar. The three men hugged one another and said their goodbyes.

Susanna watched the Mercedes pull away. After that, she decided to retire to her quarters. She took the long way on the cobblestone pathway, hoping to run into Father Juan, Mother, and the new priest.

Walking down the hall, she passed right by the three. "Ah, Susanna. We'd like you to meet Father Miguel Diaz. He'll be interning with us."

The young man smiled at her. He had such dimples that could not only melt the hearts of grandmothers, but grandfathers as well. Susanna knew the congregation would approve. His eyes were full of passion, the kind she had rarely seen—not reserved for women, but for something more holy. It was a shame, though. She blushed at this thought and felt guilty. Those kinds of feelings hadn't stirred inside her in years.

Susanna lay in her bed that night feeling restless. Her peaceful world had gone through a sudden change, by a glance from a handsome young stranger. She reminded herself of what had happened the last time she'd allowed lust to overpower her. God would certainly condemn her for such unclean thoughts about the unsuspecting young priest.

She closed her eyes and tried to go to sleep. In the distance, she heard again the voice of the man she'd heard earlier, the man who had dropped off Father Miguel. Her sleep was haunted by that voice until she opened her eyes to the early light.

CHAPTER FORTY-FOUR

THE FACT THAT THE COFFEE CROPS WEREN'T PULLING IN what they should have pulled in during the past months disturbed Antonio. They had plummeted to a new low over the last few weeks while he and the girls were vacationing in Europe. The States were going through a serious inflation, causing his profits to decrease, and all his mental wrestling had not presented a solution to the problem.

Antonio hoped Javier had some ideas. He and Pedro were due to arrive at any moment. Antonio arose from his desk chair and paced the hardwood floors. Not only did the decline in profits irk him, but handling the delicate issue of Isabella with Javier was also gnawing at him. Javier had made it quite clear from the time she was a baby that issues concerning Bella were no one's business but his own. Antonio had respected that through the years, even when Carlotta insisted on sending Bella away. Antonio disagreed with that decision, and knew the effect it would have on his goddaughter.

As he pondered this new situation, he heard a slight knock on the study door. "Come in, come in!" Pedro and Javier were ushered into his study by the butler. "I'm so glad to see you both." The three men shook hands and then embraced. "Did you see Miguel off to the convent?"

"My son—the priest—is settled," Javier replied.

"Good. Can I get either of you a drink?" They both declined. "All right, then. Let's get business out of the way. I have tickets to the opera tonight, but first, I thought we could go out for a nice dinner."

"Excellent," Javier replied.

"Is that safe? I've heard the streets around here have become quite violent these days," Pedro said.

"My dear boy, do you really think anyone is going to attempt to kill any of us? Are you kidding? I *am* this city. The people around here need me. They worship me. However, they will not for long, if I don't start generating a larger cash flow. It appears that, with inflation in the United States, the price of our coffee and other goods is becoming so expensive that it has been necessary to lay off workers. We need to find a way to make more money. Any suggestions?"

"I *do* have an idea," Javier said hesitantly.

"Go on."

"Cocaine."

"I don't think so, Javier. I'm beginning to get tired of our illegal trade. It's not so cheap to pay off Immigration and the police any longer. Besides, I understand the *federales* are coming down harder than usual at the checkpoints. Emilio called this morning to tell me that a large shipment of marijuana had been confiscated. Needless to say, I wasn't happy to hear it."

"I'm aware of the situation. I've already got someone looking into that for us. But listen to me. What little extra expense it costs us to keep the *federales* quiet will be made up in the quantity of sales we'll be doing. Antonio, we have the means to grow prosperous crops. I say that this is our ticket to taking over where the Italians left off."

"We can never play their game."

"No, but maybe we can play *with* them. Rumor has it that Tarrantino wants to make some kind of deal with us."

"I don't want to take on new partners—not after the Levine fiasco. The only reason none of us ever wound up dead after that was because the little mother had cultivated so many enemies, no one really gave a care. It's another thing with the wops. They're a lot like us when it comes to loyalty. Even if they hate the man in the hot seat, they'll blow your brains out if you look at 'em cross eyed."

"So we don't go with the Italians. But I'm telling you, Antonio, there is enough in this white powder business to go around. You, me, and the Italians have no need to step on each other's toes. I say it's worth a shot, unless you have any better ideas."

"What do you think, Pedro?"

"I'm with Javier."

"Of course," Antonio mumbled. "Fine. I respect your ideas. I'll think about this carefully."

"That's all we're asking."

"Good. Now there is something else we need to talk about."

"What is that?"

"Isabella."

"Bella? You saw her when you were in France, didn't you?"

"I did."

"How is she?"

"Beautiful and smart as ever. Did you know about her important horse trials in Italy next month? Doing well in them will mean she will only be closer to her dream of going to the Olympics. She believes that she could go to Barcelona in '92. "

"I did hear about it."

"Do you want to explain why you didn't respond to her invitation? She's very hurt."

Javier's mouth flew open. "What? She hasn't called or written in over a month."

"Not true, according to her. She says that not only did she write, but she also phoned while you were away. Carlotta told her that the two of you were going to visit Stefan during that time, because he's playing in some sort of soccer tournament."

"That crazy bitch. She's done it again—put another wedge between my daughter and me. I tell you, I've had it with her."

"What are you going to do?" Pedro asked, glancing between Antonio and Javier.

"It's not what I'm going to do. I've already had the problem taken care of. I understand that the spa she's visiting has had problems with the steam room."

"That's a shame," Antonio said.

295 | P a g e

"Yes it is. Expect to attend the funeral, gentlemen, sometime next week, and then I am going to go to Italy to see my daughter at her event and to heal from the loss of my wife."

"That's the best idea you've had in quite some time," Antonio chuckled.

After the situation with Carlotta was taken care of, and Javier returned from Italy, he planned to bring Stefan home and start being a loyal father again. He only hoped it wasn't too late.

*****

AS THE THREE MEN LEFT THE STUDY AND WALKED

separately to their quarters, Pedro felt elated that Antonio had asked him his opinion. Of course, Pedro would never go against what Javier wanted, but it felt good all the same.

Pedro walked through the garden to the guesthouse, and he caught sight of a striking young woman glancing through a magazine by the pool. At first, he didn't realize who it was. Then he took a second look and recognized Felicia. He'd never paid much attention to either of Antonio's girls before. He was always too busy with Javier's business. But seeing her for the first time in this light, Pedro couldn't help staring at her.

She must have felt his eyes on her. Felicia looked up, and their gaze met. "Pedro?" she asked.

"Hello, Felicia. How are you?"

"Good. Come here and sit down," she said, patting the seat next to her.

Pedro had had plenty of women over the years, but there had only been one he even remotely considered becoming serious with, and she'd left him after he made it quite clear that his business came first and always would. But this creature, although far too young for him, was so gorgeous that he knew he had to have her. The obstacle would be Antonio.

"You'll be going to the opera with us this evening. No?" she asked.

"Yes, I believe so."

"Excellent. I love the opera, don't you?"

"I do."

"I mean, it's so romantic and full of drama."

"It is." He smiled.

"I suppose I should start getting ready," she said. She stood and wrapped a colorful sarong around her bikini. She turned around and winked at him as she headed for the house.

Pedro fell back into the lounge chair, letting out a loud sigh. He knew this was one woman not soon forgotten.

*****

THE WARM WATER FELT GOOD ON ANTONIO'S SKIN as he showered for the evening's festivities, thinking that perhaps Javier's suggestion about the cocaine business was not such a bad idea after all. He really wasn't interested in getting more involved in the distribution of drugs. Yet he knew that going legitimate was impossible. He hadn't even been able to do it for the one woman he'd never stopped loving.

Antonio wished he'd insisted on being a part of Alejandro's life. Now Alejandro would be a young man. Even if Antonio decided to come back into his son's life, would Alejandro let him? After all, the boy believed his father was dead. Marta had seen to that. The thought broke his heart each time it came to mind.

He dressed, noticing his reflection in the mirror. Age had set in around his eyes, and his hair loss had become more prevalent in recent years. He hated the idea of getting old, and growing old alone sounded even worse. But he would be damned before he would beg Marta to come back to him, especially after all this time.

"Papa, the car is out front," Felicia yelled into his room.

"Be right there."

As they moved into the back seat of the limousine, Antonio noticed his youngest daughter's low-cut red dress. Rosa at least had the good sense to wear something elegant, black and simple. But Felicia looked to be flaunting. He wanted to yell at her to go back into the house and change. However, it was not worth the shame he knew that would cause her.

Antonio also observed that Pedro's eyes kept resting on his youngest daughter. He would make certain he spoke to Javier about reminding this renegade adopted son of his to stay away from Felicia. Throughout dinner Antonio remained quiet, watching the interaction between these two. They were flirting, but not so overtly that anyone would notice, except an overly protective father.

"I almost forgot, Antonio," Javier said. "This letter came for you to my house this week." Javier pulled a small envelope out of his coat pocket.

"Why would someone send your mail to Javier's house?" Rosa asked.

Antonio fumbled for an answer, knowing there was only one reason anyone would send his mail to Javier's. It would have to be from Marta. "Maybe they lost our address and know how close I am with Javier," he replied.

Rosa looked at him queerly, eyebrows raised. Antonio stuck the letter inside his coat. "Aren't you going to read it, Papa?"

"No, not now. It's time to go."

Once they had taken their seats inside the opera house, Antonio excused himself, retreating to the lobby. He pulled the letter from his coat pocket, and with trembling hands, looked for the return address. There was none. His heart sank once he opened it and read the contents of the letter. While his eyes scanned the handwritten words, tears fell down his cheeks.

Dear Señor Espinoza,

I am so sorry to bother you, but I thought you should know. I was a very close friend of Marta Peña and I'm your son's Godmother. I feel it is my duty to inform you of the sad events that have taken place in the last month concerning Marta and Alejandro.

Antonio could read no further after seeing the words "shot and killed." He felt a bullet of pain pierce his own heart, leaving it empty.

CHAPTER FORTY-FIVE

PEDRO'S MIND RACED WITH THOUGHTS OF WHAT FELICIA'S father would do if he discovered the two of them in bed together. Pedro would savor the memory of the previous night for a long time. He discovered, after returning from the opera, that Felicia was talented at more than putting on makeup and fixing her hair.

"Good morning," she whispered as she sat up in bed, her tousled hair dangling seductively around her face. "How are you?" She curled the small hairs on his chest around a finger.

"I'm fine," he replied. He kissed the top of her head, pressed against his chest. "I'd be better, though, if your father's face didn't keep haunting me."

"Don't you worry about Papa. By now, he's already gone over his figures, taken his morning walk through the fields, and smacked a couple of maids on the rear. I'll handle my father."

She slid down Pedro's body. Before he could protest, she moved her tongue along his engorging shaft in a slow, deliberate pattern. His fingers entwined in her hair, playing with it in order to keep from reaching orgasm too quickly. He yearned to prolong this pleasure as long as he could.

"Don't stop," he cried out as she lifted her head up and looked at him. "Please," he begged. She winked as she straddled him. His hands fondled her full breasts, her nipples soon erect to his touch. She moaned in ecstasy. She bent over him so that he could lick and suck all the more easily. As he did, her slow movements became more rapid. Pedro couldn't take much more. Not wanting it to end, he rolled her over and now was in control, holding her hands down against the mattress. "Shhh," he whispered. Aching to kiss every part of her, he tenderly placed his lips on her body beginning with her forehead, moving to her ears, her lips, arms and shoulders, fingers, stomach, legs and feet.

She stretched her body out, enjoying this prolonged and delicate attention. For the first time in Felicia's young life, a man wanted to please her. Most of the men she'd been with—boys, really—had expected her to do all the work. She felt that if there was such a thing as love on this godforsaken earth, she'd found it right here with Pedro's mouth, which was now probing her center of pleasure.

With his tongue, he did the equivalent of what she'd already done to him. He moved it across her moist skin while his hands played with her breasts. As he did so, Felicia found herself in an erotic heaven she never thought possible. Unable to delay her climax any longer, she exploded, laughing and crying at the same time.

Pedro smiled at the angel beneath him, this angel full of so much devilment.

"Oh, no, you don't," she said. "We're not through."

"What do you mean?"

"You know what I mean."

"No, I don't," he replied, wearing a smirk on his golden face.

"Yes, you do." Felicia pushed him back down on the bed.

"Now, I think we've had enough for one day, don't you? I'm certain Javier and Antonio will be wondering where I am by now."

"I'm the boss here, and you're not finished."

"Really?" Pedro teased her.

"Really." She again took him in her mouth and he gave up the fight, knowing she was right. It took only a matter of minutes for him to reach completion. Sated, they lay together.

"Now hurry and get out of here. I've got to figure out what I'm going to say to the Patróns about why I slept in so late."

"When will you be back?"

"I'm not sure. But I will be back," he replied as he walked past her on his way to the shower, smacking her bare bottom.

She laughed, throwing on the jeans and sweatshirt she'd worn to the guesthouse the night before—under the guise of going for a midnight stroll along the beach. She'd feared her incessantly nosy sister would find her and question her. "Goodbye," she said, peeking into the shower at Pedro. He was not at all boyish, like so many of the men she'd already been with. His slightly rugged face contained a wisdom Felicia longed to attain. Everyone thought of her as the dumb, pretty one, and Rosa as the intelligent, creative one. She decided that morning that Pedro was the perfect man for her in every way. Regardless of the fight her father would give her, she was going to make Pedro Torres hers and only hers. No one would stand in her way.

CHAPTER FORTY-SIX

ORANGE AND YELLOW LEAVES FELL FROM BRANCHES OF THE elm trees outside the convent. Susanna felt the crispness of the autumn air as she washed down the front patio, humming a hymn from that morning's mass. Since Father Miguel had come to the convent, her spirits had risen dramatically. He spoke about the Lord with a fervor she'd never experienced before.

The two had become friends in the three weeks since his arrival. They visited often, speaking of important passages from the Bible, and discussing their meanings. As Father Miguel spoke, Susanna would often dream about her youth, knowing that if she were the same girl she'd been fifteen years earlier, Father Miguel wouldn't be serving the Lord now.

"Susanna," the deep voice resounded behind her. She felt herself blush as she rose from her knees on the rough stones.

"Oh, hello, Father," she answered.

"I wanted to let you know that Evening Mass has been changed this evening. I'm moving it up to five o'clock instead of six. I'm expecting a phone call tonight from my sister in France. She usually calls around six-thirty."

"All right, Father. Thank you. Are you and your sister close?"

"Yes. Bella and I call each other weekly, taking turns. The calls usually don't interfere with Mass, but last week she said that her horse trainer had changed her training to an earlier time, so now she phones before she rides."

"She's an equestrienne, then?"

"Yes, and a good one too. She'll be riding in a major horse trials in a couple of weeks. She hopes to make the Olympic team for Barcelona."

"Are you going to her event?"

"I wish I could, but I'm needed here. She knows how much I want her to win, but it will be televised, so I'll be able to watch it in my room."

Relieved that he wasn't going to be leaving, Susanna replied, "I would love to watch it as well."

"Of course, you're more than welcome to join me."

"Thank you, Father."

They both turned around as the sound of Mother Superior's voice rang out, echoing through the open corridor. "Father, it's urgent. It's your father. He's on the telephone."

"Javier?"

"Yes. You must come now."

Susanna watched as Father Miguel followed Mother Superior up to the office of the church where he could take the phone call. The pace of her heart quickened. Had she heard Father Miguel call his father "Javier?" No. It could not be. And Father Miguel's sister— Bella? Bella Rodriguez? Javier and Cynthia's daughter? Impossible. The night that Father was brought to the convent rushed back to her, when she was certain she'd recognized the voice of one of the men dropping him off, but no, it could not be. Father Miguel's last name was Diaz. She said a silent prayer that her past was not catching up with her.

CHAPTER FORTY-SEVEN

EMILIO OPENED THE DOOR TO HIS BROTHER'S OFFICE.
"You wanted to see me?"

Antonio sighed. "Yes."

Antonio looked haggard. His eyes drooping, bags underneath them. He was slouched over in his chair. "I did."

"Here I am."

"Sit down."

There was a tone in Antonio's voice, Emilio had never heard before—sad—not quite sad, more beaten than anything. Emilio sat. "You're worrying me,"

"I have to go to Mexico again. Carlotta had a heart attack and is dead."

"This is what's upsetting you? That witch that Javier married is dead and you're upset by it?"

Antonio shook his head and waved his hand. "I could care less about her. Out of respect for my friend, I will attend her funeral and normally I would request that you make an appearance as well.

308 | P a g e

However, I have something far more important for you to do, and because of this situation with Javier and because I am still planning on leaving for Italy next week, I have to ask you to take care of this."

"Of course. What is it?"

Antonio stood and walked over to the bar in the corner of the room and made himself a drink. He swallowed it all before pouring another one and then sitting back down where he set his drink on the desk and placed his hands folded in front of him. He seemed to choose his words carefully as he started to speak slowly. "Have you ever been in love?"

"What?"

"I would guess that you have not. However, I have loved not only once with my whole heart to Lydia, but there was also another love in my life." He sighed. "A very powerful love."

"You've had many women, I'm sure." Emilio was sourly thrown back to that painful memory of witnessing Antonio take his beloved Marianna. "Why are you telling me this?"

"I have done many horrible things, and there is still time for me to make some of them right."

"Jesus, Antonio, you sound like a wounded woman." Emilio knew he was pushing it by speaking to his brother this way, but he wanted to slap the man. He was usually so strong. Was *El Patrón* breaking for some reason? Was he losing his mind? If so, Emilio would be able to take it all over with ease.

"No, I am a wounded man and there are things that need to be done and I'm telling you what those things are."

Emilio waited, not knowing what to say.

"This other woman that I loved died recently."

"Sorry." This was so strange. Emilio shifted uneasily in his chair.

"This woman had my son."

Emilio gasped and fell back into his chair as if he'd been punched. "What did you say?"

"I have a son. His name is Alejandro Peña and he lives in Los Angeles." Antonio handed him a piece of paper. "His address is in there. You are to go there and check on him. Make certain he is all right and keep an eye on him for awhile until you hear back from me."

"Excuse me? I don't understand."

Antonio raised his voice finally. "You don't have to understand. What you have to do is go and check on my son, and leave it at that. He's lost his mother and all I want to do right now is make certain that he is all right. After that, I'll figure out what to do."

"How old is this boy?" Emilio asked.

"Almost twenty."

Another gasp. "I see. Fine." Emilio took the address and walked out the door. He made it to his Maserati and slammed his hands against the wheel. Antonio had a son? *Antonio had a son.* With this news, Emilio knew he would have to find a way to use this boy—this Alejandro Peña—to help him destroy his brother, because he wouldn't allow some bastard prodigy his brother now seemed to want to claim, to disrupt his plans to become *El Patrón*.

****

EMILIO LIKED LOS ANGELES: THE NIGHTCLUBS WERE GREAT, drugs were abundant, and women crawled all over him. He'd been partying for a few nights and had heard through the grapevine that his brother was trying to locate him. *Fuck Antonio.* But he knew that Antonio would track him down if he didn't report back to him before too long.

Emilio believed strongly that he would still be the *Patrón* and run the entire operation one day, and that day would come soon. His mind was already working on how the kid might be manipulated into being of great service to his own plans.

He drove past the address his brother had given him. "Down and out in little Tijuana," he muttered through the blasting sounds coming from the rented limousine's loudspeakers.

He decided to ask around about the kid and see if he could dig up any information. The first couple of places where he stopped were markets, and no one wanted to give him the time of day. The people he came across were poor Mexicans, who didn't like this rich guy coming around.

He finally pulled the limousine over to a group of young men, standing on a street corner. They all glared at him as he pulled up and got out.

"Hey *ése*, what you want round here?" one kid asked him. "You want some weed, man?"

"No way man. This dude, he want some blow, don't you?" another kid asked.

"Actually, I'm looking for a guy," Emilio replied.

"Hey, man, I guess we can't help you then."

Emilio pulled out a wad of cash. At the same time, he flashed the gun he carried in his holster. The young men looked at each other.

"You ain't no cop, is you, cuz?"

"No, I'm not the police. I'm looking for an old friend."

"Who you lookin' for?"

"A kid named Alejandro Peña." Emilio could see in their eyes that the name registered.

"What you want with Alex, *ése*?"

"I wanna talk to him."

"He ain't available to be talking to. If you wanna talk to Alex, you gotta talk to me first."

"Is that so?" Emilio was feeling out the punk kid, not too sure how far he could push him. His instincts told him not to push too hard while all his buddies were still around.

"Yeah, man, so what's it gonna be? Either you talk to me or take a hike."

"Can we go for a drive and talk?"

"Oh, sure man. Like I'm gonna get in your car. What you think, I'm crazy or sometin'? No way, *ése*."

"My business with Alejandro is private. I wouldn't want to embarrass him by talking in front of his amigos." Emilio could see the kid's doubt. He was looking him over again, full of suspicion.

"I dunno who you think you talkin' to, man. But me and Alex are big people 'round here. I ain't talkin' to you no more. You had your chance. I don't like your business. I think you'd be a smart guy if you got the fuck out of here 'fore my friends and I have to mess you up or sometin'."

Emilio put his hand over the revolver inside his jacket. He wanted to shoot this little smartass then and there, right in front of his amigos. But he knew he needed this punk to lead him to Antonio's son.

"No problem, *amigo*. I'm leaving," He announced, slowly backing away and walking around to the side of his car.

*****

"HEY MAN, THERE WAS THIS GUY LOOKIN' FOR YOU TODAY," Hector told Alejandro.

"Oh, yeah, who?" Alex mumbled, not looking up at his friend. He was reading through a book of poems his mother used to read to him when he was a little boy. She'd been dead nearly a month, and his pain was as sharp as the day he watched her die. Elisa had begged him to move in with them and stay for a while, but he really hadn't felt like living with anyone. Besides, he couldn't bear to part with the home in which he was raised. It still contained so many memories of his mother that at times he would pretend she wasn't dead, but on a vacation somewhere. She always talked about taking a trip. Maybe that's where she really was, and this was a terrible nightmare.

"Didn't you hear me, man? I said some rich guy was out looking for you today. You in some trouble I don't know 'bout?"

"No, I have no idea who it would be. Probably a mistake or something."

"No way, this guy wanted you. Don't worry though, I didn't tell him nothing."

"What do you think he wanted?"

"I dunno, said it was important. Maybe he wanna make a big deal or something. You know, *ése*, we big men round here now. Word is getting out."

"I doubt it. Besides, I think I want out." Alex couldn't help the nagging guilt he still felt over his mother's death. If only she had known that he wasn't angry with her before she died. But she hadn't known, and he'd been so cruel to her the night before. God, he hoped she knew how sorry he was. He missed her so much. Money didn't matter to him the way it did before she was killed. Buying a mansion for himself didn't hold the same appeal without her around.

"You what? You crazy or something? We're starting to make some cash. You can't back out now. No way. Besides, you gotta pay the rent somehow, and you ain't gonna do it flipping burgers at McDonald's."

Hector had a point. He also wanted to continue saving enough money to go to college, in hopes of making restitution for the pain he'd caused his mother. "Yeah, maybe so. It's my mother, though. She wanted more for me, you know? She's probably tossing in her grave, knowing what we been doing this past year."

"I don't mean your mama no disrespect or anything like that, but she's gone. There's nothing you can do, and we both know she'd want you to make it. If we keep it up, we're *gonna* make it, man, both of us—like we talked 'bout. Besides, we don't sell nothing to our own kind. We ain't poisoning our families, only the *gringos*, blacks, and whoever else wants a piece—as long as it ain't our own."

Hector was right about that. In a way, it made sense. Poison the rest of the world, but keep their own people straight, and one day they would rule—the Hispanic nation would rule. "Maybe you're right."

"Yeah, I'm right and you know it, too. You'll see man. I guarantee this guy today was looking to score big. Our man Jay may have turned him onto us."

"He hasn't said anything to me about it."

"Hey amigo, I know it's been rough lately. Someone could talk shit to you and you wouldn't notice."

"I know. You think this man will come back again looking for me?" Alex was intrigued by the prospect of a big spender out to make a deal with him. Maybe they were becoming more powerful than he'd realized.

"Yeah man, he'll be back. He'll definitely be back. This guy was looking to score big, and he had the cash to do it with."

"Then why didn't he just talk to you?" Alex asked closing his book and walking over to get a Coke out of the fridge.

"I dunno. You the smart one. Maybe he hear you the business man in our game—and he look all biz, you know—so maybe he figure he better talk to you."

"Whatever," Alex replied.

"Whatever? You wait, *ése*, I got a feeling this thing with this moneybags is gonna be real good for us. Real good."

"Like I said, amigo, whatever." Alex gulped down the rest of his Coke, wondering about the mysterious moneyman.

*****

EMILIO SPOTTED THEM FROM A BLOCK AWAY. IT WAS THE smartass, and the other one had to be Alejandro. They were laughing and pushing each other from side to side, kicking a can down the trash-ridden street, looking pretty much like best friends. Emilio had been following Smart Ass for a day now, knowing he would eventually lead him to the kid.

"Follow those kids," he told the driver of the limo. "When they stop, you stop and don't move again until they're both in the car." Emilio glanced at his bodyguard and occasional assailant. Rico didn't smile, but then again he never did. He hardly ever spoke, but he was useful at what he did.

The limo pulled up next to the boys. They were pointing at it, laughing about who might be inside. "Hey, maybe it's *Dinero*," Alex commented.

"No way, it's that *Charlie's Angels* chick. You know the hot one with the hair. She come looking for me. You know she hear I'm real good and everythin'."

"Who, Farrah Fawcett?"

"Yeah, that's the chick. She's so foxy." Hector whistled at the limo.

"You wish."

"You know it, man. You know and I know it ain't Farrah Fawcett. It's that guy lookin' for you."

They stopped. Emilio rolled the window down halfway. He leaned back in the seat so the boys couldn't get a look at his face and stuck a double-barreled, sawed off shotgun out of the cracked window.

"Get in the car," he ordered in his husky voice. He could see the boys look at each other, paralyzed by fear. "If you don't want to die right here in this sewer, you'll get the fuck in the car."

The driver stepped out and opened the limousine side door. The boys' mouths dropped wide open. Looking at the giant, they didn't waste any time scrambling to get inside the car, even though their instincts told them both to run like hell. It was pretty clear that the guy's threat was no bluff.

Alex was not the kind of man to have his nerves shaken up, but he broke into a nervous sweat. Who was this guy and what did he want? Alex had never ridden in a limousine. It smelled like new leather and alcohol. There was a small bar, and the guy with the gun had a drink in his other hand. He wore dark sunglasses and didn't say a word, his lips pursed together, his hair back in a tight ponytail as slick as his black suit. Unable to see his eyes, Alex wondered what he was looking at. He didn't think the man wanted to kill them. If he'd wanted to do that, he would've done it while they were on the street. Why go through this huge ritual of getting them inside the car? He wondered if Jay had something to do with this. He was the only one Alex knew with enough cash to rent a limo. But why? Why would he do that? Unless he wanted to screw him and Hector over. But for him to do that he would have had to meet with their connection, and that probably hadn't happened.

"Like a drink?" the man asked, reaching for a glass. His fingernails were long and polished to the point of being borderline feminine, and Alex wondered if he was possibly a homosexual who'd kidnapped them for a good time. He shifted slightly in his seat.

"No, thank you. What I want to know is what we're doing here," Alex said, tired of this man's game. The man didn't speak for a couple of minutes and Alex wondered if he had made him angry. Alex looked at Hector who'd lost all color in his face and hadn't moved since they'd gotten into the car.

"I have a business proposition for you."

"Really? And what is that?"

"I've been watching you. Heard a lot of good things about you. I understand your business and I think together we could make a lot of money."

"What business?" Alex asked.

"Let's not play head games, amigo. I am a very busy man."

"How do I know you're not a cop?"

"How many cops you know drive around in limos?"

"Why do you want to make a deal with us? There's gotta be a lot more guys out there bigger than we are."

"True, but I like you. You're one of us. You don't sell to your own kind, at least this is what I've heard."

"You hear correctly, but where do you get your information?" Alex still wasn't too comfortable with the man and especially the gun sitting on his lap.

"I've got a lot of friends, and I'd like you two to join the ranks of our organization."

"What organization?"

"Allow me to introduce myself. My name is Emilio Espinoza. My brother is the one and only Antonio Espinoza."

Alex recognized the name. He knew the man was major in the coffee and emerald business. He'd also heard the name passed around in circles involving drugs. Somebody at one point told him if they wanted to get into doing some big-time business then they would need to get involved in the Espinoza clan. But he also heard that it was a difficult thing to break into the family ranks.

"I have heard of you." Alex tried to sound unimpressed.

The man chuckled. "You've heard of us. We are only one of the most powerful families in Central and South America. We do huge business in various degrees with the United States and portions of Europe."

"What type of business?" Alex interrupted.

"As if you didn't know. My brother and I have heard some things about you and your small but profitable business. We'd like to help you grow, and in return we make a nice amount as well. What do you think?"

"I don't know what to think. I'm not sure what you're asking of us."

"We want you to distribute for us in Los Angeles. It's gotten to be too much work to do by myself. I'm constantly flying back and forth from here to the Bahamas and to Colombia. We have a very lucrative gambling business in the South Pacific that is requiring more of my attention. Business is booming and I'm finding I don't have the time to do it all. I did a little investigating and decided you gentlemen would be perfect for the job. I like dealing with my own kind. I figure brothers in culture are less likely to screw each other than brothers in nothing at all."

"What do you want us to distribute?"

"A little of this, a little of that. We have some large crops of Acapulco Gold growing in the Andes, and we're getting involved in the coca business."

"Cocaine?" Alex asked.

"You got it. I know you are a little young and have a lot to learn, but that's not an obstacle. I want to prove to you I'm serious. Like I already said, I've checked you out and I know what you'd be good at. Alejandro, my friend, you have a head for business. I can feel it, see it. Here's ten thousand dollars. I want you to take it, buy some nice clothes on Rodeo Drive. I think once you learn something about finance, you'll be a major asset to us."

The man handed him ten thousand dollars, in one hundred dollar bills. Alex stared at the money. He'd never in his life held that much money in his hand. The most he'd held at one time was a thousand because any profit they'd made was turned around and put back into the business. Hector nudged Alex.

"And of course I couldn't forget about you, Hector. My guardsman." Hector moved in his seat a little. "That's right, boys. In the type of business we're involved in, and the quantities we'll be dealing with, we're going to need a militia crew. And it will be up to you, Hector, to manage and train them. Most of these men will be young like yourselves. They will be illegals and brought over here. You will give them a job on the street peddling and finding various contacts. They will also help move the drugs into the States through various means. Alex will then learn how to launder money through legit businesses. I know you have a friend over at USC, named Jay. I've checked him out, and his family is in the jewelry business. We'll see if we can't set up something with him. But I don't want anyone to do anything without my permission. Do we have a deal?" Emilio handed Hector an equal amount of cash. "Get rid of that mustache, too. We're professionals, not gangsters."

Hector rubbed the skinny mustache he'd been trying to grow for months, his face flushed from embarrassment.

"What do we get out of it?" Alex asked, trying to put the money out of his mind and get to the facts.

"A nice place to live, women, money, power, whatever you want. Can you handle it?"

"I think so."

"Good." Emilio shook Alex's hand and then Hector's, who was smiling, dumbfounded. "Now, here's your new address. I think you boys will be happy there. Don't worry about the rent. It's already been taken care of. You'll both be provided with cars as well, so I suggest if you don't have driver's licenses, you look into it. Here is my private line while I'm in Los Angeles. If you need anything, I mean anything—money, clothes, whatever, you call me." Emilio removed his glasses and his brown eyes gleamed at the canary he knew he'd just swallowed. Staring at Antonio's son with his plan already set into motion, Emilio knew it was only a matter of time before the empire was his.

The boy looked a lot like Antonio—a good-looking young man— definitely from the Espinoza lineage. He loved the idea of using the kid to destroy Antonio.

CHAPTER FORTY-EIGHT

ANXIETY PUMPED ADRENALINE THROUGH ISABELLA'S BODY.
She and Delilah were in Italy for the horse trials that would be their ticket onto the Olympic Equestrian Team for France. Their dressage test had been nearly flawless two days earlier, and yesterday's stadium jumping had gone well. She'd had neither time nor technical faults.

However, the cross country course was difficult and she was a bit worried. She and Jean Luc had walked it a few times, and if she was honest with herself, there were some technical questions out there that she needed to think through, in order to make the right decisions. Jumps 18, 19, and 20 were three ditches with a bounce in between each one. The last ditch was well over six feet wide, and then there was the drop that was also over six feet. Yes, she'd practiced and worked up to this for years. Yes, her horse was capable. Delilah lived for the open course, but Bella's nerves were beginning to eat away at her. This was her opportunity, and she could not screw it up.

Her father and Stefan had arrived three nights earlier. She hadn't had much chance to visit with them, but there seemed to be an

understanding that the conflict between them was over. She'd told
her father that she was sorry she couldn't make it home for
Carlotta's funeral, which had been held only days earlier. Bella
couldn't exactly say that she felt terrible over the loss of her
stepmother, but she did feel awful for both her brothers, especially
for Miguel. At least for Stefan, he never really knew his mother
anyway. The child had been handed off to a wet nurse, from what
Isabella had heard, almost immediately after his birth. Since Bella
had seen the child over the past couple of days, he hadn't even
mentioned his mother. Bella was working on her sign language in
order to communicate better with her younger brother.

She had spoken to Miguel, who told her that her mother's funeral
was light on guests and over with quickly and quietly. He said that he
couldn't stay away from his church for long and that his mother
wanted nothing more of him than to become a priest with a
congregation, and by returning within days to the church he would
be abiding by her wishes. Bella knew her brother well enough to
know he was hurting and she wished she could be with him. Aware
of his pain, she would succeed in these trials that she knew he would
by watching and hopefully ease his heart.

"You ready, *ma chérie?*" Jean Luc asked, walking into the dressing
area as Bella finished buttoning up her rat-catcher.

She stood in front of the mirror and fastened bobby pins into her
hair. "Ready," she replied.

Jean Luc held her helmet in his hands. He put his arms around
Bella, his protégée, before they walked to the stalls where Delilah

awaited—as polished as Bella and very nearly as anxious. The horse seemed to understand that this was a bigger deal than normal.

"Now, eyes up. Whatever you do, don't look down," Jean Luc instructed.

"Listen to you," Bella replied. "You sound as if you're talking to a beginner."

"I know. I am so sorry. You'll be fine. Just remember when we walked the course that you need to half halt before that bank. Once she gets a head of steam on her, she can be unruly. You know this."

"Jean Luc, I've walked that course every day now for the past five days. I've played it in my head over and over again. I've dreamt the strides. I've counted the steps, everything. I've done the technical questions over and over and the pacing. It's all right here." She tapped the side of her head, hoping she was as convincing as she sounded.

"All right, I know, I know. You and the mare will be brilliant as always, *chérie*."

They reached the barn. Delilah stood in the crossties waiting for her. Already saddled, Jean Luc reached for her bridle, undid her halter and slid the bit into the horse's mouth.

As Bella approached Delilah, the mare bent her head down as if she were listening intently to what her rider was saying. "This is it, my love." Bella patted her mare's neck. "This is our chance." She kissed the horse on her face, and Delilah rubbed her head against Bella in response.

"All right, you two, let's go," Jean Luc ordered. They headed to the warmup arena. It would be their turn in thirty-five minutes. As their time came, Jean Luc smiled up at Bella. "You can do it. Show the world what you're made of." Bella gave Delilah a quick pat and they trotted off to the start box.

"And riding for France this afternoon is Isabella Rodriguez on Samson's Delilah, owned by the Rodriguez family and trained by Jean Luc Bateau," came the announcement.

Bella nodded her head at the officials, the clocked ticked down on the ten count and the buzzer sounded as the time began to click off the clock. Eleven horses out of nineteen had gone before her. No one had run a clean course so far. Some hadn't made the time, one had fallen off at the bank she was concerned about, and there had even been one refusal. At the level she was competing at, that shouldn't have been the case.

Moving at near steeplechase speeds, Bella knew that her job was to maintain balance and think with logic. The course was running smoothly but her horse's speed was faster than she wanted it to be, and the two struggled for a minute for control. "Not now, girl," Bella shouted as the wind picked up blowing strongly past her ears. "Not now. I'm the boss. Come on, come on big girl..." Talking to the mare was a given on the course. It seemed to calm both her and Bella. As they flew up the bank, Bella focused on the next three jumps—all ditches with each one widening, and then they would be headed for the drop. The ditches went smoothly, and as they cleared the third one, Bella gave an audible squeal. "Good girl!" She maintained focus heading for the bank and gave the mare a half halt. "Easy, easy, whoa," she said, feeling like they had this.

Bella leaned back with her seat as Delilah plummeted over and started down off the drop. One slight misjudge. One second, one tiny mistake, and Delilah's back left leg caught as Bella shifted off balance. It all changed for horse and rider in that split second as Delilah suffered a high speed rotational fall, spinning overhead. Bella flew over her mare's neck. Water, sweat, fear, and a painful scream traveled through the air.

*****

STUNNED BY THE SCENE HE'D WITNESSED ON THE TELEVISION, Miguel cried aloud, seeing his sister lying on the ground, not moving. Paramedics reached her quickly, soon followed by Javier, Antonio, and Jean Luc. The broadcast went to a commercial.

Susanna wanted to comfort Father Miguel. But she did not know how as she sat in her own state of silent anxiety. She had seen the faces of the men who had rushed to Isabella's side.

When the broadcast returned, the commentator announced that Isabella had been taken to St. Michael's Hospital by ambulance. There was no indication of the extent of her injuries, only that she remained unconscious.

"It is a truly terrible tragedy," the British reporter commented.

Miguel left his quarters at once. Susanna found him inside the church lighting several candles and repeating the rosary. She joined

327 | P a g e

him, lighting candles for Father Miguel and Isabella, and one for herself. Then she knelt before the statue of the Virgin Mary. Her heart was heavy at the knowledge that Father Miguel's presence at the convent had rendered her safe haven no longer safe. She would have to leave. Her perfect priest had ties into a not-so-perfect family. She shivered at the thought of seeing Antonio's face on the television screen.

"Are you cold?" Miguel asked.

"No, upset. I'm sorry about the accident."

"I must go. I have to be with her."

"Of course. I'll go tell Mother Superior and Father Juan what has happened. I'm sure they'll make the arrangements for you, unless you'd like me to."

"Thank you, Susanna. I would be grateful."

Back in her small living quarters, Susanna picked up her phone to dial the airlines.

She made Miguel's reservation and then made one for herself on a separate flight. She'd saved enough money from her meager wages over the years to afford this one extravagance.

Her thoughts were confused about how to break the news to the church elders, so she decided to leave a note on her bed, as if she didn't know that Miguel was also leaving. She directed the note to Father Juan, Father Miguel, and Mother Superior:

I have heard some very disturbing news concerning my family. They need me now. Thank you for all of your kindness. The information about your trip to Italy is on your desk, Father. God bless. I will not be returning.

Susanna

The woman the nuns had named Susanna left quietly and walked to the bus station for the ride into Mexico City where she would wait for tomorrow's trip to come. Like Father Miguel, she too, was going to Italy. What Father Miguel didn't know was that he'd made an impact on her. Lately he'd been speaking to her about family and familial love, and although she wanted to put the past behind her, a part of her ached for what had been stolen from her, and today on that television screen when she had seen Antonio Espinoza's face, she knew it was a sign from God. No longer would she hide behind a name that didn't belong to her. She was going to Italy to see if her daughters were there as well. Lydia Espinoza was alive and ready to take back what was rightfully hers, and to execute her revenge on the man she once called husband. The one she believed who had tossed her into a whorehouse so many years ago to rot amongst the rats and mongrels, and to suffer the poison shot into her veins. He would pay dearly for all she'd lost and she thanked God for sending her this sign as she closed her eyes, falling asleep on the bus. For the first time in years, Lydia had no haunting nightmares.

CHAPTER FORTY-NINE

BY TWO O'CLOCK IN THE MORNING, BELLA STILL HADN'T responded to treatment, a full twelve hours following the accident. Javier sat in a chair in the corner of her hospital room, with Pedro close beside him. Antonio and his daughters, as well as Jean Luc and his partner Pierre, waited in a room down the hall.

Upon completion of the surgical procedure for internal bleeding, the doctors indicated that it might be a day or so before Bella would wake up. She did not appear to be in a coma. However, her left leg had been crushed pretty badly by the horse's fall. When she did wake up, she would have to go back into surgery so that they could try to repair it.

"Will she be all right?" Javier heard himself ask.

"We believe so," the doctor replied pensively.

"What does that mean?"

"We're not sure if Isabella will have the use of her left leg."

Javier sank back into the chair next to her bed. The doctor told him that he was sorry, but that he would do everything possible for her.

When Pedro heard the news, he talked it over with Antonio, who immediately made phone calls to find the best orthopedic surgeon for the procedure, and to have him flown in. Pedro knew better than anyone that the loss of her leg would amount to killing her. Horses and riding were her life. Javier was too immobilized by despair to think clearly, and so Pedro and Antonio took it upon themselves to do what was necessary to keep from breaking Bella's heart.

"I've found an excellent orthopedic surgeon," Antonio told Pedro as they walked down the hall to get coffee.

"Where?"

"Not far. He's in Holland. He'll be here first thing in the morning."

"Thank God. What does he think?"

"He doesn't know without seeing the X-rays first, and talking to the doctors here. But I'm told he's the best."

"I hope so. Otherwise, Bella will never ride again. We both know what that'll do to her."

Antonio nodded in agreement. Sipping their coffee, the men huddled together in silence, knowing that the next few days would be some of the toughest they and their families would ever endure.

*****

WHEN BELLA WOKE FROM THE SURGERY, THE FIRST PERSON she called out for was Miguel.

Miguel shifted from one foot to the other. He didn't want to be the one to tell her about her leg.

"You must tell me, Miguel. Am I all right?" She looked tiny amongst all the tubes and the medical apparatus, her face wan from loss of blood. Miguel had arrived at the hospital shortly before she was taken in for her second operation, with only minutes to hold her hand and pray.

It was the duty of the priest to comfort those who lay in hospital beds and, at times, to advise them of their condition. But here was the friend who'd become his baby sister. Telling her the one thing that could break her heart would take more courage than he thought he possessed.

"Bella," he picked up her hand. A silent prayer spun in his mind over and over again. He was looking for strength from God.

"What is it? I know something is wrong."

He rubbed his forehead and sighed. "Your left leg has been badly injured. It appears that Delilah fell directly on top of the femur, and severed some nerves as well."

Bella stared at him, her eyes wide. In the doorway stood her father and Pedro. They entered the room.

"You're awake," her father exclaimed, shooting a glance at Miguel.

"Papa, what's wrong with my leg?"

"Nothing. The doctors fixed you up. You'll be fine."

"You're lying to me. I know it."

"It's the drugs that are making you feel that way," Pedro interrupted.

"No, it's not. Is it, Miguel?" She looked at the one man in her life that would never lie to her.

He painstakingly shook his head.

"Get out!" she cried. "All of you get out!"

"Please, let me tell you what the doctor said..." Javier tried to reason with her.

"I know what he said. He said that I'll never ride again, didn't he?"

"Bella, listen to your father," Pedro urged her.

"Get out," Bella shouted in the strongest voice she could muster in her weakened state.

She lay there, angry and tormented by the fate that had befallen her, a sense of loneliness overwhelming her. She might never ride again. No one had to tell her that. She knew it the minute she woke up.

Bella went over and over what had happened at the trials. What had gone wrong? She wondered how Delilah was. Luc would know. He'd be taking care of Delilah. Thoughts finally drifted into dreams as a drugged sleep took hold of her.

When she awoke, Bella saw Rosa sitting in the chair next to her bed, sketching.

"What are you doing?" she asked.

"Well, hello, sleepyhead. I decided to come visit you, but you've been out for quite some time. It's a good thing I brought my pad and charcoal with me."

"What are you drawing?"

Rosa paused, hesitant to show her friend. She finally picked up the pad and turned it around to face Bella.

Bella stared at the drawing, tears forming. "It's beautiful."

"I didn't mean to upset you. It's only that you look so perfect when you were riding, that I thought you should have this."

The drawing was of Bella mounted on Delilah, sailing over an oxer. Rosa had captured their images perfectly.

She set the pad down and took Bella's hands. "You have always been there when I needed you, Bella. Now it's my turn. When my mother died, you were the only one who didn't chide me or ask me to speak. You accepted my silence for what it was. I think you would've been the only one to accept it for the rest of my life, if that's what I'd chosen to do. You *will* ride again, Bella. *I know you will.* Not only will you ride again, but you will also go on to be the best."

"I don't know."

"Well, *I* do. Life throws challenges our way to see if we can overcome them. We may not know why. There is no explanation for some of the things God allows to happen to us."

"What are you talking about?" Bella asked, knowing there was some personal meaning to Rosa's statement.

"Nothing," she answered, rubbing Bella's arm. "But I promise that no matter what life challenges us with, we can make it through. We can, my dear friend, we really can." Rosa looked away and stared out the window, trying to believe her own words. The painful memory of what had been done to her as a child confronted her each day. She made vain attempts to deal with that memory, but she knew that her life's challenge would never disappear until she made sure that the demon who had done such criminal acts to her had been fully repaid for his cruelty.

CHAPTER FIFTY

JAVIER WAS ENRAGED WITH MIGUEL FOR HIS BETRAYAL.
"How dare you tell Bella about her condition."

"I am Bella's friend and brother. I will not lie to her."

"Lie? Is that what you think I'm doing? Pardon me, priest, but I was protecting her. She is too fragile right now to be told anything about her condition."

"Do you consider your daughter an imbecile? She knew something was wrong the minute she woke up and she wanted someone to clarify it for her. She deserves that much after what she's been through."

"What she deserves is to rest and to be told only when she can handle it."

"My goodness, Papa, she is not so fragile that she's going to fall apart."

Javier held up his hand. "Do not call me Papa. I am not your father. Understand?"

"Yes," Miguel whispered. He stared at the only man who'd actually treated him well as a child, who seemed proud of him for his accomplishments. The only father he had ever known.

"Good, because you are nothing more than the bastard son I took on after being fool enough to fall in love with your whore of a mother."

Disbelieving, hurt beyond measure, Miguel stood up, shaking his fist at Javier. "You will regret saying that one day. I promise you. "

"Is God going to strike me dead?"

*****

THE DRIZZLE CHILLED LYDIA AS SHE WRAPPED THE CHEAP sweater around herself. She caught a glimpse of her newly blonde hair in the hotel room's small mirror, and rather liked the change. It hadn't been too difficult to find out the name of the hospital in which Isabella was being treated. All she had to do was scavenge through the papers from a few days ago.

She stationed herself in a café across the street from the private hospital, as she knew she could spot her family undetected from there. Just that morning she'd seen Antonio enter the hospital, and the rage she'd felt alarmed and surprised her. She thought her anger at him had dissipated after living so many years with the nuns. He hadn't changed much over the years—a little heavier, a little less hair. Otherwise, there was no mistaking him. She had yet to see Emilio, and wondered why she hadn't. She was curious about how he'd responded to her disappearance. Was Antonio so stupid that he thought she'd never come back for her revenge? Perhaps he assumed that she died in the fire at the brothel. Or maybe he'd intended to have her killed initially but his henchmen didn't have the heart to carry through with his plan. Then it hit her. The reason she hadn't seen Emilio was because Antonio had done away with him, too.

As she stared at the front doors of the hospital, she saw a pretty young woman walk out. Her head was down, her shoulder-length dark hair falling across her face. Lydia gasped. She knew that this was her daughter.

Rosa looked up as the drizzle turned into rain, pulling an umbrella from her tote bag. Tears ran down Lydia's face as she realized what she'd lost. Was destiny so cruel as to keep her from her own children? Even during those years when she could have returned to them, her fear of Antonio had kept her away. She watched Rosa walk down the street, and Lydia swore that fear would no longer conquer her need. To be with her children once again was more important than the fears for her own safety. Soon, Antonio would know she was alive, and her children would understand what an evil man their father was.

CHAPTER FIFTY-ONE

IT WAS NEARLY A MONTH BEFORE BELLA COULD LEAVE
the hospital. Severely depressed, she left Europe, leaving her dreams behind. Her father and the doctors had finally owned up to her fate, but what was worse was when she'd learned from Jean Luc the fate of Delilah.

He'd taken her hand in his. "I am so, so sorry, *chérie.*" A tear slid down his face.

Bella couldn't cry or speak. She didn't want to believe the words Jean Luc spoke. She shook her head vehemently.

Jean Luc squeezed her hands. "She was a beautiful creature. One of God's finest, and God blessed you and me with her. I know it is painful, Bella, but I promise she didn't suffer."

Bella knew this couldn't be true. Her horse would've suffered greatly from the broken leg she'd suffered. The irony of it. They were both rendered paralyzed in a moment, in a second, and Bella would give anything at that moment to be put in the ground with her horse—her sweet, sweet big girl. Life held no meaning for her if she couldn't have Delilah and if she couldn't ride. Bella finally spoke. "Where is she?"

"I had her flown home to France and buried on my property. When you feel better, you can come and say goodbye to her."

Bella nodded. Still no tears. Jean Luc stood and kissed her on the cheek as the doctor came in to see her. "I will be in touch, *ma chérie.* I love you. You will be happy again. I promise you."

Bella kissed him back, knowing his promise was said with only good intent, but she knew she would never be happy again.

Since that day a couple of weeks ago, when Jean Luc told her of Delilah's fate, Bella had become even more despondent, saddened that she could not ever again ride her beautiful mare, never again hear her whinny as approached her stall. And when she'd received a letter from Miguel explaining that he needed to return to his parishioners, she became even more withdrawn.

She knew that there was more to Miguel's story than he had told her. But what was it? When she asked her father why Miguel had left so abruptly, he said nothing, but the sourness of his face told her everything. Once again, her father had exerted his power—this time, over the one person in the world she trusted.

He'd sent away her best friend—her brother—and *expected* her to understand. The last place she wanted to be now was in her father's home. France was her real home. Being in Mexico with her father and Pedro would be lonely. She prayed to a God she no longer believed in for someone to put an end to her misery.

CHAPTER FIFTY-TWO

"I ONLY TOLD YOU TO CHECK ON HIM, TO MAKE SURE THAT
he was doing all right. For God's sakes, his mother just died, and you
go giving him money, setting him up as our main West Coast
distributor? My God, Emilio, have you gone out of your mind? I don't
want him involved in our business. The boy has a chance to go
straight, and you mess around with his life." Antonio rubbed his
temples and paced back and forth in his office, the pounding of a
migraine headache beginning to seize his mind.

"I did what you told me. I checked him out, discovered he was
already hooked up to dealing and in the business whether you want
him to be or not. He's a smart kid. He knows how to handle himself. If
we hadn't brought him in, sooner or later, somebody else would've. If
he was going to be in our business anyway, wouldn't you rather he
dealt with us than with some other operation? At least now, we can
look after him, make sure he's doing all right. He's under our
control."

"Jesus Christ, he's my *son*, Emilio." Antonio grabbed his brother by
his shirtfront and pulled him close. "The last thing I wanted for my
son was to bring him into this filthy business. I wanted something
better for the boy." He shoved Emilio away in anger and disgust.

"I told you, he's already *in* this business. Besides, has it really been all that bad? Look around you. You couldn't ask for anything better than this, could you?" Emilio motioned to the Waterford crystal and the elegant sculptures in the office.

Maybe Emilio did make some sense, but Antonio still wanted a legitimate life for his only son. The drug business was too dangerous. Antonio felt partially responsible for Marta's death. If anything were to happen to Alejandro because of his involvement in this business, he would never forgive himself.

Even though Antonio was in an ideal position, he had to have an armed guard with him at all times, and always had to check to make sure that he wasn't being followed. But at least he wasn't on the streets—much less the streets of Los Angeles, basically alone. Yes, the money was good, but what a life. Antonio didn't want his son living like this. Still, perhaps it was the only way he could get to know the boy.

"You have made some valid points. I'm pleased my son is all right, but I don't want him knowing I'm his father. Understand? As far as he's concerned, this is about business. I would also like to set up a meeting with him and this other kid. What's his name?"

"Hector?"

"Yes, that one."

"Are you sure you'll be up to this? Won't it be hard to handle?"

"Don't worry about me. Do it. I don't want the meeting here, though. Make it at Javier's place. Work out the details and let me know."

"I'll take care of it." Emilio straightened his Armani suit jacket and left the room.

"And another thing," Antonio shouted after him, "I'm warning you, if you say anything to anyone about my being this boy's father, I will personally see to it you never speak to anyone else again."

"I'm your brother, for God's sake. I would never do anything to harm you," Emilio shouted back.

Antonio sat back down. His brother needed to be kept in check. Emilio was becoming what appeared to be a loose cannon. Not good. He lit a cigar and pinched it between his thumb and forefinger. He looked forward to the day when he would come face to face with his son, now a young man. He could cope with that. Antonio only hoped that he could hide the love he felt for Alejandro. He did not want the boy to know the truth. The fear of being hated by this child horrified him; And the truth was that his only son had every reason to despise him.

*****

ALEX TOOK PART OF THE MONEY EMILIO HAD GIVEN HIM AND enrolled in business classes at Santa Monica Community College. He wanted to make his mother proud of him, even though he knew he could not escape the drug business. He would at least become good at it. He would not be some streetcorner drug pusher ever again. He added English literature and humanities to his course load.

He settled down to long hours of studying. He'd never been that great as a student before, but things were different now. He had a goal to work for. With his mother gone, he also needed something to dominate his thoughts.

Emilio had flown up a few times to talk business with Alex and Hector. He'd gone back to Colombia two days earlier, after making a run with Hector, teaching him where to find and how to handle illegal immigrants.

They had a few coyotes working for them who would bring the illegals into the States to their door. In return, Hector would set them up in cheap accommodations and get them started selling for them. Hector liked being in charge, managing a group of what he called the *little people*. This term irritated Alex, who reminded Hector that it hadn't been so long ago since they, too, were *little people*. Alex tried to stay clear of that part of the business. He didn't like treating people as if they were cattle. He felt as if he was betraying his own kind.

Emilio told him he didn't want Alex selling the drugs, which suited him. He wanted him to learn how the business worked, and he *was* learning. School consumed him, not to mention lectures from Emilio on how money laundering was carried out. To Alex, this was safer and far less emotionally draining than selling drugs on the street: out of sight, out of mind. The ruthlessness bug hadn't bitten him as it had his counterpart, Hector. He also found money laundering rather intriguing.

The apartment Emilio had set them up in was posh. It was in the Hollywood Hills, overlooking a good portion of the city. Hector's mother didn't question where all the money was coming from. Unlike Marta, Elisa didn't care, as long as her son took care of her. And Hector made sure that happened. He'd moved her and her husband into a small but pleasant home in the Fairfax district, and provided her monthly with a substantial amount of money, courtesy of Emilio.

Alex put his head down on his financial reports, his eyes tired of numbers and words. Hector came stumbling in. Between running the show and partying, Hector was rarely home. When he *was* available, Alex was too busy studying to hang out with him. On the few occasions when Alex was up to going out, Emilio seemed to be in town. Alex noticed how friendly Emilio and Hector had become in a matter of months. In a way, Alex felt as if he was losing his best friend to Emilio. It was difficult to understand, because Emilio was probably fifteen years older than they were. But Hector was rapidly getting used to money, and Emilio always had a lot on him, ever willing to pass it around.

"Hey, how's it going, Alejandro? Studying hard?" Hector patted Alex on the shoulder and smiled. His eyes were bloodshot and he smelled of tequila.

Alex closed his book. "I'm working on it. Looks like you had a successful day."

"Yeah. I'm getting the hang of this boss-man stuff. You should see those little *peons*. They shake in their shoes when they see me coming."

"Uh-huh." Alex was unimpressed by Hector's brazen harshness.

"You want a drink?" Hector stumbled over to the bar to pour himself another shot of tequila.

"No." Alex picked up his books and started to walk into the small den off the living room.

"Hey, sit down, man. I got something to tell you. Besides, you should take a break." Hector motioned for Alex to sit.

"What?"

"We're gonna be taking a trip."

"Where? Why?"

"To meet the *man*, that's why. Emilio phoned this morning and clued me in. He said the *Patrón* wants to meet us personally. We'll be flying down to Puerto Vallarta in the morning where we gonna take a boat down to some palace type place these guys own in Costa Careyes. They want to make sure we get all of this, you know. We are moving up in the world." Hector headed for his room.

Alex sat on the sofa in disbelief. Things like this didn't happen to a couple of lowlife kids from the *barrio*. It sounded way too good to be true.

"Hey, amigo, why don't you put the book away tonight and we'll go out and party?" Hector called out to Alex.

"Nah, I'm tired. You should take it easy, if we're leaving early in the morning."

"Fuck that, man. You know you really ought to try and enjoy all our new riches. Shit like this don't happen every day."

Hector was right. *Shit* like this didn't happen every day. There was a catch somewhere. For now, Alex would go along for the ride, hoping he didn't crash on his way to discovering what the catch was.

CHAPTER FIFTY-THREE

"BUT I DON'T WANT A PARTY," BELLA TOLD HER FATHER.

"It will make you feel better. You've always loved parties. And this one will be in your honor."

"My honor? Honor for *what*? Please Papa, don't give me a party. I don't want people seeing me in this thing," she replied, referring to her wheelchair.

"You're being foolish. Everyone knows that your wheelchair is only a temporary device. Please, consider allowing me to give you this party. Do it for me."

"For you?" Bella turned the wheelchair around to face the window in the front room overlooking the ocean below. Her father had brought her to the vacation house—she'd always loved staying here in the past, but now, nothing mattered.

"Yes."

"For you? That's funny and sad, Papa, because I've tried for years to do everything for you. I went away for you, to a school where you could forget all about me. I became a world-class rider to make you proud of me. I received excellent marks in school for you. I did everything to please you. Now look at me. I'm confined in a wheelchair, my horse is dead, and my dreams destroyed. Right now, Papa, I don't want to do anything for you, or for me, or for anyone else."

Javier walked over to the window and bent down to Bella. He leaned over and kissed her on the cheek, tears in his eyes. She turned her face away from him. He sighed. "Whatever you like." He left the room.

Pedro, who'd been within hearing distance in the kitchen, approached Bella. He too bent down, but lacked the kindness her father had bestowed upon her. He grabbed her shoulders, "Let me tell you something. That man loves you with all his heart and soul. He regrets ever hurting you. In fact, it is the biggest regret of his life. You will quit pitying yourself. You will let him throw you a party, and you will start allowing the physical therapist to work with you, and you *will* get better. I do not want to hear any protests. I'm going to see your father now and tell him that you've changed your mind."

Pedro left the room leaving Bella stunned and slightly ashamed of herself. But how dare Pedro speak to her like that? Who did he think he was? There was a knot in her stomach for the way she'd treated her father. In that aspect, maybe Pedro was right. Her father was only trying to make her happy.

Bella decided to go down to the stables. She hadn't seen a horse since her accident. She struggled with her wheelchair to get there, her arms sore, but she finally made it. Her childhood horse Salsa was still stabled there, eating and aging. All of the family's retired horses came to live at the vacation home in Costa Careyes after retirement. It had been a standing joke within the family that once a horse earned his keep for the Rodriguez family he would live the rest of his life in style. She was happy Salsa had been brought here to live out his final years. If only Delilah could have also had the same fortune...

Salsa peeked his head out in curiosity as he watched his girl rolling down the stable aisle in what must've seemed to him a strange contraption. He devoured the carrot she offered him, placing his face in her arms when finished with his treat. She hugged him back and as she felt the his breath upon her neck, she broke into tears. The horse remained in Bella's arms, as if he understood that was what she needed. He nuzzled her as she patted him gently. Horses had been her life for so long that the possibility of never riding one again was something she could not bear to imagine. Her father was a good man and she knew he loved her, but it didn't take away what she'd endured and his love couldn't fulfill the life she'd expected to live.

*****

THE HACIENDA WAS FILLED WITH AN AIR OF FESTIVITY, festooned with decorations in pink and white, flowers adorning each room. Isabella prepared for the party in her room with her nurse Maria, who'd been helping her with her physical therapy. Butterflies fiddled around in her stomach as she thought about the guests and what their reactions to her disability might be. She refused to allow anyone to pity her. She also regretted the fact that Miguel was unable to come. She'd sent him a letter inviting him, but he'd responded that he was busy working on a new crusade to fight crime in their country. This bothered her. He normally wouldn't have missed this party for anything. He'd also enclosed something very disturbing in his letter to her. It was a small article from a radical newspaper, claiming that her father worked with the Colombians transporting drugs. The article also claimed that the recent elections had been fixed, in order for her father to win, remaining in control, since he was in favor of those who supported their world of wealth. Bella ripped the article up and tried to dispel it from her thoughts. She was angry with Miguel for sending it to her. She could not believe that her father could be corrupt. But she'd also overheard a conversation between two of the cooks some days earlier, gossiping about what they knew of their employer's source of wealth.

"What is troubling you so?" her nurse asked, interrupting Bella's thoughts as she brushed her hair up into a chignon.

"It's nothing." She fell silent, but then decided to continue. It had been a long time since she'd confided in anyone. "I heard something terrible about my father."

"What on earth are you talking about?"

"I don't know if I should say anything. It's probably nothing, really."

"Listen to me. If it's bothering you so much, you need to tell somebody."

Bella sighed, and fiddled with the bracelet on her arm, while she spoke. "The other day, I was in the kitchen. I overheard some of the cooks talking about Papa and my godfather. They were saying that Papa and Antonio are involved in drug trafficking and killing people. You know those death squads you hear people talking about? They were saying that Antonio orders them and that Papa is also involved in seeing those types of orders are carried out."

"Oh, child, none of that's true. You pay no mind to idle gossip. They're bored idiots, who need to make up stories out of jealousy. People who have wealth like your father and godfather are always targets of malicious lies. You need not listen to such talk or worry your pretty head about it. Who was saying these awful things?"

"I don't know. I think it was Jorge and Horacio."

"If you ever hear them saying such things again, I want you to come straight to me and let me know, all right? That kind of poison need not be spread here in your father's home. I promise you that they're nothing but silly rumors."

"Are you sure?"

"Of course. Come now, let's finish getting you dressed. You don't want to be late for your own party, do you?"

"No." That was a lie, but she would do this for her father. She thought about what Maria had told her, and the denials that her father was involved in any wrongdoing. But in the back of Bella's mind, the thought still remained, a bit quieter now, but still there. Was her father a corrupt man?

CHAPTER FIFTY-FOUR

ANTONIO PACED BACK AND FORTH IN THE LARGE CONFERENCE
room. He would meet his son face to face today. Would the boy
recognize him? Would he look into Antonio's eyes and know who he
was? Maybe he should have called the whole thing off, but it was too
late now. They were scheduled to arrive at any moment.

Javier walked into the room, smoothing back what little hair he
had left. "I've just been informed they've arrived."

"Could you pour me a Scotch?" Antonio asked him.

"You all right? You seem uptight. This is only to meet our new
West Coast distributors. Emilio assures me they're good men to go
with. He checked them out. Why so tense?"

Antonio sighed. He hadn't wanted to tell Javier the truth yet about
who the new West Coast distributor was and how it had all come
about, but he had known that he and Marta had a child together and
Antonio couldn't help wondering if Javier would recognize the fact
that they were father and son. If so, he would feel betrayed and
Antonio did not want that.

"I will be, once you get me that Scotch." His hands shook as he reached inside his suit pocket for his cigarette case. Lighting a cigarette, he took a long drag.

Javier went to the marble bar and poured his friend the Scotch, straight up. Antonio swallowed it in one gulp and slammed the glass down. After finishing the drink he told the news to his *compadre.*

"The man coming her in minutes is your son?"

"Yes."

"And he has no idea that you're his father."

"Yes."

"Dios Mio."

"Yes."

"What are you going to do?"

"For now, nothing. Put the boy to work. Maybe in time when trust is there between us on that level I will tell him. For now, it will only backfire on me and us. I'm certain he has a strong hatred for his father." He sighed. "For me, and I don't know if I can take that. Can you keep this a secret?"

Javier nodded. "Of course." He walked over to the bar and made himself a drink in an obvious attempt to swallow and digest this unsettling news, but Antonio knew him to be true and a man of his word. This could only strengthen their bond. Lies would break their partnership apart. Antonio knew enough about deceit to be aware of that fact.

A few minutes later, a handful of men walked in, Emilio in front. Alex had grown in size, and his face had matured a great deal, but his eyes still resembled his father's. He stood out from the other two, far more elegant than either of them. For such a young man who'd never been provided the lavish lifestyle or riches he'd been entitled to, he'd grown up with the same grace and elegance characteristic of his mother. His demeanor was that of a gentleman. Antonio wanted to wrap his arms around him and shout to the world, *"This is my son."* Instead, he suppressed his feelings as he reached out his hand. "Hello, gentlemen. I am Antonio Espinoza, and this is my friend and business associate, Javier Rodriguez."

Alex shook his hand first. It was as strong as he'd expected. Antonio studied him to see if there were any signs of recognition in Alex's eyes. There were many similarities between himself and his son: the high cheekbones and dark eyes. Did Alex notice them as well?

"Hey there, Antonio. I'm Hector Sanchez." The bumbling idiot shoved his hand into Antonio's, obviously embarrassing Alex, whose face turned red as he nudged his associate away.

Antonio didn't like this kid, since he could see that he was an ordinary greaser. He also seemed high as a kite and tipsy as well. Antonio recognized the same symptoms in his brother Emilio. Unlike his confederates, Alex appeared straight and coherent. Antonio had been in the industry long enough to tell who was using and who wasn't. Dammit if Emilio wasn't high on cocaine at that moment. Antonio wanted to shake him.

"Hey, why don't we all have a drink?" Emilio said. He was already pouring himself a shot at the bar.

"Emilio, sit down. We are not here to socialize. We're here for a meeting. Please, gentlemen, won't you take a seat?" Antonio motioned to the long table and chairs. As he did, two bodyguards slipped into the room, standing on each side of the door.

"We appreciate your coming down here so that could meet with the newest members of our team," Javier began after they'd all been seated. "Emilio has said some very good things about you."

"Hey, no problem, *amigo*. We were glad to come," Hector replied.

"Excellent," Antonio remarked. "I understand that Emilio has gotten you both set up. From this point on, you will be answering to me." He directed his words to Alex.

"Cool, Patrón," Hector said.

"No, not *you*." Antonio's voice crackled with harshness. "You will do the job you've been assigned up to do with Emilio. You will be checking in with him. Alejandro, I expect you to keep perfect records of all transactions. I expect you to show them to no one but myself or Javier."

Emilio raised his eyebrows. Antonio noticed, but did not change his wording.

"Of course," Alex replied. He was relieved that his dealings with Emilio would be limited from now on. He liked this Antonio Espinoza. There was something about him that comforted Alex. He didn't understand it, as he didn't comprehend why he and Hector had become the chosen ones. Pieces in this puzzle still didn't fit, as far as Alex was concerned, but he had nothing to lose. Besides, this position offered him the money and power he needed to seek his

355 | P a g e

long-lost father and make him pay the dues he owed him and his mother.

Alex felt an immediate respect for Antonio. He also liked Javier. The two exuded a sense of power, wealth, and dignity. They were different from Emilio, who was merely ostentatious and crude. The meeting lasted about an hour. To Alex, it seemed more a formality than the meeting of minds Emilio had led them to expect.

Stepping out of the office, Antonio patted Alex on the shoulder. "You, my son, have a great future with us. Now Javier and I would like you to stay on for the evening. We're having a party for my goddaughter. Javier will square you away with your accommodations."

Alex smiled back. "Of course, we'd love to stay. I'm sorry about Hector, though. Sometimes, he can be somewhat rude."

"Don't worry about him. He doesn't even realize what he's doing. He's an ignorant fool. I hate to run off. But I need to make sure everything is in order for the party. It's very important that Bella have a good time."

Alex nodded his head, "Of course, do whatever you need to do. I'll be fine."

"I meant what I said about your future. I need someone young and honest to know the inner workings of our business. And to be completely truthful, my trust in my brother is fading rapidly."

Alex, not knowing what to say, smiled as he watched his new boss walk toward the front of the mansion. The meeting and the exchange of words puzzled him. Why him? He had no answers, but he believed this man, who sounded so sincere. Yet he couldn't help pondering what this was all about.

CHAPTER FIFTY-FIVE

ISABELLA WAITED FOR HER FATHER'S MEETING TO ADJOURN.
People were arriving for the party, but fear kept her away from the
front entrance and the garden, where the festivities were under way.

Pedro walked up behind her as she put on her scarlet lipstick. "It's
time to greet your guests."

"I don't want to."

"I know, but you will have a good time. It's possible for this one
evening, you can actually forget your suffering."

"Oh, really? How is that possible while I'm sitting in this thing?"

"Try. Your father went to a lot of trouble. I'll stay by your side.
You'll be fine."

"All right," she replied, rolling her eyes and preparing to swallow
her pride, since she was sure that murmurings about her accident
would reach her ears shortly, and pitying looks would follow. Pedro
rolled her out through the veranda doors and down the ramp built
for her while they were all still in Italy, awaiting her dismissal from
the hospital. He'd had ramps and elevators put in both houses.

Much to Bella's surprise, friends she hadn't seen in years were there. They smiled at her and were pleasant. It almost felt good to be around people again, but she was not about to let Pedro know that.

Her father and godfather approached them. "Ah, you look gorgeous," Antonio said, bending down to kiss her cheek. "The girls were looking for you."

"Where are they?" Bella had been looking forward to seeing Rosa. Felicia didn't matter, one way or the other. Her behavior was amusing, but her manner soon became wearying.

"Well, it would appear that my youngest is being accosted by suitors at this point," Antonio remarked. They all glanced over to the pool, where Felicia was surrounded by a group of eager young men. Felicia noticed them looking in her direction and waved.

"And Rosa, where is she?"

Antonio frowned. "I see that Rosa is speaking to our newest business partner. Here, why don't I take you over, and introduce you?" Before anyone could protest, Antonio was pushing Bella through the group in a rather hurried fashion.

"Bella," Rosa exclaimed. "It's so good to see you up and about."

Bella smiled sheepishly, and then looked up at the handsome young man who'd been speaking to Rosa.

"I see you've met Alejandro," Antonio said.

"Yes, Papa. He was telling me that he's recently started working for you, running one of your businesses in the States." Rosa smiled at her father knowingly. She was quite observant, and had noticed everything she could during her days as a mute. She knew that her father's business was not exactly legal, but it didn't bother her as she knew it would her naive friend, Bella.

Alex shook Bella's hand. "Hello," she said, "I'm Isabella Rodriguez."

"It's very nice to meet you, Isabella, and thank you for allowing me to attend your party."

"I'm pleased you could come," she replied.

Instead of simply shaking her hand, Alex took it and kissed it. Antonio mused that the chemistry between them could hardly go unnoticed by anyone in close proximity.

"Come on, Papa, let's get a glass of wine," Rosa said.

Reluctantly, Antonio agreed.

"It is your birthday? I'm afraid I don't have a present for you."

"No. It's not my birthday." Bella was not sure how she should answer his question. She decided to be honest. She told him about the accident, her horses, how she missed riding, and how her father had hoped that this party would lighten her spirits.

"Is it working?" He grinned.

"You know what? Amazingly, it is."

"Good. Looks like everyone is beginning to sit down for dinner. Would you like to sit by me?"

"I'd love to, but my father has arranged the seating." She smiled at him.

"Understood. Save me a dance when the music starts?"

Her smile suddenly turned into a frown, since she was reminded again of her handicap. "Did my father send you to talk to me, to try to make me feel better?"

"Of course not."

"Then why *are* you talking to me?" She didn't believe him. It made sense now. Why else would a handsome young man want any part of her?

"I like you. I find you interesting, sweet, and to be honest, very beautiful."

"I know my father well enough to know that he would do something like this. He wants me to be happy. To be normal. I'll never be normal again. I certainly don't need your pity or charity, Señor Peña."

"I don't pity you, and your father isn't paying me. This is the first time I've ever met your father, and to be honest, I don't like your accusations. My mother did not bring me up to be a shallow man."

"But I'm in a wheelchair. My legs may never be useful to me again."

"Do you think that changes a person inside? Do you think that would keep me from wanting to get to know you?"

"I don't know. I think I've changed a lot since the accident." She still didn't know if she believed him, but she wanted to.

"Maybe, but perhaps you've changed less than you think. I would also place bets that you'll not only walk again, but I'll bet money that you'll also ride again. Your face lit up when you were talking about your horses."

Bella looked down at her hands, which she twisted around a strand of pearls dangling from her neck. People had been telling her the same thing ever since her accident. But not until now, when a man she'd only known for barely an hour had said these same words, did she actually believe they might be true. She lifted her head up and smiled. "You're right." Even if he were only acting for her sake, for the moment it was the best she'd felt since before the accident, and for now she would take this man at his word and hope he wasn't telling her lies.

"I know I am. Now, are you going to save me that dance when dinner is over?"

"In case you hadn't noticed, I can't dance these days."

"Sure you can. I'll show you how."

"Oh, really. All right, if you insist."

"I do insist."

They both went to their separate tables. Bella was seated between Pedro and her father, Alex between Antonio and Emilio.

Throughout dinner, Isabella noticed Alex's eyes darting in her direction. She tried not to look, knowing that if she did, it would be inappropriate. But a couple of times she slipped, and their eyes locked. For the first time all evening, she wondered if the black chiffon dress she wore was cut too low. She lifted the sleeves back onto her shoulders. Throughout her years in France, she hadn't concentrated much on her looks. Boys hadn't been of much interest to her. The horses came first, and they didn't care whether she wore makeup or curled her hair. The only times she had ever dressed up and worn makeup were when her family visited or during important school functions.

She slid a wispy piece of her hair that had fallen over her eyes back into her chignon, all the while trying to concentrate on eating the lobster dinner.

Bella noticed Pedro watching her, shooting pained grimaces at Alejandro. He was behaving stupidly being an overly protective uncle.

Dinner finally ended with coffee to complement the strawberry cake the cook had made for her. Tears came to her eyes as she watched her father slice the cake. The party she'd dreaded so much had been worth it.

The band finished setting up, the music began to play, and within minutes, Alex stood before her. "May I have this dance? That is, if your father wouldn't mind?"

Javier smiled and nodded his head at both of them. The band was playing *Guantanamera*. The center of the garden filled up with guests. Alex pushed Bella's chair into the center, where he spun the chair around in time with the music. She laughed.

Lies or not, Alejandro made her laugh and he was fun. Bella wished she could stay in that moment forever, where she could forget that her legs did not work and that she was a woman like any other.

CHAPTER FIFTY-SIX

PEDRO WATCHED BELLA ALL NIGHT WITH ALEX, AS FELICIA tried everything she could to distract him, but all her wiles were useless. Pedro hated the fact that those two never left each other from the moment Antonio introduced them. He now stood in the alcove off the balcony, getting drunk, continuing to watch them down below.

Emilio interrupted Pedro's thoughts. "Where have you been? I've been looking for you all night."

"Up here," Pedro replied.

"I can see that. But why?"

"I'm not feeling all that festive."

"I don't understand. It's a wonderful party. Business went well. What is there for you to be upset about? Bella is having a terrific time. She's quite a young woman."

It was as if Emilio enjoyed rubbing salt into Pedro's wound. Pedro glared at him.

"Ah, I see, that's it. You don't like the fact that she's all grown up. It's all right. They all grow up at one time or another. You should be thankful your *niece* has grown up the way she has. She's someone you can be proud of. And, my youngest niece has grown up quite nicely as well, but I've seen that you've noticed that yourself. I would be careful with Felicia, though. Antonio is quite protective of those girls."

Pedro turned from the balcony's wall, spilling his drink in the process. "What I don't like," he slurred, "is that hoodlum hanging all over my Bella. What is between Felicia and me is none of your concern."

Emilio laughed. "No, it's not my concern. I'm only giving you fair warning. Tell you what, I'll let you stand guard here over *your* Bella. When you sober up, come see me. I think you and I can be of great benefit to one another."

*****

AFTER BEING FORBIDDEN TO SEE BELLA AND BANISHED FROM the entire Rodriguez family by Javier, Miguel buried himself in his work for the church. He was anguished about not being able to stay in touch with his sister. He'd written to her, but each one of his letters were returned, unopened. He was certain that had been the doing of Javier or Pedro. Bella had written to him twice a week, telling him about her progress and pleading with him to write her. Her letters then started coming once a week, and finally stopped. If

God had allowed him to hate, he would have hated Javier for tearing him away from the one person who meant something to him.

A few months after the letters stopped coming, right before the holidays, Miguel was transferred to Guatemala, where a small church had been conducting services without a priest. Apparently, the former parish priest disappeared shortly after being found in bed with a fifteen-year-old parishioner. The boy claimed their affair had been going on for well over a year and that the priest was paying him money in exchange for the boy's sexual favors. Rumor had it that the priest, who'd purportedly fled the country, was more than likely six feet under, after some cruel and unusual punishment from some irate parishioners. When he'd first heard about this scandal and its aftermath, Miguel shuddered in abhorrence. He knew that he would have to work very hard gaining the trust of his new flock.

One afternoon while practicing his sermon for that evening's mass, one of his parishioners, a man in his late thirties named Julio, came to see him. He was tall and muscular, weathered from the sun, but his eyes bright with youth as if he knew he had a purpose.

"How can I help you, Julio?" Miguel asked him.

"Well, Father, I'm not sure if you're aware of who I am." Julio seated himself in the chair across from Miguel's desk.

"I don't know exactly what you mean."

"I am important, but to these people, you are far more important. I think that together, we can help each other."

"What are you trying to say?"

"How do you feel about all the drugs being smuggled through our country?" Julio asked.

Miguel fingered the cross around his neck, a gift from Bella after he graduated from the seminary. "I'm aware that it is a problem and I do not like it."

"Problem? It is more than a problem. Our people are losing jobs, even losing their lives, because a few wealthy hoodlums are using Guatemala as a landing strip for their drug trade, which extends into Miami and South Carolina."

"I see."

"Whatever I say to you is confidential?"

"Of course. I am bound by the Church and by God to tell no one of our conversation—if that is what you wish."

"That's exactly what I wish."

"All right, you have my word."

"I am working with the Drug Enforcement Agency with the United States government. We need your help."

"What? But how?" Miguel's fingers tightened around the cross.

"We know of the relationship you've had with the Rodriguez and Espinoza families."

"Yes, but that relationship no longer exists."

"We also know that. Are you aware that Antonio Espinoza and Javier Rodriguez are using their affiliation with the PRI party and other legitimate fronts to deal in huge amounts of drugs?"

"I had an idea that might be true, yes."

"At first, we were talking about marijuana, but now we're looking at large sums of cocaine. It is men like these who live in great luxury, while bringing Central and South America down to new depths of poverty and degradation. They must be stopped."

"How can I help?"

"Speak out."

"I'm only a priest in a tiny church in the jungles here. I don't see what I can do."

"You know both families. I believe we can derive a lot of information from you. Not only that, but people trust you. I've seen what you've done with the people here in such a short time, after what happened with the priest before you. These people were disillusioned. They thought God had failed them, turned against them. But in a matter of weeks, you've changed that. We've been looking for someone like you—someone respectful, courageous, intelligent, and likable. The DEA will fund your lectures, which will begin with the smaller towns and cities of Central and South America, and then eventually reach the larger cities. The last thing we want is to see Javier Rodriguez in office again. Espinoza and Rodriguez are smart. They know exactly how to steal, hide, and cheat."

Miguel nodded his head.

"Can your conscience allow you to let good, God-fearing people go on dying due to their corruption?"

Miguel also had the feeling that more than his conscience would get the better of him. The fact that his life would be on the line was something to consider. Although the DEA and those who worked for them were considered righteous, Miguel had heard stories about the Guatemalan militia and their infamous torture sessions—stories that frightened him. Taking his time before he made his decision, he rose and walked to the window, and stood looking out at the huts and shacks of the community he served.

Turning to Julio, he said, "I'll do it."

"Good. I knew we could count on you. The campaign will begin with tomorrow's mass."

"Excuse me?"

"Beginning tomorrow, you will be waging a war with two of the largest crime families in our part of the world. What better way than to begin in your own backyard? I expect that the Bible has something to say about the evils of corruption, Father."

"Yes, the Bible has plenty to say on that topic, but I need to follow the missal."

"I am sure the missal for tomorrow's mass will contain something that you can translate into your homily that will discuss corruption."

Miguel slowly nodded. "I will study and see what I can do."

"Good. I suggest you study it carefully. I've noticed that many in this country seem to listen when God speaks."

"Yes," Miguel replied.

"Good day, Father. I'll see you at Mass. Afterwards I'll give you a proposed schedule we've worked out for you. Then, I must leave for some time. I have other plans to set into motion. I will be in touch, as well as one of my partners."

Miguel watched the man leave his church, pondering his proposition and the fact that he had accepted it. How could he attempt to tear down a family who'd given him so much opportunity? Then he remembered Javier's words ordering him to leave Bella alone and get out of their lives, the returned letters, and Bella's distraught words asking why he hadn't written. He remembered his mother and the nagging thought that her death didn't appear to upset his stepfather the way he thought it might have, and it nagged at him that there was a possibility that Javier may have given orders for his mother to be killed. Miguel was resolved. He knew that a higher purpose dictated what he had to do. He'd have to expose Bella's father as the man he truly was. He didn't know if he could do that to her, but he also knew that his life now belonged to God—and God wanted him to seek justice for a weary nation.

CHAPTER FIFTY-SEVEN

LYDIA PLANNED HER REVENGE IN A SINGLE ROOM ABOVE A
bar in Calí, a place designed for tourists. She worked as a waitress
there, using her tips to pay for her room that had become her
fortress. She took precautions and time daily to disguise herself for
fear of anyone from her past recognizing her. She thought about
changing locales to plan for her revenge, but her mind constantly
raced with thoughts of her daughters and all the years lost to her,
and her need to be close to them, even without them knowing, won
out now over her safety.

Yet, she also kept constant in her mind that if anyone involved
with Antonio and his business were to find out she was alive, she'd
be killed quickly, and so, she had remained closeted in her hideaway.
Although she'd wanted desperately to see her daughters while she
was in Italy, her logic overcame her impulsiveness and convinced
her to wait until the time was right. And that was exactly what she
was doing. She knew that in the game she was playing, timing was
everything.

*****

"WHAT IS BETWEEN YOU AND ISABELLA?" FELICIA WHINED
to Pedro.

"What?" he asked, distracted as he stared out the window of their hotel room. He needed to get away from everything, so he'd rented the room for the night. Javier and Antonio had asked Alejandro to stay on at the house for a week after the party, in order for him to get to know their operation. It sickened Pedro to have to be a witness to the infatuation growing between Bella and Alex.

"You heard me. You'd think you were her father, the way you've been stewing over her and this Alex kid. Or worse, you'd think you were her lover."

He turned around and raised his arm to slap her.

"Go ahead. Hit me. You know I like it rough."

He lowered his hand, instead fingering her erect nipples through her low-cut, black blouse. She smiled back at him, her cat-like eyes narrowing into slits of desire. Pedro pulled her blouse open and ravaged her breasts with his mouth. Felicia leaned back onto the bed, enjoying every bit of Pedro's furious sexual performance.

When they were finished, Pedro thought he'd feel better, but he didn't. If anything, he felt more dissatisfied than ever as he rolled over and looked down at Felicia next to him. She was great in bed, but as far as ever being the mother of his children, no way. He knew he could never love her as he loved Bella.

*****

ADRENALINE CHARGED THROUGH ROSA'S VEINS. THE ART
dealer in France whom Bella had found for her finally returned her
call, telling her that he liked her work and wished to represent her.

"We would like to have you do a show here in Paris and one in
New York. Are you ready?" Marc Honoré asked.

"I'm not sure."

"Do you have a number of pieces that could be shown?"

"Yes," Rosa replied, thinking of all the paintings she had stored in
her art room that her father had built for her, not long after her
mother's death.

"Excellent. I would like you to ship them to me. I will pick out the
best of them, and we will then complete the other arrangements."

"Thank you so much."

"No, thank *you*. I believe you are going to do wonderful things
with your art."

She hung up the phone and ran upstairs, excited. She bumped into
Emilio along the way. How she dreaded these days he was in their
house. It became like a chamber of darkness—a prison where her
every move had to be planned in order to avoid him and his
intimidating tactics. But as she looked into his eyes today, there was
nothing he could do or say to spoil the elation she felt. It was as if her
chains were disintegrating, and she might actually escape the
dreadful hell in which he had imprisoned her for so long.

"Where are you going in such a hurry?"

"None of your business," she spat as she tried to get around him.

He grabbed her arm and squeezed it tightly. "I think it is."

She attempted to yank her arm out of his grasp, sending a burning sensation through it. "No, it isn't. And if you don't let go of me, you sick pervert, I'll scream my head off and tell my father everything you've already done to me."

He slowly let go of her. He applauded. "My, my, you give such a good performance, you little whore. Go tell your father. He'll never believe you. You're nothing but a whore, like your mother was."

Rosa kept on walking, not giving him the satisfaction of any reply. He called her a whore a few more times, until a maid appeared down the hall and he turned to leave. Ha! For the first time his incessant bullying hadn't brought tears to her eyes. No longer did she need to fear this devil that disguised himself in the form of a man. She was filled with the power of her own success.

*****

"WHAT KIND OF BUSINESS ARE YOU IN WITH MY FATHER AND Antonio?" Bella asked while Alex rolled her toward the stalls on their daily outing. They'd spent quite a bit of time together over the past few months, as Alex flew down to Mexico for business on a frequent basis and their friendship was growing.

"Oh, we do some exporting into the States with the coffee and agricultural products. I'm also working in conjunction with the PRI party, helping your father get elected to the presidency. It looks as though I may be moving here to Mexico soon to further help your father." Alex wasn't sure how much she knew about her father's business, but he certainly didn't want her knowing that he was nothing more than a drug dealer.

"Really? What other kinds of agricultural products do you export other than the coffee?"

"You know a little of this, a little of that."

"No, I *don't* know. Why don't you tell me?"

Bella was beautiful, but she was intelligent as well. Most women would've left it alone, but not this one. She didn't miss a beat.

"A variety of agricultural crops. Tomatoes, oranges, bananas, peppers, those types of products."

"Really? I was unaware that my father had any crops. I thought I knew all about his business."

"Apparently you don't."

"I guess you're right, but..."

Alex had to put an end to her unexpected interrogation. He came around front of her chair and planted an untimely kiss right on her lips.

Taken by surprise, she resisted at first, then relaxed and kissed him back. When they finally pulled away, they were both speechless.

After a few moments of silence, she said, "You did that to shut me up, didn't you?"

"I did it because I wanted to."

"That may be true, but it also got me to stop asking you questions."

"I don't feel right, talking about my business with your father to you. I don't think he'd care too much for that."

"Maybe not, but sooner or later I'll find out why you're such a mystery."

Alex hoped that she never would.

The next day, Alex set out again on his walk with Bella. Only this time, he had a different agenda in mind. She laughed as he pretended they were a racecar team, popping wheelies and driving the chair as fast as his legs would carry the two of them.

"Slow down," Bella squealed.

"Slow down? You want me to slow down?"

"Yes," she giggled.

"Err." He came to a screeching stop and walked around to the front of the chair. "Am I moving too fast for you, *Señorita* Rodriguez?"

"Yes," she answered, trying to catch her breath—which she'd lost more from laughing than from the ride itself.

"Do you trust me, Bella?"

"Yes." She brushed her hair back behind her shoulders.

"Do you trust yourself?"

"What kind of question is that?"

"Answer me." He crossed his arms and leaned back on his heels.

"I don't know. I guess I do."

"Good. Take my hand and stand up."

"Alex."

"All you have to do is believe in yourself."

"But the doctors…"

"Those doctors don't know your spirit very well. Trust me and trust yourself. I wouldn't let you fall. I've talked to your therapist and she says that you're very strong and getting stronger every day. Here, I'll wheel you over there to the grass." He pointed to the lawn, surrounded by roses, mums, and dandelions. In the center stood a water fountain with a statue by Giambologna.

"No. I can't do this." She shook her head.

"You can. Come on."

"Why are you doing this to me? Why are you trying to change things between us? You know I can't do this. I'll never be normal. I'll never be a woman for you. Not in the way that you want. Take me back, Alex. Now."

She was such a stubborn girl, and he hated it when she pitied herself in this way. "You will stand. You will walk. Why are you fighting me on this? Try? What do you have to lose? Stop feeling sorry for yourself, and start making things better for yourself."

"Feeling sorry for myself? Is that what you think?"

Alex knelt down and faced her, his hands resting on her knees. "Yes, Bella. It is what I think. You're a strong, determined woman, but your determination is headed in the wrong direction. Don't determine that you're going to be stuck in this chair forever. If you do, that's what will happen."

"Then you wouldn't want to be my friend or...she paused. "Is that what you're saying?"

"You're beautiful, charming, intelligent and your friendship means everything to me, but if you are convinced that you'll never walk and you allow yourself to be a victim, then I don't know if I can be a part of your life."

Bella shoved his hands from her knees. "I was right about you all along. You don't want to be with me because I'm in a wheelchair. You want a walking, dancing Bella."

"Of course I do. As I said before whether or not you're in the chair doesn't change who you are inside. What you make of the chair and your attempt to create a better life for yourself is what makes you who you are. It's when you stop trying that you'll start dying."

"You are so ignorant. Go away. I don't want your help, or your lectures. You may think you're helping me, but you're not. Go away."

"Bella, please. I'm sorry. Please. Maybe not today but you have to promise me you'll try to walk again and not for me or your father, but for yourself.

"Leave me alone. Now!" she yelled.

Pedro came up behind them and wrapped his hands around the handles of the chair. "I think she asked you to go away," he said, his eyes trained on Alex.

"Don't do this, Bella." Alex said ignoring Pedro's presence.

She looked away from him.

After a minute of silence with the watchdog glaring at him, Alex started to walk away. He called back to her. "I won't give up on you, Bella. Don't give up on yourself." He hoped she would listen to his words. He was aware that if she gave up on herself, that she would surely give up on the two of them ever having a relationship. Alex knew that he was falling in love with her and the thought of losing her hurt, but more than that, the thought of her losing herself hurt even worse.

CHAPTER FIFTY-EIGHT

JULIO ARRANGED FOR MIGUEL TO TRAVEL TO A DIFFERENT city almost every day. Today he was in Monterrey, and today would be his thirty-second speech. He was more nervous than usual. The rural areas he'd spoken in brought in the poor, and they were the people who wanted change. However, Monterrey was home to many wealthy people who liked the distance from Mexico City, people who lived in villas and elaborate haciendas and liked the expensive lives they led. He might not be as welcome here as in other places. But it would be a good warmup for the audience Julio had told him would be present in Mexico City. That talk was scheduled for a little more than a week later.

He stepped inside the city's cathedral, glad to see that the gathering was good-sized. This pleased him, and gave him much needed confidence.

He placed his Bible on the pulpit and faced the crowd, his eyes catching glimpse of a young boy of maybe thirteen and his spirit and his faith renewed with the freshness and innocence of this boy. He was on a mission to save children like this one in the audience from succumbing to the evils of drugs and perversion.

"There is only one salvation." He paused and raised his right hand high. "And, that is in Jesus Christ our Lord. There are those out there who deem themselves higher than the Lord and they steal from you, and they deceive you and your families. They kill the innocent, and they reap the wealth. But their evil does not go unnoticed, my friends. Psalms 37; versus 1-4—*Fret not because of evildoers, Be not envious toward wrongdoers. For they will wither quickly like the grass, And fade like the green earth. Trust in the Lord and do good; Dwell in the land and cultivate faithfulness. Delight in yourself in the Lord; And he will give you the desires of your heart.*" With each word spoken, Miguel's voice raised an octave and his strength grew, for the words he spoke were the truth.

"You see, these men who destroy in the name of wealth and power will wither away, but it is good people like you who keep your faith in the Lord who will thrive. However, we must fight against this evil that threatens our cities, our children, and our livelihoods. Drugs and money are the products of evildoers and these men that I speak of, and many of you have heard their names, will be done away with. They come from prominent families and they threaten your very lives. It is time to take their power away and take back our beautiful country from such corruption."

Miguel went on to speak in this manner for over an hour, quoting more verses, speaking of real situations caused by the implosion of drugs being funneled through the country. At one point, he went so far as to name the Espinoza family as being behind much of the corruption. He still had yet to name Javier as a culprit, but by the time he made his way to Mexico City he knew he would be able to do that as well. The people knew of whom he spoke. The implications made were not subtle.

After shaking parishioners' hands and speaking one on one with many of them, Miguel was escorted back to his hotel room where his supper would be brought to him and he could get a night's rest before leaving early in the morning for the next town. He sipped a glass of red wine brought to him by the man assigned to him as his bodyguard. He sighed heavily after taking a long sip and wondered if word had spread about his confrontational speeches. He felt certain that by the end of next week in Mexico City, his words would have spread throughout the entire country.

Julio also warned Miguel that his life might be in danger as he traveled the country. His remarks created great hostility and angered many influential people. But Miguel no longer feared reprisal, for with each sermon, his belief in what he was doing grew stronger. It no longer concerned him about whom he was speaking out against. The evil he wished to see destroyed was far more important.

*****

THE TEN DAYS THAT ALEX WAS AWAY FROM BELLA BEFORE Christmas were difficult, and not knowing if she would ever speak to him again made it more difficult. He didn't realize how close they'd become until they were apart. It was the first time he'd felt happy since before his mother died, and how quickly his mood had changed with her anger and fear. He had to do something to fix things between them and it had to be something big.

He knew that Antonio and Javier were pleased with his work. He'd become adept at laundering drug money through a local family jewelry business. He was also learning how to manipulate accounting procedures.

However, he also knew that Isabella wouldn't approve of these business dealings. He wrote her to say that he was raising campaign funds in the States for her father, who was considering running for President with the *Partido Revolucionario Institucional*, the leading Mexican political party. He didn't know if she would read his letter, but he sent it anyway. In it he apologized for the way he'd spoken to her, but told her that he still believed that she could walk. He told her how much he missed her and he prayed that they could continue their friendship. He hoped she would believe the lies he told about what he did for her father.

Javier was gaining favor with the elite as well as the population at large. Those in power were touting him as a man who would become the first president without any taint of corruption. His status as governor was also helping his political prospects. Things looked good for the coming election, but if Bella and the majority of the population knew the truth about Javier and Antonio's dealings, his chances of winning the election would surely diminish.

Alex enjoyed Bella's naiveté. It lent her a certain sweetness. But he also realized it could harm her in the long run. He wished he could

383 | P a g e

tell her the truth, but that would be impossible if he wanted to keep seeing her.

Instead, he concentrated on his work and on finding a perfect Christmas gift for Bella. One that would please her so she'd have to forgive him and get over the argument they'd had. He was making great money working for Antonio and Javier and he'd been stashing it away. He knew exactly what he wanted to buy her, but he wondered if it was too extravagant. He decided to ask Javier, who agreed that the gift was a wonderful idea.

"Let me tell you, I don't think you have enough money to buy her a horse of the caliber she's used to," Javier told him, when Alex phoned one evening from Los Angeles to discuss the prospect. He added with a chuckle: "And I understand she's quite angry with you."

"Yes, well, maybe that will change with this gift. How much could a horse cost? A couple of thousand dollars?"

Javier laughed aloud. "My dear boy, you are streetwise, but there are some things that you're so ignorant about it's funny. I suggest that I buy her the horse, and you buy her a new saddle. We gave the saddle she used to own to the school after her accident."

"Well, I... It's that I really wanted to buy her the horse."

"All right. Let me put it to you this way, Alejandro. Do you have a few hundred thousand dollars to spare on a horse for my daughter?"

Alex's mouth fell open. "No, I didn't realize..."

"Of course you didn't. The gesture itself is quite noble. You must be falling pretty hard for my daughter."

"I like her a lot, sir."

"Of course you do. Your idea is brilliant, but I think I'll give you an early Christmas present. I'll buy the horse for Bella, and you buy her the saddle. I know you have your mind set on buying the horse for her, so I'm going to give you a list of some contacts I have in the horse business. You will have the joy of finding Bella the perfect mount. As soon as you think you've found it, give me a call and I'll wire the money. But trust me when I tell you that you don't have much time. You'll be booking a lot of flights, because when you're in the horse business, my boy, you have to play like the players."

Alex wasn't sure what Javier meant, but he had the feeling he would soon find out. After getting the names and numbers he needed from Javier, he hung up, dazed by the conversation but excited all the same.

The search proved exhausting. After a week, Alex knew the difference between Holsteiners, Trakkheners, Thoroughbreds, and Selle Francais. He could distinguish between grays, bays, and chestnuts. He began to fancy himself quite the horse connoisseur. He flew from coast to coast, from Miami to the Hamptons, and back to California. After looking at some one hundred different show jumpers, he came across what he'd been searching for, a seventeen hands, bay Holsteiner mare. To Alex, she was the most exquisite animal he'd ever seen—amazingly powerful with big, sweet eyes that reflected a gentle spirit. She was six years old, and her potential was clear when he witnessed her rider sail over various jumps.

Alex knew this young mare was the right one and she had wonderful bloodlines. He got the selling price down to $125,000, and made arrangements to have her shipped from the Florida stables to her new home in Mexico. They paid extra to ensure the mare's arrival by Christmas.

He phoned Javier, who thanked him, telling him he trusted Alex's judgment; he would not need to fly up to look at her for himself. The money was transferred from a Swiss bank account to the owner's account, the transaction swift and neat, and Alex returned to Los Angeles. The mare was on her way to Mexico for Christmas. Alex, his heart filled with anticipation, followed close behind, leaving a disgruntled Hector in charge of operations. Alex felt guilty about leaving everything for Hector to do, but Emilio assured him that it would be all right for the holidays. This would be Alex's second Christmas without his mother. The year before he could barely recall, as his life had recently taken a new path, and he'd begun his studies. This Christmas he wouldn't need to study to escape from his pain of being without his mother over the holidays. This year he would be with Bella, if she would still have him, and thinking about her surprise gift warmed his heart.

*****

"HOW DARE YOU BECKON ME LIKE A SERVANT! WHAT IN THE hell do you want anyway?" Pedro bellowed at Emilio—whose eyes danced with amusement at Pedro's agitation.

"Well," Emilio began as he paced across the floor of the suite he'd rented in Miami Beach for the week, "It would appear, my friend, that you and I have some common interests."

"I doubt that."

"Don't be so quick to jump to conclusions." Emilio shook a finger at him. "I guarantee you'll want to hear what I have to say."

"I'm listening, but I don't have a lot of time," Pedro replied, glancing down at his gold Rolex.

"Alejandro Peña is a thorn in both our sides."

"I don't have any problems with Alex."

"Right. You love seeing him with your precious Isabella. You're hoping the two of them will marry."

"Bella's interest in the boy is over with. Besides, she is like my baby sister. I'm seeing someone else, anyway."

"I'm dubious that she's lost interest in Alejandro so quickly. In six months time those two have gotten quite close. And you may have another woman in your bed, but I also know you covet Isabella Rodriguez as your own. And, that boy will not go away easily."

"Fuck you."

"No, fuck you, because if you were a real man, you'd admit that what I'm saying is true. You can't stand Alex. You can't stand him being near Bella. The thought of him touching her fills you with rage."

"Shut up."

"You wouldn't be so angry if what I'm saying weren't true."

"I don't have to listen to any more of this." Pedro stormed toward the door.

"No, you don't. But if I were you, I'd reconsider. Your secret is safe with me. I also know how to get rid of Alejandro for good. On top of that, I know how to wipe him from Bella's memory." Pedro spun around. "I thought that would get your attention."

"Why? What's your motive?" Pedro asked.

"Let's say, it's personal and necessary."

"I think you're setting me up."

"Think what you want, but I'm telling you, if we work together, we can eliminate that little thorn in our side. Why don't you take the time to listen to what I have to say? If it makes sense to you, we can pull that thorn free. If not, we'll have a troublesome sore for the rest of our lives."

Pedro reached for the door, but something stopped him as he turned the handle. Maybe it was the image of that thorn constantly sticking into his flesh, infecting him from the inside out. Or maybe it was the image of Bella in Alex's bed. He stopped and turned around.

*****

JULIO SPOTTED HER BEHIND THE BAR. HE NEVER FORGOT A face, and there was something special about the woman who was filling up the blender of margaritas. He sat waiting for his DEA contact, who was late as usual. Julio smiled at the bartender as she poured his margarita. After his meeting with the agent was over, he'd work on her for a while to see if he could convince her to spend the evening with him.

An hour passed. No DEA contact. The pretty bartender came over. "Can I get you another drink?"

She didn't look him in the eye.

"Yes, as a matter of fact, you can." It suddenly hit him who she was. She'd aged somewhat. But since he was a man who never forgot a face, he knew when and where he'd seen this one, years ago. He was trained to remember faces.

Luck had struck him like a club on the head. He was looking at the face of Lydia Espinoza. He'd seen her in the society columns, had even met her at a party where he parked cars when he first started working with the DEA. It had been his first assignment to scope out the cars that the money men drove. He came up with a few tidbits, but more than anything, he'd remembered Lydia Espinoza's long legs stepping out of a black Mercedes.

He couldn't believe it. When he'd read of her death, he actually felt a sense of sadness, along with horror at the fact that someone so young and beautiful should suffer such a tragic death. But she hadn't died. Here she was in the flesh. It had to be her. And thus, the false reports of her death had to be the doing of Antonio.

He wasn't sure how he was going to approach her, but he knew that she was Lydia Espinoza and that he could pump a lot of information out of her. When she brought the drink over, Julio forgot all about the agent who'd stood him up. Instead, he concentrated on his newfound gold mine.

"Why don't you sit down and join me for a drink?"

"No, thank you. I've got to work anyway."

"When do you get off?"

"I don't know."

She was curt and cold and he wasn't sure how he'd break her, but he would. He took notice of the cross around her neck.

"I'll wait."

"No. I'm not interested." She wiped down the counter and turned her back to him.

"You go to church?"

She didn't answer.

"Catholic?"

No response.

"My uncle was a priest. Good man. I miss him. I loved the church. I still do. I travel a lot though, and so I go when I can."

She turned around and this time looked at him. "What do you do?"

"I actually do some work for the government and the church. I'm involved with Father Miguel Diaz. You may have heard of him."

There was a hint of recognition in her eyes and a pained look on her face. She immediately regained her composure and nodded.

"We're on a crusade to save this country from the filth that has invaded it. The drugs, those in power with all the wealth, the violence. I'm certain you know what I speak of."

She turned away from him again. "I live a simple life."

"Most of us do or try to, but with the greedy and evil amongst us, it's all we can do to maintain a simple life. Many of us never seem to get our fair share."

"I wouldn't know about that. I keep to myself."

"Yes. Well, I must be going. If you're interested, I'll be at mass this evening at Our Lady of Guadalupe. I would love to see you there."

She didn't respond and Julio walked out of the bar, knowing that even if Lydia didn't show up at mass tonight, he'd gotten under her skin. And in the days to come, she would prove to be a wonderful ally.

CHAPTER FIFTY-NINE

IT WAS CHRISTMAS EVE DAY AND SOON BELLA WOULD
receive Regala. The mare had been delivered in the early hours of the
morning from a nearby stable where she'd been cared for a day until
her unveiling. Javier had picked Alex up, and together they'd gone to
inspect the new horse. Javier seemed duly impressed. "Quite a job
you've done, my boy."

"Thank you," Alex replied. "I looked at a lot of horses, *Señor*
Rodriguez. *A lot* of horses, but the minute I saw her, I knew she was
the one for Bella."

"Did you get the saddle to go along with her?"

Alex nodded. Not only had he bought Bella a saddle, but the
saleswoman in the tack shop had also sold him every conceivable
accessory. Regala had new day sheets, winter blankets, fly masks,
bridles, and halters—anything and everything that a horse and rider
might need. Alex had spent a good portion of his recent earnings on
these gifts for Bella. But she was worth it.

Before the others arrived for the evening, Javier urged Alex to go
and see Isabella. She was seated in the courtyard, wrapped in a

shawl. A breeze tousled her hair. She was reading a book when he came upon her.

She flinched as he surprised her. "Hello," she said coolly.

"Hi. I want to tell you again how..."

She held her hand up. "I know that you're sorry, and you were right. Everything you said to me that day was right. And, I'm sorry that I wouldn't try and that I said those things to you."

Alex placed a finger on her lips. "No more apologies. Let's move on."

She nodded. "Let's move on."

Alex kissed her hand and then her cheek. He wiped the tears from her face. "Come on, the rest of the family should be arriving soon."

"Family?" Pedro asked, walking up behind them. "Who are you calling family? If I remember correctly, this is not your family. You work for the family, but this isn't your family."

"Pedro," Bella scolded. "Don't speak to him like that."

"Bella, can't you see what he's trying to do to you? You wanted no part of him two weeks ago and now he manipulates his way back into your life. Are you blind that all this man wants is to be a part of this family for the wealth and the power? He doesn't care about you."

Alex clenched his fists. "You son of a bitch. That is a lie."

"Alex," Bella pleaded.

"That's enough." Javier had come into the courtyard upon hearing the men's raised voices.

Pedro glared at Alex and pointing at him said, "He's a weasel, a rotten weasel and he will ruin this family. If he is staying here for Christmas, I'm leaving until he's gone."

Javier crossed his arms and glared at Pedro. "Then, I suppose you better go ahead and leave."

Pedro stormed away. Javier put an arm around Alex. "I'm sorry. I didn't know he felt threatened by you. I'll speak to him. Now leave this bad business behind and come inside. I can see that you two have done away with your problems. That's wonderful."

With Pedro gone, and the welcoming arms of Javier and Isabella that received him, Christmas Eve was perfect. The house was decorated in traditional Christmas colors, candles lit the rooms, and the scent of pine and holly rod filled the air. Antonio, Rosa, and Felicia had flown in to join them for the holidays. This pleased Alex. He felt he really had a family.

Shortly after dinner, Antonio asked Alex if he'd like to take a walk with him. Alex looked at Bella, who was seated on the couch, gossiping with Rosa. Felicia had gone to her room to watch television. She was sullen and unhappy for some reason. Javier, who truly loved the magic of the holidays, was off in the kitchen, making preparations for the next day's feast. He always cooked Christmas dinner. It was customary for him to allow the servants time off, and he worked nearly twenty-four hours to see that his grand presentation turned out perfectly—a ritual that had always endeared him to Cynthia.

Alex and Antonio headed out for a walk through the gardens.

"You're a good man, Alejandro."

"Thank you."

"Next week after the holidays, Javier and I have some business to take care of. We are going to Germany. There's some interesting business prospects there. I'll fill you in upon our return if it all works in our favor. We're sending Pedro to Guatemala to set up some new business. As you know, we need Emilio in Los Angeles, but we also need someone we can trust to stay here and oversee our interests from this end. We discussed it today. Javier and I trust you. We think it would be a good idea for you to fill this spot while we're away."

"Thank you. Of course I'll do it."

"Good. You'll stay here in Mexico and oversee things. I'll have Emilio keep you informed of what is happening in both Colombia and Los Angeles."

"Fine."

"There's a catch." Alex looked at him quizzically. "You'll have to play babysitter."

"Babysitter?"

"To Bella. You'll also have to promise me not to touch her, or else there'll be hell to pay." Antonio winked at the boy. "But then again, what her father and godfather don't know won't hurt them."

"I wouldn't think of touching her," Alex replied.

"You say that now, but wait until you're alone with her."

*****

THE NEXT MORNING, PRESENTS WERE PASSED AROUND AND opened. Alex loved the hunting knife Bella gave him. She'd had it specially made for him with turquoise—his birth stone adorning the handle and his initials inserted within the turquoise in red coral.

"Thank you," he said, handling the knife, truly touched by the gesture.

"I saw you one day down near the stables whittling a piece of wood and I thought that maybe you would like to have a special knife to do that with."

He came over to her and kissed her on the cheek. It was sweet of her to notice the little things about him. He felt himself blushing. Something about this girl did that to him. When he didn't hand her a present, he knew that she had to be wondering where her gift from him and her father was.

When everything had been opened, Javier got up from the sofa and walked over to Bella. "I suppose you're wondering what we've gotten for you?" He pointed in Alex's direction. Bella didn't answer, but smiled, knowing that something big was coming. "You see, Alex and I collaborated on a gift."

"Really?"

"Really," Alex said. He got up and brought Bella's wheelchair into the room. "Get in," he said.

"What?"

"You heard him," her father said.

They went down the path heading to the stables. Upon reaching the stables there, in the cross ties next to the head groom, stood the new mare.

"Bella, this is your new mare, Regala," Alex announced proudly.

"What?" She looked back and forth between Alex and her father. "What do you mean, this is my new horse? Why are you doing this to me? What do you expect from me?"

"What's the problem?" Javier asked. "We thought you'd be pleased with her."

"Is she the wrong color?" Alex asked.

"Are you a fool? Can't you see that I can't ride? I can't walk! What are you two trying to do? Drive me mad? Because if so, it's working. I don't want this horse. Send her back. The only horse I want is buried in the ground in France where I can't even visit her grave."

Alex placed a hand on her shoulder. "I know that she isn't Delilah, but in time you'll love her. I'm certain of it. Come on, pet her. She's very kind, very sweet—like you." Alex walked over to the mare and patted her on the neck. She turned her head and nuzzled him.

"Alex went to a lot of time and trouble to find the right horse for you. At least come and see her," Javier said.

"Alex wasted his time. What is it that you two don't understand? I can't ride! My legs don't work!"

"Your father has found an experienced trainer who works with people with disabilities. You'll be riding in no time."

"You call that riding? That's not riding, Alex. Do me a favor and stop trying to make me forget that I have a handicap. Don't buy me

397 | P a g e

anything and don't do anything more for me. Papa, take me back into the house, please!"

"Bella," Javier pleaded. "You're being childish."

"No, I'm being realistic. I want to go back inside."

Javier came back around behind the chair and put his hands on the bars to push her back to the house. There were tears in his eyes. "I'm sorry," he muttered to Alex.

"Wait, Bella!" Alex tossed his arms in the air. "I won't try and do anything more for you. I haven't been trying to make you forget that you're handicapped. You won't allow yourself to forget even if that was what I was trying to do. Your stubbornness and your mind have convinced you that you're a cripple. I wanted you to realize that everything we do is about choices and you can make the choice to do everything you can to live your life to the fullest while in that chair or you can make the choice to remain in the chair. It's up to you. But I can see you don't want or need my help."

"You're right, Alex, I don't. You can take your pity and self righteousness and leave me alone."

Javier took Alex aside. "Let her cool off. She'll settle down."

Alex shook his head. "I think I better leave. I'm sorry that I was tough on her."

"No. She needs to hear it. Thank you. Don't go. Antonio will be upset if you leave and so will I. Stay. Have dinner with us. Let me take her in, and maybe after a rest she'll behave better. Take a walk. The cool breezes are nice this time of year down on the water. It

398 | P a g e

helps to clear the mind. If you want, grab a *cerveza* out of the refrigerator in the tack room."

"Thank you."

Alex watched as Javier and Bella made their way back up the path. He went into the tack room, grabbed a handful of hay pellets for the horse and brought it out to her. She eagerly took them from his palm. He then led her back into her stall and put a day sheet on her. She was a spectacular animal. How could Bella be so stubborn and blind? He grabbed the beer out of the refrigerator and took the walkway down to the sand below and made his way to the ocean where he took his shoes off and walked along the shoreline, kicking up the cold water spray. He'd thought that this Christmas again without his mother would be impossible to endure, but then he'd met Antonio and Javier and his life had changed so drastically. And, of course when he'd laid eyes on Isabella, he knew that he would never be the same. Her handicap wasn't a factor to him. Not at all. She was bright, sweet, funny and the most beautiful woman he'd ever seen. He wanted to be with her, and love her, but she wouldn't allow that. He thought last night, after they'd talked, that things would be different and her focus wouldn't be on what she couldn't do but what she could do. He'd been wrong. Bella would certainly shut him out now.

*****

THE EVENTS AT JAVIER'S ON CHRISTMAS EVE HAD PEDRO
in a rage. He knew that Emilio was staying in town because Antonio
was here, and from his room at Javier's he'd seen Emilio make a
quick appearance on Christmas Eve. Pedro followed him back to the
house and he'd been biding his time before he was sure what he
wanted to do was the right thing. He banged on the door of the villa
overlooking the Bay of Banderas.

"Who the hell is it?" Emilio yelled.

"Pedro."

"What the fuck do you want?" He flung the door open.

Pedro stumbled inside, smelling like booze.

"You're all fucked up. Can't you see I'm busy? Go home."

Pedro took notice of the two scantily clad women, neither of
whom appeared older than sixteen. Pedro nodded in their direction.

"Everyone deserves a good Christmas present," Emilio observed
with a derisive snort. "You want some *fun,* too?"

"No. I want Alejandro Peña dead."

Emilio slammed Pedro up against the wall and whispered,
"Everyone has ears and mouths—including whores—especially
whores." He looked behind him. The women drifted out of sight. " I
already told you that I would take care of him. Get your ass back to
the house before anyone notices you're gone. Someone might want
to know why, on Christmas night, you need to be out of the house.
Keep your fucking mouth shut. I know for a fact that Javier and my

brother are leaving in a few days. We'll take care of the situation then."

"I'm supposed to fly to Guatemala then."

"And I'm supposed to go back to Los Angeles, but I promise you, we'll take care of this first. Now go home."

"Home? I don't have a home. Javier kicked me out because of Alejandro. He told me to come back after Christmas."

Emilio snorted and put his arm around Pedro, "*Mi casa es su casa, amigo.*"

"No thank you. I'll be at a hotel. I'll call you tomorrow. I want this situation handled."

"Whatever you need, amigo. But, I'll call you." He winked at him.

Pedro left the villa. He hated Emilio but not as much as he hated Alejandro. He had no idea why Emilio didn't want the kid around, but he apparently didn't and his reasons didn't matter to Pedro. All that mattered was that Alejandro would soon be forever out of their lives.

CHAPTER SIXTY

ALEX THOUGHT ABOUT ALL THAT HAD OCCURRED IN HIS LIFE
over the past year. It was as if he belonged amongst the Espinoza and
Rodriguez families, and not for the mere purpose of business. They
had become his family. He owed this reclaimed sense of security lost
with his mother's death to Antonio. Alex sensed a connection with
Antonio, as if he'd known him in another life. He had heard about the
theories of karma and reincarnation in a religious class he'd taken
and had to wonder if they might not hold some truths.

But now he walked alone down to the stables. Bella hadn't spoken
to him since Christmas and it didn't look like that would change
anytime soon. It had been a week and now both Antonio and Javier
were off doing business elsewhere, and he was stationed here as an
unwelcome guest. The New Year had passed and he hadn't really
celebrated, other than to have dinner with Javier and a sullen Bella.
He'd overheard her tell her father that she didn't need Alex watching
over her while they were gone and didn't understand why he was
staying.

That had hurt. Javier explained that he was a trusted employee and had become a good friend and that he would be using his office to balance various records and books. Javier's words had healed the hurt a bit, but the silence coming from the woman he was falling in love with was angry and thick.

He didn't know where she was at the moment, probably in her room reading again. She spent a lot of time doing that. He'd even bought her new books and had set them on her dresser when she wasn't close by. She hadn't returned them to him, so maybe she was softening some.

As he turned the corner into the closed-in stable area, cutting off the breeze that had sent a chill through him, that familiar scent of horse, fresh cut hay and manure wafted his way. He liked it, the earthiness of it. He'd made his way to the stables every day. It had become a ritual to go and see the mare that Bella denied. He'd be sad to see the horse go. He'd already placed a call to the original stable she'd come from and the old owners had forwarded him information about someone else interested in the horse. Alex then had called the people and they were still interested and excited that she was again for sale.

Heading for the tack and feed room to retrieve Regala's treats, he stopped, surprised.

There was Bella, in front of Regala's stall, feeding her a carrot. She looked up at him.

"I've found a new home for her," he said.

"So soon?"

"Yes."

"She is lovely," she said.

"Yes, she is."

"Maybe I should keep her."

"That's up to you," Alex replied and approached her, not allowing the tinge of hope he felt come through in his voice.

"I didn't think I could love another horse after Delilah, and I'm not sure that I can, or at least not the way I did with her."

"Of course not. No one is expecting that from you, Bella."

"I suppose if I keep her, then you should call that trainer you were talking about."

Alex didn't reply.

Bella reached up and put her hands around the bars on the stall. She tightened her grip on the bar and pulled with a groan. Alex went behind her and placed his hands under her arms.

"No. I have to do this alone."

Alex removed his hands and watched in awe as Bella grasped the bars even tighter, her hands turning red and with every ounce of strength she could muster, she pulled herself up. She stood for several seconds until she collapsed back into her chair, tears sprung to her eyes.

He knelt down next to her. "You're a stubborn woman."

She laughed between her sobs. "Call the people who want the horse and tell them we're keeping her. I'm going to ride again."

****

ALEX WAS PLEASED THAT BELLA HAD A CHANGE OF HEART.
After leaving the stables and having lunch together, she phoned the physical therapist and told her she wanted to continue therapy and be more aggressive with it. She then asked for the phone number of the horse trainer Alex had told her about and she set up a time for him to come by and see her and the horse. After all the activity she was exhausted and had gone into rest before dinner.

In his gratefulness he felt that his mother had something to do with all that was happening to him. He knew his mother's spirit was there in the room with him, loving him as she always had. And he knew she was at peace. She was letting him know that things were all right with her. He sat down on the bed in the guest room he was sleeping in at Javier's hacienda, thinking of her, of her soul, of his loss, and at the same time, appreciative for the joy he had so suddenly found.

Hearing a sound, he looked up to find Bella, seated in her wheelchair, just inside the doorway to his room, more radiant than he'd ever seen her, her long hair pulled back in a braid. She wore a pink silk blouse with black linen pants.

"I thought you were resting," he said.

"I was, but I was so excited after this morning that I couldn't fall asleep. I thought I'd clean up and come to see you."

"I'm glad that you did. You look beautiful. How do you feel?"

"Fine."

"How about you? Are you all right? You seem sad," she said.

"I'm fine. I was..." He paused and looked out the window away from her and then down at his hands.

"That's all right, you don't have to tell me. I don't want to intrude on your privacy."

"No, really. You're not. I was thinking about my mother."

Isabella rolled her chair over to him and touched his arm. "I think about mine often, too. You must miss her."

"Very much. She was a wonderful woman. She raised me all by herself. My father deserted us before I was born. He was a wealthy man, and she worked for him. I don't know all the details, but I do know that the bastard left us. My mother suffered over the years, slaving for us to get by."

"I'm so sorry. How horrible for you. I didn't know."

He faced her and with a fury building inside of him whenever he thought of his father out there somewhere, he said, "If I ever meet my father, it'll be a sorry day. I have nothing but contempt for him."

*****

THE FOLLOWNG MORNING, BELLA AND ALEX TOOK A WALK down to the beach to enjoy the sunlight bouncing off the ocean. A roll of waves crept up and sprayed the rocky shoreline. Alex looked at Isabella, sitting next to him on a rock. They'd left her chair on the path and he'd carried her across the sand. She was scheduled for a therapy session again that afternoon, so Alex didn't want to push her. Her skin glistened as water splashed against her and she laughed. He laughed with her and wiped the droplets of water from her face.

Moments later her laughter halted and she turned to him, growing serious. "You wouldn't believe how corrupt things are down here," she said. "I've tried talking to my father, but he brushes me off, as if I were some dumb girl. I know my family could do something to help our people, but my father concentrates on making more and more money. I think he does *some* good things. I'm sure of it. I don't know exactly what they are..." She hesitated. "My father is a good man. It's hard for me to imagine him as being a part of the corruption. I try to ignore what we are, but the reality of it is getting harder and harder to avoid each and every day. What do you think, Alex? Do you think there are any honest politicians anywhere? Is my father like the everybody else?"

"I doubt it. But that doesn't make your father a bad man. It only makes him human."

"I suppose you're right. Can I ask you a favor?"

Alex hesitated. "What kind of favor?"

"I know that my brother is speaking in Mexico City in a few days and there is talk that his sermons are on the corruption and how we can change what's happening here in Mexico. I haven't seen or heard from him since the accident, and I really need to see him."

"I don't know, Bella. I think we should talk to your father about this first."

"I'm not a child any longer, and if you won't escort me, then I'll do it on my own. You said I was a stubborn woman. I want to go to Mexico City to see my brother. Will you take me or not?"

Alex sighed. "All right. I'll take you."

At that moment a large wave crashed against the rock they were sitting on, soaking both of them.

"Oh no." She ducked away from the wave.

Alex scooped her up, as they started to laugh again. He was concerned by her request, knowing that Javier wouldn't approve, but he also knew that she would find a way to get to Mexico City on her own. If he didn't allow her to go, it might ruin what they were finally building together.

While Bella was occupied with her physical therapist, he tried to reach Antonio to discuss the situation, but couldn't locate him. He didn't want to upset Javier. He contemplated his next move. He couldn't stand Emilio, but he was Antonio's brother and he had brought him and Hector into the operation. Maybe he should ask his advice. Instead he called Hector.

"Shit, man, take her. They love you, those *Patrónes*. Even if they find out, you know it'll work out. Plus, man, maybe you'll get laid."

"Go to hell. It's not like that."

"Oh yeah, 'cause she can't walk and stuff. Why you want her so bad, then?"

"I'm sorry I called you."

"I just teasing, Cuz. I seen her. She's gorgeous, but be careful. Take her to see her brother. It will make her happy and I don't think anyone would be too mad at you for making the Señor Rodriguez's daughter happy. Good luck, Cuz. Gotta go, Emilio is on his way over. We got a meeting with some new buyers tonight. It's getting big. Real big."

"Right. Listen. Don't mention our conversation to Emilio."

"No *problema*. You do your thing."

Alex hung up the phone, not sure if taking advice from Hector was a good idea, but he did want to hear it from someone else that it was an okay thing to do. Even though, Alex figured it probably wouldn't please Javier. The facts were that Alex wanted to take Bella to Mexico City, away from the watchful eye of the servants. And that he desperately wanted to be completely alone with her.

CHAPTER SIXTY-ONE

MORE THAN TWO HUNDRED PEOPLE SAT IN THE PEWS OF THE church where Father Miguel delivered his sermon in the city of Cuernavaca, a place of spiritual roots and more wealth than most of the places he'd spoken in, other than the seaside resort type areas where his audiences were small. However, they'd been growing with each lecture, and today the audience before him was proof that the crusade was working.

His next stop would be Mexico City. With each town and city in which he spoke, Miguel's convictions grew. Julio had shown him the pictures of innocent slain victims, including women and children, all murdered in the name of money and drugs. And with each returned letter he received from his sister, his belief in what he was doing became stronger.

"The politicians of this country do not work in the name of God. They are not trying to better your circumstances at home. They are not working for the people." He went on to quote from the Book of Romans. He then recited a list of names he believed were enemies of the people and enemies of the Lord. Javier Rodriguez was one of those names.

After the hour-and-a-half service was over, Miguel was drained. As he lay his head down on his pillow that night, he wondered how much time he had left to live. He knew that the implications of his crusade could have deadly consequences for him. He imagined that sooner or later, regardless of his bodyguards, his enemies would catch up to him.

*****

PEDRO RUBBED HIS PALMS TOGETHER, EYEING EMILIO. They were seated at an outdoor café in Los Angeles. Emilio had insisted Pedro come there to see him, in order to put their plan into play. Pedro didn't like L.A. Too many people, too many noises. He preferred the serenity his country held for him rather than the glamour of the big American city. Plus, he didn't like Americans and their pompous attitudes. They had no culture, no history. It was with disdain that Pedro sat across from a man he would normally consider an enemy, or at the very least an opponent. But he had nowhere else to turn.

"We've been struck with luck, my friend. I had one plan at first on how to deal with Alejandro, but it seems that something interesting has happened, and a new plan has been created with great ease." Emilio winked at a buxom blonde who set their hamburgers down.

"What the hell are you talking about?"

"I've been told that Alejandro and Isabella are taking a trip together, while Antonio and Javier are away."

"I don't know anything about this. There's no way Javier would ask them to go on a trip anywhere. Isabella isn't even aware of her father's businesses. I certainly doubt he'd have her travel with one of his *thugs*."

"He asked him to stay with her and not you."

Pedro's grip tightened around his cola. He snarled. "That's because he had me ending business elsewhere."

"Which I can see that you're doing."

"Fuck you, Emilio. You asked me here. You said that you had a plan. What is it? Quit wasting my time, because I do have business elsewhere, and the sooner I get out of this place the happier I'll be."

"Yes, you do have business elsewhere. In Mexico City."

"Since when do you tell me where I'm supposed to be?"

"Since you decided to join me in eradicating the thorn in our side."

Pedro looked out at the street, cars speeding by. He closed his eyes and sighed. "Tell me."

"Isabella misses her brother. As you know, Father Diaz is causing quite a problem for us. He is working with the DEA from what our sources say, and he is vigilant in his efforts to bring us down."

"He's a priest. He can't hurt us. Leave him alone." Pedro had always liked Miguel. In a way he understood the boy's need for revenge. He remembered himself at that age and leaving his father's home, only to return to kill him and find refuge in another family. What Miguel had chosen to do was not much different. Javier had banished him from the family. He'd chosen the church and his country as his new family, and hoped the death of the positive reputation of the man he once called father would thoroughly tarnish his reputation and bring him down from his throne. It couldn't be done. Javier and Antonio retained too much wealth and too much power for Miguel to ever succeed. However, Pedro, although against the crusade and angry that the DEA was using the kid, respected him and understood him for it.

"Can't hurt us? The little people listen to God, and even some of the big people. He's *hurting* us."

"What does this have to do with Isabella and Alejandro? I don't see how Miguel is a part of the destruction of that peon with an ego too big for him."

Emilio lit a cigarette, offered one to Pedro who hesitated before taking it. By the time they were finished with their smokes, Emilio had laid everything out and explained how Miguel fit into the plan. Pedro shook his head, not ready to agree to it.

"This is the best way to get him out of our lives and to get him away from Isabella. Isn't that what you want?"

"You have more than the motive of getting rid of Alejandro at stake."

"True. But, you have to admit, it is necessary that we do this."

After listening to Emilio and taking into consideration what he had to say, he finally nodded his head in agreement. By the following day's end, Alejandro would no longer be a problem.

CHAPTER SIXTY-TWO

ALEX HAD BEEN ABLE TO CONVINCE THE SERVANTS AND others at Javier's hacienda that he was taking Bella to see her father. He knew that if he were caught in this lie, he could possibly be banished from the business and the family. But when he saw the adoration in Bella's eyes when she spoke of her brother, he knew that bringing her to Mexico City was the right thing to do.

She smiled sweetly at him as she turned from the hotel's reception desk, a message in her hand. She rolled her chair over to him and handed him the note. "My brother received my message this morning and he'd be delighted to see us today."

"I'm so happy for you," Alex said and bent down, giving her a kiss on the cheek, after reading over the message. "We better get going, though. The note says he'll be expecting us at one o'clock and that's only a half an hour away."

"Good, good." She clapped her hands. "Can we walk? I want to enjoy the city. Do we have time?"

"Perhaps. I don't think it's too far. It's a residence only a few blocks from here. I think that's a great idea." He smiled at her.

As he rolled her out into the bright, crisp day, Bella turned her head to the side. "I noticed that you brought the knife that I gave you for Christmas."

Alex laughed. "You notice everything. I love it. I know it's for whittling, but for the time that we're here in Mexico City it's also for protection. I brought it because we're here alone and I have to make sure that nothing happens to you."

"Nothing will happen to me."

"I know, especially since I have this knife." He felt for it in his back pocket.

As they crossed the street, a group of children around ten or so, clamored around them, some behind them, some in front, laughing and gawking at Bella's chair. Alex told them to go away.

They arrived at the home where Father Miguel was staying. A guard stood at the entrance and after they identified themselves, let them through. Following another guard, a bald, angry looking large man dressed in black, Alex rolled Bella through the entry and down the hall leading to Miguel's' room. The guard's dark eyes never met either one of theirs, and Alex found it odd that he was the one protecting Miguel. However, what Miguel was doing was dangerous, and Alex knew it was almost as dangerous for him to be here. He was, in fact, a part of the group the priest was trying to destroy. He was also Isabella's brother and Alex could not deny her this visit.

The bodyguard said to Bella, "Father Miguel has asked that you wait here for a moment. He has something to say to your guest first."

She looked puzzled and turned her face up to Alex. "I don't understand."

"It's all right. I'll go in and see him. I'm certain it will only be a moment."

"I suppose if that's what my brother has requested, then I'll wait."

"I'll wait with you, *Señorita*," the bodyguard said.

Something about the way the man said it didn't sit well with Alex, but he went inside the door that the bodyguard opened for him and closed it behind him.

The priest had his chair turned so that the high back of it was facing Alex. The room was a study, and Alex assumed that Miguel was looking through the books on the shelves he faced.

Alex cleared his throat. "Father. Hello. I was told that you wanted to see me. I'm Alejandro Peña. You obviously know that I've escorted your sister here to see you. She's very excited about the visit." He paused waiting to see if he'd receive a response from Miguel. "That said, if you want to tell me what you need of me, it would probably be nice to get the anticipation over for Isabella."

Miguel still did not turn around or say anything. Alex brought his palms up to his face as in prayer and breathed deeply, letting out a long sigh, figuring that the priest wanted to take up the fact that Alex worked for the very enemy he wanted to destroy. He was sure that Miguel had asked around about who he was and discovered that he wasn't simply Isabella's friend.

"Listen, Father Diaz, I'm only here as a friend of Isabella's. I have no ulterior motives. She desperately wants to see you. She's missed you a great deal, and my goal is to make her happy. The time with you means so much to her."

Alex thought he heard a type of gurgling sound as if maybe Miguel was clearing his throat, but it wasn't exactly like that. Alex approached the desk and the chair. "Please, Father, what do you need from me?" Alex asked.

When Miguel didn't respond again, Alex hesitantly came closer to the desk. He blinked and then stared at the object on the desk, half hidden under a stack of papers. It took him almost a minute to register what he was seeing. He felt his back pocket. *His* knife was missing. The kids on the street. He picked up the knife on the desk. The one Bella had given him. It *was* his. *His* initials were there on the knife and it was covered in blood. He went around to the other side of the desk to the chair the priest was in. The man looked at him, his eyes filled with horror as his body shuddered and all of the life left him. Blood streaked down the front of his white cassock, looking like a sacrificial lamb that had been slaughtered. Alex shook his head and backed away from the scene, his stomach dropping filled with nausea. "No, no, no," he moaned.

A tap at the door sounded. It opened and in came Isabella, who saw that her brother's throat had been slit and his tongue pulled through the back of his mouth in what was known in the drug world as a Colombian necktie. She froze and as it registered what she was seeing, and as she looked at Alex holding the knife, she howled.

The bodyguard plowed through the door, knocking a stunned Alex to the ground and taking the knife from his hand. Soon after, the bodyguard from outside and another man were in the room. One of them hit Alex hard across the head. The room whirled and Bella's screams resounded in his ears as his world went black.

*****

ALEJANDRO GAGGED FROM THE ROTTEN FECAL STENCH inside the dismal cell. He retched, holding his stomach, which contained nothing but bile. No one had brought food to him in more than forty-eight hours. After he'd lost consciousness, he found himself being slapped awake, a group of policemen standing over him. Bella was nowhere in sight and he kept asking for her, but they ignored his pleas.

They dragged him to his feet, handcuffing him. His mind shouted, "This is all a mistake." However, he knew that his protests would be useless.

His body ached from the beating he'd endured. But Alex knew that the worst punishment was yet to come—the knowledge that Bella thought him a murderer and not only a killer, but the one who savagely destroyed her brother. He hadn't cried since the death of his mother, but now it was all he could do to keep from collapsing in despair.

The worst of it was that Alex knew they would never achieve the dreams and plans they'd made together. He hugged himself tightly, closing his eyes, hungry for Bella's warmth—warmth he knew he'd never feel again.

CHAPTER SIXTY-THREE

THE FIRST MEETING BEHIND THE BACKS OF ANTONIO AND JAVIER

had been called. Emilio knew which buttons to push, and how to get away with pushing them. Seated in the large conference room inside the warehouse where the drugs were stored was a group of about twenty men, most of them uneducated, who'd come to America to make their dreams come true. They'd discovered the hard way that it wasn't as easy as they had once thought.

These men were the drug pushers, the foot soldiers of the organization, the ones on the street. They risked their lives, and the threat of being sent back to Mexico if they were caught hung over their heads. Emilio and Hector had plans for all of them in their new regime.

The men all sat around a long, wooden table, fidgeting and looking at each other nervously. No one had ever called them for a meeting before. Hector usually met with them on the street and brought them the drugs they needed to sell.

"Hello, gentlemen. Thank you for coming," Emilio began. "I'm sure you're all wondering why you are here."

The young men stared at him, full of fear and curiosity.

"You're here because you have a new job to do. You now work for me and Hector. Your orders will not come from my brother, Señor Espinoza, or from Javier Rodriguez. They will come directly from me from now on. But all this is to be kept quiet. When we tell you to do something, you will do it. Things are going to change around here. You will report directly to Hector every day. You will pick up your product on a daily basis. In the evening, you'll bring us what you do not sell, including the day's take. Then the shift will change. Whoever works evenings will take their cut, and come back in the morning. You will account for everything spent, and every ounce sold. There will be no stealing within this organization. Do you understand? Up 'til now, things have been way too flexible. We've gotten wind that some of you have been stealing drugs and money from us."

"We don't like that," Hector chimed in.

The men looked at each other, not quite understanding the implications of what was being said in this cold, dim room. One of the young men, Juan, who was considered more courageous than the others, interrupted the proceedings. "This don't sound right to me. I think I don't want to be a part of this."

"Really now? Well, Juan, I don't think you have to worry about that," Hector sneered. "Remember when I said we heard some of you men have been stealing from us? We heard it was you, man."

Juan looked surprised. "Me? No way. I never stole from you. I always gave you your money and did everything right."

"We'd like to believe you, but we don't," Hector answered him curtly. Then, as if time had slowed to a standstill, Hector pulled out a .22 from his long, dark coat and shot the man in the head. Blood spurted everywhere. Juan's head rolled forward as he slumped in his chair, life completely drained from him. The other men gasped, and then quickly fell silent, looking away from the ghastly scene.

"Does anyone else have a problem with us?" Emilio quietly asked them, but the men were too dumbfounded to mutter a response.

"Good," Emilio said, a slow smile creeping across his face. "Clean this mess up, and get rid of him. Business will begin tomorrow. You can have today off. If anyone speaks of what went on here today, they'll wind up the way Juan did."

The two men swept out of the building, high as kites on the coke they'd been doing all morning, ready to cause more trouble to bring down their empire by transferring its source of power.

"Now, my friend, we fly to Bogotá, and then on to Guatemala." Emilio winked at Hector. He knew from experience that the other man was high at that moment from not only the drugs but also from the killing. Emilio could tell by the look in his henchman's eyes that he'd loved it—loved the feeling, loved the power, and couldn't wait until he could do it again. Emilio would be certain to see that Hector got that chance.

*****

SORROW SO PAIN FILLED IT HELD BELLA'S HEART IN A VISE and swept through her entire body, while disillusionment and tears clouded her vision. Pedro sat across from her inside the hotel suite that had only two days before been adjoined by Alex's suite. Now Pedro was staying there. Directly after seeing her brother slain, and after Alex was arrested, she was taken by the bodyguard and another man. They stayed with her until Pedro arrived a couple of hours later. He'd told her that her father was being notified and would be leaving Europe with Antonio soon. They expected them that afternoon.

Her world had changed in those two days and she could hardly speak to Pedro at that moment. She wanted nothing more than to curl up and die. How could the man that she loved, or thought she loved, kill her brother? Her beloved and dear brother. She didn't understand. A thought crossed her mind time and again: she wondered just how corrupt her family was. She was beginning to believe the stories she heard about them, and now she wondered if her own father hadn't asked Alex to kill Miguel. She didn't want to think such a horrible thought, but she couldn't help herself. She could not believe that Alex had done this. *Why?* He was not a cold, evil man. At least she'd thought that. He claimed he cared for her. Yet, she saw him there, with the knife in his hand with her brother's blood on it, and until Alex had gone in there alone, her brother had been guarded. None of this made sense.

Placing her face in her palms, Bella cried uncontrollably. "I can't believe this. Why? Why would he do this? Did my father order this? Is that why? I know that everything you say you do with my father, everything Alex has tried to tell me that all of you do for him and Antonio is legitimate, but I have ears and a brain, and I no longer believe you."

"Bella, that may be so. You will have to speak to your father on these issues. I feel you should be more aware of what goes on in this family and business. If it were my choice you would know everything." He took her hand. "But I know that your father had nothing to do with this, or Antonio either. Alex was pathologically jealous."

Emilio interrupted as he entered the room. He'd arrived that morning. He walked over to Bella and placed a hand on her shoulder. He stood above her in an authoritative manner. "I believe there was a side to this young man you were quite unaware of. He hated the thought of your being close to any other man—even one whom you thought of as your brother and friend. Even a *priest*."

"If that's the truth, then why do this almost in front of me? If he was so jealous and did this out of love, why so brutal and why while I was there?"

Pedro nodded his head in agreement. "That is a good question. It troubles me, too."

Emilio shot him a grave look.

"However, it is possible that he's plain crazy, and had it in his mind to rid you of all the men in your life, even including your father and myself. Are you aware that his mother was killed in Los Angeles a couple of years ago? She was shot down. They never found the killer and at the time Alejandro was nowhere to be found. It is possible that this boy has kept his dark side hidden so well from us that we were all fooled by him. I truly believe him insane."

Bella shook her head. "That is ridiculous," she exclaimed. "Are you implying he murdered his own mother? I cannot believe or listen to any more of this."

"It's true," Pedro said.

"I'm going to see him."

"No!" Emilio ordered her.

"I'm going, Emilio. I have to talk with Alex."

Emilio paced the floor, the oak planks creaking beneath his heavy feet. He shot Pedro a glance, then turned and left the room.

"If you insist on going, I'll drive you," Pedro said. There was no way he was going to allow Bella to see Alex without him there, and by the look in Emilio's eyes, he knew that they would have to make certain that Bella accepted their lies.

*****

THE HORRENDOUS CRIES ESCAPING FROM THE PRISON CELLS pricked Bella's nerves. Already distressed over Miguel's murder and Alex's imprisonment, the disturbing sensation she felt as Pedro rolled her along those cold corridors assailed even the marrow of her bone.

A prison guard, who looked as if he'd been stuffed into his uniform, came around behind the chair after he explained to Pedro that only one of them at a time could see Alejandro.

The guard escorted her into a small room, where she was told Alex would be brought to her. "Usually we don't allow anyone to see the prisoners. But since you're the governor's daughter, well…"

"Thank you for your cooperation." Bella had telephoned the prison before they left and insisted she be able to speak to Alex. She even offered a bribe if necessary.

Once inside the room, she sat in one of the chairs at opposite ends of a small wooden table. It was dank, and smelled worse than a trash bin. Alex was led in, shackled on his feet, his arms handcuffed in front of him. His head was down, but when he raised it, he looked straight into her eyes. She gasped. She could see that he'd been badly beaten. Dried blood trickled down his chin. His right eye was swollen closed and purple, the other one half closed and bloodshot. His face was bruised almost beyond recognition.

"My God!" Bella exclaimed.

"Shhh," he said. "I'm all right." The guard shoved him down into the chair opposite her. She got up to go to him.

"No," The guard ordered her. "It is against prison rules." She sat back down, not taking her eyes off Alex. She nodded at the guard, who turned to leave the room.

"I'll be right outside," he told her.

She couldn't say anything at first, her mouth gaping open.

"I must look pretty bad?" he asked.

"Oh, Alex does it hurt?"

"I'm fine." He winced.

"The police? Did they do this to you?"

He nodded.

"Look at me, Alejandro. We don't have much time I know what I saw. My brother…" She choked on her words. "Did you do that? Did you kill him?"

He shook his head. "No." He looked up at her. "I love you, Isabella. You have to believe me." Although he'd never uttered those words aloud, he'd thought about his feelings for Bella quite a bit the last two days, and what had occurred, brought him to the need to voice it. If she heard him say it, then maybe it would make things right between them. Maybe she would believe him. "I would never do anything to hurt you. I know how much you loved your brother. I couldn't kill him or anyone."

Bella closed her eyes, tears coming down her face. "Then how? Who?"

"I don't know. You have to believe me. Someone set me up."

"The knife? Your knife?"

"Those kids, when we were walking to meet your brother, I think one of them took it. The knife was in the room when I went in. On the desk. I swear."

"Am I to believe a child did that?"

The prison guard opened the door. "Your time is up. Say goodbye."

Bella unlocked the brakes on her chair. She rotated it toward the door.

"Tell me that you believe me, Bella. Please, you have to help me."

Not looking at him, she said, "I don't know what to believe."

Pedro was right there to take the handles of the wheelchair and escort her out of the prison.

She wanted to believe Alex. Needed to, but the proof and now the story of the children. Maybe he was crazy as Pedro suggested. Her mind understood that possibility, but her heart would never accept it.

*****

WHEN ANTONIO HEARD THE NEWS THAT HIS SON WAS imprisoned for murdering Miguel, he immediately cut short his trip in Europe, where he and Javier had been meeting with a group of wealthy and powerful Germans who were eager to do business with them instead of with the Italian mafia.

On board the jet, Javier poured himself his third large shot of tequila and offered some to Antonio, who refused. "I cannot understand this. First of all, why would Alex take Bella to Mexico City without speaking with one of us? I want to kill him for that alone. Why would he murder Miguel? You must imagine how this will look to all of those he'd been spreading his rhetoric to. Once the connection is made between Alex and you and then possibly me, it will be bad. Pedro has told me that Bella was witness to the carnage. For God's sake, he didn't just cut his throat; he pulled his tongue through the back of his head! What kind of man did you bring on board our operation?" Javier shot back the booze and slammed his hand against the tray in front of him.

"That man is my son."

"What if he's not? It may not be so. Have you considered this?"

"Alejandro is my son. Marta was his mother. Look at the boy and you know he's mine. I told you he was mine and that's the end of the discussion."

"Maybe Alejandro knows you're his father. Maybe this is his revenge. Could he want to destroy this operation, this business, your family and mine out of his hatred for you? What if he knows? It would make sense."

"He doesn't know."

"How can you be sure of that?"

Antonio glared at his lifelong friend. "Because I know." He thumped his chest. "I also know he didn't murder your stepson. The boy is not a killer. He has his mother's heart."

Javier was not convinced as he poured himself another drink. He'd known Antonio since they were boys and he knew that what existed in the man's heart was not always good. He could kill without thought. He ordered people to be sent to their graves on a regular basis. How could Antonio expect Javier to believe that if it was true that Alex was indeed the man's son, that the boy would not be like his father?

Afraid to further press the issue with an already cross Antonio, Javier remained quiet for the rest of the flight home. A thought crossed his mind several times on the way back to Mexico, and upon seeing his distraught daughter and hearing her cries, this thought, he knew would have to put into effect. It was time for him to part ways with his best friend and partner Antonio Espinoza.

****

AFTER FLYING FOR FIFTEEN HOURS, ANTONIO HAD HIS driver take him straight to the prison in Mexico City, where Alex was being held. Javier had gone to the hotel to see Isabella.

"Alejandro Peña is not allowed to see visitors." The warden met Antonio at the entrance. He was a tall man, slight in build, with narrow dark eyes, and greasy hair. His eyes seemed to nearly close as he spoke.

Antonio immediately sized him up as a miserable functionary. "I believe you will allow me to see him."

"No, *Señor*, as I have already explained, no one is allowed in to talk to him."

Antonio got in the man's face and stared straight into his eyes. "My name is Antonio Espinoza. Does that name mean anything to you? Because it should. I am allowed to see *Señor* Peña. Odd, but people who give me a difficult time always have such terribly bad luck. I would certainly regret your having bad fortune the rest of your life."

The warden's hands shook as he nodded his head. He turned around, and motioned for Antonio to follow him. When they arrived at the small interrogation room and Alex was seated across the table from him, Antonio was shocked to see the cuts and bruises on Alejandro's face and noticed that he looked much thinner than he had ten days before, when Antonio had left for Germany.

"My God. What have they done to you?" Antonio blurted.

"Tried to kill me," Alex answered in a weak voice that sounded as if it was coming from a broken heart.

"I know you didn't murder Miguel."

"You're the only one who does."

"And the murderer, of course. Do you know who that is?" Antonio placed his hands on the table.

"I don't know." Alex looked away from Antonio.

"Are you positive?"

"Yes. I know, or I think that the man who was supposedly his bodyguard was involved."

"Do you know the man's name?"

"No."

"I'll find out. I'm already working on getting you out of here. Whoever did this to you probably would go so far as to have you killed, if needed. With me, you'll be protected. You stay here and I'm certain that you'll die."

"But how? There is no way they're going to let me out. The entire country is seeking my blood."

"There isn't anything money can't buy. Including innocence."

"But I *am* innocent."

"I know that. If I didn't think you were, I might let you rot in here. Killing a priest is a terrible sin, indeed. I wouldn't want to be any part of that. If things go the way I want them to, you will be out of here in forty-eight hours. No trial. Nothing. You will be vindicated on all charges."

"Can we keep this quiet?" Alex asked.

"We'll have to, for awhile."

"Good."

"Stay careful and awake. I have a lot of work to do. I'll be back tomorrow. Don't worry, though. No one is going to hurt you anymore." Antonio walked over and placed his hands reassuringly on Alex's shoulders.

*****

"BELLA, I LOVE YOU AND I WANT TO MARRY YOU. I PROMISE that I'll take good care of you," Pedro beseeched her, knowing that time was of the essence. With the return of Javier and Antonio, Pedro felt the chase of fear in his stomach. If they knew what he and Emilio had done, they would be killed.

After Javier had shown up at the hotel, Pedro played it like Emilio had told him to. Emilio had promised Pedro that he would get Bella, and in return Pedro would help in handing over the business to Emilio. This part had not been as difficult as Pedro thought when Emilio suggested it.

"Once Javier is there, tell him that you think maybe it would be best for him to sever ties with Antonio. That if the people of the country wanted someone to blame and started looking into Alex's ties, then it would all come back to Antonio and not Javier."

Javier had said that it was already a consideration.

Now all Pedro had to do was convince Bella that he was the right man for her. Once this was all behind them, he would take her back to France where she loved the country and they could have a different life than what they'd been leading in Mexico. By taking her there, she would never find out the truth about Miguel's death. It was something that still pained Pedro. He hadn't liked Emilio's idea, but he'd gone along with it, seeing that the ends did justify the means. He'd done as Emilio advised that day at the outdoor café in Los Angeles.

"I've already spoken to the man who is Miguel's bodyguard. Seems his loyalties can be swayed with the right amount of money. You're to take one hundred thousand American dollars in cash, which I have right here." Emilio had patted a leather briefcase, next to him.

Pedro set down his cola. "Am I to buy Miguel's death?"

"No. You're to buy Bella's love and your freedom from the nuisance that has been infiltrating *your* family. Alejandro will have that knife he always carries, the one Bella gave him. I have already instructed the bodyguard on how to handle the entire situation. All you have to do is take the money to him."

"Why can't you do this?"

"I have other business to conduct. As you are putting your plans into action, I have some things to do here to make sure my future goes as planned."

"I don't know. I don't like having Miguel murdered."

"What will you hate more? Isabella with Alejandro's ring on her finger? He *will* marry her if you don't do this. Can't you see the way they look at each other? Don't be a fool."

Pedro had taken the money and flown to Mexico City that evening, where he met with the man who had been Miguel's bodyguard and gave him the money. He would be damned before he'd let his princess marry a hoodlum like Alex, even if it meant shedding the blood of a man he thought highly of.

And now Pedro heard his Bella say," But Pedro, you're like a father or a brother to me, not a husband. I can't marry you."

"In time you will learn to love me that way. And until then, we don't need to be physically intimate, if that's what you're worried about."

She blushed and looked away. "I can't walk. You wouldn't want me as a wife." She couldn't believe what he was suggesting. She was trying to make excuses and be kind to him, but the thought of being his wife was upsetting. She had no idea he felt this way about her. She hoped her father would hurry back from the hotel restaurant where he'd gone for a cup of coffee.

"Stop that. I've seen you with the physical therapist and I know you've been holding out on your family."

"You've been spying on me?" Anger welled inside her. She had been taking a few steps here and there with the therapist, but she had made her promise to keep it from her family. She wanted to surprise her father on his fiftieth birthday, which was only a couple of weeks away.

"Of course not. I saw one day when I was taking a walk through the garden. I didn't say anything then because I know you, and I knew that you would want to be the one to tell the family. I'm sorry."

She studied him and continued to listen.

"I will take care of you. You know I will. Your father would be so pleased."

"No. I don't want to marry you. I can't think of you like that."

Pedro's face turned an angry red. "Are you still thinking of Alejandro? Let me tell you, Alejandro is going away for a very long time, for the rest of his life, if they don't put him to death first. He killed your brother. He is a beast, an insane beast. You don't love him and he never loved you. Get him out of your head. You will be happy with me. Don't be foolish."

A knock sounded at the door.

"Yes?" Bella asked.

"It's your godfather."

"Go and let him in," Bella ordered Pedro.

He walked to the door and as he opened it to let Antonio in, he turned back to her before walking out. "You don't have to make a decision right now. Think about it. I know how unhappy you've been lately."

"What was that all about?" Antonio asked after Pedro left the room.

"Nothing."

"Would you care to join me for a walk? I think we have something to talk about." Antonio asked.

Bella nodded and left the hotel with her godfather, hoping he would have the answers she was looking for.

*****

JULIO MOVED LYDIA INTO THE STUDIO HE'D RENTED IN
downtown Calí, within six weeks after meeting her. At first she'd
been cold and difficult. But he'd found common ground in talking
with her about her faith. And now, he knew more about this woman
than any other he'd ever met. Their faith was a common ground. But
they'd found a passion in each other that, although many would have
considered it sinful, they'd found it heavenly.

After not having been with a man for eleven years, Lydia craved
him by her side. She matched his insatiability perfectly.

One night lying in bed after making love, Julio began to question
her about her background and where she was from. They'd had
several *cervezas* and he'd told her he loved her. She hadn't replied,
but he didn't expect her to. Instead she told him about her life and
what had happened to her over the last ten years.

She told him about the kidnapping, the whorehouse, the drugs,
the convent, Father Miguel, and then her determination about
retrieving what was rightfully hers. In particular, she wanted to take
back the love of her daughters.

Julio told her about working with the DEA and being a part of the
Guatemalan militia, along with their plan to wipe out drug dealers.
He told her about his involvement with Father Miguel.

Lydia smiled at him knowingly. Although she'd never alluded to it
during all the years she'd been with Antonio, she knew all about his
business operations. She also knew that anything could be done for a
price, including getting drugs into neighboring countries. She felt

sure that Julio was part of that corruption in his own way, but it didn't really matter to her. What mattered was that she was lying next to this man whom she felt comfortable with, and he loved her.

"What do you want from me?" she asked. "You're not in my bed only for love."

"Maybe not, but you do know that I love you, Lydia."

"Yes." She sighed.

He reached for her hand and brought it to his lips. She smiled sadly at him. "But this here, what we have between us isn't solely about love, is it?"

He shook his head. "Maybe you can or can't help me. Maybe you know or could tell me something about Antonio or his crew that I haven't heard. What do you have to lose? They think you're dead."

Hearing this from him upset her and reinforced her anger. The thought of her children thinking she was dead infuriated her. "I can't believe he went to such lengths to get rid of me. Why not simply ask me for a divorce if he hated me so much?"

"Not his style, but neither is what he's done to you. It seems far too cruel to even be the work of Antonio. His family is very important to him. He's ruthless, but..." Julio paused. "Do you know anyone else involved who might have wanted you gone?"

She considered the question seriously for the first time. Although she hated the thought, one name came to her: "Emilio."

"Emilio? His brother?"

"Yes."

"Why?"

"The baby."

"Baby?"

Lydia had left that one detail out of her story. She'd never told anyone this story—not the nuns, not Father Miguel, no one. But here she was, pouring out the last eleven years of her life to a near stranger, who had taken over her life with passion and a sense of renewal. The relief that engulfed her after she told him the story about the affair with Emilio and then her pregnancy and what had happened afterwards made her positively euphoric. She'd released it, and together they held each other, as she cried tears of freedom.

After that night, Julio and Lydia joined ranks. Julio taught her the ways of his world, how to spy, tap phone lines, and investigate potential informants. She learned quickly, like a child greedy for knowledge.

On the days when he was out, he asked her to keep a low profile. "You're too close to your old home," he told her one evening. "I know that you ventured out this afternoon to spy on your daughters out shopping. I was watching."

"I am sorry. They didn't spot me. I know how to disguise myself well now. I really want to see my girls."

"In time, love. Keep patient."

She abided by his rules for a couple of weeks, until she could no longer wait. She found a spot near her old home where she could park the small car Julio allowed her to use and then she'd follow whichever daughter would leave first, if only to get a glimpse.

Felicia had a certain pattern: she liked to shop. She bought a lot of makeup, clothes, and lingerie. Lydia smiled as she watched her bounce along the streets of stores, still every bit the mischievous girl with the flirty eyes. She was captivating. It was impossible not to notice all the men leering at her. It made Lydia want to slap their faces, but Felicia smiled back at her admirers, unfazed by their blatant stares. In fact, she seemed to welcome them. This troubled Lydia, who prayed that her youngest daughter was not too promiscuous, even though she suspected that Felicia was.

Rosa had a very different routine. Each day, she would go to the park or the library, where she studied art or worked on one project or another. Lydia could never get close enough to catch a glimpse of exactly what it was her daughter was working on, but she still felt enormously proud of her, seeing her working so hard. They always had a bodyguard in tow.

After spying on them for a few weeks, Lydia decided to back off once she'd investigated one more avenue. She'd witnessed Rosa going into a doctor's office each week. It was the only time that a bodyguard didn't shadow her daughter. The next time she followed Rosa closer than she ever had before, she passed by a door that read *Dr. Martinez, Psychiatrist.*

Lydia was bothered about why her oldest daughter needed to see a psychiatrist. She decided to put her new skills to the test. She knew that what she was about to do was wrong, but she had to. She had to find out what was troubling her daughter.

*****

ROSA HAD MADE A CONSCIOUS DECISION TO GET WELL.

The nightmares and broken sleep, the binge eating she did in those hours that she couldn't sleep, and the fantasies she had about torturing and killing her uncle plagued her and came through in her art. Although, her violent pieces of artwork had interested a dealer and agent, she longed to paint serene pieces. Painting was her life, and although she loved it, each time she sat down with a brush and paints she relived the traumas of the past, and she wanted it to stop. She needed to get well for her own sanity. She'd started seeing Dr. Martinez a month earlier, and last week had begun telling him about her uncle.

As she sat across from the middle-aged doctor who spoke in hushed tones, she became comfortable enough with him to tell him what her uncle had put her through. The therapist listened intently. It felt so good to tell someone at last, and have that person tell her that none of it was her fault. Her relief was great and the hour passed quickly. As she left his office, she barely noticed the woman seated in his waiting room, reading a magazine. The woman wore dark glasses and kept her head down. *Another one of the shamed,* Rosa thought as the door closed behind her.

*****

ROSA HAD BEEN SO CLOSE FOR A MOMENT. LYDIA WANTED to touch her, talk to her, embrace her. But the time was not right, and she'd had to clasp her hands together hard when her oldest daughter walked by, just so she wouldn't touch her. She'd had to bite the inside of her mouth, afraid that if she said anything, that it would all escape her. She hadn't, though, and after a few more moments in the waiting room, Lydia stepped inside Dr. Martinez's office, having fabricated a story of an abusive, alcoholic husband to justify her being there.

Her recent relationship with Julio had taught her many things in a short amount of time. Bugging offices was fairly easy, and that's what she'd done the night before. She didn't necessarily need to make this appointment with the doctor, but she'd already taken enough of a risk the night before by breaking and entering, then planting the bug inside his office. She knew that she could easily reach under the chair she sat on and retrieve the small device when the doctor wasn't looking. Her opportunity came within fifteen minutes of the start of their session when the doctor was paged on his beeper.

"One moment please," he told her as he held up a hand. "I hate to do this, but I really need to return this call. I have a patient I'm very concerned about."

"No problem," Lydia replied. The doctor closed the door behind him when he went into a separate office to make the phone call.

Lydia quickly retrieved the bug, quietly got up, and left the doctor's office without leaving any explanation.

Within a few hours, she knew exactly why Rosa was seeing a doctor. The words she heard her daughter speak horrified her. The truth hit Lydia with the force of a hurricane and she hated Emilio for what he'd done to her daughter. His name had come to mind, but she'd never believed he would have done this to her or her child. She had always thought that Emilio loved her. Maybe it had been a woman's intuition that had made her utter his name the other night in bed with Julio, but to accept it as truth and then to hear further that he'd raped her child after she was gone, made her physically ill.

When she was finished vomiting, she pieced it all together. Emilio had been the one who had her kidnapped. As she listened to her daughter's sweet voice and heard her tears of shame, Lydia realized further that it had been Emilio all along who'd set her up. He'd gotten rid of her because she had stopped fitting into his plans. Her anger was now focused on the right man.

CHAPTER SIXTY-FOUR

THE SMALL AIRCRAFT CIRCLED THE LANDING STRIP IN THE middle of the overgrown jungle. Emilio glanced over at Hector, asleep on the seat across the aisle, smiling through his drug-induced bliss. Emilio slapped him across the face. "Wake up, *pendejo*. We're here."

Hector sat up straight and rubbed the side of his face like a scolded puppy. "That hurt, man."

"Shut up."

The pilot brought the small plane down. It rolled roughly across the dirt strip, bouncing and jostling the load of drugs it carried, as well as the plane's three occupants.

Once the plane came to a stop, Emilio looked around, but didn't see anyone. "Hold on," he said to the pilot and stepped out of the plane. He heard his name being called, and looked across the strip towards an old metal shack, where he could see Julio and another guy waiting. Emilio waved. He went back to the plane. "We're all clear."

The pilot and Hector got out. "Do you want us to start unloading?" Hector asked him.

"Let me take care of business first." Emilio waved a hand at him as he went to meet Julio, who was walking towards them. He had a good feeling that business with this Julio would prove to be fruitful. At first, Emilio had been on the alert about Julio, since they'd met one another at a bar in Mexico City a couple of months back, while Emilio had been there doing some business transactions for Antonio. More grunt work, but not for long. Emilio had gotten to talking with Julio. He liked the guy, and Julio seemed to know the right people. More importantly, he had the right amount of dollar bills.

Their last meeting was shortly after Emilio staged the hit on Miguel and the setup of Alejandro. He and Julio met in Mexico City at a strip joint. After a few drinks, a sample of the cocaine Emilio was pushing on his new business partner, and some talk of big money and large amounts of drugs, the talk turned toward the murdered priest.

"This Alejandro kid, he worked for you didn't he?" Julio asked.

"We had some ties, but he was a bit of a problem."

"What do you mean?" Julio ordered another round of drinks.

"You know, a trust thing, really. He has a thing for the governor of Jalisco's daughter—Javier Rodriguez."

"The priest was her stepbrother? No?"

"Oh, yes. They were close, those two, ever since they were little kids." The combination of cocaine and tequila fueled Emilio's arrogance.

"Then why would this man murder the priest like that?"

Emilio glanced around the bar, then leaned in and lowered his voice. "He didn't."

"What do you mean he didn't kill the priest?"

"Nothing, man. Let's finish up our business. I have somewhere else I need to be." Emilio realized that divulging what they'd done to Alex and Miguel might not be such a good idea, even if this man was on his side. Secrets got out and he was regretting that he'd said anything. Thankfully, Julio didn't pursue it.

"I like you, Julio. You're going to be a big part of my business."

Julio smiled in agreement. They finished their drinks, sealed the deal and went their separate ways, with the plan to meet in Guatemala and make their trades.

It hadn't taken long for them to set up this big shipment. Apparently, Julio was making inroads with the Gambino family. And Emilio, unlike his brother, had nothing against the Cosa Nostra, as long as they could make a mutually profitable deal.

Emilio liked to think of himself as being much smarter than Antonio for not going against the tide, but flowing with it. Everyone with any brains in organized crime knew you needed the Italians as partners in order to really get anywhere. And Emilio was banking on Julio to guide him in their direction.

They shook hands. "Do you have the money?" Emilio asked.

"Back there," Julio replied, pointing to the shack. "And you?"

"It's all there."

"Can I take a look?"

"Be my guest. But my guys aren't going to unload until I see the color of your money."

"No problem."

They walked over to the plane together. Julio looked inside, tore open one of the clear plastic bags, and tasted the coke. "Mhhmm. This is good *yao*. Exactly like the sample."

"I told you that it would be. Emilio Espinoza is as good as his word."

"Okay, amigos, I believe we're ready to make a deal. Come with me." He motioned for Emilio to follow him.

Emilio looked back at Hector and the pilot, nodding his head.

Another plane was moved out of a hangar. Emilio could see that the pilot looked American. He knew that this was the transfer plane. Julio motioned for him to pull it up next to Emilio's plane. Emilio looked quizzically at Julio.

"Don't look so worried. The faster we get this stuff out of here and into Miami, the better off we'll all be."

Emilio relaxed a little, but he knew he wouldn't feel completely safe until he was back on Colombian soil. He entered the metal shack behind Julio. Before the door could close, he was grabbed from behind and kicked in the back of his knees. A knife was placed at his throat and he was bound and gagged with duct tape by four husky thugs. Julio put a hand on his shoulders and seated him in a rickety old chair with a spotlight shining directly in his eyes.

"Now, pendejo, we have some business to deal with," Julio said.

Emilio struggled in his seat, his eyes wild and dilated, his fear obvious to everyone in the room. All he could make out were shadows of people. No faces, only shadows surrounding him. He heard a loud boom and realized it was a gunshot. A few seconds later, Hector was seated next to him, bound and gagged as well. They'd killed the pilot.

"Now," Julio began, "we have some things to settle. See, you said something the other day that has me curious about the murder of Father Diaz." Julio pulled the gag from Emilio's mouth.

"What? I don't understand," Emilio replied, sweat slipping down his back.

"I think you do. Who killed Father Diaz?"

"Alejandro Peña. What is going on here? I thought..."

"Wrong answer," Julio yelled his voice high and shrill, his eyes wild. He looked back into the wall of shadows where one muscular hoodlum came forward out of the dark abyss, a machete in his hand. Julio nodded his head and the sharp instrument was brought down abruptly against Emilio's thumb. He screamed in agony as blood shot from the missing appendage. Julio placed the tape back over Emilio's mouth.

Julio walked to where Hector was sitting and pulled the tape off his mouth. Hector shook visibly. Tears formed in Hector's eyes as he realized that his chances of getting out of here alive were not too good.

"You don't look like a liar to me. I'm having a real hard time believing that Alejandro Peña murdered the priest. Why don't you tell me who did it?" Julio said. "Weren't you Alejandro's good friend? How quickly loyalties change. Maybe it is time for you to remember your friend."

Hector couldn't look over at Emilio, but knew that if he had a prayer of getting out alive, he'd have to squeal.

"Emilio Espinoza and Pedro Torres killed him."

"Good boy. You may now die a painless death." The shadow appeared again, this time with a revolver and placed it at Hector's right temple. Hector said a frantic prayer. Shortly after that, blood and brains were scattered all over both the floor and Emilio.

"Why would you do that? Why murder the priest?" Julio tore the tape from Emilio's mouth.

He screamed out. "My thumb! My fucking thumb! Why the fuck did you do this? Why?" His eyes darted to his dead *compadre.*

"I'm asking the questions and you have choices here; you can answer them and possibly see the light of day, or you can die a very excruciating death via a Colombian necktie."

"What? Come on now!" Emilio tried to make out the others in the room, his eyes sly and cagey, his mind in a state of confusion. The pain from his missing thumb, putting him in a stunned state.

"Fuck you," Emilio spat.

Julio motioned for one of the shadows in the dark to come forward. A large man with a machete approached Emilio. The man threw Emilio to the ground and turned him around so that he was face up. Julio nodded his head and the man placed the machete under Emilio's pecker.

"Maybe you want to think a little harder about that? You ready to answer some questions for me?"

Emilio closed his eyes. He nodded.

"Excellent."

Julio took out a tape recorder and pressed "record." He knelt down next to Emilio.

"Did Alejandro murder the priest? And don't tell me he did, because I've been fortunate enough to find the priest's former bodyguard. After you slipped in our conversation the other day, I went looking for answers. It was a good thing I did, because I had already made plans to have Alejandro killed, but you saved the kid, and so did the big mouthed bodyguard who showed up after Father Miguel's murder in a whorehouse, all liquored up and ready to talk about how he'd made so much money. What happened, Emilio?"

"We set him up."

"Who did?"

"Me and another *hombre* in our operation, Pedro Torres."

"Why?"

Emilio groaned in pain and fear. He didn't respond right away.

"Why?" Julio screamed.

"Because Pedro has this obsession with the girl," Emilio cried out.

"Who? The governor's daughter?

"*Yes*—Isabella. I don't understand why, but I don't really care," he whimpered.

"If you didn't care, then why do it?"

"Pedro wanted Alex gone and so did I."

"Why would you want him gone?"

"I would think that's obvious to you," Emilio moaned. "He's a problem for me. The kid is too smart and too loyal to my brother. I needed to get rid of anyone who might stand in my way."

"Don't you think your brother might stand in your way?" Julio asked. "Why kill the priest?"

"That's one of the reasons I had the priest done away with." Emilio choked out the words. He couldn't believe he was telling Julio all of this but he had no other way. Maybe this man would let him go free, if he told him everything he wanted. "The priest, he's been making problems for us. You know about that. He's had an effect on anyone in this business transporting from Latin America."

Julio nodded. "Exactly." He smiled.

"I needed to get rid of him for that reason. I also knew to cause a rift between the two *Patróns* so that things would start to break down. My brother would feel the pressure, especially without his keeper."

"Javier?"

"Yes."

"How did you kill the priest and frame the kid?"

"You said you knew the answer to that. You talked to the bodyguard."

"I need to hear it from you."

Emilio shook his head. He couldn't take anymore. The henchman inched the machete further into his pecker. "I paid him a lot of money."

"Did you pay extra for the Colombian necktie?"

Emilio could no longer look at Julio. He simply nodded.

"Thank you for being so honest, Emilio. We have one more thing to discuss."

Emilio closed his eyes again, dizzy and disillusioned.

Julio took a photograph from his jacket pocket and held it in front of Emilio's tear-stained eyes. "Do you recognize this woman? You ought to. She's your brother's wife, the one you got pregnant and then rid yourself of when she interfered with your plans. Remember?" Emilio's muffled cries were his only answer. "The man with his arm around her shoulder in the picture is me, of course. You thought she died when that whorehouse your boys put her into went up in smoke, didn't you? Well, sorry to say for you, *hombre,* that Lydia is very much alive. She's back in Calí, at our place, waiting for me. She's glad to be with a man who treats her right for a change—someone who won't force an abortion on her, like you did. Someone who won't sell her as a prostitute, like you did. Someone who won't rape her small daughter over and over again, like you did."

Emilio's opened his eyes wide.

"Yes, we know all about that, too." Julio snapped his fingers once. Another man came forward and pinned Emilio to the ground, not that he could go anywhere, Julio liked seeing this maggot squirm and the fear in his eyes. "Oh, and I lied. You won't live, and my friends will not be nice about the way you die. Instead of a Colombian necktie like you had inflicted upon my dear friend Father Diaz, my friends are going to sever what you have considered your *manhood,* and instead of choking on your tongue as my friend suffered, you will have to choke on what has seemed to mean the most to you throughout the years."

"You bastard!" Emilio screamed.

"That's right, I am a bastard," Julio answered him calmly and stood.

"Fuck you!"

"Finish him off," Julio ordered and headed for the door of the shack. "Enjoy hell, Emilio." As Julio opened the door he heard Emilio's screams that only a moment later were muffled as Julio got on the plane and headed back to Calí to tell Lydia she was free to go home.

CHAPTER SIXTY-FOUR

ANTONIO NEEDED REST BEFORE ALEJANDRO ARRIVED.
He'd received word that the boy had been released from the prison
in Mexico City in the middle of the night and had been transported to
a private landing strip. There, Antonio's jet waited to take him back
to Colombia. Antonio fretted all night that something could go wrong
with the transport, but now, knowing that his son was out of prison
and in the air, he felt better.

He wasn't sure how long, moments or hours, before he was
awakened by a noise coming from the cracked open French doors in
his room. He rubbed his eyes and tried to focus on what looked to be
the silhouette of a woman outside his door. He reached for his
glasses on the nightstand. Putting them on, he could see that there
was a woman standing at the door, with the light of dusk streaming
around her form, making her appear ghostly, her dress billowing in
the breeze.

"Who's there?" he asked, hearing his own voice tremble. There
was no answer. Something about the apparition, the woman,
whatever it was, was frightening and yet there was also something
very familiar about her. When she didn't respond, he got up to see

for himself. He walked toward the door, trepidation in his step. His hand stretched out, still shaking. What was it about this figure? Was he dreaming? It didn't feel like a dream. He was walking and feeling and his mind was spinning. He asked again, "Who are you? What do you want? I *demand* to know."

Reaching the door and putting his hand out to turn the handle and further open the door, the figure simultaneously placed her hand on the doorknob opposite him. Antonio pulled his hand back as if it had been scalded. He took a step back and as the figure eased the door open, he took yet another step back his eyes widening with recognition. He shook his head and blinked several times. "I, I, Lyd, Lyd, Lydia?" he stammered in a whisper, not sure himself if her name escaped his lips. "Oh my God."

She reached out and touched him on the chest, her hand warm, tears in her eyes. He had to still be sleeping. This was a dream. Had to be a dream.

Lydia took her hand from his chest and stroked his cheek.

"No. How? I don't understand. Is it you? Who are you? What is this? A joke?"

"No, Antonio." She finally spoke.

Antonio felt his mouth drop wide open. It was *her* voice, and *her* touch and *her* eyes and *her* body. My God, this was his wife, the woman he thought dead for over a dozen years. He brought his hand to her hair and touched the end strands—like silk, still. He stepped back again and brought both his hands over his eyes and shook his head. "How? Why? Where?"

"There is so much to say. I assure you, it is me, and I am alive. Please sit down."

He did as she instructed and nearly fell back into the chair in what had once been *their* suite. She sat opposite him and took his hands in hers. His still shook. Hers were so warm and so alive.

"It is you! Isn't it?" he cried.

"Yes." She nodded. Together they sat for several minutes before either one could say another word, both of them in tears and so wrapped in emotion and confusion that no words could be found.

Antonio's heart raced when Lydia spoke again. "I need to tell you everything. Please listen and wait until I'm finished to say anything. I know that you have and will have many questions, but I believe when you hear what I have to say, many of them will be answered." She wiped away the tears running down his face, kissed him on the forehead. Her lips were tender and soft. She again took both his hands in hers and relayed to him the horror and the pain and even the peace she'd found during the past decade. She told him of the betrayal with Emilio and the knowledge that she had in regard to Marta and his son—and how that pain had caused her to seek solace in his brother's arms, and because of that betrayal she'd wound up nearly dead, addicted for a time to heroin and prostituted out. She told of the nuns, their kindness and how the meeting and mentoring of Father Miguel led her out of despair and rekindled the need in her to seek out her old life and make peace with her past and wreak vengeance on those who'd dealt her the cruel blows. Lydia explained to him that for years she'd believed Antonio to be the mastermind behind her "death," and the events that precipitated from it, and how, because of her beliefs, she'd feared ever coming home and being a part of her daughters' lives. She'd feared *him*. But, in the arms of Julio, and through his resources she'd discovered the truth: that Emilio had done this to her and her family.

Antonio sat, stunned, and let her speak for nearly an hour. There were still some pieces missing when she was through. Antonio's emotions ranged from fear, to hatred, sadness, anger, pity and finally to love. He couldn't believe she had endured all that she had, thinking that he had done this to her. He didn't respond, only listened and surprising himself, he actually understood his wife better at that moment than he ever had. It wasn't rage he felt toward her. Too many years had passed and he could recognize his own wrongdoings, and his part in what had happened to her.

"My God, Lydia, if I had only known." He withdrew his hands from inside hers and took her hands in his. "I never meant to hurt you so. If I'd only known," he sobbed. "If I thought you were alive, I would have looked, I would have found you."

"I know. I know that now."

"Can you, will you forgive me?"

"I already have, Antonio."

He leaned in and kissed her cheek. Pulling away, the anger came rushing back as the implications of his brother's deceit hit him. "I will kill Emilio for this. I will cut his goddamn heart out."

"No. There is no need."

"What? What do you mean? Of course there is. He betrayed, me, you, this family, his nieces."

"Yes. However, I have taken care of Emilio."

Antonio didn't respond. He had no idea what she meant. He watched as she took a tape recorder out of the bag she carried. "You need to hear this." First she played Rosa's confession to the therapist. Together, they listened in silence. Then they both wept.

"Oh, God, no, no, no," Antonio bellowed. "How could I never even suspect he was *this* monster? How could I not protect my child or you? Oh, dear God." Antonio's body trembled and with wracking sobs he fell back in the chair. After a moment he looked at Lydia again. "I don't know why you ask me to spare him, but I will break that evil bastard in two. I will destroy him." He stood and paced the floor.

"No, I told you that you won't need to." He stopped and stared at her, crazed by what he'd already heard. He watched as Lydia put another tape in. It was one that Julio had given to her after Emilio and Hector's execution. Julio's words and those on the tape had been difficult to hear, but she knew they were necessary.

"I knew you'd need some proof," Julio had told Lydia. He'd reached out, touching her shoulder. "I'm the wrong man for you. We both know that. You go home. You go back to your family."

"What about your investigation?" Lydia had asked him, afraid of what would happen to Antonio.

"I have to tell you something, Lydia. I've been a DEA agent for the government in the States up until now. But since the work has become so dangerous lately, I've also been working for the Italian

Mafia. They paid me all the money I made from stealing Emilio's last drug shipment, in order to make sure I had Emilio killed. They were afraid his rogue operation would interfere with their own drug trade. It worked well for me. I was able to seek revenge for Father Miguel, who I know we both loved, and I killed the man who stole your life from you. My work is complete here in Colombia and in Mexico. Now I've made enough to retire on. But I must change my name and my identity, because the DEA will be very angry that I had Emilio killed, instead of bringing him in as a witness against Antonio and Javier, and the Italian mafia will look for me, too. I know too much about too many governments and too many criminals. They're all the same though, aren't they?" He'd laughed and then turned somber again. "I'll have to live my life on the run from now on, even have plastic surgery to alter my features enough to escape from all of them and even then I will have to always be looking behind me. As much as I love you, and God, you know that I do," he said, stroking her face, "I know that kind of life wouldn't be any good for you. You've lived it long enough. Go home. Don't worry about me or the DEA. Your husband is a mastermind. It wouldn't matter how many years they pursued him, he'll always find some way out."

"Emilio is dead, isn't he?" Antonio asked her after the tape played out. "They didn't spare him."

"He's dead."

Antonio felt nothing for his brother. Nothing at all. He embraced Lydia. "I am so sorry you suffered so."

"I want to see my daughters."

457 | P a g e

"Of course. I do think they'll need to be prepared."

"I understand. When?"

"Tomorrow. Come here at noon."

"All right. I'll be staying at Las Brillas."

"May I keep the tape?"

"Yes."

Antonio saw Lydia out the door, and had a car brought around for her. No one noticed her leaving. He was still in shock over the story she'd told and the tapes he'd heard. His emotions were a mixed brew. But one thing he knew for sure as he fingered the tape, his son would soon be free of any questions that others had regarding his innocence.

*****

ALEX LOOKED AT ANTONIO, SEATED ACROSS FROM HIM IN the office. Everything in the room was dark, from mahogany desks and wall panels, to the plush burgundy sofa next to the bookshelves. Alex watched his mentor, who looked drawn and older than he had only a few days before when he'd come to see him in prison.

"Are you feeling all right?" Alex asked him.

"Yes, of course. I've received some surprising news, that's all," Antonio replied.

"What kind of news?"

"We'll talk about it later. Right now we have guests."

Antonio stood up as Javier, Bella, and Pedro were ushered into the room. Pedro glanced anxiously at all of them, his hands in his slack's pockets. Bella looked at Alex, but he couldn't get a sense of what she was feeling. Her face showed nothing and when his eyes caught hers and tried to hold them in a gaze she looked away. Alex wondered if she doubted his innocence.

"Sit down, please," Antonio said.

"I don't understand why we're here," Javier replied. "I definitely don't understand why you got him out of prison." He pointed at Alex. "He murdered my stepson and he's made us a family divided. I can't see how we can go on as partners or think of each other as family any longer after this fiasco. I'm not willing to throw my political career away because of his insane criminal act."

"Please, sit down," Antonio ordered, his voice stern.

Bella in her chair looked away from the other four seated around the desk.

"This young man you are so ready to condemn was indeed set up."

"I can't believe that. The proof against him is too strong," Javier said. "My daughter saw him standing over Miguel with her own eyes, his bloodied knife in his hands."

"I think you'll change your mind after you hear this." Antonio pulled a tape recorder out of a desk drawer and placed it on top of the desk. He turned it on.

"Who killed Father Miguel?" a man's voice asked. "Who set up Alejandro Peña?"

A gasp and moan rang out over the recorder and then they heard Emilio's voice answering. "It was me, and Pedro Torres."

"Who is Pedro Torres?"

"He's a man who works for us. For Antonio and Javier."

Antonio turned the tape off.

"That's a lie," Pedro screamed. "He's lying. Where is that bastard? Where is Emilio?" He stood and paced the floor, perspiration beading around his hairline.

"Where Emilio is, is none of your concern. Sit down," Antonio ordered.

Antonio turned the tape back on and played out the section in regard to why Pedro wanted Alejandro out of the way and what Emilio's motives were.

"Is that true, Pedro?" Bella asked.

"Of course not," Pedro replied.

It was Javier who spoke next, his voice gravely and low. "I accepted you as my son. I loved you, trusted you. Now I'm asking you to leave."

"He was ruining you anyway," Pedro shouted. "Miguel Diaz was defaming you. Emilio and I did you a favor." Pedro placed his hands in his face and when he looked back up he had turned red. "Listen to me, this boy..." He pointed at Alex. "He is going to ruin this family. I was doing it for the family and for you, Bella." He knelt down next to her.

She slapped him hard across the face. "For me?"

Pedro brought his hand up to his face. "For you. He is a lowly street thug. He is not worthy of your presence, and he will never fit into this family."

Bella shook her head. Alex watched her face twist into something he had never seen her express.

"Go, Pedro. Leave this family and stay away," Javier replied. Pedro got up from the chair and silently started to leave the room.

"You're going to let him go?" Bella screamed. "After what he did?"

"Calm down. He'll rot in his own hell, trust me."

"Trust you? He murdered Miguel, and Alex was blamed for it."

"Isabella, I know Pedro. He will suffer more without this family than he would in a prison cell."

Pedro looked back pleadingly at Javier who gave him nothing back. He turned again and headed toward the door. "I'll go," he muttered.

"You will go nowhere, you bastard," Bella said.

Pedro turned back around as Bella pointed a small pistol, etched with mother of pearl on the handle, squarely at his chest.

"Bella, no!" Alex yelled. As he reached out to grab the gun from her, she pulled the trigger, the echo of the bullet bounced off the wall, and the men in the room watched in awe as Pedro Torres, his face twisted into a mixture of disbelief and horror, collapsed to the floor.

****

BELLA'S SHOT DIDN'T MISS. SHE'D HIT PEDRO DIRECTLY IN

the heart and he died within minutes. Her skills as a crack shot had come from her days of archery in school, and she had fully intended to kill Pedro after what he'd done to her brother and the man she loved.

Alex rushed to her side as Antonio made a phone call. Javier and Antonio ushered Alex and Bella out of the office and into the living room. It didn't take long before Bella understood that the phone call her godfather made was to a couple of men who arrived quickly and with stealth, removed Pedro's body from the house.

She'd had her suspicions about Pedro and his possible involvement since Mexico City a few days before, and she'd thought about it for the past three days. When Antonio had shown up at the hotel to take her for a walk after Pedro pleaded for her hand in marriage, she confided in her godfather.

"Don't you think it odd, godfather?" She'd asked.

"Indeed. Not only is it odd, it's abhorrent behavior. He should not be looking at you with the eyes of a man in that way. He's known you since you were a baby. He's eighteen years older than you. Your father will have to speak to him on this issue."

"Yes, *Patrón.* I will. Can I ask you something?"

"Of course."

"Do you think Alex killed my brother?"

"No. I do not. I know this young man and he is not a killer." He rolled her chair inside a corner café, where he ordered them each *panuelos* and Mexican cocoa. "Bella, what's more important is, do you think Alex is guilty of this crime?"

She hesitated before shaking her head. "I can't believe that he could or would do it."

"I don't know who did this, but we will find out, my child. However, for now, I fear for you."

"Why?"

He sighed. "Bella, your father and I have many enemies. Some of the things you have heard about us are true."

She nodded, knowing that her fears about her father and Antonio were truths. Could she accept this? Did she even have a choice? For now, all she could do was listen.

He'd taken a case from the satchel he carried. It looked to be a jewelry box, but a bit larger. "I know that you have people who watch over you, but this is in case you ever need it. Our families have more enemies than ever, suspicious that your father or I may have asked Alejandro to murder Miguel. I assure you that is not the case. I was always very fond of your brother and am deeply troubled and saddened by his death. I may not always do the right thing according to the law, but Bella, I am a man of God. I am human and have sinned more times than I can say, but my love for God and for your brother was true. I hope you believe that."

She nodded, tears in her eyes. The thought of Miguel and his passing would be a wound she knew she would never quite recover from. It was like a part of her soul had been ripped from her.

Antonio handed her the box. "This is for you. It is possible that someone might take out their hatred of our families by trying to hurt the innocent."

She'd opened the box, and found a small hand pistol inside, the handle decorated in mother of pearl. She gasped. "I don't know if I should accept this."

He took her free hand. "You must accept it. It's for your own good, and I know that you know how to use it." He smiled at her, and she'd recalled the times he had taken her and his girls bird hunting on the occasions when they came to visit her in France. She'd been a natural and proud of what she could do with a gun. Then, of course, there were her archery lessons from school that helped her aim. But having a gun was different than archery or bird hunting. It was the real thing for the real thing—her own protection. She knew better than to deny her godfather's gift, and so she'd taken it.

Today that gift had helped her seek vengeance for her brother, and now she wondered, as her godfather and father went into the kitchen to make drinks to help calm everyone's nerves, if Antonio hadn't known all along that this might be how everything would play out.

Alex stood with his back to her, facing the large window that looked out upon the blue mountains. It was obvious to her by the clothes he wore, and his unkempt hair and unshaven face, that he'd only been released from prison not long ago. He was far leaner than a week earlier, his bruises still covering his face.

"I can't imagine what you've been through," she said. "It must've been horrible.

He nodded, but did not turn around. "The worst part was not knowing if you believed that I was innocent or not."

"I know, Alex, and I'm so sorry. Can you please forgive me? That day when I came to see you at the prison I was so distraught and confused, and then the guard would not let me stay long enough to hear you out. You remember. And, then, when you brought up the idea that those children might have taken your knife and done that horror to my brother, I was shocked at the thought. But I had to go, and you could not finish telling me your thoughts. I realized that afternoon what you meant to tell me about them taking the knife from your pocket and giving it to someone who would kill my brother and make it look as though you did it. Please accept my apology. I love you, Alex." The words rushed out of her.

Alex slowly turned around. "Did you say you love me?"

She bit her bottom lip and nodded, not knowing what to expect from him. "Bella, I have waited for a long time to hear you say that to me. Of course I accept your apology. There is no forgiveness necessary. I understand why you had doubts. I do."

Her voice caught in her throat as she tried to thank him.

"And, Bella."

She looked up at him.

"I love you, too." He started to walk toward her.

"No," she said, a smile widening across her face as he stopped and watch her slowly stand up.

At that moment her father and godfather walked into the room with their drinks and watched as Bella, with slow deliberation, walked to Alex. When she reached him, they threw their arms around each other. Alex bent down and covered her face in kisses, kissing her tears away. They laughed, and cried together. Both Javier and Antonio joined in.

Alex picked her up and twirled her around, disregarding his injuries. "I love you, I love you," he repeated over and over again.

She leaned her face into his chest and felt a comfort there that not even her father could ever provide for her. Bella was now certain that Alex was the man intended for her.

CHAPTER SIXTY-FIVE

ROSA AND FELICIA WERE SEATED ON THE SOFA IN THEIR father's office, both curious as to what this urgent meeting was about. Their father had summoned them, which was, in and of itself, highly unusual, especially together.

Felicia studied her freshly painted nails. "What do you think Papa wants?" she wondered aloud.

"I have no idea," Rosa replied, getting up from the sofa and walking over to the bar, where she poured herself a glass of water from a crystal carafe.

"If he wants to go on another vacation, he can forget it. I'm too old to be hanging out with my daddy."

"Right, Miss High and Mighty."

"I am."

"Yeah, you're too busy with Pedro."

"Actually I've moved on to someone my own age. Pedro was becoming a bore."

"Because he only has eyes for Isabella."

"Shut up."

Rosa laughed.

"No, I told you, it was because what I need is a real man."

"And who might that be?"

"Anyone handsome, virile, and under thirty."

"You have a one-track mind, my little sister."

"It's the only thing I'm good at."

"What are you talking about?"

"It's true. I'm not like you. You're talented. You have your art, and people genuinely like you."

"People genuinely take advantage of me."

"That, too," Felicia replied. Both sisters broke out into laughter. A pause left them both in deep thought about one another. Felicia was the first to comment, "Why have we never been closer?"

Rosa didn't know how to answer that question. She realized that she had made sure there was an insurmountable distance between them. She did it in part to keep her baby sister in the dark about the horror that had been inflicted on her. Rosa's shame had convinced her for so long that she deserved what her uncle had done to her. And she had felt that her sister, the beautiful one, should never know about something so ugly. At one point, Rosa had fretted over the possibility that their uncle could destroy Felicia as well. But as Felicia grew, Rosa could see she was far more headstrong than Rosa. Rosa's emotional stability had been destroyed with the death of her mother, leading her into a pattern of victimization.

Felicia, on the other hand, recovered more rapidly from their mother's death. She never would allow herself to be victimized. But Rosa now realized that Felicia, too, had fallen into an unfavorable trap. The outward beauty hid a deep insecurity. The more men Felicia allowed to love her, the more she thought she was worth being loved. Thus, ironically enough, her little sister, too had been a victim.

"Why haven't we ever been closer?" Rosa pondered, repeating the question. "I guess we were too busy growing up."

"Stupid, huh?"

"Definitely."

"Do you think we can change that?" Felicia asked.

"I think we can rectify anything." Rosa walked across the room. She put her arms around her younger sister, the doe eyed beauty with the flawless skin. "I love you," Rosa told her.

"And I love you, too," Felicia replied.

Their father walked into the study. He appeared nervous and edgy. There were visible lines on his face, and the dark circles under his eyes made him look much older than he ever had. "Sit down, please," he said.

Both young women sat down opposite him in front of his desk. "What is it, Papa?" Felicia asked.

"I'm not sure how to tell you this."

"What?" Rosa asked.

Antonio turned toward his eldest daughter, tears in his eyes. "Oh, *mija*, I am so sorry."

"What are you talking about, Papa?" Rosa asked, feeling a sinking sensation in her stomach.

"I apologize to both of you for not being a better father."

Rosa and Felicia glanced at each other, baffled by this display of emotion.

"There is no easy way to say this, so bear with me. At first, you may not believe anything I'm about to say, but I assure you, all of it is true. I'm going to begin by saying that we had a very terrible person within our family." He paused to wipe the corner of his eyes. "Your Uncle Emilio is someone I never really knew. He deceived me for years, pretending to be someone I could trust and love. But I was wrong. He did terrible things to this family that I am only now finding out about."

"What are you talking about, Papa?" Felicia asked, but Rosa already knew that her father had discovered the truth.

"He told many lies. He stole from me. But worst of all, he stole from you."

"Papa?" Rosa said. It sounded more a plea than a question. She shook her head, hoping that if he knew what her uncle had done to her, he wouldn't reveal it to her sister.

"It's all right, child." He folded his hands in front of him on the desk. "What I have to say will only become a reality when you see with your own eyes. I am as shocked and confused as you both will be."

"Papa, you're scaring me," Felicia said.

"I have some wonderful news that comes from a tragedy. The tragedy is what Emilio took from us many years ago. I don't know how to say this, so I am just going to say it." He sighed heavily. "Rosa, Felicia, your mother is alive."

"What?" they responded in unison.

"I know it sounds unbelievable, but I have seen her with my own eyes. She is truly alive. Emilio had your mother kidnapped all those years ago. There never was a car accident. She was brutally abused, and suffered for many long, hard years. She has been living in a convent for most of the past ten years, recovering from the brutality Emilio inflicted upon her."

"What?" Rosa said. "No! Why? I don't understand."

Felicia's face was pale.

"I know, my sweets, it sounds like the ranting of a mad man, but I am not. I know it sounds ludicrous..."

"But it's true." Lydia finished his sentence as she walked through the door. She stood there, with both of her daughters staring in disbelief, not knowing how to react.

Rosa's eyes widened and her jaw dropped. She couldn't speak.

"Mama?" Felicia stuttered.

"Yes, it is." Lydia walked over to her daughters.

Rosa stood up slowly out of her chair. Vertigo nearly overcame her, but she managed to stay on her feet. She couldn't believe she was staring into the face of her mother.

Lydia held out her hands. Rosa took them. She still could not utter a sound. Tears clouded her vision. She touched her mother's face and hair. Lydia smiled at her. It *was* her.

"Mama! Oh God, Mama! Mama."

Her mother pulled her in tight and held her. "I've missed you, *mija*. I have missed you so much." She stroked her hair as she'd done when her daughter was a child. She even smelled like she had when Rosa had been a child—like gardenias.

Felicia approached them and Lydia opened her arms to include her youngest daughter. The women stood there in that embrace for several minutes and with all the time they'd lost from each other's lives they could have remained there for the rest of their lives. For each one there, the girls who had now grown into women and for the woman who had had a good portion of her life stolen from her, they'd found themselves whole again.

The three cried, speechless, in that embrace as their emotions overwhelmed them. "Mama, Mama!" Felicia kept repeating the word, laughing and regressing back to the age when her mother had been taken from her.

Antonio watched, guilty about not having investigated Lydia's death more thoroughly, allowing her life to be lost to the hands of his insane brother.

After some time, the three women sat down together, staring unbelievingly at one another. There was so much catching up to do, so much explaining, so much damage to be undone. The four of them sat talking for hours into the night. Food was brought into them at dinnertime. Felicia and Rosa could not believe what their mother had faced all those missing years.

Finally, late in the evening, Felicia stood up. "I'm sorry, but I'm exhausted."

"Of course. We have the rest of our lives to spend catching up," Lydia said. She hugged her youngest daughter good night.

"Mama?" Felicia asked hesitation in her voice.

"Yes, *mija*?"

She glanced away, almost as if she were ashamed. "Would you do something for me?"

"Of course. I would do anything."

"Will you tuck me in my bed and sing to me like you did when I was a little girl."

Lydia rose and took Felicia's hand. "Come on, *mija*, let's put you to bed."

Rosa stood up as well.

Antonio stopped her and whispered, "Your mother and I need to speak with you. Will you stay and wait?"

"Yes." Rosa had an idea what they wanted to speak to her about.

Her stomach twisted into knots as she heard her mother's voice coming from her sister's room, singing lullabies that she had not heard in many years. Again, tears came to her eyes and her father sat down by her, wrapping his arms around her. She laid her head on his shoulder.

After some time her mother returned and sat down on the other side of her.

"You know, don't you?" Rosa asked. "You know what he did to me."

"We know," Antonio said, squeezing his daughter's hand. "I wish you had told me. I wish I could've protected you."

"It's not your fault, Rosa," Lydia interrupted him. "None of this was your fault."

"I know. Finally I know that," Rosa managed to say. With those words, Rosa for the first time felt a true sense of relief, as if nothing bad could ever reach her again. She hugged her parents, and thanked God her mother had been returned to her.

*****

ANTONIO, EXHAUSTED FROM THE LAST FEW DAYS, HAD made a decision after seeing that his life had turned into a mountain of deceit. He must tell Alejandro the truth. He'd feared this day, but he knew the time had come.

The two walked among the coffee crops, as they'd become accustomed to doing over the weeks that Alex had been staying with him.

"I can't believe it," Alex exclaimed, hearing about Lydia. "I never wanted to say this, because I knew he was your brother, but I always thought Emilio was a bad seed."

"You have the same instincts as your mother." Antonio replied.

"Well, yes." Alex stopped walking. He faced Antonio. "How did you know that? About my mother having good instincts?"

"There's something else which I think you're going to find quite amazing. I'm not sure how you'll take this. I can only pray you won't hate me."

"Hate you? You're like a father to me." But as he said it, and meant it, a sinking feeling spread from his brain down and settled into his gut.

Antonio looked into Alex's eyes and said, "I am your father."

Alex didn't respond at first. Finally through gritted teeth, he said, "That isn't funny, Antonio."

"It's not meant to be. I'm telling you the truth. Your mother and I were lovers."

"That's impossible." He shook his head, his denial vehement. "My father was a coldhearted man who abandoned my mother. That's not you."

"No, Alex. Your mother was a good, decent woman who did not agree with the way I made a living. After I thought my wife had died, she came here for a couple of weeks. I even saw you once in Los Angeles, when you were a little boy. I wanted to marry her, then bring you home. But I lied to her. I made her a promise that I would become a legitimate businessman. She found out that I had no intention of ever keeping that promise, so she left, doing everything in her power to keep me away from you. She felt I would be a bad influence on you."

"I don't believe you," Alex's voice raised. "No. No. I don't believe you! Why are you saying these things? What the hell is wrong with you?"

"I'm sorry." Antonio reached out to touch Alex on the shoulder. He pulled away. "Alex, It's all true. I didn't even know about you until after your birth and I wanted desperately to go to you and your mother. But I was afraid she would refuse me, and I was right. I sent her money over the years. It was the only thing she would accept from me. Please believe me when I say that I have always loved you. I've always wanted you here with me. But I respected and loved your mother. And I would never have gone against her wishes—even if it meant I couldn't see you."

Alex stared at him for several seconds. This was like a hazy dream, where everything stood still—air particles, life—all of it. He felt off balance and shaken. "If what you say is true, then why did you find me, finally?" Alex asked, his voice laden with disbelief and anger. "Why would you think that I would ever want anything to do with you?" he yelled. "Why are you telling me these lies, Antonio? What do you want from me?"

"I know this is hard to take, but please listen to me. I am not lying to you. When your mother died, I wanted to reach out and take care of you, make sure you were all right. I sent Emilio to find you. Nothing more. He took it upon himself to bring you into our business. I wanted so much more for you than a life filled with wrongdoings and deceit. It was all a part of Emilio's plan to ruin my life. Believe me when I say that I only sent Emilio to watch over you, that's all. By the time I learned what Emilio had done, it was too late. I learned that you had already fallen into this trap. I figured that if you wanted to choose this life, then you should at least be under my care."

"I don't want to hear any more!" Alex was now screaming at Antonio, his face colored by fury, his fists clenched and ready to strike. "My mother was right about you. If you'd wanted me, wanted to be a part of my life, you would have been. Life was difficult for my mother and me. And you know what? She was right, and so are you. I never needed you then, and I don't need you now! Stay away from me! Stay the hell away and out of my life. I don't want to be a part of you or your business. You disgust me!"

Antonio watched as Alex turned and ran back to the house, his vision blurred by the tears his deceit caused, and he knew he was watching the son he wanted so badly in his life run right out of it.

CHAPTER SIXTY-SIX

LONG STEMMED RED ROSES WERE DELIVERED TO BELLA
the next morning, the card inside reading, *This is the first of a long list of surprises to come. Love, Alex.*

Throughout the day, every hour on the hour, Bella received another gift. The roses came first, then a beautiful violet silk dress with an open back and plunging neckline. The dress epitomized elegance and sensuality. Silver shoes and a matching purse came along in a smaller box an hour later.

Another hour went by, and a pair of one-carat diamond stud earrings arrived. After that, a matching diamond necklace and bracelet. Bella drifted between shock and elation. Each gift contained a small card that read, *I love you. Alex.* The last card contained information on where she should meet him for dinner that evening: Fernando's, a small, exclusive restaurant set against the cliffs, overlooking Banderas Bay in Puerto Vallarta. He would have a car sent to drive her up from her father's home in Costa Careyes. She glanced at her watch. Alex had flown from Colombia into Puerto

Vallarta the night before and had contacted her, but they hadn't seen each other yet, and she was dying with anticipation.

"Two hours before the car will be here," she cried. She wanted to look her best, and was a bit miffed that he'd given her such short notice. Then she looked around her room and saw all the beautiful gifts Alex had sent her throughout the day and her arrogance vanished.

Her father walked into her room and found her flitting around, searching for a bottle of nail polish. "Did you go on a shopping spree today?"

"No, Papa. Alex sent these to me. I'm supposed to meet him for dinner this evening."

"Ah, of course." Javier smiled. "Alejandro sent you these things?"

"Yes. Isn't he wonderful?"

"If I didn't know better, I'd think you were in love." A faint pink color rose to Bella's cheeks. "You don't need to defend yourself," Javier said, "I'm happy for you. Even though I wish you were still a little girl. It seems like only days have passed instead of years. And now, before I have a chance to blink, you turn into a woman."

"Oh, Papa!" Bella walked over and hugged her father. "I'll always be your little girl."

"This is true." Javier pulled away and kissed her on the forehead. "I believe you have a dinner engagement. You'd better hurry up. I'll have the car ready when you are."

"Thank you, Papa."

Javier left the room, his heart swollen with happiness, but yet tainted by a small amount of pain—the kind only a father feels when he knows he's lost his daughter to another man.

*****

ALEX WAS WAITING AT THE TABLE WHEN BELLA ARRIVED.
She looked stunning, her long, dark hair cascading down her back in shining waves. The dress fit her petite figure the way Alex hoped it would, and he could smell her scent as he stood to greet her.

"You take my breath away," he told her. "You are so beautiful."

She had left her wheelchair in the car and was obviously determined to try and start making it through her days with only the use of the cane.

They began with drinks and Oysters Rockefeller, and soon moved on to a main course of filet mignon. Candlelight bounced off the bay windows, casting a glow on the bay outside and also onto Bella. The quaint restaurant was decorated in traditional old Spanish style with wrought iron chandeliers, dark wood crown molding, and clean white tablecloths. A fire in the fireplace in the center of the room burned brightly, and a harp was being played in the background. Everything was perfect.

"This is beautiful, all you've done for me. Thank you." Bella said.

"I would do *anything* for you, Bella."

"I'm starting to believe you." She winked at him. "Tell me, Alex, what this is all about? All of the gifts, the dinner, all of the romance."

She smiled. "If I didn't know better, I might think you're trying to seduce me."

"Aren't you forward tonight? This is not about anything. Does it have to be a special occasion for me to want to give you gifts and take you to dinner?"

"I am still suspicious, Alejandro Peña! You are up to something."

He laughed, picking up his glass of wine.

"There's something more than this surprise I know you're hiding, Alex. There's something bothering you."

"What makes you say that?" Alex asked, setting his glass back down.

"I see it. I know."

"You're psychic?"

"No, I am a woman and we have good intuition. Tell me."

"You are too perceptive." He sighed and didn't say anything for a moment. He took a sip from his wine and setting it back down, he said, "You're correct, there is something on my mind." He traced the rim of his wine glass with a long manicured finger. "It's my father."

"Your father. What about him? You told me he deserted you and your mother when you were a baby."

"Antonio is my father." There was no other way to say it.

"What?"

"It's true. I didn't believe it myself, but there were too many things he said that convinced me. Besides busying myself with finding only the best that money could buy for you today, my mind has played the scene I had with Antonio, with *my* father yesterday, over and over again."

"Tell me about it."

Alex told Bella everything—from what his mother had told him when he was a boy, to the scene with Antonio only the day before. She listened intently and when he finished, his eyes were misted over.

"You love him, don't you?" she asked him.

"Yes. No. I definitely do not love that man."

She held up her hand. "Don't lie to me, Alex. Of course you love him. I've seen how close you two have become. What happened to you and your mother wasn't fair, but he *does* love you, and he wants to be a father now. Don't you think you can let him? I believe you can. In fact, I *know* you can. Alejandro, you're a compassionate man. Bitterness isn't a part of you. Don't allow it into your heart. It will ruin you."

"I don't know."

"Yes, you do. All you have to do is listen to your heart. Think about it. I believe it would please your mother."

"I will think about it. Why are you so smart?"

"Luck."

"Right."

They both laughed as their dessert was placed before them: a bowl of beautiful strawberries with fresh cream.

"What's this? Only one bowl?" Bella mused, lifting an eyebrow.

"I intend to let you have most of them."

"Oh, I'm sure."

Alex elaborately dipped the ripe fruit in the smooth, white cream. He then reached across the table, placing it gently in her mouth. When she bit down she felt something hard and cold in the center of the berry. What she hadn't noticed was that the berry had been sliced to fit the small trinket inside it.

"What's this?" she exclaimed.

"What?" Alex tried to act as surprised, but appeared sheepish.

"Oh my God!" She wiped off a beautiful, two carat, princess cut diamond ring.

Alex reached for the ring and then her hand. He got up from his chair and knelt down on one knee. "Isabella Rodriguez, since the first day I laid eyes on you, I haven't been able to stop thinking of you. I knew you were the one for me. Your strength, your intelligence, your kindness with all you meet—especially with your horses..." He reached up and wiped the tears now coming down her face. "Your love for your family—all of it has made me certain and cemented in my heart and soul how much I love you. I want to love you for the rest of my life. I want to have children with you. I want to grow old with you. I want to be your best friend and you mine. I want to argue with you and then make love with you. I respect you. You challenge me. You make me a better man. I cannot even think of a life without you." He shook his head. "I can't. So please, please, I beg you, will you marry me, Isabella?"

Bella couldn't answer, the words catching in her throat. At first, she began to nod her head, and then finally blurted out, "Yes. Of course I will marry you."

Alex stood and brought her to her feet, kissing her. "You have made me the happiest man in the world, in the universe, in the heavens, everywhere!" He kissed her again—sweetly, slowly.

"We need to tell our families," she said as he held her close.

"I asked your father this morning for your hand, so he is aware." He smiled. "Besides, you *are* my family, now."

"You *have* a family, too."

Alex looked away. He knew she was right.

"For me, Alex. No, do it for yourself."

He nodded. "All right. But first, there is something I want to *do* to you." He smiled and grabbed her hand. He slid the ring onto Bella's finger.

She took his face in her hands and leaned in, her lips meeting his in a soft, luscious kiss that sent a vibration of lust and love through each of them. She pulled away from him and looking into his eyes said, "And there is something I'd like to do to you."

He smiled. "I was going to try and be a gentleman and ask you. I even thought we might want to wait until our wedding night."

"I don't want to wait."

He took a key out from his coat pocket and placed it on the table as he stood to help her out of her chair.

"What's this?" she asked.

"A suite at Las Brisas."

"You were hoping I wouldn't hold you to that chivalry stuff and make an honest woman out of me."

"I was hoping."

She laughed.

He turned serious. "Bella, to me you are already my wife in my heart. There is not a day that will pass that I won't love you and hold you in my soul. You are a part of me." He kissed her again and then hand in hand, he escorted her out of the restaurant.

*****

ANTONIO HAD BEEN FILLED WITH EVERY CONCEIVABLE emotion during the past few days. Joy filled him every time he saw his daughters together with their mother, becoming reacquainted. But the sadness of losing the son he never really had filled him with grief, too. And each time he and Lydia spent time trying to talk, there was a distance that had never been there before. They were like strangers who had known each other once, long ago. Each of them realized that there was no turning back time. Too much damage had occurred. There could be no going back for either one of them.

As he sat in the garden pondering the losses he'd suffered throughout the years, Antonio was shocked to hear a male voice say, "Father."

Antonio whipped around to see Alex standing behind him. "I know that I was very angry the other day. And, I'm still hurt about your lies, but you *are* my father. And as much as I hate to admit it,

I've grown to love you over the last year and a half, as if you really were my father."

Antonio stood up from the wooden bench where he was sitting. He reached for Alex and grabbed him, embracing the larger yet younger man, who didn't respond at first, until he swore he saw a vision of his mother standing next to one of the rose bushes. She smiled, nodding her head. He hugged his father back.

"I suppose we need to let the others in on our secret," Antonio said.

"I suppose so, but first I want you to know that Bella and I are getting married."

"Oh, this is wonderful! I am so happy. This is the happiest, best news!" Antonio cried. He pulled Alex in again to him and held him tight for a long time, neither one of them saying anything, but in that embrace expressing emotions that had been bottled up for years. "I think we should meet with Lydia and your sisters this evening."

"Fine. I have to say one more thing, and I need your blessing on this. I have already spoken to Javier and received his."

"Alejandro?"

"Bella and I don't want any part of the business. We want our families as one and we will respect and love you, but we can't be a part of what is wrong in your and Javier's world any longer. We plan to move to France. Bella was happy there. We want to start a horse farm and Bella has already contacted Jean Luc, her old trainer, who has offered to help us. Bella wants to go and see where Delilah is buried—pay her respects—and we want to settle down there in the countryside."

Antonio didn't respond at first. He looked into his son's eyes and gave him the answer they both knew was right. "Of course, son. I wouldn't want anything else for you. Take your wife and be happy there. Remember though, you have to come home for Christmas, and when you start having children you may have to build me a house on your farm so that I can be a grandpapa. I understand your need. Maybe it is also time that both Javier and I rethink what it is we do with our lives."

"Thank you." Alex smiled at him, unsure of himself and the next stage of his life, which would now involve a father he'd been determined to hate until the day he died.

*****

THE FAMILY WAS GATHERED AROUND THE DINNER TABLE, Alex included. They had finished supper and the servants were clearing the plates. Their conversation had been lively and neither of the girls had asked why Alex was at the table. They'd become accustomed to his presence there, and he and Rosa had become good friends. Alex found Felicia to be somewhat annoying at times, but since the return of her mother, she seemed to have toned her behavior down quite a bit and was staying close to home while she, her sister and Lydia bonded again.

"I have something to announce," Antonio said once the table was cleared and the servants out of the room.

"Uh-oh," Rosa replied. "There can't be more."

"There is," Antonio said. The women looked at their mother, who shrugged. "As you all know, I haven't been a saint, but I have always loved all of you with everything I have."

"What is it, Papa?" Felicia asked impatiently.

"I have done many terrible deeds, committed sins against your mother that I can never take back, but out of those sins I was, actually we were all, given a gift."

"What are you talking about?" Rosa asked and glanced back at Lydia.

"There was another woman in my life many years ago. Marta."

"Who is Marta?" Felicia asked.

"My mother," Alex replied.

Lydia looked over at Alex, and smiled with happiness as she realized who Alex really was. Here was the little boy she'd wanted to hate all those years ago. But in a short amount of time since she'd been reunited with her family, she'd come to know Alex somewhat. He was a kind young man who she'd noticed liked to smell the flowers in the garden and play with the many dogs on the property. "She worked for Javier years ago," Lydia answered.

Antonio nodded. "Yes. And I had an affair with her."

"Oh, my God," Rosa muttered, realizing who Alex was.

"Isn't that what all you men do?" Felicia asked nonchalantly. "Big deal. You had an affair."

"Alex is our brother," Rosa told Felicia.

"That's right," Antonio told them. Alex looked down at the table.

"Are you serious?" Felicia asked.

"One hundred percent." Antonio said.

Lydia laughed.

They are certainly a crazy family, but I guess they're mine, Alex thought as he glanced around, from face to face.

CHAPTER SIXTY-SEVEN

Six Months Later

Costa Careyes, Mexico

"IT LOOKS AS THOUGH WE ARE TO BE IN-LAWS," JAVIER SAID, finishing off his third tequila, sitting outside on Javier's veranda at the vacation house, overlooking the jungles and the ocean. It was two nights before Alex and Bella's wedding, and the *Patróns* saw it fit for them to celebrate in honor of the occasion.

"You know, I always knew we'd wind up being a family one way or another."

"You *loco pinche pendejo*! I only wish Cynthia were here to see this, see all the changes we've gone through and now to see our children married. She would rejoice in this." Javier poured another shot of tequila and tossed it down, swallowing back his tears at the same time.

"Yes, she would," Antonio replied.

"What are you and Lydia going to do?" Javier asked, thinking of the women each of them had loved as young men. The women who had given them beautiful children and sacrificed so much of themselves for their families.

"Too much time has passed. We have both changed. I still love her. She's the mother of my children, and I think we could be together again, but I know for her she doesn't feel the same way. She's suffered greatly and I'm in part to blame. I don't expect her to try and love me as her husband ever again. She's going to Paris with Rosa for her art show and then, on to New York."

"I am sorry, *amigo*. Maybe in time…"

Antonio shook his head. "I don't know. Maybe…"

"What about Felicia?"

"You know my youngest daughter. She's so full of life. She needs a big city to entertain her."

"Where did she convince you to send her?"

"New York," Antonio said, laughing. "Says she's going to try modeling. At least her mother will be in the same city before long, but I don't know if anyone of us can ever control that girl."

"She is a wild one, but good for her. What about you?" Javier asked.

"Me?"

"Yes."

"I've still got you. And if our children do right by us, we'll be grandpapas soon enough." Antonio smiled and shook his head at the possibility of grandchildren. Where had time gone? "I'm not old enough for this."

"You said it." Javier poured his best friend and business partner of twenty-five years more tequila from the bottle they shared. As they sat together, getting drunk and watching the sun slowly make its

491 | P a g e

descent, they reflected on life in that satirical way that only best friends who had suffered with one another, laughed together, and would die for one another, can.

"So what do you think the next twenty-five years have in store for us?" Javier asked, slurring his words.

"I don't know that I *want* to know the answer to that one," Antonio replied. The two laughed as they raised their glasses together, in celebration of the lives they had already lived.

About the Author

A.K. Alexander lives in San Diego, Ca with her husband, three children and many animals. She is working on her next novel. The author also writes under the name Michele Scott.